# NOVEL LEARNING SERIES®

# Dear John

For Teacher Resources,
visit NovelLearningSeries.com.

# Also by Nicholas Sparks

*The Notebook*

*Message in a Bottle*

*A Walk to Remember*

*The Rescue*

*A Bend in the Road*

*Nights in Rodanthe*

*The Guardian*

*The Wedding*

*Three Weeks with My Brother*
(with Micah Sparks)

*True Believer*

*At First Sight*

*The Choice*

*The Lucky One*

*The Last Song*

*Safe Haven*

*The Best of Me*

# Other Books in the Novel Learning Series

*A Bend in the Road* by Nicholas Sparks (student edition)

*Frankenstein* by Mary Shelley (student edition)

*The Last Song* by Nicholas Sparks (student edition)

*The Notebook* by Nicholas Sparks (student edition)

*Three Weeks with My Brother: A Memoir* by Nicholas and Micah Sparks (student edition)

*A Walk to Remember* by Nicholas Sparks (student edition)

# NICHOLAS SPARKS

NOVEL LEARNING SERIES®

## Dear John

GRAND CENTRAL
PUBLISHING

NEW YORK    BOSTON

Student Guide copyright © 2013 by Willow Holdings, Inc.
and Hachette Book Group, Inc.
*Dear John* is copyright © 2006 by Nicholas Sparks

*Dear John* was originally published by Hachette Book Group.

Grand Central Publishing
Hachette Book Group
237 Park Avenue, New York, NY 10017
www.HachetteBookGroup.com

Printed in the United States of America

RRD-C

First Student Guide Edition: April 2013
10  9  8  7  6  5  4  3  2

Grand Central Publishing is a division of Hachette Book Group, Inc.
The Grand Central Publishing name and logo is a trademark of
Hachette Book Group, Inc.

The Novel Learning Series is a registered trademark of Willow Holdings, Inc.

The Hachette Speakers Bureau provides a wide range of authors for speaking events. To find out more, go to www.hachettespeakersbureau.com or call (866) 376-6591.

The publisher is not responsible for websites (or their content) that are not owned by the publisher.

The Library of Congress has cataloged the hardcover edition of
*Dear John* as follows:
Sparks, Nicholas
Dear John / Nicholas Sparks.—1st ed.
p. cm.
1. Soldiers—Fiction.  2. Long-distance relationships—Fiction.
I. Title.
PS3569.P363D43 2006
813'.54—dc22

ISBN 978-1-4555-2944-5 (student guide)

*For Micah and Christine*

# Acknowledgments

The Novel Learning Series gratefully acknowledges the contributions of the following people: Micah Sparks, Susan Copeland, Kallie Shimek, Emily Griffin, Melissa Nicholas, Rich Wasowski, Deborah Sloan, Rachel Bressler, and Pete Knapp.

# Contents

# Contents

# Contents

# Dear John

# Introduction to the
# Novel Learning Series®

The purpose of the Novel Learning Series® is threefold:

1. to provide you with an opportunity to read and analyze a novel independently,
2. to provide study questions and writing prompts that are aligned with the Common Core State Standards for English Language Arts, and
3. to prepare you for rigorous high-stakes tests, such as the SAT and ACT, by providing multiple-choice questions that are similar in both form and content to the questions on those tests.

The first part of this book contains the novel *Dear John*, which is divided into nine sections for the purpose of this guide: the prologue and chapter 1; chapters 2 and 3; chapters 4 and 5; chapters 6 through 8; chapters 9 through 11; chapters

12 and 13; chapters 14 and 15; chapters 16 through 18; and chapters 19 and 20 and the epilogue. After each of these nine sections of the novel, there is a series of multiple-choice questions. You should read the chapters of the novel first and then answer the questions. The information following each question explains *how* to answer the preceding question. If you are confident in your answer, use this information to confirm your thought process. If you are unsure of how to answer the question, the explanation can guide your decision-making process.

The final part of this guide contains critical reading questions related to a given passage, short answer assignments, and essay assignments. A rubric—a list of various essay elements and descriptions used to gauge quality in essay responses—is also provided. The rubric and the guide to understanding the rubric are designed to walk you through the writing process as you organize your thoughts and craft your response.

At this time, please turn the page, read the prologue and chapter 1, and answer the questions that follow.

# Prologue

What does it mean to truly love another?

There was a time in my life when I thought I knew the answer: It meant that I'd care for Savannah more deeply than I cared for myself and that we'd spend the rest of our lives together. It wouldn't have taken much. She once told me that the key to happiness was achievable dreams, and hers were nothing out of the ordinary. Marriage, family...the basics. It meant I'd have a steady job, the house with the white picket fence, and a minivan or SUV big enough to haul our kids to school or to the dentist or off to soccer practice or piano recitals. Two or three kids, she was never clear on that, but my hunch is that when the time came, she would have suggested that we let nature take its course and allow God to make the decision. She was like that—religious,

*3*

I mean—and I suppose that was part of the reason I fell for her. But no matter what was going on in our lives, I could imagine lying beside her in bed at the end of the day, holding her while we talked and laughed, lost in each other's arms.

It doesn't sound so far-fetched, right? When two people love each other? That's what I thought, too. And while part of me still wants to believe it's possible, I know it's not going to happen. When I leave here again, I'll never come back.

For now, though, I'll sit on the hillside overlooking her ranch and wait for her to appear. She won't be able to see me, of course. In the army, you learn to blend into your surroundings, and I learned well, because I had no desire to die in some backward foreign dump in the middle of the Iraqi desert. But I had to come back to this small North Carolina mountain town to find out what happened. When a person sets a thing in motion, there's a feeling of unease, almost regret, until you learn the truth.

But of this I am certain: Savannah will never know I've been here today.

Part of me aches at the thought of her being so close yet so untouchable, but her story and mine are different now. It wasn't easy for me to accept this simple truth, because there was a time when our stories were the same, but that was six years and two lifetimes ago. There are memories for both of us, of course, but I've learned that memories can have a physical, almost living presence, and in this, Savannah and I are different as well. If hers are stars in the nighttime sky, mine are the haunted empty spaces in between. And unlike her, I've been burdened by questions I've asked myself a thousand times since the last time we were together. Why did I do it? And would I do it again?

It was I, you see, who ended it.

On the trees surrounding me, the leaves are just beginning

their slow turn toward the color of fire, glowing as the sun peeks over the horizon. Birds have begun their morning calls, and the air is perfumed with the scent of pine and earth; different from the brine and salt of my hometown. In time, the front door cracks open, and it's then that I see her. Despite the distance between us, I find myself holding my breath as she steps into the dawn. She stretches before descending the front steps and heads around the side. Beyond her, the horse pasture shimmers like a green ocean, and she passes through the gate that leads toward it. A horse calls out a greeting, as does another, and my first thought is that Savannah seems too small to be moving so easily among them. But she was always comfortable with horses, and they were comfortable with her. A half dozen nibble on grass near the fence post, mainly quarter horses, and Midas, her white-socked black Arabian, stands off to one side. I rode with her once, luckily without injury, and as I was hanging on for dear life, I remember thinking that she looked so relaxed in the saddle that she could have been watching television. Savannah takes a moment to greet Midas now. She rubs his nose while she whispers something, she pats his haunches, and when she turns away, his ears prick up as she heads toward the barn.

She vanishes, then emerges again, carrying two pails—oats, I think. She hangs the pails on two fence posts, and a couple of the horses trot toward them. When she steps back to make room, I see her hair flutter in the breeze before she retrieves a saddle and bridle. While Midas eats, she readies him for her ride, and a few minutes later she's leading him from the pasture, toward the trails in the forest, looking exactly as she did six years ago. I know it isn't true—I saw her up close last year and noticed the first fine lines beginning to form around her eyes—but the prism through which I view her remains for me unchanging. To me, she will always be twenty-one and I will always be twenty-three. I'd been stationed in Germany; I had yet to go to Fallujah or Baghdad or receive her letter, which I read in the railroad station in Samawah in the initial weeks of the campaign; I had yet to return home from the events that changed the course of my life.

Now, at twenty-nine, I sometimes wonder about the choices I've made. The army has become the only life I know. I don't know whether I should be pissed or pleased about that fact; most of the time, I find myself going back and forth, depending on the day. When people ask, I tell them I'm a grunt, and I mean it. I still live on base in Germany, I have maybe a thousand dollars in savings, and I haven't been on a date in years. I don't surf much anymore even on leave, but on my days off I ride my Harley north or south, wherever my mood strikes me. The Harley was the single best thing I've ever bought for myself, though it cost a fortune over there. It suits me, since I've become something of a loner. Most of my buddies have left the service, but I'll probably get sent back to Iraq in the next couple of months. At least, those are the rumors around base. When I first met Savannah Lynn Curtis—to me, she'll always be Savannah Lynn Curtis—I could never have predicted my life would turn out the way it has or believed I'd make the army my career.

But I did meet her; that's the thing that makes my current life so strange. I fell in love with her when we were together, then fell deeper in love with her in the years we were apart. Our story has three parts: a beginning, a middle, and an end. And although this is the way all stories unfold, I still can't believe that ours didn't go on forever.

I reflect on these things, and as always, our time together comes back to me. I find myself remembering how it began, for now these memories are all I have left.

# *Part I*

# Chapter 1

*Wilmington, 2000*

My name is John Tyree. I was born in 1977, and I grew up in Wilmington, North Carolina, a city that proudly boasts the largest port in the state as well as a long and vibrant history but now strikes me more as a city that came about by accident. Sure, the weather was great and the beaches perfect, but it wasn't ready for the wave of Yankee retirees up north who wanted someplace cheap to spend their golden years. The city is located on a relatively thin spit of land bounded by the Cape Fear River on one side and the ocean on the other. Highway 17—which leads to Myrtle Beach and Charleston—bisects the town and serves as its major road. When I was a kid, my dad and I could drive from the historic district near the Cape Fear River to Wrightsville Beach in ten minutes, but so many stoplights and shopping centers have been added that it can now take an hour, especially on the weekends, when the tourists come flooding in. Wrightsville Beach, located on an island just off the coast, is on the northern end of Wilmington and far and away one of the most popular beaches in the state. The homes along the dunes are ridiculously expensive, and most of them are rented out all summer long. The Outer Banks may have more romantic appeal because of their isolation and wild horses and that flight that Orville and Wilbur were famous for, but let me tell you, most people who go to the beach on vacation feel most at home when they can find a McDonald's or Burger King nearby, in case the little ones aren't too fond of the local fare, and want more than a couple of choices when it comes to evening activities.

Like all cities, Wilmington is rich in places and poor in others, and since my dad had one of the steadiest, solid-citizen jobs on the planet—he drove a mail delivery route for the post office—we did okay. Not great, but okay. We weren't rich, but we lived close enough to the rich area for me to attend one of the best high schools in the city. Unlike my friends' homes, though, our house was old and small; part of the porch had begun to sag, but the yard was its saving grace. There was a big oak tree in the backyard, and when I was eight years old, I built a tree house with scraps of wood I collected from a construction site. My dad didn't help me with the project (if he hit a nail with a hammer, it could honestly be called an accident); it was the same summer I taught myself to surf. I suppose I should have realized then how different I was from my dad, but that just shows how little you know about life when you're a kid.

My dad and I were as different as two people could possibly be. Where he was passive and introspective, I was always in motion and hated to be alone; while he placed a high value on education, school for me was like a social club with sports added in. He had poor posture and tended to shuffle when he walked; I bounced from here to there, forever asking him to time how long it took me to run to the end of the block and back. I was taller than him by the time I was in eighth grade and could beat him in arm-wrestling a year later. Our physical features were completely different, too. While he had sandy hair, hazel eyes, and freckles, I had brown hair and eyes, and my olive skin would darken to a deep tan by May. Our differences struck some of our neighbors as odd, which made sense, I suppose, considering that he'd raised me by himself. As I grew older, I sometimes heard them whispering about the fact that my mom had run off when I was less than a year old. Though I later suspected my mom had met someone else, my dad never confirmed this. All he'd say was that she'd realized she made a mistake in getting married so young, and that she wasn't ready to be a mother. He neither heaped scorn on her nor praised her, but he made sure that I included her in my prayers, no matter where she was or what she'd done. "You remind me of her," he'd say sometimes. To this day, I've never spoken a single word to her, nor do I have any desire to do so.

I think my dad was happy. I phrase it like this because he seldom showed much emotion. Hugs and kisses were a rarity for me growing up, and when they did happen, they often struck me as lifeless, something he did because he felt he was supposed to, not because he wanted to. I know he loved me by the way he devoted himself to my care, but he was forty-three when he had me, and part of me thinks my dad would have been better suited to being a monk than a parent. He was the quietest man I've ever known. He asked few questions about what was going on in my life, and while he rarely grew angry, he rarely joked, either. He lived for routine. He cooked me scrambled eggs, toast, and bacon every single morning and listened as I talked about school over a dinner he'd prepared as well. He scheduled visits to the dentist two months in advance, paid his bills on Saturday morning, did the laundry on Sunday afternoon, and left the house every morning at exactly 7:35 a.m. He was socially awkward and spent long hours alone every day, dropping packages and bunches of mail into the mailboxes along his route. He didn't date, nor did he spend weekend nights playing poker with his buddies; the telephone could stay silent for weeks. When it did ring, it was either a wrong number or a telemarketer. I know how hard it must have been for him to raise me on his own, but he never complained, even when I disappointed him.

I spent most of my evenings alone. With the duties of the day finally completed, my dad would head to his den to be with his coins. That was his one great passion in life. He was most content while sitting in his den, studying a coin dealer newsletter nicknamed the *Greysheet* and trying to figure out the next coin he should add to his collection. Actually, it was my grandfather who originally started the coin collection. My grandfather's hero was a man named Louis Eliasberg, a Baltimore financier who is the only person to have assembled a complete collection of United States coins, including all the various dates and mint marks. His collection rivaled, if not surpassed, the collection at the Smithsonian, and after the death of my grandmother in 1951, my grandfather became transfixed by the idea of building a collection with his son. During the summers, my grandfather and dad would travel by train to the various mints to collect the new coins firsthand or visit various coin shows in the Southeast. In time, my grandfather and dad established relationships with coin dealers across the country, and my grandfather spent a fortune over the years trading up and improving the collection. Unlike Louis Eliasberg, however, my grandfather wasn't rich—he owned a general store in Burgaw that went out of business when the Piggly Wiggly opened its doors across town—and never had a chance at matching Eliasberg's collection. Even so, every extra dollar went into coins. My grandfather wore the same jacket for thirty years, drove the same car his entire life, and I'm pretty sure my dad went to work for the postal service instead of heading off to college because there wasn't a dime left over to pay for anything beyond a high school education. He was an odd duck, that's for sure, as was my dad. Like father, like son, as the old saying goes. When the old man finally passed away, he specified in his will that his house be sold and the money used to purchase even more coins, which was exactly what my dad probably would have done anyway.

By the time my dad inherited the collection, it was already quite valuable. When inflation went through the roof and gold hit $850 an ounce, it was worth a small fortune, more than enough for my frugal dad to retire a few times over and more than it would be worth a quarter century later. But neither my grandfather nor my dad had been into collecting for the money; they were in it for the thrill of the hunt and the bond it created between them. There was something exciting about searching long and hard for a specific coin, finally locating it, then wheeling and dealing to get it for the right price. Sometimes a coin was affordable, other times it wasn't, but each and every piece they added was a treasure. My dad hoped to share the same passion with me, including the sacrifice it required. Growing up, I had to sleep with extra blankets in the winter, and I got a single pair of new shoes every year; there was never money for my clothes, unless they came from the Salvation Army. My dad didn't even own a camera. The only picture ever taken of us was at a coin show in Atlanta. A dealer snapped it as we stood before his booth and sent it to us. For years it was perched on my dad's desk. In the photo, my dad had his arm draped over my shoulder, and we were both beaming. In my hand, I was holding a 1926-D buffalo nickel in gem condition, a coin that my dad had just purchased. It was among the rarest of all buffalo nickels, and we ended up eating hot dogs and beans for a month, since it cost more than he'd expected.

But I didn't mind the sacrifices—for a while, anyway. When my dad started talking to me about coins—I must have been in the first or second grade at the time—he spoke to me like an equal. Having an adult, especially your dad, treat you like an equal is a heady thing for any young child, and I basked in the attention, absorbing the information. In time, I could tell you how many Saint-Gaudens double eagles were minted in 1927 as compared with 1924 and why an 1895 Barber dime minted in New Orleans was ten times more valuable than the same coin minted in the same year in Philadelphia. I still can, by the way. Yet unlike my dad, I eventually began to grow out of my passion for collecting. It was all my dad seemed able to talk about, and after six or seven years of weekends spent with him instead of friends, I wanted out. Like most boys, I started to care about other things: sports and girls and cars and music, primarily, and by fourteen, I was spending little time at home. My resentment began to grow as well. Little by little, I began to notice differences in the way we lived when I compared myself with most of my friends. While they had money to spend to go to the movies or buy a stylish pair of sunglasses, I found myself scrounging for quarters in the couch to buy myself a burger at McDonald's. More than a few of my friends received cars for their sixteenth birthday; my dad gave me an 1883 Morgan silver dollar that had been minted in Carson City. Tears in our worn couch were covered by a blanket, and we were the only family I knew who didn't have cable television or a microwave oven. When our refrigerator broke down, he bought a used one that was the world's most awful shade of green, a color that matched nothing else in the kitchen. I was embarrassed at the thought of having friends come over, and I blamed my dad for that. I know it was a pretty crappy way to feel—if the lack of money bothered me so much, I could have mowed lawns or worked odd jobs, for instance—but that's the way it was. I was as blind as a snail and dumb as a camel, but even if I told you I regret my immaturity now, I can't undo the past.

My dad sensed that something was changing, but he was at a loss as to what to do about us. He tried, though, in the only way he knew how, the only way his father knew. He talked about coins—it was the one topic he could discuss with ease—and continued to cook my breakfasts and dinners; but our estrangement grew worse over time. At the same time, I pulled away from the friends I'd always known. They were breaking into cliques, based primarily on what movies they were going to see or the latest shirts they bought from the mall, and I found myself on the outside looking in. Screw them, I thought. In high school, there's always a place for everyone, and I began falling in with the wrong sort of crowd, a crowd that didn't give a damn about anything, which left me not giving a damn, either. I began to cut classes and smoke and was suspended for fighting on three occasions.

I gave up sports, too. I'd played football and basketball and run track until I was a sophomore, and though my dad sometimes asked how I did when I got home, he seemed uncomfortable if

I went into detail, since it was obvious he didn't know a thing about sports. He'd never been on a team in his life. He showed up for a single basketball game during my sophomore year. He sat in the stands, an odd balding guy wearing a worn sport jacket and socks that didn't match. Though he wasn't obese, his pants nipped at the waist, making him look as if he were three months pregnant, and I knew I wanted nothing to do with him. I was embarrassed by the sight of him, and after the game, I avoided him. I'm not proud of myself for that, but that's who I was.

Things got worse. During my senior year, my rebellion reached a high point. My grades had been slipping for two years, more from laziness and lack of care than intelligence (I like to think), and more than once my dad caught me sneaking in late at night with booze on my breath. I was escorted home by the police after being found at a party where drugs and drinking were evident, and when my dad grounded me, I stayed at a friend's house for a couple of weeks after raging at him to mind his own business. He said nothing upon my return; instead, scrambled eggs, toast, and bacon were on the table in the mornings as usual. I barely passed my classes, and I suspect the school let me graduate simply because it wanted me out of there. I know my dad was worried, and he would sometimes, in his own shy way, broach the subject of college, but by then I'd made up my mind not to go. I wanted a job, I wanted a car, I wanted those material things I'd lived eighteen years without.

I said nothing to him about it one way or the other until the summer after graduation, but when he realized I hadn't even applied to junior college, he locked himself in his den for the rest of the night and said nothing to me over our eggs and bacon the next morning. Later that evening, he tried to engage me in another discussion about coins, as if grasping for the companionship that had somehow been lost between us.

"Do you remember when we went to Atlanta and you were the one who found that buffalo head nickel we'd been looking for for years?" he started. "The one where we had our picture taken? I'll never forget how excited you were. It reminded me of my father and me."

I shook my head, all the frustration of life with my dad coming to the surface. "I'm sick and tired of hearing about coins!" I shouted at him. "I never want to hear about them again! You should sell the damn collection and do something else. Anything else."

My dad said nothing, but to this day I'll never forget his pained expression when at last he turned and trudged back to his den. I'd hurt him, and though I told myself I hadn't wanted to, deep down I knew I was lying to myself. From then on my dad rarely brought up the subject of coins again. Nor did I. It became a yawning gulf between us, and it left us with nothing to say to each other. A few days later, I realized that the only photograph of us was gone as well, as if he believed that even the slightest reminder of coins would offend me. At the time, it probably would have, and even though I assumed that he'd thrown it away, the realization didn't bother me at all.

Growing up, I'd never considered entering the military. Despite the fact that eastern North Carolina is one of the most militarily dense areas of the country—there are seven bases within a few hours' driving time from Wilmington—I used to think that military life was for losers. Who wanted to spend his life getting ordered around by a bunch of crew-cut flunkies? Not me, and aside from the ROTC guys, not many people in my high school, either. Instead, most of the kids who'd been good students headed off to the University of North Carolina or North Carolina State, while the kids who hadn't been good students stayed behind, bumming around from one lousy job to the next, drinking beer and hanging out, and pretty much avoiding anything that might require a shred of responsibility.

I fell into the latter category. In the couple of years after graduation, I went through a succession of jobs, working as a busboy at Outback Steakhouse, tearing ticket stubs at the local movie theater, loading and unloading boxes at Staples, cooking pancakes at Waffle House, and working as a cashier at a couple of tourist places that sold crap to the out-of-towners. I spent every dime I earned, had zero illusions about eventually working my way up the ladder to management, and ended up getting fired from every job I had. For a while, I didn't care. I was living my life. I was big into surfing late and sleeping in, and since I was still living at home, none of my income was needed for things like rent or food or insurance or preparing for a future. Besides, none of my friends was doing any better than I was. I don't remember being particularly unhappy, but after a while I just got tired of my life. Not the surfing part—in 1996, Hurricanes Bertha and Fran slammed into the coast, and those were some of the best waves in years—but hanging out at Leroy's bar afterward. I began to realize that every night was the same. I'd be drinking beers and bump into someone I'd known from high school, and they'd ask what I was doing and I'd tell them, and they'd tell me what they were doing, and it didn't take a genius to figure out we were both on the fast track to nowhere. Even if they had their own place, which I didn't, I never believed them when they told me they liked their job as ditch digger or window washer or Porta Potti hauler, because I knew full well that none of those were the kinds of occupations they'd grown up dreaming about. I might have been lazy in the classroom, but I wasn't stupid.

I dated dozens of women during that period. At Leroy's, there were always women. Most were forgettable relationships. I used women and allowed myself to be used and always kept my feelings to myself. Only my relationship with a girl named Lucy lasted more than a few months, and for a short time before we inevitably drifted apart, I thought I was in love with her. She was a student at UNC Wilmington, a year older than me, and wanted to work in New York after she graduated. "I care about you," she told me on our last night together, "but you and I want different things. You could do so much more with your life, but for some reason, you're content to simply float along." She'd hesitated before going on. "But more than that, I never know how you really feel about me." I knew she was right. Soon after, she left on a plane without bothering to say good-bye. A year later, after getting her number from her parents, I called her and we talked for twenty minutes. She was engaged to an attorney, she told me, and would be married the following June.

The phone call affected me more than I thought it would. It came on a day when I'd just been fired—again—and I went to console myself at Leroy's, as always. The same crowd of losers was there, and I suddenly realized that I didn't want to spend another pointless evening pretending that everything in my life was okay. Instead, I bought a six-pack of beer and went to sit on the beach. It was the first time in years that I actually thought about what I was doing with my life, and I wondered whether I should take my dad's advice and get a college degree. I'd been out of school for so long, though, that the idea felt foreign and ridiculous. Call it luck or bad luck, but right then two marines jogged by. Young and fit, they radiated easy confidence. If they could do it, I told myself, I could do it, too.

I mulled it over for a couple of days, and in the end, my dad had something to do with my decision. Not that I talked to him about it, of course—we weren't talking at all by then. I was walking toward the kitchen one night and saw him sitting at his desk, as always. But this time, I really studied him. His hair was mostly gone, and the little that was left had turned completely silver by his ears. He was nearing retirement, and I was struck by the notion that I had no right to keep letting him down after all he'd done for me.

So I joined the military. My first thought was that I'd join the marines, since they were the guys I was most familiar with. Wrightsville Beach was always packed with jarheads from Camp Lejeune or Cherry Point, but when the time came, I picked the army. I figured I'd be handed a rifle either way, but what really closed the deal was that the marines recruiter was having lunch when I swung by and wasn't immediately available, while the army recruiter—whose office was right across the street—was. In the end, the decision felt more spontaneous than planned, but I signed on the dotted line for a four-year enlistment, and when the recruiter slapped my back and congratulated me as I went out the door, I found myself wondering what I'd gotten myself into. That was in late 1997, and I was twenty years old.

Boot camp at Fort Benning was just as miserable as I thought it would be. The whole thing seemed designed to humiliate and brainwash us into following orders without question, no matter how stupid they might be, but I adapted more quickly than a lot of the guys. Once I got through it, I chose the infantry. We spent the next few months doing a lot of simulations in places like Louisiana and good old Fort Bragg, where we basically learned the best ways to kill people and break things; and after a while, my unit, as part of the First Infantry Division—aka the Big Red One—was sent to Germany. I didn't speak a word of German, but it didn't matter, since pretty much everyone I dealt with spoke English. It was easy at first, then army life set in. I spent seven lousy months in the Balkans—first in Macedonia in 1999, then in Kosovo, where I stayed until the late spring of 2000. Life in the army didn't pay much, but considering there was no rent, no food expenses, and really nothing to spend my paychecks on even when I got them, I had money in the bank for the first time. Not a lot, but enough.

I spent my first leave at home completely bored out of my mind. I spent my second leave in Las Vegas. One of my buddies had grown up there, and three of us crashed at his parents' place. I blew through pretty much everything I'd saved. On my third leave, after coming back from Kosovo, I was desperately in need of a break and decided to head back home, hoping the boredom of the visit would be enough to calm my mind. Because of the distance, my dad and I seldom talked on the phone, but he wrote me letters that were always postmarked on the first of every month. They weren't like the ones my buddies got from their moms or sisters or wives. Nothing too personal, nothing mushy, and never a word that suggested he missed me. Nor did he ever mention coins. Instead, he wrote about changes in the neighborhood and a lot about the weather; when I wrote to tell him about a pretty hairy firefight I'd been in in the Balkans, he wrote back to say that he was glad I survived, but said no more about it. I knew by the way he phrased his response that he didn't want to hear about the dangerous things I did. The fact that I was in peril frightened him, so I started omitting the scary stuff. Instead, I sent him letters about how guard duty was without a doubt the most boring job ever invented and that the only exciting thing to happen to me in weeks was trying to guess how many cigarettes the other guard would actually smoke in a single evening. My dad ended every letter with the promise that he would write again soon, and once again, the man didn't let me down. He was, I've long since come to believe, a far better man than I'll ever be.

But I'd grown up in the previous three years. Yeah, I know, I'm a walking cliché—go in as a boy, come out as a man and all that. But everyone in the army is forced to grow up, especially if you're in the infantry like me. You're entrusted with equipment that costs a fortune, others put their trust in you, and if you screw up, the penalty is a lot more serious than being sent to bed without supper. Sure, there's too much paperwork and boredom, and everyone smokes and can't complete a sentence without cursing and has boxes of dirty magazines under his bed, and you have to answer to ROTC guys fresh out of college who think grunts like me have the IQs of Neanderthals; but you're forced to learn the most important lesson in life, and that's the fact that you have to live up to your responsibilities, and you'd better do it right. When given an order, you can't say no. It's no exaggeration to say that lives are on the line. One wrong decision, and your buddy might die. It's this fact that makes the army work. That's the big mistake a lot of people make when they wonder how soldiers can put their lives on the line day after day or how they can fight for something they may not believe in. Not everyone does. I've worked with soldiers on all sides of the political spectrum; I've met some who hated the army and others who wanted to make it a career. I've met geniuses and idiots, but when all is said and done, we do what we do for one another. For friendship. Not for country, not for patriotism, not because we're programmed killing machines, but because of the guy next to you. You fight for your friend, to keep him alive, and he fights for you, and everything about the army is built on this simple premise.

But like I said, I had changed. I went into the army as a smoker and almost coughed up a lung during boot camp, but unlike practically everyone else in my unit, I quit and hadn't touched the things in over two years. I moderated my drinking to the point that one or two beers a week was sufficient, and I might go a month without having any at all. My record was spotless. I'd been promoted from private to corporal and then, six months later, to sergeant, and I learned that I had an ability to lead. I'd led men in firefights, and my squad was involved in capturing one of the most notorious war criminals in the Balkans. My commanding officer recommended me for Officer Candidate School (OCS), and I was debating whether or not to become an officer, but that sometimes meant a desk job and even more paperwork, and I wasn't sure I wanted that. Aside from surfing, I hadn't exercised in years before I joined the service; by the time I took my third leave, I'd put on twenty pounds of muscle and cut the flab from my belly. I spent most of my free time running, boxing, and weight lifting with Tony, a musclehead from New York who always shouted when he talked, swore that tequila was an aphrodisiac, and was far and away my best friend in the unit. He talked me into getting tattoos on both arms just like him, and with every passing day, the memory of who I once had been became more and more distant.

I read a lot, too. In the army, you have a lot of time to read, and people trade books back and forth or sign them out from the library until the covers are practically worn away. I don't want you to get the impression that I became a scholar, because I didn't. I wasn't into Chaucer or Proust or Dostoevsky or any of those other dead guys; I read mainly mysteries and thrillers and books by Stephen King, and I took a particular liking to Carl Hiaasen because his words flowed easily and he always made me laugh. I couldn't help but think that if schools had assigned these books in English class, we'd have a lot more readers in the world.

Unlike my buddies, I shied away from any prospect of female companionship. Sounds weird, right? Prime of life, testosterone-filled job—what could be more natural than searching for a little release with the help of a female? It wasn't for me. Although some of the guys I knew dated and even married the locals while stationed in Würzburg, I'd heard enough stories to know that those marriages seldom worked out. The military was hard on relationships in general—I'd seen enough divorces to know that—and while I wouldn't have minded the company of someone special, it just never happened. Tony couldn't understand it.

"You gotta come with me," he'd plead. "You never come."

"I'm not in the mood."

"How can you not be in the mood? Sabine swears her friend is gorgeous. Tall and blond, and she loves tequila."

"Bring Don. I'm sure he'd like to go."

"Castelow? No way. Sabine can't stand him."

I said nothing.

"We're just going to have a little fun."

I shook my head, thinking that I'd rather be alone than revert to the kind of person I'd been, but I found myself wondering whether I would end up being as monkish as my dad.

Knowing he couldn't change my mind, Tony didn't bother hiding his disgust on his way out the door. "I just don't get you sometimes."

\*　　\*　　\*

When my dad picked me up from the airport, he didn't recognize me at first and almost jumped when I tapped him on the shoulder. He looked smaller than I remembered. Instead of offering a hug, he shook my hand and asked me about the flight, but neither of us knew what to say next, so we wandered outside. It was odd and disorienting to be back at home, and I felt on edge, just like the last time I took leave. In the parking lot, as I tossed my gear in the trunk, I spotted on the back of his ancient Ford Escort a bumper sticker that told people to support our troops. I wasn't sure exactly what that meant to my dad, but I was still glad to see it.

At home, I stowed my gear in my old bedroom. Everything was where I remembered, right down to the dusty trophies on my shelf and a hidden, half-empty bottle of Wild Turkey in the back of my underwear drawer. Same thing in the rest of the house. The blanket still covered the couch, the green refrigerator seemed to scream that it didn't belong, and the television picked up only four blurry channels. Dad cooked spaghetti; Friday was always spaghetti. At dinner, we tried to talk.

"It's nice to be back," I said.

His smile was brief. "Good," he responded.

He took a drink of milk. At dinner, we always drank milk. He concentrated on his meal.

"Do you remember Tony?" I ventured. "I think I mentioned him in my letters. Anyway, get this—he thinks he's in love. Her name's Sabine, and she has a six-year-old daughter. I've warned him that it might not be such a good idea, but he isn't listening."

He carefully sprinkled Parmesan cheese over his food, making sure every spot had the perfect amount. "Oh," he said. "Okay."

After that, I ate and neither of us said anything. I drank some milk. I ate some more. The clock ticked on the wall.

"I'll bet you're excited to be retiring this year," I suggested. "Just think, you can finally take a vacation, see the world." I almost said that he could come see me in Germany, but I didn't. I knew he wouldn't and didn't want to put him on the spot. We twirled our noodles simultaneously as he seemed to ponder how best to respond.

"I don't know," he finally said.

I gave up trying to talk to him, and from then on the only sounds were those coming from our forks as they hit the plates. When we finished dinner, we went our separate ways. Exhausted from the flight, I headed off to bed, waking every hour the way I did back on base. By the time I stirred in the morning, my dad was off at work. I ate and read the paper, tried to contact a friend without success, then grabbed my surfboard from the garage and hitched my way to the beach. The waves weren't great, but it didn't matter. I hadn't been on a board in three years and was rusty at first, but even the little dribblers made me wish I had been stationed near the ocean.

It was early June 2000, the temperature was already hot, and the water was refreshing. From my vantage point on my board, I could see folks moving their belongings into some of the homes just beyond the dunes. As I mentioned, Wrightsville Beach was always crowded with families who rented for a week or more, but occasionally college students from Chapel Hill or Raleigh did the same. It was the latter who interested me, and I noted a group of coeds in bikinis taking their spots on the back deck of one of the houses near the pier. I watched them for a bit, appreciating the view, then caught another wave and spent the rest of the afternoon lost in my own little world.

I thought about paying a visit to Leroy's but figured that nothing or no one had changed except for me. Instead, I grabbed a bottle of beer from the corner store and went to sit on the pier to enjoy the sunset. Most of the people fishing had already begun clearing out, and the few who remained were cleaning their catch and tossing the discards in the water. In time, the color of the ocean began changing from iron gray to orange, then yellow. In the breakers beyond the pier, I could see pelicans riding the backs of porpoises as they skimmed through the waves. I knew that the evening would bring the first night of the full moon—my time in the field made the realization almost instinctive. I wasn't thinking about much of anything, just sort of letting my mind wander. Believe me, meeting a girl was the last thing on my mind.

That was when I saw her walking up the pier. Or rather, two of them walking. One was tall and blond, the other an attractive brunette, both a little younger than me. College students, most likely. Both wore shorts and halters, and the brunette was carrying one of those big knit bags that people sometimes bring to the beach when they plan to stay for hours with the kids. I could hear them talking and laughing, sounding carefree and vacation-ready as they approached.

"Hey," I called out when they were close. Not very smooth, and I can't say I expected anything in response.

The blonde proved me right. She took one glimpse at my surfboard and the beer in my hand and ignored me with a roll of her eyes. The brunette, however, surprised me.

"Hiya, stranger," she answered with a smile. She motioned toward my board. "I'll bet the waves were great today."

Her comment caught me off guard, and I heard an unexpected kindness in her words. She and her friend continued down to the end of the pier, and I found myself watching her as she leaned over the railing. I debated whether or not I should stroll over and introduce myself, then decided against it. They weren't my type, or more accurately, I probably wasn't theirs. I took a long pull on my beer, trying to ignore them.

Try as I might, though, I couldn't stop my gaze from drifting back to the brunette. I tried not to listen to what the two girls were saying, but the blonde had one of those voices impossible to ignore. She was talking endlessly about some guy named Brad and how much she loved him, and how her sorority was the best at UNC, and the party they had at the end of the year was the best ever, and that the other should join next year, and that too many of her friends were hooking up with the worst kind of frat guys, and one of them even got pregnant, but it was her own fault since she'd been warned about the guy. The brunette didn't say much—I couldn't tell whether she was amused or bored by the conversation—but every now and then, she would laugh. Again, I heard something friendly and understanding in her voice, something akin to coming home, which I'll admit made no sense at all. As I set aside my bottle of beer, I noticed that she'd placed her bag on the railing.

They had been standing there for ten minutes or so before two guys started up the pier—frat guys, I guessed—wearing pink and orange Lacoste shirts over their knee-length Bermuda shorts. My first thought was that one of these two must be the Brad that the blonde had been talking about. Both carried beers, and they grew furtive as they approached, as if intending to sneak up on the girls. More than likely the two girls wanted them there, and after a quick burst of surprise, complete with a scream and a couple of friendly slaps on the arm, they'd all head back together, laughing and giggling or doing whatever it was college couples did.

It may have turned out that way, too, for the boys did just what I thought they would. As soon as they were close, they jumped at the girls with a yell; both girls shrieked and did the friendly slap thing. The guys hooted, and pink shirt spilled some of his beer. He leaned against the railing, near the bag, one leg over the other, his arms behind him.

"Hey, we're going to be starting the bonfire in a couple of minutes," orange shirt said, putting his arms around the blonde. He kissed her neck. "You two ready to come back?"

"You ready?" the blonde asked, looking at her friend.

"Sure," the brunette answered.

Pink shirt pushed back from the railing, but somehow his hand must have hit the bag, because it slid, then tumbled over the edge. The splash sounded like a fish jumping.

"What was that?" he asked, turning around.

"My bag!" the brunette gasped. "You knocked it off."

"Sorry about that," he said, not sounding particularly sorry.

"My purse was in there!"

He frowned. "I said I'm sorry."

"You've got to get it before it sinks!"

The frat brothers seemed frozen, and I knew neither of them had any intention of jumping in to get it. For one thing, they'd probably never find it, and then they'd have to swim all the way back to shore, something that wasn't recommended when one had been drinking, as they obviously had been. I think the brunette read pink shirt's expression as well, because I saw her put both hands on the upper rail and one foot on the bottom.

"Don't be dumb. It's gone," pink shirt declared, putting his hand on hers to stop her. "It's too dangerous to jump. There might be sharks down there. It's just a purse. I'll buy you a new one."

"I need that purse! It's got all my money in there!"

It wasn't any of my business, I knew. But all I could think as I leapt to my feet and rushed toward the edge of the pier was, Oh, what the hell . . .

# Questions and Explanations for the Prologue and Chapter 1

The questions in this book serve multiple purposes. Not only are they designed to check your comprehension and understanding of *Dear John*, but they also encourage you to think critically about the text. It's important not only to know what happens in the novel, but also to be able to analyze the text and make connections outside of it. In addition, the questions check your knowledge of essential literary terms and your knowledge of standard grammar and usage rules, as well as your vocabulary. The formats of the questions mirror those found in important standardized tests, such as the ACT and SAT.

You should do your best to answer each question. If you are having difficulty, a detailed explanation to guide your reasoning process is provided after each question. It is designed to teach you *how* to answer the question rather than just providing you with the correct answer. Reading the explanation will be beneficial even if you are certain of your response; use it to verify that you have the correct response.

The ten questions on the prologue and chapter 1 focus on grammar and usage, vocabulary, literary terms, comprehension, style, and characterization. Some of the questions combine two or more of these areas, requiring you to synthesize your knowledge, make inferences, and interpret the text. The questions are designed to determine both your current level of understanding of the novel and your ability to answer higher-level questions.

**The following sentence tests correctness and effective expression. Part of the following sentence is underlined; beneath the sentence are four ways of phrasing the underlined material. Select the option that produces the best sentence. If you think the original phrasing produces a better sentence than any of the alternatives, select choice A.**

1. John Tyree loved Savannah Lynn Curtis and he ended their relationship.

   A. John Tyree loved Savannah Lynn Curtis and he ended

   B. John Tyree loved Savannah Lynn Curtis, he ended

   C. John Tyree loved Savannah Lynn Curtis, but he ended

   D. Although John Tyree loved Savannah Lynn Curtis, he ended

For choice A to be correct, the original sentence must be free of errors or the original wording must be better than the other choices. Otherwise, substitute the suggested changes in place of the underlined words and compare them to the original.

Choice B eliminates the conjunction, resulting in the creation of a comma splice. A comma splice is when a comma is used to connect two main clauses without using a coordinating conjunction. A comma splice is also one kind of a run-on sentence—for example, "John likes *The Lord of the Rings*, Jane prefers *Twilight*." Each clause in this example is a complete thought, so connecting them with only a comma is incorrect. The error can be corrected in two different ways: by using a comma and a coordinating conjunction to create a compound sentence, a sentence with two or more main clauses ("John likes *The Lord of the Rings*, but Jane prefers *Twilight*"), or by using a comma and a subordinating conjunction to create a complex sentence, a sentence with one main clause and at least one dependent clause ("John likes *The Lord of the Rings*, although Jane prefers *Twilight*"). Stylistically, a complex sentence is usually preferable to a compound sentence.

Choice C eliminates the run-on sentence in the original and switches the conjunction from *and* to *but*, demonstrating a contrast that emphasizes the difference between feelings and actions and creating a grammatically correct compound sentence.

Choice D adds the subordinating conjunction *although*, turning the first part of the sentence into an introductory adverbial clause, which creates a complex sentence.

**Question 2 tests your vocabulary. Choose the word that, when inserted in the sentence, best fits the meaning of the sentence as a whole.**

2. When John, the narrator of the novel, addresses the readers with the words "but let me tell you," he is using a _____ form of diction.

    A. formal

    B. general

    C. colloquial

    D. technical

The word *diction* refers to word choice. *Formal* diction, choice A, is an elevated form of impersonal language that usually appears in written form. It can be considered stuffy and impersonal.

*General* diction, choice B, refers to the words of educated native speakers. This is the most common form of written expression.

*Colloquial* diction, choice C, refers to the informal language of the average native speaker. Colloquial diction tends to be spoken rather than written and can include slang, contractions, and second-person pronouns; it is personal in nature.

*Technical* diction, choice D, refers to the words used by specialists in particular fields and often includes vocabulary that may be unfamiliar to the average audience.

**Question 3 asks you to analyze how an author's choices contribute to overall structure and meaning.**

3. The prologue of *Dear John* opens with a question. This stylistic technique produces all of the following effects EXCEPT:

    A. establishing a conversational tone for the text

    B. introducing an important thematic topic of the novel

C. fully developing the protagonist

D. engaging the reader

Three out of the four choices are effects of the opening question and can be eliminated. If the question sounds like the narrator is actually asking you, the reader, a question, then it is creating a conversational tone, and you can eliminate choice A. If one of the important ideas in the novel appears to be about the true nature of love, eliminate choice B. If the question enables you to get a thorough understanding of John, the main character, eliminate choice C. And if the question is thought provoking, encouraging you to continue reading, eliminate choice D.

**Question 4 tests your knowledge of literary terms.**

4. "Beyond her, the horse pasture shimmers like a green ocean." Identify the literary term used in this sentence.

A. allusion

B. metaphor

C. personification

D. simile

Knowing about figures of speech will help you answer this question. An *allusion*, choice A, is an indirect reference. Some of the most common types of allusions are historical (when someone meets his Waterloo, it's a reference to Napoleon); biblical (such as John Coffey in *The Green Mile* being a Christ figure); mythological (a reference to a Greek or Roman myth, such as a character being said to have the Midas touch); and literary (a reference to a character in a work of literature, such as a couple being compared to Romeo and Juliet). A *metaphor*, choice B, is a comparison between two unlike things without using a connective word—for example, "Michael Phelps was a flying fish in the pool." *Personification*, choice C, is giving a human characteristic to a nonhuman thing, such as in "Opportunity knocked on the door." And a *simile*, choice D, is a comparison of two unlike things using a connective word, such as *like*, *as*, or *than*—for example, "She looked as fresh as the morning snow."

**Question 5 checks your comprehension and your ability to understand the use of metaphor.**

5. When discussing memories, John states, "If hers are stars in the nighttime sky, mine are the haunted empty spaces in between." This comparison creates each of the following effects EXCEPT:

   A. comparing the couple's time together to the beauty of a star

   B. recognizing that some things are both beautiful and unattainable

   C. contrasting the way two people can remember the same event

   D. establishing the duality of light and darkness that will permeate the novel

You can determine the correct answer by eliminating the choices that are effects of the metaphor or by realizing which one is an incorrect description of the effect. If the memories of their time together and his memories of Savannah herself can be considered beautiful, then comparing the memories to stars shining at night is an effect of the metaphor, and you can eliminate choice A. If John and readers realize that Savannah is as distant and unattainable as a star, then eliminate choice B. If the starlight and contrasting darkness between stars parallels the distance between the past and the present, as well as the differences between the way John and Savannah view their memories, eliminate choice C. And if the motifs of light and darkness pervade all of the prologue and chapter 1, thus suggesting or introducing a recurring thematic topic throughout the novel, eliminate choice D.

**Question 6 asks you to make an inference based on strong and thorough textual evidence.**

6. Based on their words and actions in chapter 1, John's relationship with his father while he was in high school can best be described as _____.

    A. loving

    B. strained

    C. intellectual

    D. carefree

A *loving* relationship, choice A, is based on mutual respect and understanding. A *strained* relationship, choice B, is tense and full of conflict. An *intellectual* relationship, choice C, is extremely rational, illustrating a meeting of the minds between the two. A *carefree* relationship, choice D, is lighthearted and cheerful.

**Question 7 checks your understanding of literary terms.**

7. John claims, "I was as blind as a snail and dumb as a camel." Which literary term is he using to describe himself?

   A. hyperbole

   B. metaphor

   C. personification

   D. simile

Knowledge of literary terms will enable you to answer this question. *Hyperbole*, choice A, is using overexaggeration to make a point. An example would be, "Everyone who reads this learning guide will know what *hyperbole* is because hyperbole will be explained a bazillion times." A *metaphor*, choice B, is a comparison between two unlike things without using a connective word—for example, "Michael Phelps was a flying fish in the pool." *Personification*, choice C, is giving a nonhuman thing a human characteristic, such as in "Opportunity knocked on the door." And a *simile*, choice D, is a comparison of two unlike things using a connective word, such as *like*, *as*, or *than*—for example, "She looked as fresh as the morning snow."

**Question 8 checks your comprehension.**

8. According to John, one fact more than any other makes the army work. What is it?

   A. Soldiers are programmed killing machines.

   B. Soldiers are extremely patriotic.

   C. Soldiers fight to keep their friends alive.

   D. Soldiers view the army as a career.

Understanding John's belief of why an army works is crucial to getting to know his character. A close reading of the chapter will enable you to know the correct answer. If you are not sure, reread the paragraph on page 22 where John describes his growing up as a member of the Army.

**Question 9 asks you to analyze the impact of specific details on meaning.**

9. What is the primary significance of the author's inclusion of the following statement in chapter 1: "if schools had assigned these books [by Stephen King and Carl Hiaasen] in English class, we'd have a lot more readers in the world"?

    A. It tells us that John didn't get a chance to read contemporary authors during his high school years.

    B. It states the most important thematic topic of the novel.

    C. It illustrates that the army did a better job of educating John than the public schools did.

    D. It reveals insights into John's character.

This question asks you to think about the implications of a particular statement. Although more than one of the answers may be true, the question is asking for the "primary significance" of the statement. If you think that mentioning the type of reading material that John was assigned during high school is the most important part of this detail, select choice A. If you think the main idea presented in the novel is allowing students to read contemporary fiction in the classroom, select choice

B. If elevating the army and belittling high schools is the main point of the sentence, select choice C. And if the statement provides insight into John's character by showing the type of reading material he values and the connections he can make between his life and to the world in general, select choice D.

**Question 10 asks you to analyze textual evidence to make an inference regarding character development.**

10. What is the primary reason that John dives off the pier after the purse?

    A. He wants to show off.

    B. He does it because he's intrigued by and interested in the brunette.

    C. His army training taught him that it's the right thing to do.

    D. He is making a conscious effort to embarrass the fraternity boys.

Although you might be able to make a case for more than one answer, the question asks you for the best choice. If you believe John is truly just showing off, select choice A. If John is interested in the brunette and wants to do this because of her smile and her friendly voice, select choice B. If he believes it's the right thing to do, based on what he was taught in the service, select choice C. And if John wants to belittle the guys whom he refers to as fraternity boys, select choice D.

# Chapter 2

I suppose I should explain why I jumped into the waves to retrieve her bag. It wasn't that I thought she would view me as some sort of hero, or because I wanted to impress her, or even because I cared in the slightest how much money she'd lost. It had to do with the genuineness of her smile and the warmth of her laugh. Even as I was plunging into the water, I knew how ridiculous my reaction was, but by then it was too late. I hit the water, went under, and popped to the surface. Four faces stared down at me from the railing. Pink shirt was definitely annoyed.

"Where is it?" I shouted up at them.

"Right over there!" the brunette shouted. "I think I can still see it. It's going down..."

It took a minute to locate it in the deepening twilight, and the surge of the ocean was doing its best to drive me into the pier. I swam to the side, then held the bag above the water as best I could, despite the fact that it was already soaking. The waves made the swim back to shore less difficult than I'd feared, and every now and then I'd look up and see the four people following along with me.

I finally felt bottom and trudged out of the surf. I shook the water from my hair, started up the sand, and met them halfway up the beach. I held out the bag.

"Here you go."

"Thank you," the brunette said, and when her eyes met mine, I felt something click, like a key turning in a lock. Believe me, I'm no romantic, and while I've heard all about love at first sight, I've never believed in it, and I still don't. But even so, there was something there, something recognizably real, and I couldn't look away.

Up close, she was more beautiful than I'd first realized, but it had less to do with the way she looked than the way she *was*. It wasn't just her slightly gap-toothed smile, it was the casual way she swiped at a loose strand of hair, the easy way she held herself.

"You didn't have to do that," she said with something like wonder in her voice. "I would have gotten it."

"I know." I nodded. "I saw you getting ready to jump."

She tilted her head to the side. "But you felt an uncontrollable need to help a lady in distress?"

"Something like that."

She evaluated my answer for a moment, then turned her attention to the bag. She began removing items—her wallet, sunglasses, visor, a tube of sunscreen—and handed them all to the blonde before wringing out the bag.

"Your pictures got wet," said the blonde, flicking through the wallet.

The brunette ignored her, continuing to wring one way and

then the next. When she was finally satisfied, she took back the items and reloaded her bag.

"Thank you again," she said. Her accent was different from that of eastern North Carolina, more of a twang, as if she'd grown up in the mountains near Boone or near the South Carolina border in the west.

"No big deal," I mumbled, but I didn't move.

"Hey, maybe he wants a reward," pink shirt broke in, his voice loud.

She glanced at him, then back at me. "Do you want a reward?"

"No." I waved a hand. "Just glad to help."

"I always knew chivalry wasn't dead," she proclaimed. I tried to detect a note of teasing, but I heard nothing in her tone to indicate that she was poking fun at me.

Orange shirt gave me the once-over, noting my crew cut. "Are you in the marines?" he asked. He tightened his arms around the blonde again.

I shook my head. "I'm not one of the few or the proud. I wanted to be all that I could be, so I joined the army."

The brunette laughed. Unlike my dad, she'd actually seen the commercials.

"I'm Savannah," she said. "Savannah Lynn Curtis. And these are Brad, Randy, and Susan." She held out her hand.

"I'm John Tyree," I said, taking it. Her hand was warm, velvety soft in places but callused in others. I was suddenly conscious of how long it had been since I'd touched a woman.

"Well, I feel like I should do something for you."

"You don't need to do anything."

"Have you eaten?" she asked, ignoring my comment. "We're getting ready to have a cookout, and there's plenty to go around. Would you like to join us?"

The guys traded glances. Pink-shirted Randy looked down-right glum, and I'll admit that made me feel better. *Hey, maybe he wants a reward.* What a putz.

"Yeah, come on," Brad finally added, sounding less than thrilled. "It'll be fun. We're renting the place next to the pier." He pointed to one of the houses on the beach, where half a dozen people lounged on the deck out back.

Even though I had no desire to spend time with more frat brothers, Savannah smiled at me with such warmth that the words were out before I could stop them.

"Sounds good. Let me go grab my board from the pier and I'll be there in a bit."

"We'll meet you there," Randy piped up. He took a step toward Savannah, but she ignored him.

"I'll walk with you," Savannah said, breaking away from the group. "It's the least I can do." She adjusted the bag on her shoulder. "See you all in a few, okay?"

We started toward the dune, where the stairs would lead us up to the pier. Her friends lingered for a minute, but when she fell in step beside me, they slowly turned and began making their way down the beach. From the corner of my eye, I saw the blonde turn her head and glance our way from beneath Brad's arm. Randy did too, sulking. I wasn't sure that Savannah even noticed until we'd walked a few steps.

"Susan probably thinks I'm crazy for doing this," she said.

"Doing what?"

"Walking with you. She thinks Randy's perfect for me, and she's been trying to get us together since we got here this after-noon. He's been following me around all day."

I nodded, unsure how to respond. In the distance, the moon, full and glowing, had begun its slow rise from the sea, and I saw

Savannah staring at it. When the waves crashed and spilled, they flared silver, as if caught in a camera's flash. We reached the pier. The railing was gritty with sand and salt, and the wood was weathered and beginning to splinter. The steps creaked as we ascended.

"Where are you stationed?" she asked.

"In Germany. I'm home on leave for a couple of weeks to visit my dad. And you're from the mountains, I take it?"

She glanced at me in surprise. "Lenoir." She studied me. "Let me guess, my accent, right? You think I sound like I'm from the sticks, don't you."

"Not at all."

"Well, I am. From the sticks, I mean. I grew up on a ranch and everything. And yes, I know I have an accent, but I've been told that some people find it charming."

"Randy seemed to think so."

It slipped out before I could catch myself. In the awkward silence, she ran a hand through her hair.

"Randy seems like a nice young man," she remarked after a bit, "but I don't know him that well. I don't really know most of the people in the house all that well, except for Tim and Susan." She waved a mosquito away. "You'll meet Tim later. He's a great guy. You'll like him. Everybody does."

"And you're all down here on vacation for a week?"

"A month, actually—but no, it's not really a vacation. We're volunteering. You've heard of Habitat for Humanity, right? We're down here to help build a couple of houses. My family's been involved with it for years."

Over her shoulder, the house seemed to be coming to life in the darkness. More people had materialized, the music had been turned up, and every now and then I could hear laughter. Brad, Susan, and Randy were already surrounded by a group of coeds drinking beer and looking less like do-gooders than college kids trolling for a good time and a chance to hook up with someone of the opposite sex. She must have noticed my expression and followed my gaze.

"We don't start until Monday. They'll find out soon enough that it's not all fun and games."

"I didn't say anything..."

"You didn't have to. But you're right. For most of them, it's their first time working with Habitat, and they're just doing it so they have something different to put on their résumé when they graduate. They have no idea how much work is actually involved. In the end, though, all that matters is that the houses get built, and they will. They always do."

"You've done this before?"

"Every summer since I was sixteen. I used to do it with our church, but when I went off to Chapel Hill, we started a group there. Well, actually, Tim started it. He's from Lenoir, too. He just graduated and he'll start on his master's degree this fall. I've known him forever. Instead of spending the summer working odd jobs at home or doing internships, we thought we could offer students a chance to make a difference. Everyone chips in for the house and pays their own expenses for the month, and we don't charge anything for the labor we do on the houses. That's why it was so important that I get my bag back. I wouldn't have been able to eat all month."

"I'm sure they wouldn't have let you starve."

"I know, but it wouldn't be fair. They're already doing something worthy, and that's more than enough."

I could feel my feet slipping in the sand.

"Why Wilmington?" I asked. "I mean, why come here to build houses, instead of somewhere like Lenoir or Raleigh?"

"Because of the beach. You know how people are. It's hard enough to get students to volunteer their time for a month, but it's easier if it's in a place like this. And the more people you have, the more you can do. Thirty people signed up this year."

I nodded, conscious of how close together we were walking. "And you graduated, too?"

"No, I'll be a senior. And I'm majoring in special education, if that's your next question."

"It was."

"I figured. When you're in college, that's what everyone asks you."

"Everyone asks me if I like being in the army."

"Do you?"

"I don't know."

She laughed, and the sound was so melodic that I knew I wanted to hear it again.

We reached the end of the pier, and I grabbed my board. I tossed the empty beer bottle into the garbage can, hearing it clank to the bottom. Stars were coming out overhead, and the lights from the houses outlined along the dunes reminded me of bright jack-o'-lanterns.

"Do you mind if I ask what led you to join the army? Given that you don't know whether you like it, I mean."

It took me a second to figure out how to answer that, and I shifted my surfboard to my other arm. "I think it's safest to say that at the time, I needed to."

She waited for me to add more, but when I didn't, she simply nodded.

"I'll bet you're glad to be back home for a little while," she said.

"Without a doubt."

46

"I'll bet your father is glad, too, huh?"

"I think so."

"He is. I'm sure he's very proud of you."

"I hope so."

"You sound like you're not certain."

"You'd have to meet my dad to understand. He's not much of a talker."

I could see the moonlight reflected in her dark eyes, and her voice was soft when she spoke. "He doesn't have to talk to be proud of you. He might be the kind of father who shows it in other ways."

I thought about that, hoping it was true. While I considered it, there was a loud scream from the house, and I caught sight of a couple of coeds near the fire. One of the guys had his arms wrapped around a girl and was pushing her forward; she was laughing and fighting him off. Brad and Susan were snuggling together nearby, but Randy had vanished.

"You said you don't know most of the people you'll be living with?"

She shook her head, her hair sweeping her shoulders. She swiped at another strand. "Not too well. We met most of them for the first time at the sign-up, then again today when we got here. I mean, we might have seen each other around campus now and then, and I think a lot of them know each other already, but I don't. Most of them are in fraternities and sororities. I still live in a dorm. They're a nice bunch, though."

As she answered, I got the feeling she was the kind of person who would never say a bad thing about anyone. Her regard for others struck me as refreshing and mature, and yet, strangely, I wasn't surprised. It was part of that indefinable quality I'd sensed about her from the beginning, a manner that set her apart.

47

"How old are you?" I asked as we approached the house.

"Twenty-one. I just had a birthday last month. You?"

"Twenty-three. Do you have brothers and sisters?"

"No. I was an only child. Just me and my folks. My parents still live in Lenoir, and they're happy as clams after twenty-five years. Your turn."

"The same. Except for me, it's always been just me and my dad."

I knew my answer would lead to a follow-up about the status of my mother, but to my surprise, it didn't come. Instead she asked, "Was he the one who taught you to surf?"

"No, I picked that up on my own when I was a kid."

"You're good. I was watching you earlier. You made it look so easy, graceful even. It made me wish I knew how."

"I'd be happy to teach you if you want to learn," I volunteered. "It's not that hard. I'll be out tomorrow."

She stopped and fixed her gaze on me. "Now, don't make offers you're not sure you intend to keep." She reached for my arm, leaving me speechless, then motioned toward the bonfire. "You ready to meet some people?"

I swallowed, feeling a sudden dryness in my throat, which was just about the strangest thing that had ever happened to me.

The house was one of those big three-storied monsters with the garage on the bottom and probably six or seven bedrooms. A massive deck circled the main level; towels were slung over the railings, and I could hear the sound of multiple conversations coming from all directions. A grill stood on the deck, and I could smell the hot dogs and chicken cooking; the guy leaning over it was shirtless and wearing a do-rag, trying to come across as urban cool. It wasn't working, but it did make me laugh.

*Dear John*

On the sand out front, the fire was set into a pit, with several girls in oversize sweatshirts seated in chairs circling it, all pretending to be oblivious to the boys around them. Meanwhile, the guys stood just beyond them, looking as if they were trying to pose in a way that accentuated the size of their arms or sculpted abs and acting as if they didn't notice the girls at all. I'd seen all this at Leroy's before; educated or not, kids were still kids. They were in their early twenties, and lust was in the air. Throw in the beach and beer, and I could guess what would happen later; but I would be long gone by then.

When Savannah and I drew near, she slowed before pointing. "How about over there, by the dune?" she suggested.

"Sure."

We took a seat facing the fire. A few of the other girls stared, checking out the new guy, before retreating into their conversations. Randy finally wandered toward the fire with a beer, saw Savannah and me, and quickly turned his back, following the example of the girls.

"Chicken or hot dog?" she asked, seemingly oblivious to all of this.

"Chicken."

"What do you want to drink?"

The firelight made her look newly mysterious. "Whatever you're having's fine. Thanks."

"I'll be right back."

She headed toward the steps, and I forced myself not to follow. Instead I walked toward the fire, slipped off my shirt, and laid it over an empty chair, then returned to my seat. Glancing up, I saw do-rag flirting with Savannah, felt a surge of tension, then turned away to get a better grip on things. I knew little about her and knew even less about what she thought of me.

49

Besides, I had no desire to start something I couldn't finish. I was leaving in a couple of weeks, and none of this would amount to anything. I told myself all those things, and I think I partially convinced myself that I'd head home just as soon as I finished eating, when my thoughts were interrupted by the sight of someone approaching. Tall and lanky, with dark hair that was already receding parted neatly to the side, he reminded me of those guys you met from time to time who looked middle-aged from birth.

"You must be John," he said with a smile, squatting in front of me. "My name's Tim Wheddon." He extended his hand. "I heard what you did for Savannah—I know she was grateful you were there."

I shook his hand. "It's nice to meet you."

Despite my initial wariness, his smile was more genuine than either Brad's or Randy's had been. Nor did he mention my tattoos, which was unusual. I suppose I should mention they weren't exactly small and covered most of my arms. People have told me I'll regret it when I'm older, but at the time I got them, I really didn't care. I still don't.

"Do you mind if I take a seat?" he asked.

"Help yourself."

He made himself comfortable, neither crowding me nor sitting too far away. "I'm glad you could come. I mean, it's not much, but the food's good. Are you hungry?"

"Actually, I'm starved."

"Surfing will do that to you."

"Do you surf?"

"No, but spending time in the ocean always makes me hungry. I remember that from being on vacation as a kid. We used to go to Pine Knoll Shores every summer. Have you been there?"

"Only once. I had all I needed here."

"Yeah, I suppose you did." He motioned to my board. "You like the long boards, huh?"

"I like 'em both, but the waves here are better suited for the long ones. You need to ride in the Pacific to really enjoy a short board."

"Have you been there? Hawaii, Bali, New Zealand, places like that? I've read they're the ultimate."

"Not yet," I said, surprised he'd know about them. "One day, maybe."

A log crackled, sending small sparks up to the sky. I brought my hands together, knowing it was my turn. "I hear you're here to build some homes for the poor."

"Did Savannah tell you that? Yeah, that's the plan, anyway. They're for a couple of really deserving families, and hopefully they'll be in their own homes by the end of July."

"That's a good thing you're doing."

"It's not just me. But hey, I wanted to ask you something."

"Let me guess, you want me to volunteer?"

He laughed. "No, nothing like that. That's funny, though— I've heard that before. People see me coming and usually they run the other way. I guess I'm way too easy to read. Anyway, I know it's a long shot, but I was wondering if you know my cousin. He's stationed at Fort Bragg."

"Sorry," I said. "I'm posted in Germany."

"At Ramstein?"

"No. That's the air force base. But I'm relatively close. Why?"

"I was in Frankfurt last December. I spent Christmas there with my family. That's where we're originally from, and my grandparents still live there."

"Small world."

"Have you learned any German?"

"Not a bit."

"Me neither. The sad thing is, my parents are fluent and I've heard it at home for years, and I even took a class in it before I went. But I just didn't get it, you know? I think I was lucky to pass the class, and all I could do was nod at the dinner table and pretend I understood what everyone was saying. The only saving grace was that my brother was in the same boat, so we could feel like morons together."

I laughed. He had an open, honest face, and despite myself, I liked him.

"Hey, can I get you anything?" he asked.

"Savannah's taking care of it."

"I should have guessed. Perfect hostess and all that. Always has been."

"She said you two grew up together?"

He nodded. "Her family's ranch is right next to ours. We went to the same schools and attended the same church for years, and then we were at the same university. She's kind of like my little sister. She's special."

Despite the sister comment, I got the impression by the way he said "special" that his feelings ran a little deeper than he was letting on. But unlike Randy, he didn't seem at all jealous about the fact that she'd invited me here. Before I could puzzle over it, Savannah appeared on the stairs and stepped onto the sand.

"I see you met Tim," she said, nodding. In one hand were two plates with chicken, potato salad, and chips; in the other were two cans of Diet Pepsi.

"Yeah, I just wanted to come over and thank him for what he did," Tim explained, "then decided to bore him with family stories."

"Good. I was hoping you two would have a chance to meet." She held up her hands; like Tim, she ignored the fact that I was shirtless. "The food's ready. Would you like my plate, Tim? I can go up and get another."

"Nah, I'll get it," Tim said, standing. "Thanks, though. I'll let you two dig in." He brushed the sand from his shorts. "Hey, it was nice meeting you, John. If you're in the area again tomorrow or whenever, you're always welcome."

"Thanks. Nice meeting you, too."

A moment later, Tim was heading up the stairs. He didn't look back, merely called out a friendly hello to someone going in the opposite direction, then bounded up the rest of the way.

Savannah handed me the plate and some plastic utensils, switched hands and offered me a soda, then took a seat beside me. Close, I noticed, but not quite close enough to touch. She propped her plate on her lap, then reached for her can before hesitating. She held up the can.

"You were drinking beer earlier, but you said to get whatever I was getting, so I brought you one of these. I wasn't quite sure what you wanted."

"The soda's fine."

"You sure? There's plenty of beer in the coolers, and I've heard about you army guys."

I snorted. "I'm sure," I said, opening my can. "I take it you don't drink."

"I don't," she said. No defensiveness or smugness in her tone, I noted, just the truth. I liked that.

She ate a bite of her chicken. I did the same, and in the silence, I wondered about her and Tim and whether she was aware of how he really felt about her. And I wondered how she felt about him. There was something there, but I couldn't figure it out, unless Tim was right and it was a sibling-type thing. I somehow doubted that was the case.

"What do you do in the army?" she asked, finally putting down her fork.

"I'm a sergeant in the infantry. Weapons squad."

"What's it like? I mean, what do you do every day? Do you shoot guns, or blow things up, or what?"

"Sometimes. But actually, it's pretty boring most of the time, at least when we're on base. We assemble in the morning, usually around six or so, make sure everyone's there, and then we break into squads to exercise. Basketball, running, weight lifting, whatever. Sometimes there's a class that day, anything from assembling and reassembling our weapons, or a night-terrain class, or we might head to the rifle range, or whatever. If nothing's planned, we just head back to the barracks and play video games or read or work out again or whatever for the rest of the day. Then we reassemble at four o'clock and find out what we're doing tomorrow. Then we're done."

"Video games?"

"I work out and read. But my buddies are experts at games. And the more violent the game, the more they like it."

"What do you read?"

I told her, and she considered it. "And what happens when you're sent to a war zone?"

"Then," I said, finishing my chicken, "it's different. There's guard duty, and things are always breaking and need to be fixed, so you're busy, even when you're not out on patrol. But the infantry are the forces on the ground, so we spend a big chunk of our time away from camp."

"Do you ever get scared?"

I searched for the right answer. "Yeah. Sometimes. It's not

like you're walking around terrified all the time, even when things are going to hell all around you. It's just that you're . . . reacting, trying to stay alive. Things are happening so fast that you don't have time to think much of anything except doing your job and trying not to die. It usually affects you afterward, once you're clear. That's when you realize how close you came, and sometimes you get the shakes or puke or whatever."

"I'm not sure I could do what you do."

I wasn't sure if she expected a response to that, so I switched topics. "Why special education?" I asked.

"It's kind of a long story. You sure you want to hear it?"

When I nodded, she drew a long breath.

"There's this boy in Lenoir named Alan, and I've known him all my life. He's autistic, and for a long time no one knew what to do with him or how to get through to him. And it just got to me, you know? I felt so bad for him, even when I was little. When I asked my parents about it, they said that maybe the Lord had special plans for him. It didn't make any sense at first, but Alan had an older brother who was so patient with him all the time. I mean always. He never got frustrated with him, and little by little, he helped Alan. Alan's not perfect by any stretch—he still lives with his parents, and he'll never be on his own—but he's not as lost as he was when he was younger, and I just decided that I wanted to be able to help kids like Alan."

"How old were you when you decided that?"

"Twelve."

"And you want to work with them in a school?"

"No," she said. "I want to do what Alan's brother did. He used horses." She paused, collecting her thoughts. "With autistic kids . . . it's like they're locked into their own little worlds, so usually school and therapy are based on routine. But I want to show them experiences that can open new doors for them. I've seen it happen. I mean, Alan was terrified of the horses at first, but his brother kept trying, and after a while, Alan got to the point where he would pat them or rub their noses, then later even feed them. After that, he started to ride, and I remember watching his face the first time he was up there...it was just so incredible, you know? I mean, he was smiling, just as happy as a kid could be. And that's what I want these kids to experience. Just...happiness, even if it's only for a short while. That's when I knew exactly what I wanted to do with my life. Maybe open a riding camp for autistic kids, where we can really work with them. So maybe they can feel that same happiness that Alan did."

She put down her fork as if embarrassed, then set her plate off to the side.

"That sounds wonderful."

"We'll see if it happens," she said, sitting up again. "It's just a dream for now."

"I take it you like horses, too?"

"All girls love horses. Don't you know that? But yes, I do. I have an Arabian named Midas, and it kills me sometimes that I'm here when I could be off riding him."

"The truth comes out."

"As it should. But I'm still planning to stay here. I'll ride all day, every day, when I get back. Do you ride?"

"I did once."

"Did you like it?"

"I was sore the next day. It hurt to walk."

She giggled, and I realized I liked talking to her. It was easy and natural, unlike with so many people. Above me, I could see Orion's belt; just over the horizon on the water, Venus had appeared and glowed a heavy white. Guys and girls continued to tramp up and down the stairs, flirting with booze-induced courage. I sighed.

"I should probably get going so I can visit with my dad for a while. He's probably wondering where I am. If he's still awake, that is."

"Do you want to call him? You can use the phone."

"No, I think I'll just head out. It's a long walk."

"You don't have a car?"

"No. I hitched a ride this morning."

"Do you want Tim to drive you home? I'm sure he won't mind."

"No, that's okay."

"Don't be ridiculous. You said it was a long walk, right? I'll have Tim drive you. Let me get him."

She raced off before I could stop her, and a minute later Tim was following her out of the house. "Tim is happy to take you," she said, looking way too pleased with herself.

I turned toward Tim. "You sure?"

"No problem at all," he assured me. "My truck's out front. You can just put your board in the back." He motioned to the board. "Need a hand?"

"No," I said, rising, "I got it." I went to the chair and slipped on my shirt, then picked up my board. "Thanks, by the way."

"My pleasure," he said. He patted his pocket. "I'll be back in a second with the keys. It's the green truck parked on the grass. I'll meet you out front."

When he was gone, I turned back to Savannah. "It was nice meeting you."

She held my gaze. "You too. I've never hung out with a soldier before. I felt sort of...protected. I don't think Randy'll give me any trouble tonight. Your tattoos probably scared him away."

I guess she had noticed them. "Maybe I'll see you around."

"You know where I'll be."

I wasn't sure whether that meant she wanted me to come visit again or didn't. In many ways, she remained a complete mystery to me. Then again, I barely knew her at all.

"But I am a little disappointed that you forgot," she added, almost as an afterthought.

"Forgot what?"

"Didn't you say that you'd teach me how to surf?"

If Tim had any inkling of the effect Savannah had on me or that I'd be visiting again the next day, he gave no indication. Instead he focused mainly on the drive, making sure he was heading in the right direction. He was the kind of driver who stopped the car even when the light was yellow and he could have sailed through.

"I hope you had a good time," he said. "I know it's always strange when you don't know anyone."

"I did."

"You and Savannah really hit it off. She's something, isn't she? I think she liked you."

"We had a nice conversation," I said.

"I'm glad. I was a little worried about her coming down here. Last year her parents were with us, so this is the first time she's been on her own like this. I know she's a big girl, but these aren't the kind of people she usually hangs out with, and the last thing I wanted was for her to be fending off guys all night."

"I'm sure she could have handled it."

"You're probably right. But I get the feeling that some of these guys are pretty persistent."

"Of course they are. They're guys."

He laughed. "I guess you're right." He motioned toward the window. "Which way now?"

I directed him through a series of turns, then finally I told him to slow the car. He stopped in front of the house, where I could see the light from my dad's den glowing yellow.

"Thanks for the ride," I said, opening my door.

"No problem." He leaned over the seat. "And listen, like I said, feel free to stop by the house anytime. We work during the week, but weekends and evenings are usually clear."

"I'll keep that in mind," I promised.

Once inside, I went to my dad's den and opened the door. He was peering at the *Greysheet* and jumped. I realized he hadn't heard me come in.

"Sorry," I said, taking a seat on the single step that separated the den from the rest of the house. "Didn't mean to scare you."

"It's okay," was all he said. He debated whether to set aside the *Greysheet,* then did.

"The waves were great today," I commented. "I'd almost forgotten how fantastic the water feels."

He smiled but again said nothing. I shifted slightly on the step. "How'd work go?" I asked.

"The same," he said.

He lapsed back into his own thoughts, and all I could think was that the same thing could be said about our conversations.

# Chapter 3

Surfing is a solitary sport, one in which long stretches of boredom are interspersed with frantic activity, and it teaches you to flow with nature, instead of fighting it...it's about getting in the *zone.* That's what the surfing magazines say, anyway, and I mostly agree. There's nothing quite as exciting as catching a wave and living within a wall of water as it rolls toward shore. But I'm not like a lot of those dudes with freeze-dried skin and stringy hair who do it all day, every day, because they think it's the be-all and end-all of existence. It isn't. For me, it's more about the fact that the world is crazy noisy almost all the time, and when you're out there, it's not. You're able to hear yourself think."

This is what I was telling Savannah, anyway, as we made our way toward the ocean early Sunday morning. At least, that's what I thought I was saying. For the most part, I was just sort of rambling, trying not to be too obvious about the fact that I really liked the way she looked in a bikini.

"Like horseback riding," she said.

"Huh?"

"Hearing yourself think. That's why I like riding, too."

I'd shown up a few minutes earlier. The best waves were usually early in the morning, and it was one of those clear, blue-sky days portending heat that meant the beach would be packed again. Savannah had been sitting on the steps out back, wrapped in a towel, the remains of the bonfire before her. Despite the fact that the party had no doubt gone on for hours after I'd left, there wasn't a single empty can or piece of trash anywhere. My impression of the group improved a bit.

Despite the hour, the air was already warm. We spent a few minutes in the sand near the water's edge going over the basics of surfing, and I explained how to pop up on the board. When Savannah thought she was ready, I waded in carrying the board, walking beside her.

There were only a few surfers out, the same ones I'd seen the day before. I was trying to figure out the best place to bring Savannah so she'd have enough room when I realized I could no longer see her.

"Hold on, hold on!" she shouted from behind me. "Stop, stop..."

I turned. Savannah was on her tiptoes as the first splashes of water hit her belly, and her upper body was immediately covered in gooseflesh. She appeared to be trying to lift herself from the water.

"Let me get used to this..." She gave a few quick, audible gasps and crossed her arms. "Wow. This is *really* cold. Holy cow!"

*Holy cow?* It wasn't exactly something my buddies would say. "You'll get used to it," I said, smirking.

"I don't *like* being cold. I *hate* being cold."

"You live in the mountains where it snows."

"Yeah, but we have these things called jackets and gloves and hats that we wear to keep warm. And we don't thrust ourselves into arctic waters first thing in the morning."

"Funny," I said.

She continued to hop up and down. "Yeah, real funny. I mean, geez!"

*Geez?* I grinned. Her breathing gradually began to even out, but the gooseflesh was still there. She took another tiny step forward.

"It works best if you just jump right in and go under instead of torturing yourself in stages," I suggested.

"You do it your way, I'll do it mine," she said, unimpressed with my wisdom. "I can't believe you wanted to come out now. I was thinking sometime in the afternoon, when the temperature was above freezing."

"It's almost eighty degrees."

"Yeah, yeah," she said, finally acclimating. Uncrossing her arms, she took another series of breaths, then dipped maybe an inch. Steeling herself, she slapped a bit of water on her arms. "Okay, I think I'm getting there."

"Don't rush for me. Really. Take your time."

"I will, thank you," she said, ignoring the teasing tone. "Okay," she said again, more to herself than me. She took a small step forward, then another. As she moved, her face was a mask of concentration, and I liked the way it looked. So serious, so intense. So ridiculous.

"Quit laughing at me," she said, noting my expression.

"I'm not laughing."

"I can see it in your face. You're laughing on the inside."

"All right, I'll stop."

Eventually she waded out to join me, and when the water was up to my shoulders, Savannah climbed on the board. I held it in place, trying again not to stare at her figure, which wasn't easy, considering it was right in front of me. I forced myself to monitor the swells behind us.

"Now what?"

"Do you remember what to do? Paddle hard, grab the board on both sides near the front, then pop up to your feet?"

"Got it."

"It's kind of tough at first. Don't be surprised if you fall, but if you do, just roll with it. It usually takes a few times to get it."

"Okay," she said, and I saw a small swell approaching.

"Get ready . . . ," I said, timing it. "Okay, start paddling . . ."

As the wave hit us, I pushed the board, giving it some momentum, and Savannah caught the wave. I don't know what I expected, except that it wasn't to see her pop straight up, keep her balance, and ride the wave all the way back to shore, where it finally petered out. In the shallow water, she jumped off the board as it slowed and turned with dramatic flair toward me.

"How was that?" she called out.

Despite the distance between us, I couldn't look away. Oh man, I suddenly thought, I'm in real trouble.

"I did gymnastics for years," she admitted. "I've always had a good sense of balance. I suppose I should have said something about that while you were telling me I was going to wipe out."

We spent more than an hour in the water. She popped up every time and rode the waves to shore with ease; though she couldn't steer the board, I had no doubt that if she wanted to, she would be able to master that in no time.

Afterward, we returned to the house. I waited out back while she went upstairs. While a few people had risen—three girls were on the deck staring at the ocean—most were still recovering from the night before and nowhere to be seen. Savannah emerged a couple of minutes later in shorts and a T-shirt, holding two cups of coffee. She sat beside me on the steps as we faced the water.

"I didn't say you'd wipe out," I clarified. "I just said that if you did, you should roll with it."

"Uh-huh," she said, her expression mischievous. She pointed to my cup. "Is your coffee okay?"

"Tastes great," I said.

"I have to start my day with coffee. It's my one vice."

"Everyone's got to have one."

She glanced at me. "What's yours?"

"I don't have any," I answered, and she surprised me by giving me a playful nudge.

"Did you know that last night was the first night of the full moon?"

I did but thought it best not to admit it. "Really?" I said.

"I've always loved full moons. Ever since I was a kid. I liked to think that they were an omen of sorts. I wanted to believe they always portended good things. Like if I was making a mistake, I would have the chance to start over."

She said nothing else about it. Instead she brought the cup to her lips, and I watched as the steam wreathed her face.

"What's on your agenda today?" I asked.

"We're supposed to have a meeting sometime today, but other than that, nothing. Well, except for church. For me,

I mean. And, well, whoever else wants to go. Which reminds me—what time is it?"

I checked my watch. "A little after nine."

"Already? I guess that doesn't give me much time. Service is at ten."

I nodded, knowing our time together was almost up.

"Do you want to go with me?" I heard her ask.

"To church?"

"Yeah. To church," she said. "Don't you go?"

I wasn't sure what to say. It was obviously important to her, and though I got the impression that my answer would disappoint, I didn't want to lie. "Not really," I admitted. "I haven't been to church in years. I mean, I used to go as a kid, but..." I trailed off. "I don't know why," I finished.

She stretched her legs out, waiting to see if I would add more. When I didn't, she arched an eyebrow. "So?"

"What?"

"Do you want to go with me or not?"

"I don't have any clothes. I mean, this is all I have, and I doubt if I have enough time to go home, shower, and get back in time. Otherwise I would."

She gave me the once-over. "Good." She patted my knee, the second time she'd touched me. "I'll get you some clothes."

"You look great," Tim assured me. "The collar's a little snug, but I don't think anyone will be able to tell."

In the mirror, I saw a stranger dressed in khakis and a pressed shirt and tie. I couldn't remember the last time I'd worn a tie. I wasn't sure I was happy about any of this or not. Tim, meanwhile, was way too chipper about the whole thing.

"How'd she talk you into this?" he asked.

"I have no idea."

He laughed and, leaning over to tie his shoes, winked. "I told you she likes you."

We've got chaplains in the army, and most of them are pretty good guys. On base, I got to know a couple of them fairly well, and one of them—Ted Jenkins—was the kind of guy you trusted on the spot. He didn't drink, and I'm not saying he was one of us, but he was always welcome when he showed up. He had a wife and a couple of rugrats, and he'd been in the service for fifteen years. He had personal experience when it came to struggles with family and military life in general, and if you ever sat down to talk with him, he really listened. You couldn't tell him everything—he was an officer, after all—and he ended up coming down fairly hard on a couple of guys in my platoon who admitted their escapades a bit too freely, but the thing was, he had this kind of presence that made you want to tell him anyway. I don't know what it was other than the fact that he was a good man and a hell of an army chaplain. He talked about God just as naturally as you might talk about your friend, not in that preachy, irritating way that generally turns me off. Nor did he press you to attend services on Sundays. He sort of left it up to you, and depending what was going on or how dangerous things got, he might find himself talking to either one or two people or a hundred. Before my platoon was sent to the Balkans, he probably baptized fifty people.

I'd been baptized as a kid, so I didn't go that route, but like I said, it had been a long time since I'd been to service. I'd stopped going with my dad a long time ago, and I didn't know what to expect. Nor can I honestly say I was looking forward to it, but in the end, the service wasn't that bad. The pastor was low-key, the music was all right, and time didn't drag by the way it always seemed to when I was little. I'm not saying I got much out of it, but even so, I was glad I went, if only so I could talk about something new with my dad. And also because it gave me just a bit more time with Savannah.

Savannah ended up sitting between Tim and me, and I watched her from the corner of my eye as she sang. She had a quiet, low-key singing voice but was always in tune, and I liked the way it sounded. Tim stayed focused on the scriptures, and on the way out, he stopped to visit with the pastor while Savannah and I waited in the shade of a dogwood tree out front. Tim looked animated as he chatted with the pastor.

"Old friends?" I asked, nodding toward Tim. Despite the shade, I was getting hot and could feel trails of perspiration beginning to form.

"No. I think his dad was the one who told him about this pastor. He had to use MapQuest last night to find this place." She fanned herself; in her sundress, she reminded me of a proper southern belle. "I'm glad you came."

"So am I," I agreed.

"Are you hungry?"

"Getting there."

"We have some food back at the house, if you want some. And you can give Tim his clothes back. I can tell you're hot and uncomfortable."

"It's not half as hot as helmets, boots, and body armor, trust me."

She tilted her head up at me. "I like hearing you talk about body armor. Not a lot of guys in my classes talk like you. I find it interesting."

"You teasing me?"

"Just noting for the record." She leaned gracefully against the tree. "I think Tim's finishing up."

I followed her gaze, noticing nothing different. "How can you tell?"

"See how he brought his hands together? That means he's getting ready to say good-bye. In just a second, he's going to put his hand out, he'll smile and nod, and then he'll be on his way."

I watched Tim do exactly as she predicted and amble toward us. I noted her amused expression. She shrugged. "When you live in a small town like mine, there's not much to do other than watch people. You begin to see patterns after a while."

There'd probably been too much Tim-watching in my humble opinion, but I wasn't about to admit it.

"Hey there..." Tim raised a hand. "You two ready to head back?"

"We've been waiting for you," she pointed out.

"Sorry," he said. "We just got to talking."

"You just get to talking with anyone and everyone."

"I know," he said. "I'm working on being more standoffish."

She laughed, and while their familiar banter put me momentarily outside their circle of intimacy, all was forgotten when Savannah looped her arm through mine on our way back toward the car.

Everyone was up by the time we got back, and most were already in their bathing suits and working on their tans. Some were lounging on the upper deck; most were clustered together on the beach out back. Music blasted from a stereo inside the house, coolers of beer stood refilled and ready, and more than a few were drinking: the age-old cure for the hangover headache. I passed no judgment; a beer sounded good, actually, but given that I'd just been to church, I figured I should pass.

I changed my clothes, folding Tim's the way I'd learned in the army, then returned to the kitchen. Tim had made a plate of sandwiches.

"Help yourself," he said, gesturing. "We have tons of food. I should know—I'm the one who spent three hours shopping yesterday." He rinsed his hands and dried them on a towel. "All right. Now it's my turn to change. Savannah will be out in a minute."

He left the kitchen. Alone, I looked around. The house was decorated in that traditional beachy way: lots of bright-colored wicker furniture, lamps made with seashells, small statues of lighthouses above the mantel, pastel paintings of the coast.

Lucy's parents had owned a place like this. Not here, but on Bald Head Island. They never rented it out, preferring to spend their summers there. Of course, the old man still had to work in Winston-Salem, and he and the wife would head back for a couple of days a week, leaving poor Lucy all alone. Except for me, of course. Had they known what was happening on those days, they probably wouldn't have left us alone.

"Hey there," Savannah said. She'd donned her bikini again, though she was wearing shorts over the bottoms. "I see you're back to normal."

"How can you tell?"

"Your eyes aren't bulging because your collar's too tight."

I smiled. "Tim made some sandwiches."

"Great. I'm starved," she said, moving around the kitchen. "Did you grab one?"

"Not yet," I said.

"Well, dig in. I hate to eat alone."

We stood in the kitchen as we ate. The girls lying on the deck hadn't realized we were there, and I could hear one of them talking about what she did with one of the guys last night, and none of it sounded as though she were in town on a goodwill mission for the poor. Savannah wrinkled her nose as if to say, *Way too much information,* then turned to the fridge. "I need a drink. Do you want something?"

"Water's fine."

She bent over to grab a couple of bottles. I tried not to stare but did so anyway and, frankly, enjoyed it. I wondered whether she knew I was staring and assumed she did, for when she stood up and turned around, she had that amused look again. She set the bottles on the counter. "After this, you want to go surfing again?"

How could I resist?

We spent the afternoon in the water. As much as I enjoyed the up-close-Savannah-lying-on-the-board view I was treated to, I enjoyed the sight of her surfing even more. To make things even better, she asked to watch me while she warmed up on the beach, and I was treated to my own private viewing while enjoying the waves.

By midafternoon we were lying on towels near, but not too near, the rest of the group behind the house. A few curious glances drifted in our direction, but for the most part, no one seemed to care that I was there, except for Randy and Susan. Susan frowned pointedly at Savannah; Randy, meanwhile, was content to hang out with Brad and Susan as the third wheel, licking his wounds. Tim was nowhere to be seen.

Savannah was lying on her stomach, a tempting sight. I was on my back beside her, trying to doze in the lazy heat but too distracted by her presence to fully relax.

"Hey," she murmured. "Tell me about your tattoos."

I rolled my head in the sand. "What about them?"

"I don't know. Why you got them, what they mean."

I propped myself on one elbow. I pointed to my left arm,

which had an eagle and banner. "Okay, this is the infantry insignia, and this"—I pointed to the words and letters—"is how we're identified: company, battalion, regiment. Everyone in my squad has one. We got it just after basic training at Fort Benning in Georgia when we were celebrating."

"Why does it say 'Jump-start' underneath it?"

"That's my nickname. I got it during basic training, courtesy of our beloved drill sergeant. I wasn't putting my gun together fast enough, and he basically said that he was going to jump-start a certain body part if I didn't get my act in gear. The nickname stuck."

"He sounds pleasant," she joked.

"Oh yeah. We called him Lucifer behind his back."

She smiled. "What's the barbed wire above it for?"

"Nothing," I said, shaking my head. "I had that one done before I joined."

"And the other arm?"

A Chinese character. I didn't want to go into it, so I shook my head. "It's from back in my 'I'm lost and don't give a damn' stage. It doesn't mean anything."

"Isn't it a Chinese character?"

"Yes."

"Then what does it mean? It's got to mean something. Like bravery or honor or something?"

"It's a profanity."

"Oh," she said with a blink.

"Like I said, it doesn't mean anything to me now."

"Except that maybe you shouldn't flash it if you ever go to China."

I laughed. "Yeah, except that," I agreed.

She was quiet for a moment. "You were a rebel, huh?"

I nodded. "A long time ago. Well, not really that long ago. But it seems like it."

"That's what you meant when you said the army was something you needed at the time?"

"It's been good for me."

She thought about it. "Tell me—would you have jumped for my bag back then?"

"No. I probably would have laughed at what happened."

She evaluated my answer, as if wondering whether to believe me. Finally, she drew a long breath. "I'm glad you joined, then. I really needed that bag."

"Good."

"What else?"

"What else what?"

"What else can you tell me about yourself?"

"I don't know. What do you want to know?"

"Tell me something no one else knows about you."

I considered the question. "I can tell you how many ten-dollar Indians with a rolled edge were minted in 1907."

"How many?"

"Forty-two. They were never intended for the public. Some men at the mint made them for themselves and some friends."

"You like coins?"

"I'm not sure. It's a long story."

"We've got time."

I hesitated while Savannah reached for her bag. "Hold on," she said, rummaging through it. She pulled out a tube of Coppertone. "You can tell me after you put some lotion on my back. I feel like I'm getting burned."

"Oh, I can, huh?"

She winked. "It's part of the deal."

I applied the lotion to her back and shoulders and probably went a bit overboard, but I convinced myself that she was turning pink and that having a sunburn of any sort would make her work the next day miserable. After that, I spent the next few minutes telling her about my grandfather and dad, about the coin shows and good old Eliasberg. What I didn't do was specifically answer her question, for the simple reason that I wasn't quite sure what the answer was. When I finished she turned to me.

"And your father still collects coins?"

"All the time. At least, I think so. We don't talk about coins anymore."

"Why not?"

I told her that story, too. Don't ask me why. I knew I should have been putting my best foot forward and tossing out crap to impress her, but with Savannah that wasn't possible. For whatever reason, she made me want to tell the truth, even though I barely knew her. When I finished she was wearing a curious expression.

"Yeah, I was a jerk," I offered, knowing there were other, probably more accurate words to describe me back then, all of which were profane enough to offend her.

"It sounds like it," she said, "but that's not what I was thinking. I was trying to imagine you back then, because you seem nothing like that person now."

What could I say that wouldn't sound bogus, even if it was true? Unsure, I opted for Dad's approach and said nothing.

"What's your dad like?"

I gave her a quick recap. As I spoke, she scooped sand and let it trail through her fingers, as if concentrating on my choice of words. In the end, surprising myself again, I admitted that we were almost strangers.

"You are," she said, using that nonjudgmental, matter-of-fact tone. "You've been gone for a couple of years, and even you admit that you've changed. How could he know you?"

I sat up. The beach was packed; it was the time of day when everyone who planned to come was already here, and no one was quite ready to leave. Randy and Brad were playing Frisbee by the water's edge, running and shouting. A few others wandered over to join them.

"I know," I said. "But it's not just that. We've always been strangers. I mean, it's just so hard to talk to him."

As soon as I said it, I realized she was the first person I'd ever admitted it to. Strange. But then, most of what I was saying to her sounded strange.

"Most people our age say that about their parents."

Maybe, I thought. But this was different. It wasn't a generational difference, it was the fact that for my dad, normal chitchat was all but impossible, unless it dealt with coins. I said nothing more, however, and Savannah smoothed the sand in front of her. When she spoke, her voice was soft. "I'd like to meet him."

I turned toward her. "Yeah?"

"He sounds interesting. I've always loved people who have this . . . passion for life."

"It's a passion for coins, not life," I corrected her.

"It's the same thing. Passion is passion. It's the excitement between the tedious spaces, and it doesn't matter where it's directed." She shuffled her feet in the sand. "Well, most of the time, anyway. I'm not talking vices here."

"Like you and caffeine."

She smiled, flashing the small gap between her two front teeth. "Exactly. It can be coins or sports or politics or horses or music or faith . . . the saddest people I've ever met in life are the ones who don't care deeply about anything at all. Passion and satisfaction go hand in hand, and without them, any happiness is only temporary, because there's nothing to make it last. I'd love to hear your dad talk about coins, because that's when you see a person at his best, and I've found that someone else's happiness is usually infectious."

I was struck by her words. Despite Tim's opinion that she was naive, she seemed far more mature than most people our age. Then again, considering the way she looked in her bikini, she probably could have recited the phone book and I would have been impressed.

Savannah sat up beside me, and her gaze followed mine. The game of Frisbee was in full swing; as Brad zipped the disk, a couple of others went running for it. They both dove for it simultaneously, splashing in the shallows as their heads collided. The one in red shorts came up empty, swearing and holding his head, his shorts covered in sand. The others laughed, and I found myself smiling and wincing simultaneously.

"Did you see that?" I asked.

"Hold on," she said instead. "I'll be right back." She trotted over to red shorts. He saw her approaching and froze, as did the guy next to him. Savannah, I realized, had pretty much the same effect on every guy, not just me. I could see her talking and smiling, turning that earnest gaze on the guy, who nodded as she spoke, looking like a chastised adolescent. She returned to my side and sat again. I didn't ask, knowing it wasn't my business, but I knew I was telegraphing my curiosity.

"Normally, I wouldn't have said anything, but I asked him to keep his language in check because of all the families out here," she explained. "There are lots of little kids around. He said he would."

I should have guessed. "Did you suggest he use 'Holy cow' or 'Geez' instead?"

She squinted at me mischievously. "You liked those expressions, didn't you."

"I'm thinking of passing them on to my squad. They'll add to our intimidation factor when we're busting down doors and launching RPGs."

She giggled. "Definitely scarier than swearing, even if I don't know what an RPG is."

"Rocket-propelled grenade." Despite myself, I liked her more with every passing minute. "What are you doing tonight?"

"I don't have any plans. Well, except for the meeting. Why? Did you want to bring me to meet your father?"

"No. Well, not tonight, anyway. Later. Tonight, I wanted to show you around Wilmington."

"Are you asking me out?"

"Yeah," I admitted. "I'll have you back whenever you want. I know you've got to work tomorrow, but there's this great place that I want to show you."

"What kind of place?"

"A local place. Specializes in seafood. But it's more of an experience."

She wrapped her arms around her knees. "I usually don't date strangers," she finally said, "and we only met yesterday. You think I can trust you?"

"I wouldn't," I said.

She laughed. "Well, in that case, I suppose I can make an exception."

"Yeah?"

"Yeah," she said. "I'm a sucker for honest guys with crew cuts. What time?"

# Questions and Explanations for Chapters 2 and 3

The ten questions on chapters 2 and 3 focus on grammar and usage, vocabulary, comprehension, literary terms, style, and characterization. Some of the questions combine two or more of these areas, requiring you to synthesize your knowledge, make inferences, and interpret the text. The questions are designed to determine both your current level of understanding of the novel and your ability to answer higher-level questions.

The following sentence tests your ability to recognize grammar and usage errors. The sentence contains either a single error or no error at all. If the sentence contains an error, select the one underlined part that must be changed to make the sentence correct. If there is no error, select choice D.

1. Although <u>it's</u> frustrating for John to eat every meal in
          <sub>A</sub>
   silence, the silence is essential to his <u>father's</u> comfort,
                                               <sub>B</sub>
   with <u>it's</u> sense of order and familiarity. <u>No error</u>
      <sub>C</sub>                                             <sub>D</sub>

Each of these choices checks the use of the apostrophe. The contraction *it's* is a combination of the words *it is* (or *it has*). Use the substitution method to determine if the words *it is* or *it has* make sense in the sentence. Choice B checks the use of an apostrophe to show possession. A singular noun demonstrates possession with an apostrophe and an *s*—for example, "the boy's book, the girl's letter, the surfer's board." If you want the pronoun *it* to show possession, just add an *s*—for example, "the cat hurt its paw."

> **Question 2 tests your vocabulary. Choose the word that, when inserted in the sentence, best fits the meaning of the sentence as a whole.**

2. "It was one of those clear, blue-sky days \_\_\_\_\_ heat that meant the beach would be packed again."

   A. exacerbating

   B. mitigating

   C. nullifying

   D. portending

This question tests your comprehension and your vocabulary. *Exacerbating*, choice A, means worsening or aggravating. *Mitigating*, choice B, means lessening. *Nullifying*, choice

C, means negating or abolishing. *Portending*, choice D, means foreshadowing.

**Question 3 tests your knowledge of literary terms.**

3. "I felt something click, like a key turning in a lock." Identify the literary term used to describe the moment when John's eyes met Savannah's.

    A. allusion

    B. metaphor

    C. personification

    D. simile

Knowing about figures of speech will help you answer this question. An *allusion*, choice A, is an indirect reference. Some of the most common types of allusions are historical (when someone meets his Waterloo, it's a reference to Napoleon); biblical (such as John Coffey in *The Green Mile* being a Christ figure); mythological (a reference to a Greek or Roman myth, such as a character being said to have the Midas touch); and literary (a reference to a character in a work of literature, such as a couple being compared to Romeo and Juliet). A *metaphor*, choice B, is a comparison between two unlike things without using a connective word—for example, "Michael Phelps was a flying fish in the pool." *Personification*, choice C, is giving a nonhuman thing a human characteristic, such as in "Opportunity knocked on the door." And a *simile*, choice D, is a comparison of two unlike things using a connective word, such as *like*, *as*, or *than*—for example, "She looked as fresh as the morning snow."

**Question 4 asks you to analyze the impact of specific details on character development.**

4. What is the significance of including the following thought at the end of chapter 2: "All I could think was that the same thing could be said about our conversations"?

   A. It illustrates John's growing frustration with the lack of conversation between his father and himself.

   B. It reveals John's anger regarding his father's refusal to talk to him.

   C. It demonstrates John's father's desire to give his son the silent treatment.

   D. It shows John's ability to make connections between the past and the present.

Chapter 2 ends with John reflecting about conversations between his father and him. If John's thoughts illustrate a sense of frustration and sadness that they do not have lengthier, more in-depth conversations, select choice A. If John's tone is angry because his father is determined not to talk to him, select choice B. If John's comment is meant to illustrate that John's father is punishing him by refusing to speak to him, select choice C. If John's ability to recognize that their conversations have always been this way is of prime importance, select choice D.

**Question 5 asks you to analyze the impact of specific details on the development of character.**

5. What is the most significant conclusion you can draw regarding John's observation, the morning after the bonfire, that "there wasn't a single empty can or piece of trash anywhere"?

   A. Savannah cleaned up after the students in order to impress John.

   B. Tim is a very strict leader.

   C. John misjudged the students and recognizes that he did so.

   D. Randy cleaned up to make John jealous.

If you think Savannah tidied up in order to influence John's opinion, select choice A. If the cleaned area is probably the result of Tim's leadership, select choice B. If John realizes the students are more responsible than he initially thought and realizes that he may have slightly misjudged them, select choice C. If Randy probably cleaned up in order to fuel the fire of jealousy, select choice D.

**Question 6 checks your understanding of literary terms.**

6. When walking to the beach next to the pier, John states, "The steps creaked as we ascended." What literary term is used in this description?

   A. allusion

   B. metaphor

   C. onomatopoeia

   D. simile

An *allusion*, choice A, is an indirect reference. Some of the most common types of allusions are historical (when someone meets his Waterloo, it's a reference to Napoleon); biblical (such as John Coffey in *The Green Mile* being a Christ figure); mythological (a reference to a Greek or Roman myth, such as a character being said to have the Midas touch); and literary (a reference to a character in a work of literature, such as a couple being compared to Romeo and Juliet). A *metaphor*, choice B, is a comparison between two unlike things without using a connective word—for example, "Michael Phelps was a flying fish in the pool." *Onomatopoeia*, choice C, is a word that suggests the very sound it describes, like *buzz*, *sizzle*, and *boom*.

And a *simile*, choice D, is a comparison of two unlike things using a connective word, such as *like*, *as*, or *than*—for example, "She looked as fresh as the morning snow."

**Question 7 checks your understanding of literary terms.**

7. Sitting by the fire with Savannah, John notices that a "log crackled." What figure of speech is used to describe the sound?

   A. hyperbole

   B. metaphor

   C. onomatopoeia

   D. personification

Knowledge of literary terms is essential to answering this question. *Hyperbole*, choice A, is using overexaggeration to make a point—for example, "Everyone who reads this learning guide will know what *hyperbole* is because hyperbole will be explained a bazillion times."

A *metaphor*, choice B, is a comparison made between two unlike things without using a connective word—for example, "LeBron James is an animal on the basketball court."

*Onomatopoeia*, choice C, is a word that suggests the very sound it describes, like *buzz*, *sizzle*, and *boom*.

*Personification*, choice D, is giving a nonhuman thing a human characteristic, such as in "Opportunity knocked on the door."

**Question 8 checks your understanding of literary terms.**

8. As Savannah acclimates herself to the cold water, John likes the way her face looks: "So serious, so intense. So ridiculous." What rhetorical figure of speech is used in this description?

   A. alliteration

   B. anaphora

   C. personification

   D. polysyndeton

*Alliteration*, choice A, is the repetition of a word's initial sound—for example, "Becky bought Bill a bad bugle." *Anaphora*, choice B, is the repetition of a word or group of words at the beginning of successive clauses or lines. An example of this might be, "I want you to know the word *anaphora*. I want you to recognize the effect of anaphora in a passage. I want you to attempt to use anaphora in your own writing."

*Personification*, choice C, is giving a nonhuman thing a human characteristic, such as in "Opportunity knocked on the door." *Polysyndeton*, choice D, is the use of a number of conjunctions (*and, but, or, for, nor, so, yet*) in close succession, when one or more of them could be eliminated—for example, "lions *and* tigers *and* bears" and "neither snow *nor* rain *nor* heat *nor* gloom of night."

**Question 9 asks you analyze the development of a central idea.**

9. One important thematic topic addressed throughout the novel is the nature of true love. Which statement below best develops the idea of what it means to truly love another?

   A. Savannah commenting on Mr. Tyree's passion for coin collecting, saying, "Someone else's happiness is usually infectious."

   B. John reflecting on the information about his personal life that he shares with Savannah, stating, "She made me want to tell the truth."

   C. Savannah speaking to John about his father, stating, "He doesn't have to talk to be proud of you."

   D. John saying to Savannah in response to her question regarding surfing, "I'd be happy to teach you if you want to learn."

Although all of these choices develop the idea of loving another, the question is asking for the most important aspect of understanding true love.

If the spreading of happiness from one person to another is the most important aspect of loving someone, select choice A. If being open and honest with another person best illustrates the nature of true love, select choice B. If the fact that actions may speak louder than words is most significant, select choice C. And if being willing to do things for another demonstrates what is most important in true love, select choice D.

**Question 10 tests your understanding of irony.**

10. After telling John that she usually doesn't date strangers, Savannah asks if she can trust him, and he replies, "I wouldn't." This is an example of what type of irony?

    A. cosmic irony

    B. dramatic irony

    C. situational irony

    D. verbal irony

Understanding *irony*, the situation of appearance versus reality, is essential to understanding most literary texts. *Cosmic irony*, also known as irony of fate, is the situation where no matter what a character attempts to do, he or she cannot escape his or her fate. The most famous example of this is the Greek myth of Oedipus, who was fated to grow up and kill his father and marry his mother, no matter what he or anyone else tried to do to prevent it. *Dramatic irony* is when the reader knows something that the character in the text does not know. For example, the audience knows that Juliet is not really dead when Romeo discovers her body in the crypt, but he does not, and so he stabs himself. *Situational irony* is the incongruity between the expected outcome and what actually occurs. For example, Macbeth's misinterpretation of the witches' prophecies is an example of situational irony because he expects their words to mean one thing but in reality they mean something else. *Verbal irony* is meaning the opposite of what is said; sarcasm is a form of verbal irony. For example, when Mark Antony is talking about the conspirators as he stands over the body of dead Caesar, he says, "For Brutus is an honorable man." Clearly, Antony does not think Brutus is really honorable.

# Chapter 4

I was home by five, and though I didn't feel sunburned—that Southern European skin again—the burn was obvious when I showered. The water stung as it ricocheted off my chest and shoulders, and my face made me feel as if I were running a low fever. Afterward, I shaved for the first time since I'd been home and dressed in a clean pair of shorts and one of the few relatively nice button-down shirts I owned, light blue. Lucy had bought it for me and swore the color was perfect for me. I rolled up the sleeves and left the shirt untucked, then rummaged through my closet for an ancient pair of sandals.

Through the crack in the door, I could see my dad at his desk, and it struck me that for the second night in a row I'd made other plans for dinner. Nor had I spent any time with him this weekend. He wouldn't complain, I knew, but I still felt a pang of guilt. After we stopped talking about coins, breakfast and dinner were the only things we shared, and I was now depriving him even of that. Maybe I hadn't changed as much as I thought I had. I was staying in his home and eating his food, and I was just about to ask him whether I could borrow his car. In other words, pretty much leading my own life and using him in the process. I wondered what Savannah would say to that, but I think I already knew the answer. Savannah sometimes sounded a lot like the little voice that had taken up residence in my head but never bothered paying rent, and right now it whispered that if I felt guilty, maybe I was doing something wrong. I resolved that I would spend more time with him. It was a cop-out and I admitted it, but I didn't know what else to do.

When I opened the door, Dad looked startled to see me.

"Hey, Dad," I said, taking my usual seat.

"Hi, John." As soon as he spoke, he glanced at his desk and ran a hand over his thinning hair. When I added nothing, he realized that he should ask me a question. "How was your day?" he finally inquired.

I shifted in my seat. "It was great, actually. I spent most of the day with Savannah, the girl I told you about last night."

"Oh." His eyes drifted to the side, refusing to meet mine. "You didn't tell me about her."

"I didn't?"

"No, but that's okay. It was late." For the first time, he seemed to realize I was dressed up, or at least as dressed up as he'd ever seen me, but he couldn't bring himself to ask about it.

I tugged at my shirt, letting him off the hook. "Yeah, I know, trying to impress her, right? I'm taking her out to dinner tonight," I said. "Is it okay if I borrow the car?"

"Oh...okay," he said.

"I mean, did you need it tonight? I might be able to call a friend or something."

"No," he said. He reached into his pocket for the keys. Nine dads out of ten would have tossed them; mine held them out.

"You okay?" I asked.

"Just tired," he said.

I stood and took the keys. "Dad?"

He glanced up again.

"I'm sorry about not having dinner with you these last couple of nights."

"It's okay," he said. "I understand."

The sun was beginning its slow descent, and as I pulled out, the sky was a swirl of fruity colors that contrasted dramatically with the evening skies I'd come to know in Germany. Traffic was horrendous, as it usually was on Sunday nights, and it took almost thirty exhaust-fumed minutes to get back to the beach and pull in the drive.

I pushed open the door to the house without knocking. Two guys seated on the couch watching baseball heard me come in.

"Hey," they said, sounding uninterested and unsurprised.

"Have you seen Savannah?"

"Who?" one of them asked, obviously paying me little attention.

"Never mind. I'll find her." I crossed the living room to the back deck, saw the same guy as the night before grilling again and a few others, but no sign of Savannah. Nor could I see her on the beach. I was just about to go back in when I felt someone tapping my shoulder.

"Who are you looking for?" she asked.

I turned around. "Some girl," I said. "She tends to lose things at piers, but she's a quick learner when it comes to surfing."

She put her hands on her hips, and I smiled. She was dressed in shorts and a summer halter, with a hint of color in her cheeks, and I noticed she'd applied a bit of mascara and lipstick. While I loved her natural beauty—I am a kid from the beach—she was even more striking than I remembered. I caught the whiff of some lemony fragrance as she leaned toward me.

"That's all I am? Some girl?" she asked. She sounded both playful and serious, and for an instant, I fantasized about wrapping my arms around her right then and there.

"Oh," I said, feigning surprise. "It's you."

The two guys on the couch glanced toward us, then returned to the screen.

"You ready to go?" I asked.

"I've just got to get my purse," she said. She retrieved it from the kitchen counter, and we started for the door. "And where are we going, by the way?"

When I told her, she lifted an eyebrow.

"You're taking me to eat at a place with the word *shack* in the name?"

"I'm just an underpaid grunt in the army. It's all I can afford."

She bumped against me as we walked. "See, this is why I usually don't date strangers."

The Shrimp Shack is in downtown Wilmington, in the historic area that borders the Cape Fear River. At one end of the historic area are your typical tourist destinations: souvenir stores, a couple of places specializing in antiques, a few upscale restaurants, coffee shops, and various real estate offices. At the other end, however, Wilmington displayed its character as a working port city: large warehouses, more than one of which stood abandoned, and a few other dated office buildings only half-occupied. I doubted that the tourists who flocked here in the summer ever ventured toward this other end. This was the direction I turned. Little by little, the crowds faded away until no one was left on the sidewalk as the area grew more dilapidated.

"Where is this place?" Savannah asked.

"Just a little farther," I said. "Up there, at the end."

"It's kind of out of the way, isn't it?"

"It's kind of a local institution," I said. "The owner doesn't care if tourists come or not. He never has."

A minute later, I slowed the car and turned into a small parking lot bordering one of the warehouses. A few dozen cars were parked in front of the Shrimp Shack, as they always were, and the place hadn't changed. As long as I'd known it, it had looked run-down, with a broad, cluttered porch, peeling paint, and a crooked roofline that made it appear as if the place were about to fall over, despite the fact that it had been weathering hurricanes since the 1940s. The exterior was decorated with nets, hubcaps, license plates, an old anchor, oars, and a few rusty chains. A broken rowboat sat near the door.

The sky was beginning its lazy fade to black as we walked to the entrance. I wondered whether I should reach for Savannah's hand, but in the end I did nothing. While I may have had some version of hormone-induced success with women, I had very little experience when it came to girls I cared about. Despite the fact that only a day had passed since we'd met, I already knew I was in new territory.

We stepped onto the sagging porch, and Savannah pointed to the rowboat. "Maybe that's why he opened a restaurant. Because his boat sank."

"Could be. Or maybe someone just left it there and he never bothered to remove it. You ready?"

"As I'll ever be," she said, and I pushed open the door.

I don't know what she expected, but she wore a satisfied expression as she stepped inside. There was a long bar off on one side, windows that overlooked the river, and, in the main seating area, wooden picnic benches. A couple of waitresses with big hair—they hadn't seemed to change any more than the decor—were moving among the tables, carrying platters of food. The air held the greasy smell of fried food and cigarette smoke, but somehow it seemed just right. Most of the tables were filled, but I motioned toward one near the jukebox. It was playing a country-western song, though I couldn't have told you who the singer was. I'm more of a classic-rock fan.

We wove our way among the tables. Most of the customers looked as if they worked hard for a living: construction workers, landscapers, truckers, and the like. I hadn't seen so many NASCAR baseball hats since...well, I'd never seen that many. A few guys in my squad were fans, but I never got the appeal of watching a bunch of guys drive in circles all day or figured out why they didn't post the articles in the automotive section of the paper instead of the sports section. We sat across from each other, and I watched Savannah take in the room.

"I like places like this," she said. "Was this your regular hangout when you lived here?"

"No, this was more of a special-occasion place. Usually I hung out at a place called Leroy's. It's a bar near Wrightsville Beach."

She reached for a laminated menu sandwiched between a metal napkin holder and bottles of ketchup and Texas Pete hot sauce.

"This is way better," she said. She opened the menu. "Now, what's this place famous for?"

"Shrimp," I said.

"Gee, really?" she asked.

"Seriously. Every kind of shrimp you can imagine. You know that scene in *Forrest Gump* when Bubba was telling Forrest all the ways to prepare shrimp? Grilled, sautéed, barbecued, Cajun shrimp, lemon shrimp, shrimp Creole, shrimp cocktail... That's this place."

"What do you like?"

"I like 'em chilled with cocktail sauce on the side. Or fried."

She closed the menu. "You pick," she said, sliding her menu toward me. "I trust you."

I slipped the menu back into its place against the napkin holder.

"So?"

"Chilled. In a bucket. It's the consummate experience."

She leaned across the table. "So how many women have you brought here? For the consummate experience, I mean."

"Including you? Let me think." I drummed my fingers on the table. "One."

"I'm honored."

"This was more of a place for me and my friends when we wanted to eat instead of drink. There was no better food after a day spent surfing."

"As I'll soon find out."

The waitress showed up and I ordered the shrimp. When she asked what we wanted to drink, I lifted my hands.

"Sweet tea, please," Savannah said.

"Make it two," I added.

After the waitress left, we settled into easy conversation, uninterrupted even when our drinks arrived. We talked about life in the army again; for whatever reason, Savannah seemed fascinated by it. She also asked about growing up here. I told her more than I thought I would about my high school years and probably too much about the three years before enlistment.

She listened intently, asking questions now and then, and I realized it had been a long time since I'd been on a date like this; a few years, maybe more. Not since Lucy, anyway. I hadn't seen any reason for it, but as I sat across from Savannah, I had to rethink my decision. I liked being alone with her, and I wanted to see more of her. Not just tonight, but tomorrow and the next day. Everything—from the easy way she laughed to her wit to her obvious concern for others—struck me as fresh and desirable. Then again, spending time with her also made me realize how lonely I'd been. I hadn't admitted that to myself, but after just two days with Savannah, I knew it was true.

"Let's get some more music going," she said, interrupting my thoughts.

I rose from my seat, rummaged through my pockets for a couple of quarters, and dropped them in. Savannah put both hands on the glass and leaned forward as she read the titles, then picked a few songs. By the time we got back to the table, the first was already going.

"You know, I just realized that I've done all the talking tonight," I said.

"You are a chatty thing," she observed.

I freed my utensils from the rolled-up paper napkin. "How about you? You know all about me, but I don't know anything about you."

"Sure you do," she said. "You know how old I am, where I go to school, my major, and the fact that I don't drink. You know I'm from Lenoir, live on a ranch, love horses, and spend my summers building homes for Habitat for Humanity. You know a lot."

Yeah, I suddenly realized, I did. Including things she hadn't mentioned. "It's not enough," I said. "Your turn."

She leaned forward. "Ask what you will."

"Tell me about your parents," I said.

"All right," she said, reaching for a napkin. She wiped the condensation from her glass. "My mom and dad have been married for twenty-five years, and they're still happy as clams and madly in love. They met in college at Appalachian State, and Mom worked at a bank for a couple of years until she had me. Since then, she's been a stay-at-home mom, and she was the kind of mom who was there for everyone else, too. Classroom helper, volunteer driver, coach of our soccer team, head of the PTA, all that kind of stuff. Now that I'm gone, she spends every day volunteering for other things—the library, schools, the church, whatever. Dad is a history teacher at the school, and he's coached the girls volleyball team since I was little. Last year they made it to the state finals, but they lost. He's also a deacon in our church, and he runs the youth group and the choir. Do you want to see a picture?"

"Sure," I said.

She opened her purse and removed her wallet. She flipped it open and pushed it across the table, our fingers brushing.

"They're a little ragged at the edges from being in the ocean," she said, "but you get the idea."

I turned the photo around. Savannah took more after her father than her mother, or had at least inherited the darker features from him.

"Nice-looking couple."

"I love 'em," she said, taking the wallet back. "They're the best."

"Why do you live on a ranch if your dad is a teacher?"

"Oh, it's not a working ranch. It used to be when my

grandfather owned it, but he had to sell bits and pieces to pay the taxes on it. By the time my dad inherited it, it was down to ten acres with a house, stables, and a corral. It's more like a great big yard than a ranch. It's the way we always refer to it, but I guess that conjures up the wrong image, huh?"

"I know you said you did gymnastics, but did you play volleyball for your dad?"

"No," she said. "I mean, he's a great coach, but he always encouraged me to do what was right for me. And volleyball wasn't it. I tried and I was okay, but it wasn't what I loved."

"You loved horses."

"Since I was a little girl. My mom gave me this statue of a horse when I was really little, and that's what started the whole thing. I got my first horse for Christmas when I was eight, and it's still the best Christmas gift I've ever received. Slocum. She was this really gentle old mare, and she was perfect for me. The deal was that I had to take care of her—feed her and brush her and keep her stall clean. Between her, school, gymnastics, and taking care of the rest of the animals, that was pretty much all I had time for."

"The rest of the animals?"

"When I was growing up, our house was kind of like a farm. Dogs, cats, even a llama for a while. I was a sucker when it came to strays. My parents got to the point where they wouldn't even argue with me about it. There were usually four or five at any one time. Sometimes an owner would come, hoping to find a lost pet, and he'd leave with one of our recent additions if he couldn't find it. We were like the pound."

"Your parents were patient."

"Yes," she said, "they were. But they were suckers for strays, too. Even though she'd deny it, my mom was worse than me."

I studied her. "I'll bet you were a good student."

"Straight A's. I was valedictorian of my class."

"Why doesn't that surprise me?"

"I don't know," she said. "Why?"

I didn't answer. "Did you ever have a serious boyfriend?"

"Oh, now we're getting down to the nitty-gritty, huh?"

"I was just asking."

"What do you think?"

"I think," I said, dragging out the words, "I have no idea."

She laughed. "Then... let's let that question go for now. A little mystery is good for the soul. Besides, I'd be willing to bet you can figure it out on your own."

The waitress arrived with the bucket of shrimp and a couple of plastic containers of cocktail sauce, set them on the table, and refilled our tea with the efficiency of someone who'd been doing it for way too long. She turned on her heels without asking whether we needed anything else.

"This place is legendary for its hospitality."

"She's just busy," Savannah said, reaching for a shrimp. "And besides, I think she knows you're grilling me and wanted to leave me to my inquisitor."

She cracked the shrimp and peeled it, then dipped it in the sauce before taking a bite. I reached in the pail and set a couple on my plate.

"What else do you want to know?"

"I don't know. Anything. What's the best thing about being in college?"

She thought about it as she filled her plate. "Good teachers," she finally said. "In college, you can sometimes pick your professors, as long as you're flexible with your schedule. That's what I like. Before I started, that was the advice my dad gave me. He said to pick classes based on the teacher whenever you can, not the subject. I mean, he knew that you had to take certain subjects to get a degree, but his point was that good teachers are priceless. They inspire you, they entertain you, and you end up learning a ton even when you don't know it."

"Because they're passionate about their subjects," I said.

She winked. "Exactly. And he was right. I've taken classes in subjects I never thought I'd be interested in and as far away from my major as you can imagine. But you know what? I still remember those classes as if I were still taking them."

"I'm impressed. I thought you'd say something like going to the basketball games was the best part about being in college. It's like a religion at Chapel Hill."

"I enjoy those, too. Just like I enjoy the friends I'm making and living away from Mom and Dad and all that. I've learned a lot since I left Lenoir. I mean, I had a wonderful life there, and my parents are great, but I was...sheltered. I've had a few eye-opening experiences."

"Like what?"

"Lots of things. Like feeling the pressure to drink or hook up with a guy every time I went out. My first year, I hated UNC. I didn't feel like I fit in, and I didn't. I begged my parents to let me come home or transfer, but they wouldn't agree. I think they knew that in the long run I'd regret it, and they were probably right. It wasn't until some time during my sophomore year that I met some girls who felt the same way I did about those types of things, and it's been a lot better ever since. I joined a couple of Christian student groups, I spend Saturday mornings at a shelter in Raleigh serving the poor, and I feel no pressure at all to go to this or that party or date this or that guy. And if I do go to a party, the pressure doesn't get to me. I just accept the fact that I don't have to do what everyone else does. I can do what's right for me."

Which explained why she was with me last night, I thought. And right now, for that matter.

She brightened. "It's kind of like you, I guess. In the past couple of years, I've grown up. So, in addition to both of us being expert surfers, we have that in common, too."

I laughed. "Yeah. Except that I struggled a lot more than you did."

She leaned forward again. "My dad always said that when you're struggling with something, look at all the people around you and realize that every single person you see is struggling with something, and to them, it's just as hard as what you're going through."

"Your dad sounds like a smart man."

"Mom and Dad both. I think they both graduated in the top five in college. That's how they met. Studying in the library. Education was really important to both of them, and they sort of made me their project. I mean, I was reading before I got to kindergarten, but they never made it seem like a chore. And they've talked to me like I was an adult for as long as I can remember."

For a moment, I wondered how different my life would have been had they been my parents, but I shook the thought away. I knew my father had done the best he could, and I had no regrets about the way I'd turned out. Regrets about the journey, maybe, but not the destination. Because however it had happened, I'd somehow ended up eating shrimp in a dingy downtown shack with a girl that I already knew I'd never forget.

After dinner, we headed back to the house, which was surprisingly quiet. The music was still playing, but most people were relaxing around the fire, as if anticipating an early morning. Tim sat among them, engrossed in earnest conversation. Surprising me, Savannah reached for my hand, halting me in my tracks before we reached the group.

"Let's go for a walk," she said. "I want to let dinner settle just a little before I sit down."

Above us, a few wispy clouds were spread among the stars, and the moon, still full, hovered just over the horizon. A light breeze fanned my cheek, and I could hear the ceaseless motion of the waves as they rolled up the shore. The tide had gone out, and we moved to the harder, more compact sand near the water's edge. Savannah put a hand on my shoulder for balance as she removed one sandal, then another. When she finished, I did the same, and we walked in silence for a few steps.

"It's so beautiful out here. I mean, I love the mountains, but this is wonderful in its own way. It's . . . peaceful."

I felt the same words could be used to describe her, and I wasn't sure what to say.

"I can't believe that I only met you yesterday," she added. "It seems like I've known you much longer."

Her hand felt warm and comfortable in mine. "I was thinking the same thing."

She gave a dreamy smile, studying the stars. "I wonder what Tim thinks about this," she murmured. She glanced at me. "He thinks I'm a little naive."

"Are you?"

"Sometimes," she admitted, and I laughed.

She went on. "I mean, when I see two people heading off on a walk like this, I'm thinking, Oh, that's sweet. I'm not thinking they're going to hook up behind the dunes. But the fact is, sometimes they do. I just never realize it beforehand, and I'm always surprised when I hear about it later. I can't help it. Like last night, after you left. I heard about two people here who did just that, and I couldn't believe it."

"I would have been more surprised if it hadn't happened."

"That's what I don't like about college, by the way. It's like a lot of people don't believe these years really count, so you're allowed to experiment with...whatever. There's such a casual view about things like sex and drinking and even drugs. I know that sounds really old-fashioned, but I just don't get it. Maybe that's why I didn't want to go sit by the fire like everyone else. To be honest, I'm kind of disappointed in those two people I heard about, and I don't want to sit there trying to pretend that I'm not. I know I shouldn't judge, and I'm sure they're good people since they're here to help, but still, what was the point? Shouldn't you save things like that for someone you love? So that it really means something?"

I knew she didn't want answers, nor did I offer any.

"Who told you about that couple?" I asked instead.

"Tim. I think he was disappointed, too, but what's he going to do? Kick them out?"

We had gone a good way down the beach, and we turned around. In the distance, I could see the circle of figures silhouetted by the fire. The mist smelled of salt, and ghost crabs scattered to their holes as we approached.

"I'm sorry," she said. "I was out of line there."

"About what?"

"For being so...upset about it. I shouldn't pass judgment. It's not my place."

"Everyone judges," I said. "It's human nature."

"I know. But...I'm not perfect, either. In the end, it's only God's judgment that matters, and I've learned enough to know that no one can presume to know the will of God."

I smiled.

"What?" she asked.

"The way you talk reminds me of our chaplain. He says the same thing."

We strolled down the beach, and as we neared the house, we moved away from the water's edge, into the softer sand. Our feet slipped with every step, and I could feel Savannah tighten her grip on my hand. I wondered whether she would let go when we got close to the fire, and I was disappointed when she did.

"Hey," Tim called out, his voice friendly. "You're back."

Randy was there, too, and he wore his usual sulky expression. Frankly, I was getting a bit tired of his resentment. Brad stood behind Susan, who was leaning into his chest. Susan seemed undecided about whether to pretend to be happy, so she could learn the details from Savannah, or to be upset for Randy's benefit. The others, obviously indifferent, went back to their conversations. Tim stood and made his way toward us.

"How was dinner?"

"It was great," Savannah said. "I got a taste of local culture. We went to the Shrimp Shack."

"Sounds like fun," he commented.

I strained to detect any undercurrent of jealousy but found none. Tim motioned over his shoulder and went on. "Do you two want to join us? We're just winding down, getting ready for tomorrow."

"Actually, I'm a bit sleepy. I was just going to walk John to his car, and after that I'll turn in. What time do we need to be up?"

"Six. We'll have breakfast and be at the site tomorrow by seven-thirty. Don't forget your sunscreen. We'll be out in the sun all day."

"I'll remember. You should remind everyone else."

"I have," he said. "And I'll do it again tomorrow. But you just wait—some folks won't listen and they'll get fried."

"I'll see you in the morning," she said.

"All right." He turned his attention to me. "I'm glad you came by today."

"Me too," I said.

"And listen, if you find yourself bored in the next couple of weeks, we could always use an extra hand."

I laughed. "I knew it was coming."

"I am who I am," he said, holding out his hand. "But either way, I hope to see you again."

We shook hands. Tim went back to his seat, and Savannah nodded toward the house. We made our way toward the dune, stopped to put our sandals back on, then followed the wooden pathway, through the sea grass, and around the house. A minute later, we were at the car. In the darkness, I couldn't make out her expression.

"I had a good time tonight," she said. "And today."

I swallowed. "When can I see you again?"

It was a simple question, expected even, but I was surprised to hear the desire in my tone. I hadn't even kissed her yet.

"I suppose," she said, "that depends on you. You know where I am."

"How about tomorrow night?" I blurted out. "I know of another place that has a band, and it's a lot of fun."

She tucked a strand of hair behind her ear. "How about the

night after? Would that be okay? It's just that the first day at the site is always . . . exciting and tiring at the same time. We have a big group dinner, and I really shouldn't miss it."

"Yeah, that's fine," I said, thinking it wasn't fine at all.

She must have heard something in my voice. "Like Tim said, you're welcome to come by if you'd like."

"No, that's okay. Tuesday night's fine."

We continued to stand there, one of those awkward moments I'll probably never get used to, but she turned away before I could attempt a kiss. Normally, I would have plunged ahead just to see what happened; I may not have been open about my feelings, but I was impulsive and quick to action. With Savannah, I felt oddly paralyzed. She didn't appear to be in any hurry, either.

A car passed by, breaking the spell. She took a step toward the house, then stopped and put her hand on my arm. In an innocent gesture, she kissed me on the cheek. It was almost sisterly, but her lips were soft and the scent of her engulfed me, lingering even after she pulled back.

"I really did have a good time," she murmured. "I don't think I'll forget about today for a long, long time."

I felt her hand leave my arm, and then in a whisper she vanished, retreating up the stairs of the house.

At home later that night, I found myself tossing and turning in bed, reliving the events of the day. Finally I sat up, wishing I had told her how much our day had meant to me. Outside my window, I saw a shooting star cross the sky in a brilliant streak of white. I wanted to believe it was an omen, though of what, I wasn't sure. Instead, all I could do was replay Savannah's gentle kiss on my cheek for the hundredth time and wonder how I could be falling for a girl that I'd met only the day before.

# Chapter 5

"Mornin', Dad," I said, staggering into the kitchen. I squinted in the bright morning light and saw my dad standing in front of the stove. The smell of bacon filled the air.

"Oh . . . hi, John."

I plopped myself on the chair, still trying to wake up. "Yeah, I know I'm up early, but I wanted to catch you before you headed off to work."

"Oh," he said. "Okay. Let me just get a bit more food going."

He seemed almost excited, despite this wrinkle in the routine. It was times like these that let me know he was glad I was home.

"Is there any coffee?" I asked.

"It's in the pot," he said.

I poured myself a cup and wandered to the table. The newspaper lay as it had arrived. My dad always read it over breakfast, and I knew enough not to touch it. He had always been funny about being the first to read it, and he always read it in exactly the same order.

I expected my dad to ask how the evening had gone with Savannah, but instead he said nothing, preferring to concentrate on his cooking. Noting the clock, I knew Savannah would be leaving for the site in a few minutes, and I wondered whether she was thinking about me as much as I was thinking about her. In the rush of what was no doubt a chaotic morning for her, I doubted she was. The realization made me ache unexpectedly.

"What did you do last night?" I finally asked, trying to get my mind off Savannah. He kept on cooking as if he hadn't heard me. "Dad?" I said.

"Yeah?" he asked.

"How'd it go last night?"

"How'd what go?"

"Your night. Anything exciting happen?"

"No," he said, "nothing." He smiled at me before turning a couple of slices in the pan. I could hear the sizzling intensify.

"I had a great time," I volunteered. "Savannah's really something. We actually went to church together yesterday."

Somehow I thought he'd ask more about it, and I'll admit that I wanted him to. I imagined that we might have a real conversation, the kind that other fathers might have with their sons, that he might laugh and maybe crack a joke or two. Instead, he turned on another burner. He sprayed a small frying pan with oil and poured in the egg batter.

"Would you mind putting some bread in the toaster?" he asked.

I sighed. "No," I said, already knowing that we'd eat in silence. "No problem at all."

\* \* \*

I spent the rest of the day surfing, or rather, trying to surf. The ocean had calmed overnight, and the small swells were nothing to get excited about. Making matters worse, they broke nearer to shore than they had the day before, so even if I did find a few worth riding, the experience didn't last long before the waves petered out. In the past, I might have gone to Oak Island or even driven up to Atlantic Beach, where I could catch a ride out to Shackleford Banks in the hope that I'd find something better. Today, I just wasn't in the mood.

Instead, I surfed where I had the previous two days. The house was a little way down the beach, and it looked almost uninhabited. The back door was closed, the towels were gone, and no one passed by the window or stepped out on the deck. I wondered when everyone would be getting back. Probably around four or five o'clock, and I had already made the decision that I'd be long gone by then. There was no reason to be here in the first place, and the last thing I wanted Savannah to think was that I was some kind of stalker.

I left around three and swung by Leroy's. The bar was darker and dingier than I remembered, and I hated the place as soon as I walked in the door. I had always thought of it as a pro bar, as in professional alcoholics bar, and I saw the proof as lonely men sat hovering over glasses of Tennessee's finest, hoping for refuge from life's problems. Leroy was there, and he recognized me when I walked in. When I took a seat at the bar, he automatically brought a glass to the beer tap and began filling it.

"Long time no see," he commented. "You keeping out of trouble?"

"Trying," I grunted. I glanced around the bar as he slid the glass in front of me. "I like what you've done with the place," I said, motioning over my shoulder.

"Good. It's all for you. You gonna eat anything?"

"No. This is fine, thanks."

He wiped the counter in front of me, then flipped the rag over his shoulder and moved away to take someone else's order. A moment later, I felt a hand on my shoulder.

"Johnny! What're you doing here?"

I turned and saw one of the many friends I had come to despise. That's the way it was here. I hated everything about the place, including my friends, and I realized that I always had. I had no idea why I'd come, or even why I'd ever made this a regular hangout, other than the fact that it was here and I had no place else to go.

"Hey, Toby," I said.

Tall and scrawny, Toby took a seat beside me, and when he turned to face me, I saw that his eyes were already glassy. He smelled as if he hadn't showered in days, and his shirt was stained. "You still playing Rambo?" he asked, his words slurred. "You look like you've been working out."

"Yeah," I said, not wanting to go into it. "What are you doing these days?"

"Hanging out, mainly. For the last couple of weeks, anyway. I was working at Quick Stop until a couple of weeks ago, but the owner was a real ass."

"Still living at home?"

"Of course," he said, sounding almost proud of the fact. He tipped the bottle and took a long drink, then focused on my arms. "You look good. You been working out?" he asked again.

"A little," I said, knowing he didn't remember he'd already asked.

"You're big."

I couldn't think of anything to say. Toby took another drink.

"Hey, there's a party tonight at Mandy's," he said. "You remember Mandy, right?"

Yeah, I remembered. A girl from my past who lasted less than a weekend. Toby was still going on.

"Her parents are up in New York or someplace like that, and it should be a real banger. We're just having a little pre-party to get us in the proper mood. You want to join us?"

He motioned over his shoulder toward four guys at a corner table littered with three empty pitchers. I recognized two from my past life, but the others were strangers.

"I can't," I said, "I'm supposed to be meeting my dad for dinner. Thanks, though."

"Blow him off. It's going to be a blast. Kim'll be there."

Another woman from my past, another reminder that made me wince inside. I could barely stomach the person I used to be.

"I can't," I said, shaking my head. I stood, leaving the mostly full glass in front of me. "I promised. And he's letting me stay with him. You know how it is."

That made sense to him, and he nodded. "Then let's get together this weekend. A bunch of us are heading up to Ocracoke to go surfing."

"Maybe," I said, knowing there wasn't a chance.

"Your dad still have the same number?"

"Yeah," I said.

I left, sure that he'd never call and that I'd never return to Leroy's.

On my way home, I picked up steaks for dinner, along with a bag of salad, some dressing, and a couple of potatoes. Without a car, it wasn't easy carrying the bag along with my surfboard all the way back home, but I didn't really mind the walk. I'd done it for years, and my shoes were a whole lot more comfortable than the boots I'd grown used to.

Once home, I dragged the grill from the garage, along with a bag of briquettes and lighter fluid. The grill was dusty, as if it hadn't been used for years. I set it up on the back porch and emptied out the charcoal dust before hosing off the cobwebs and letting it dry in the sun. Inside, I added some salt, pepper, and garlic powder to the steaks, wrapped the potatoes in foil and put them in the oven, then poured the salad in a bowl. Once the grill was dry, I got the briquettes going and set the table out back.

Dad walked in just as I was adding the steaks to the grill.

"Hey, Dad," I said over my shoulder. "I thought I'd make us dinner tonight."

"Oh," he said. It seemed to take him an instant to grasp the fact that he wouldn't be cooking for me. "Okay," he finally added.

"How do you like your steak?"

"Medium," he said. He continued to stand near the sliding glass door.

"It looks like you haven't used the grill since I left," I said. "But you should. There's nothing better than a grilled steak. My mouth was watering all the way home."

"I'm going to go change my clothes."

"Steaks will be done in about ten minutes."

When he left I went back into the kitchen, took out the potatoes and the bowl of salad—along with dressing, butter, and steak sauce—and put them on the table. I heard the patio door slide open, and my dad emerged carrying two glasses of milk, looking like a cruise ship tourist. He was dressed in shorts, black socks, tennis shoes, and a flowered Hawaiian shirt. His legs were painfully white, as if he hadn't worn shorts in years. If ever. Thinking back, I'm not sure I'd ever seen him in shorts. I did my best to pretend he looked normal.

"Just in time," I said, returning to the grill. I loaded both plates with steaks and set one in front of him.

"Thanks," he said.

"My pleasure."

He added salad to his plate and poured the dressing, then unwrapped his potato. He added butter, then poured steak sauce onto the plate, making a small puddle. Normal and expected, except for the fact that he did all this in silence.

"How was your day?" I asked, as always.

"The same," he answered. As always. He smiled again but added nothing else.

My dad, the social misfit. I wondered again why he found conversation so difficult and tried to imagine what he'd been like in his youth. How had he ever found someone to marry? I knew the last question sounded petty, but it hadn't come from spite. I was genuinely curious. We ate for a while, the clatter of forks the only sound to keep us company.

"Savannah said she'd like to meet you," I finally said, trying again.

He cut at his steak. "Your lady friend?"

Only my dad would phrase it that way. "Yeah," I said. "I think you'll like her."

He nodded.

"She's a student at UNC," I explained.

He knew it was his turn, and I could sense his relief when another question came to him. "How did you meet her?"

I told him about the bag, painting the picture, trying to make the story as humorous as possible, but laughter eluded him.

"That was kind of you," he observed.

Another conversation stopper. I cut another piece of steak. "Dad? Do you mind if I ask you a question?"

"Of course not."

"How did you and Mom meet?"

It was the first time I'd asked about her in years. Because she'd never been part of my life, because I had no memories, I'd seldom felt the need to do so. Even now, I didn't really care; I just wanted him to talk to me. He took his time adding more butter to his potato, and I knew he didn't want to answer.

"We met at a diner," he said finally. "She was a waitress."

I waited. Nothing more seemed forthcoming.

"Was she pretty?"

"Yes," he said.

"What was she like?"

He mashed the potato and added salt, sprinkling it with care. "She was like you," he concluded.

"What do you mean?"

"Umm..." He hesitated. "She could be...stubborn."

I wasn't sure what to think or even what he meant. Before I could dwell on it, he rose from the table and seized his glass.

"Would you like some more milk?" he asked, and I knew he would say no more about her.

# Questions and Explanations for Chapters 4 and 5

The ten questions on chapters 4 and 5 focus on grammar and usage, vocabulary, comprehension, literary terms, style, and characterization. Some of the questions combine two or more of these areas, requiring you to synthesize your knowledge, make inferences, and interpret the text. The questions are designed to determine both your current level of understanding of the novel and your ability to answer higher-level questions.

**The following sentence tests correctness and effective expression. Part of the following sentence is underlined; beneath the sentence are four ways of phrasing the underlined material. Select the option that produces the best sentence. If you think the original phrasing produces a better sentence than any of the alternatives, select choice A.**

1. <u>As a teenager, John's father wanted</u> him to attend college but wasn't sure how to pursue the application process.

    A. As a teenager, John's father wanted

    B. When a teenager, John's father wanted

    C. As a teenager, John's father had wanted

    D. When John was a teenager, his father wanted

A dangling modifier is a word or group of words used to modify something that isn't in the sentence—for example, "Walking along the beach, a pod of porpoises came into view." In this sentence, the pod wasn't walking along the beach, so the phrase "walking along the beach" is considered a dangling modifier. To correct this error, rewrite the sentence by creating a subordinate clause with the doer of the action as the subject, such as, "While John was walking along the beach, a pod of porpoises came into view."

Three of the choices above contain dangling modifiers, so the only correct choice is the one that rights that error.

**Question 2 tests your vocabulary. Choose the set of words that, when inserted in the sentence, best fits the meaning of the sentence as a whole.**

2. Since John considered chilled in a bucket the _____ way to enjoy shrimp, he considered that preparation of the popular shellfish the _____ experience.

    A. worst...perfect

    B. ideal...most reprehensible

    C. best...consummate

    D. inferior...worst

The context clues in the sentence indicate that the two words in the set need to be synonymous.

First determine if John likes eating shrimp chilled. If he does, you can eliminate choices A and D. If he does not, eliminate choices B and C.

In choice A, *perfect* means ideal. In choice B, *most reprehensible* means deserving or receiving strong disapproval. In choice C, *consummate* means perfect or ideal. In choice D, *inferior* means substandard and below average.

**Question 3 tests your comprehension.**

3. What makes John think, "Maybe I hadn't changed as much as I thought I had"?

    A. making alternate dinner plans two nights in a row

    B. enjoying the Shrimp Shack

    C. talking with Toby at Leroy's

    D. asking his father about his mother

John is the protagonist of the novel, and his development as a character is of prime importance. If you are uncertain of the correct answer, you can eliminate the choices that do not illustrate how John has changed or are factually incorrect—for example, if John has always enjoyed eating at the Shrimp Shack, clearly no change has occurred, and you can eliminate choice B. If using the process of elimination doesn't enable you to answer the question, reread the beginning of chapter 4.

**Question 4 asks you to determine the meaning of words used in context.**

4. When describing the waitresses at the Shrimp Shack, what does John mean when he says, "they hadn't seemed to change any more than the decor"?

   A. The waitresses are old.

   B. The interior of the restaurant is in disrepair.

   C. The uniforms haven't been changed in a long time.

   D. Their hairstyles are as outdated as the furnishings in the restaurant.

The context clues in the question indicate that the pronoun *they* refers to the waitresses and the word *decor* refers to the style and layout of the restaurant. Thus, the best answer will address both the waitresses and the furnishings.

**Question 5 tests your understanding of irony.**

5. Annoyed at the service that he and Savannah are receiving at the Shrimp Shack, John mutters, "This place is legendary for its hospitality." This is an example of what type of irony?

   A. cosmic irony

   B. dramatic irony

   C. situational irony

   D. verbal irony

Understanding *irony*, the situation of appearance versus reality, is essential to understanding most literary texts. *Cosmic irony*, also known as irony of fate, is the situation where no matter what a character attempts to do, he or she cannot escape his or her fate. The most famous example of this is the Greek myth of Oedipus, who was fated to grow up and kill his father and marry his mother, no matter what he or anyone else tried to do to prevent it. *Dramatic irony* is when the reader knows something that the character in the text does not know. For example, the audience knows that Juliet is not really dead when Romeo discovers her body in the crypt, but he does not, and so he stabs himself. *Situational irony* is the incongruity between the expected outcome and what actually occurs. For example, Macbeth's misinterpretation of the witches' prophecies is an example of situational irony because he expects their words to mean one thing but in reality they mean something else. *Verbal irony* is meaning the opposite of what is said; sarcasm is a form of verbal irony. For example, when Mark Antony is talking about the conspirators as he stands over the body of dead Caesar, he says, "For Brutus is an honorable man." Clearly, Antony does not think Brutus is actually honorable.

**Question 6 checks your comprehension.**

6. After Savannah describes the type of teacher whose classes she really enjoys, John replies, "Because they're passionate about their subjects." What is the significance of his choice of words?

    A. He is bringing up her comments from earlier in the day, demonstrating that he listens to her.

B. He is introducing a new idea into the conversation, expanding their discussion.

C. He is making a connection between Savannah's teachers and her parents.

D. He is drawing a conclusion that is contrary to Savannah's.

Making connections within and between chapters enables you to understand the development of characters and themes. If Savannah had previously used the word *passionate* to discuss people she admires, select choice A. If John's comments are completely new, select choice B. If John is relating Savannah's comments about her professors to her own parents, select choice C. If his conclusions are different from Savannah's, select choice D. If you are unsure of the correct answer, you can reread chapter 4 and determine the correct answer by eliminating the incorrect choices.

**Question 7 checks your understanding of literary terms.**

7. When describing the sound of his father cooking bacon for their breakfast, John states that "I could hear the sizzling intensify." What figure of speech is used to describe the sound?

A. hyperbole

B. metaphor

C. onomatopoeia

D. personification

Again, knowledge of literary terms is essential to answering this question. *Hyperbole*, choice A, is using overexaggeration to make a point—for example, "Everyone who reads this learning guide will know what *hyperbole* is because hyperbole will be explained a bazillion times."

A *metaphor*, choice B, is a comparison made between two unlike things without using a connective word—for example, "Michael Phelps was a flying fish in the pool."

*Onomatopoeia*, choice C, is a word that suggests the very sound it describes, like *buzz*, *pop*, and *boom*.

*Personification*, choice D, is giving a nonhuman thing a human characteristic, such as in "Opportunity knocked on the door."

**Question 8 asks you to make an inference regarding character development.**

8. When leaving Leroy's, John's conclusion that Toby would not call him and that he wouldn't ever return to the bar indicate all of the following EXCEPT:

   A. that John has changed and the patrons of Leroy's haven't

   B. that John would rather spend time with Savannah than with his old friends

   C. that John is giving up drinking beer or any form of alcohol

   D. that John truly hated everything about Leroy's

Three of the four choices exist in the novel as examples of the way John has changed and matured and can be eliminated from consideration. If John recognizes that he is no longer the person who enjoys hanging out at the local bar yet the regulars at Leroy's still enjoy their time there, eliminate choice A. If John would rather spend the limited time he has on leave with Savannah than revisiting places he used to frequent, eliminate choice B. If John's decision not to return to Leroy's indicates that he has sworn off drinking, eliminate choice C. If John realizes that he hated everything about Leroy's—the people and the place itself—eliminate choice D.

**Question 9 asks you to make an inference based on strong and thorough textual evidence.**

9. All of the following are valid interpretations as to why John's father doesn't say much to him EXCEPT:

   A. He is not accustomed to having conversations with anyone.

   B. He doesn't really like John, and when you don't have something nice to say, it's better to say nothing at all.

   C. He doesn't know what to say.

   D. He is concerned about offending John.

The inference that you draw will be based on the details provided in the text, and three of the four choices can be eliminated because they are sound reasons that could potentially explain John's father's lack of speaking.

If his father is often alone, eliminate choice A. If there is any indication that John's father doesn't really like his son, eliminate choice B. If there are details to suggest that he just doesn't know the words to say or the questions to ask, eliminate choice C. And if John's father is worried that he might say the wrong thing and thus finds it easier and safer to not say anything, eliminate choice D.

**Question 10 checks your comprehension.**

10. Why does John ask his father, "How did you and Mom meet"?

   A. He is trying to embarrass his father.

   B. He has been yearning for this information for years.

   C. He is asking on behalf of Savannah.

   D. He just wants to start a conversation with his father.

Understanding the motivation behind John's actions is crucial to understanding his development as a character. A close reading of the chapter will enable you to know the correct answer. If you are unsure of the answer, reread the last page of chapter 5.

# Chapter 6

Time is relative. I know I'm not the first to realize it and far from the most famous, and my realization had nothing to do with energy or mass or the speed of light or anything else Einstein might have postulated. Rather, it had to do with the drag of hours while I waited for Savannah.

After my dad and I finished dinner, I thought about her; I thought of her again soon after I woke. I spent the day surfing, and though the waves were better than they'd been the day before, I couldn't really concentrate and decided to call it quits by mid-afternoon. I debated whether or not to grab a cheeseburger at a little place by the beach—the best burgers in town, by the way—but even though I was in the mood, I just went home, hoping that I could talk Savannah into a burger later. I read a bit of the latest Stephen King novel, showered and threw on a pair of jeans and a polo, then read for another couple of hours before glancing at the clock and realizing only twenty minutes had passed. That's what I meant by time being relative.

When my dad got home, he saw the way I was dressed and offered his keys.

"Are you going to see Savannah?" he asked.

"Yeah," I said, rising from the couch. I took the keys. "I might be late getting in."

He scratched the back of his head. "Okay," he said.

"Breakfast tomorrow?"

"Okay." For a reason I couldn't understand, he sounded almost scared.

"All right," I said. "I'll see you later, okay?"

"I'll probably be sleeping."

"I didn't mean it literally."

"Oh," he said. "Okay."

I headed for the door. Just as I opened it, I heard him sigh.

"I'd like to meet Savannah, too," he said in a voice so soft, I barely heard it.

The sky was still bright and the sun was bending light across the water when I arrived at the house. As I got out, I realized I was nervous. I couldn't remember the last time any girl had made me nervous, but I couldn't shake the thought that somehow things might have changed between us. I didn't know how or why I felt that way; all I knew was that I wasn't sure what I'd do if my fears proved correct.

I didn't bother knocking and simply wandered in. The living room was empty, but I could hear voices down the hall, and there was the usual collection of people on the back deck. I stepped out, asking for Savannah, and was told she was at the beach.

I trotted down to the sand and froze when I saw her seated near the dune, next to Randy, Brad, and Susan. She hadn't noticed me, and I heard her laugh at something Randy said. She and Randy looked as much a couple as Susan and Brad. I knew they weren't, that they were probably just talking about the house they were building or sharing experiences from the last couple of days, but I didn't like it. Nor did I like the fact that Savannah was sitting as close to Randy as she'd been to me. As I stood there, I wondered whether she even remembered our date, but she smiled when she saw me as if nothing were amiss.

"There you are," she said. "I was wondering when you'd show up."

Randy grinned. Despite her comment, he wore an almost victorious expression. *When the cat's away, the mice are at play*, he seemed to be saying.

Savannah stood and ambled toward me. She was wearing a white sleeveless blouse and a light, flowing skirt that swayed when she walked. I could see the additional color on her shoulders that spoke of hours in the sun. When she got close, she stood on her tiptoes and planted a kiss on my cheek.

"Hi," she said, circling an arm around my waist.

"Hi."

She leaned back slightly, as if evaluating my expression. "You look like you missed me," she said, her voice teasing.

As usual, I couldn't think of a response, and she winked at my inability to admit that I had. "Maybe I missed you, too," she added.

I touched her bare shoulder. "You ready to go?"

"As I'll ever be," she said.

We started toward the car and I reached for her hand,

her touch making me feel all was right with the world. Well, almost...

I straightened. "I saw you talking to Randy," I said, trying to keep my voice neutral.

She squeezed my hand. "You did, huh?"

I tried again. "I take it you two got to know each other while you were working."

"We sure did. I was right, too. He's a nice young man. After he finishes here, he's heading up to New York for a six-week internship at Morgan Stanley."

"Hmm," I grunted.

She laughed under her breath. "Don't tell me you're jealous."

"I'm not."

"Good," she concluded, squeezing my hand again. "Because there's no reason to be."

I hung on those last few words. She needn't have said them, but I couldn't be happier that she had. When we reached the car, I opened her door.

"I was thinking of taking you out to Oysters," I said. "It's a nightclub a little way down the beach. They'll have a band later, and we could go dancing."

"What are we doing until then?"

"Are you hungry?" I asked, thinking about the cheeseburger I'd passed on earlier. "A little," she said. "I had a snack when I got back, so I'm not too hungry yet."

"How about a walk on the beach?"

"Hmm...maybe later."

It was obvious that she already had something in mind. "Why don't you tell me what you want to do?"

She brightened. "How about if we go say hi to your father."

I wasn't sure I'd heard her right. "Really?"

"Yeah, really," she said. "Just for a little while. Then we can get something to eat and go out dancing."

When I hesitated, she put a hand on my shoulder. "Please?"

I wasn't all that happy about going, but the way she asked made it impossible for me to say no. I was getting used to that, I suppose, but I would rather have had her all to myself for the rest of the evening. Nor did I understand why she wanted to see my dad tonight, unless it meant she wasn't quite as thrilled as I was at the prospect of being alone. To be honest, the thought depressed me.

Still, she was in a good mood as she talked about the work they'd accomplished over the last couple days. Tomorrow, they planned to start on the windows. Randy, it turned out, had worked alongside her on both days, which explained their "new-found friendship." That's how she described it. I doubted Randy would have described his interest in the same way.

We pulled into the drive a few minutes later, and I noted the light in my father's den. When I turned off the engine, I fiddled with the keys before getting out.

"I told you my father is quiet, didn't I?"

"Yeah," she said. "It doesn't matter, though. I just want to meet him."

"Why?" I asked. I know how it sounded, but I couldn't help it.

"Because," she said, "he's your only family. And he was the one who raised you."

Once my dad got over the shock of my return with Savannah in tow and the introductions were made, he ran a quick hand over his wispy hair and stared at the floor.

"I'm sorry we didn't call first, but don't blame John," she said. "It was all my fault."

"Oh," he said. "It's okay."

"Did we catch you at a bad time?"

"No." He glanced up, then back to the floor again. "It's a pleasure to meet you," he said.

For a moment, we all stood in the living room, none of us saying anything. Savannah wore an easy smile, but I wondered if my dad even realized it.

"Would you like something to drink?" he asked, as if suddenly remembering he was supposed to play host.

"I'm fine, thanks," she said. "John tells me that you're quite the coin collector."

He turned to me, as if wondering whether he should answer. "I try," he finally said.

"Is that what we so rudely interrupted?" she asked, using the same teasing tone she used with me. To my surprise, I heard my dad give a nervous laugh. Not loud, but a laugh nonetheless. Amazing.

"No, you didn't interrupt. I was just examining a new coin I got today."

As he spoke, I could sense him trying to gauge how I'd react. Savannah either didn't notice or pretended not to. "Really?" she asked. "What kind?"

My dad shifted his weight from one foot to the other. Then, to my astonishment, he looked up and asked her, "Would you like to see it?"

We spent forty minutes in the den.

For the most part, I sat in the den and listened to my dad tell stories I knew by heart. Like most serious collectors, he kept only a few coins at home, and I didn't have any idea where the rest of them were stored. He would rotate part of the collection every couple of weeks, new coins appearing as if by magic. Usually there were never more than a dozen in his office at any given time and never anything valuable, but I got the impression that he could have been showing Savannah a common Lincoln penny and she would have been entranced. She asked dozens of questions, questions either I or any book on coin collecting could have answered, but as the minutes passed, her questions became more subtle. Instead of asking why a coin might be particularly valuable, she asked when and where he'd found it, and she was treated to tales of boring weekends of my youth spent in places like Atlanta and Charleston and Raleigh and Charlotte.

My dad talked a lot about those trips. Well, for him, anyway. He still had a tendency to retreat into himself for long stretches, but he probably said more in those forty minutes to her than he'd said to me since I'd arrived home. From my vantage point, I saw the passion she had referred to, but it was a passion I'd seen a thousand times before, and it didn't alter my opinion that he used coins as a way to avoid life instead of embracing it. I'd stopped talking to him about coins because I wanted to talk about something else; my father stopped talking because he knew how I felt and could discuss nothing else.

And yet...

My dad was happy, and I knew it. I could see the way his eyes gleamed as he gestured to a coin, pointing out the mint mark or how crisp the stamp had been or how the value of a coin might differ because it had arrows or wreaths. He showed Savannah proof coins, coins minted at West Point, one of his favorite type to collect. He pulled out a magnifying glass to show her flaws, and when Savannah held the magnifying glass, I could see the animation on my father's face. Despite my feelings about coins, I couldn't help smiling, simply to see my father so happy.

But he was still my dad, and there was no miracle. Once he'd shown her the coins and told her everything about them and how they'd been collected, his comments grew further and further apart. He began to repeat himself and realized it, causing him to retreat and grow even quieter. In time, Savannah must have sensed his growing discomfort, for she gestured to the coins atop the desk.

"Thank you, Mr. Tyree. I feel like I've really learned something."

My dad smiled, obviously drained, and I took it as my cue to stand.

"Yeah, that was great. But we should probably be going," I said.

"Oh . . . okay."

"It was wonderful meeting you."

When my dad nodded again, Savannah leaned in and gave him a hug.

"Let's do this again sometime," she whispered, and though my dad hugged her back, it reminded me of the lifeless hugs I'd received as a child. I wondered if she felt as awkward as he obviously did.

In the car, Savannah seemed lost in thought. I would have asked about her impressions of my father but wasn't sure I wanted to hear the answer. I know my dad and I didn't have the best relationship, but she was right when she'd said he was the only family I had and had raised me. I could complain about him, but the last thing I wanted to hear was someone else doing it, too.

Still, I didn't think she would say anything negative, simply because it wasn't in her nature, and when she turned to me, she was smiling.

"Thanks for bringing me by to meet him," she said. "He's got such a . . . warm heart."

I'd never heard anyone describe him that way, but I liked it.

"I'm glad you liked him."

"I did," she said, sounding sincere. "He's . . . gentle." She glanced at me. "But I think I understand why you got in so much trouble when you were younger. He didn't strike me as the kind of father who would lay down the law."

"He didn't," I agreed.

She shot me a playful scowl. "And mean old you took advantage."

I laughed. "Yeah, I suppose I did."

She shook her head. "You should have known better."

"I was just a kid."

"Ah, the old youth excuse. You know that doesn't hold water, don't you? I never took advantage of my parents."

"Yes, the perfect child. I think you mentioned that."

"Are you making fun of me?"

"No, of course not."

She continued to stare at me. "I think you are," she finally decided.

"Okay, maybe a little."

She thought about my answer. "Well, maybe I deserved that. But just so you know, I wasn't perfect."

"No?"

"Of course not. I remember quite plainly, for instance, that in fourth grade I got a B on a test."

I feigned shock. "No! Don't tell me that!"

"It's true."

"How did you ever recover?"

"How do you think?" She shrugged. "I told myself it would never happen again."

I didn't doubt it. "Are you hungry yet?"

"I thought you'd never ask."

"What are you in the mood for?"

She drew up her hair in a sloppy ponytail, then let it go. "How about a big, juicy cheeseburger?"

As soon as she said it, I found myself wondering if Savannah was too good to be true.

# Chapter 7

I must admit that you bring me to eat at the most interesting places," Savannah said, glancing over her shoulder. In the distance beyond the dune, we could see a long line of customers snaking away from Joe's Burger Stand in the middle of a gravel parking lot.

"It's the best in town," I said, taking a bite of my enormous burger.

Savannah sat close to me in the sand, facing the water. The burgers were fantastic, nice and thick, and though the French fries were a bit too greasy, they hit the spot. As she ate, Savannah stared at the sea, and in the waning light I found myself thinking that she seemed even more at home here than I did.

I thought again about the way she'd talked to my father. About the way she talked to everyone, for that matter, including me. She had the rare ability to be exactly what people needed when she was with them and yet still remain true to herself. I couldn't think of anyone who remotely resembled her in appearance or personality, and I wondered again why she'd taken a liking to me. We were as different as two people could be. She was a mountain girl, gifted and sweet, raised by attentive parents, with a desire to help those in need; I was a tattooed army grunt, hard around the edges, and largely a stranger in my own home. Remembering how she'd been with my dad, I could tell how gracefully her parents had raised her. And as she sat beside me, I found myself wishing that I could be more like her.

"What are you thinking?"

Her voice, probing yet gentle, pulled me away from my thoughts.

"I was wondering why you're here," I confessed.

"Because I like the beach. I don't get to do this very often. It's not like there are any waves or shrimp boats where I'm from."

When she saw my expression, she tapped my hand. "That was flippant," she said, "I'm sorry. I'm here because I want to be here."

I set aside the remains of my burger, wondering why I cared so much. It was a new feeling for me, one I wasn't sure I'd ever get used to. She patted my arm and turned toward the water again.

"It's gorgeous out here. All we need is a sunset over the water, and it would be perfect."

"We'd have to go to the other side of the country," I said.

"Really? You're trying to tell me the sun sets in the west?"

I noted the mischievous gleam in her eye.

"That's what I hear, anyway."

She'd eaten only half of her cheeseburger, and she slipped it into the bag, then added the remains of mine as well. After folding the bag over so the wind wouldn't blow it away, she stretched out her legs and turned to me, looking at once flirtatious and innocent.

"You want to know what I was thinking?" she asked.

I waited, drinking in the sight of her.

"I was thinking that I wished you'd been with me the last couple of days. I mean, I enjoyed getting to know everyone better. We ate lunch together, and the dinner last night was a lot of fun, but it just felt like something was wrong, like I was missing something. It wasn't until I saw you walking up the beach that I realized it was you."

I swallowed. In another life, in another time, I would have kissed her then, but even though I wanted to, I didn't. Instead, all I could do was stare at her. She met my gaze without a hint of self-consciousness.

"When you asked me why I was here, I made a joke because I thought the answer was obvious. Spending time with you just feels...right, somehow. Easy, like the way it's supposed to be. Like it is with my parents. They're just comfortable together, and I remember growing up thinking that one day I wanted to have that, too." She paused. "I'd like you to meet them one day."

My throat had gone dry. "I'd like that, too."

She slipped her hand easily into mine, her fingers intertwining with my own.

We sat in peaceful silence. At the water's edge, terns were bobbing their beaks into the sand in search of food; a cluster of seagulls broke as a wave rolled in. The sky had grown darker and the clouds more ominous. Up the beach, I could see scattered couples walking under a spreading indigo sky.

As we sat together, the air filled with the crashing of the surf. I marveled at how new everything felt. New and yet comfortable, as if we'd known each other forever. Yet we weren't even a real couple. *Nor,* a voice in my head reminded me, *is it likely you ever will be.* In a little more than a week, I'd be heading back to Germany and this would all be over. I'd spent enough time with my buddies to know that it takes more than a few special days to survive a relationship that spanned the Atlantic Ocean. I'd heard guys in my unit swear they were in love after coming off leave—and maybe they were—but it never lasted.

Spending time with Savannah made me wonder whether it was possible to defy the norm. I wanted more of her, and no matter what happened between us, I already knew I'd never forget anything about her. As crazy as it sounded, she was becoming part of me, and I was already dreading the fact that we wouldn't be able to spend the day together tomorrow. Or the day after, or the day after that. Maybe, I told myself, we could beat the odds.

"Out there!" I heard her cry. She pointed toward the ocean. "In the breakers."

I scanned an ocean the color of iron but didn't see anything. Beside me, Savannah suddenly stood up and started running toward the water.

"Come on!" she shouted over her shoulder. "Hurry!"

I rose and started after her, puzzled. Breaking into a run, I closed the gap between us. She stopped at the water's edge, and I could hear her breaths coming fast.

"What's going on?" I said.

"Right there!"

When I squinted, I saw what she'd been referring to. Three of them were riding the waves, one after the next, then disappearing from view in the shallows, only to reappear again a little ways down the beach.

"Young porpoises," I said. "They pass by the island almost every evening."

"I know," she said, "but it looks like they're surfing."

"Yeah, I suppose it does. They're just having fun. Now that everyone's out of the water, they feel like it's safe to play."

"I want to go in with them. I've always wanted to swim with the dolphins."

"They'll stop playing, or they'll just move down the beach to where you can't reach them. They're funny that way. I've seen them while surfing. If they're curious, they'll come within a few feet and give you the once-over, but if you try to follow them, they'll leave you in the dust."

We continued to watch the porpoises as they moved away from us, eventually vanishing from view under a sky that had grown opaque.

"We should probably get going," I said.

We made our way back to the car, stopping to pick up the remains from our dinner.

"I'm not sure the band will be playing yet, but it shouldn't be long."

"It doesn't matter," she said. "I'm sure we can find something to do. Besides, I should warn you, I'm not much of a dancer."

"We don't have to go if you don't want to. We could go someplace else if you'd like."

"Like where?"

"Do you like ships?"

"What kind of ships?"

"Big ones," I said. "I know this place where we can see the USS *North Carolina*."

She made a funny face, and I knew the answer was no. Not for the first time did I wish I had my own place. Then again, I was under no illusions that she'd follow me home if I did. If I were her, I wouldn't go either. I'm only human.

"Wait," she said, "I know where we can go. I want to show you something."

Intrigued, I asked, "Where?"

Considering Savannah's group had started their work only yesterday, the house was surprisingly far along. Most of the framing was already finished, and the roof had been raised as well. Savannah stared out the window of the car before turning to me.

"Would you like to walk around? See what we're doing?"

"I'd love to," I said.

I followed her out of the car, noting the play of moonlight on her features. As I stepped onto the dirt of the work site, I realized I could hear songs from a radio emanating from one of the kitchen windows of the neighbors. A few steps from the entrance, Savannah motioned around the structure with obvious pride. I moved close enough to slip my arm around her, and she tilted her head against my shoulder as she relaxed into me.

"This is where I've spent the last couple of days," she almost whispered in the nighttime quiet. "What do you think?"

"It's great," I said. "I'll bet the family is thrilled."

"They are. And they're such a great family. They really deserve this place since it's been such a struggle for them. Hurricane Fran destroyed their home, but like so many others, they didn't have flood insurance. It's a single mom with three kids— her husband ran out on her years ago—and if you met the family, you'd love them. The kids all get good grades and sing in the youth choir at church. And they're just so polite and gracious... you can tell their mom has worked hard to make sure they turn out right, you know?"

"You've met them, I take it?"

She nodded toward the house. "They've been here the last couple of days." She straightened. "Would you like to look around inside?"

Reluctantly, I let her go. "Lead the way."

It wasn't a large place—about the same size as my dad's—but the floor plan was more open, which made it seem larger. Savannah took me by the hand and walked me through each room, pointing out features, her imagination filling in the detail. She mused about the ideal wallpaper for the kitchen and the color of tile in the entryway, the fabric of the curtains in the living room, and how to decorate the mantel over the fireplace. Her voice conveyed the same wonder and joy she'd expressed when seeing the porpoises. For an instant, I had a vision of what she must have been like as a child.

She led me back to the front door. In the distance, the first rumblings of thunder could be heard. As we stood in the doorway, I drew her near.

"There's going to be a porch, too," she said, "with enough room for a couple of rocking chairs, or even a swing. They'll be able to sit out here on summer nights, and congregate here after church." She pointed. "That's their church right over there. That's why this location is so perfect for them."

"You sound like you really got to know them."

"No, not really," she said. "I talked to them a little bit, but I'm just guessing about all this. I've done that with every house I've helped to build—I walk through and try to imagine what the owners' lives will be like. It makes working on the house a lot more fun."

The moon was now hidden by clouds, darkening the sky. On the horizon, lightning flashed, and a moment later a soft rain began to fall, pattering against the roof. The oak trees lining the street, heavy with leaves, rustled in the breeze as thunder echoed through the house.

"If you want to go, we should probably leave before the storm hits."

"We don't have anywhere to go, remember? Besides, I've always loved thunderstorms."

I pulled her closer, breathing in her scent. Her hair smelled sweet, like ripe strawberries.

As we watched, the rain intensified into a steady downpour, falling diagonally from the sky. Streetlamps provided the only light, casting half of Savannah's face in shadow.

Thunder exploded overhead, and the rain began coming down in sheets. I could see the rain blowing onto the sawdust-covered floor, forming wide puddles in the dirt, and I was thankful that despite the rain, the temperature was warm. Off to the side, I spotted some empty crates. I left her side to collect them, then began to stack them into a makeshift seat. It wouldn't be all that comfortable, but it would be better than standing.

As Savannah took a seat next to me, I suddenly knew that coming here had been the right thing to do. It was the first time we'd really been alone, but as we sat side by side, it felt as though we'd been together forever.

# Chapter 8

The crates, hard and unforgiving, made me question my wisdom, but Savannah didn't seem to mind. Or pretended not to. She leaned back, felt the edge of the rear crate press into her skin, then sat up again.

"Sorry," I said, "I thought it would be more comfortable."

"It's okay. My legs are exhausted and my feet hurt. This is perfect."

Yes, I thought, it was. I thought back to nights on guard duty, when I'd imagine sitting beside the girl of my dreams and feeling all was right with the world. I knew now what I'd been missing all these years. When I felt Savannah rest her head on my shoulder, I found myself wishing I hadn't joined the army. I wished I weren't stationed overseas, and I wished I'd chosen a different path in life, one that would have let me remain a part of her world. To be a student at Chapel Hill, to spend part of my summer building houses, to ride horses with her.

"You're awful quiet," I heard her say.

"Sorry," I said. "I was just thinking about tonight."

"Good things, I hope."

"Yeah, good things," I said.

She shifted in her seat, and I felt her leg brush against mine. "Me too. But I was thinking about your dad," she said. "Has he always been like he was tonight? Kind of shy and glancing away when he talks to people?"

"Yeah," I said. "Why?"

"Just curious," she said.

A few feet away, the storm seemed to be reaching its climax as another sheet of rain broke from the clouds. Water poured off all sides of the house like waterfalls. Lightning flashed again, closer this time, and thunder crashed like a cannon. Had there been windows, I imagined they would have rattled in their casings.

Savannah scooted closer, and I put my arm around her. She crossed her legs at the ankles and leaned against me, and I felt as if I could hold her this way forever.

"You're different from most of the guys I know," she observed, her voice low and intimate in my ear. "More mature, less . . . flighty, I guess."

I smiled, liking what she said. "And don't forget my crew cut and tattoos."

"Crew cut, yes. Tattoos . . . well, they sort of come with the package, but no one's perfect."

I nudged her and pretended to be wounded. "Well, had I known how you feel, I wouldn't have got them."

"I don't believe you," she said, pulling back. "But I'm sorry—I shouldn't have said that. I was speaking more about how I'd feel about getting one. On you, they do tend to project a certain . . . image, and I suppose it fits."

"What image is that?"

She pointed to the tattoos, one by one, starting with the Chinese character. "This one tells me that you live life by your own rules and don't always care what people think. The infantry one shows that you're proud of what you do. And the barbed wire . . . well, that goes with who you were when you were younger."

"That's quite the psychological profile. Here I thought it was just that I liked the designs."

"I'm thinking about getting a minor in psychology."

"I think you already have one."

Though the wind had picked up, the rain finally began to slow.

"Have you ever been in love?" she asked, switching gears suddenly.

Her question surprised me. "That came out of the blue."

"I've been told that being unpredictable adds to the mysteriousness of women."

"Oh, it does. But to answer your question, I don't know."

"How can you not know?"

I hesitated, trying to think of what to say. "I dated a girl a few years back, and at the time, I knew I was in love. At least, that's what I'd told myself. But now, when I think back, I'm just . . . not sure anymore. I cared about her and I enjoyed spending time with her, but when we weren't together, I barely thought about her. We were together, but we weren't a couple, if that makes any sense."

She considered my answer but said nothing. In time, I turned toward her. "How about you? Have you ever been in love?"

Her face clouded. "No," she said.

"But you thought you were. Like me, right?" When she inhaled sharply, I went on. "In my squad, I have to use a bit of psychology, too. And my instincts tell me there was a serious boyfriend in your past."

She smiled, but there was something sad in it. "I knew you'd figure it out," she said in a subdued voice. "But to answer your question, yes, there was. During my freshman year in college. And yes, I did think I loved him."

"Are you sure you didn't love him?"

It took her a long time to answer. "No," she murmured. "I'm not."

I stared at her. "You don't have to tell me—"

"It's okay," she said, raising her hand to cut me off. "But it's hard. I've tried to forget about it, and it's something that I've never even told my parents. Or anyone, for that matter. It's such a cliché, you know? Small-town girl goes off to college and meets a handsome senior, who's also president of his fraternity. He's popular and rich and charming, and the little freshman is awed that he could be interested in someone like her. He treats her like she's special, and she knows that other freshman girls are jealous, so she begins to feel special, too. She agrees to go to the winter formal at one of these fancy out-of-town hotels with him and some other couples, even though she's been warned that the guy isn't as kind or sensitive as he appears to be, and that in reality, he's the kind of boy who carves notches in his bed frame for every girl he's had."

She closed her eyes, as if summoning the energy to continue. "She goes against the better judgment of her friends, and even though she doesn't drink and he happily brings her a soda, she starts getting woozy anyway, and he offers to take her back to the hotel room so she can lie down. And the next thing she knows, they're on the bed kissing, and she likes it at first, but the room is really spinning, and it doesn't occur to her until later that maybe someone—maybe him—put something in her drink and that carving another notch with her name on it had been his goal all along."

Her words began to come faster, tumbling over one another. "And then he starts groping at her breasts and her dress gets torn and then her panties get torn, too, but he's on top of her and he's so heavy and she can't get him off, and she feels really helpless and wants him to stop since she's never done this before, but by then she's so dizzy she can barely talk and can't call for help, and he probably would have had his way with her except that another couple who was staying in the room happened to show up, and she staggers out of the room crying and holding her dress. Somehow she finds her way to the lobby bathroom and keeps crying there, and other girls she'd traveled to the formal with come in and see the smeared mascara and torn dress and instead of being supportive, they laugh at her, acting like she should have known what was coming and got what she deserved. Finally she ends up calling a friend who hopped in his car and drove out there to pick her up, and he was smart enough not to ask any questions the whole way back."

By the time she finished, I was rigid with anger. I'm no saint with women, but I've never once in my life considered forcing a woman to do something she rather wouldn't.

"I'm sorry," was all I could muster.

"You don't have to be sorry. You didn't do it."

"I know. But I don't know what else to say. Unless..." I trailed off, and after a moment she turned to me. I could see the tears running down her cheeks, and the fact that she'd been crying so silently made me ache.

"Unless what?"

"Unless you want me to...I don't know. Beat the crap out of him?"

She gave me a sad little laugh. "You have no idea how many times I've wanted to do just that."

"I will," I said. "Just give me a name, but I promise to leave you out of it. I'll do the rest."

She squeezed my hand. "I know you would."

"I'm serious," I said.

She gave a wan smile, looking simultaneously world-weary and painfully young. "That's why I won't tell you. But believe me, I'm touched. That's sweet of you."

I liked the way she said it, and we sat together, hands clasped tightly. The rain had finally stopped, and in its place I could hear the sounds of the radio next door again. I didn't know the song, but I recognized it as something from the early jazz era. One of the guys in my unit was a fanatic about jazz.

"But anyway," she went on, "that's what I meant when I said it wasn't always easy my freshman year. And it was the reason I wanted to quit school. My parents, bless their hearts, thought that I was homesick, so they made me stay. But...as bad as it was, I learned something about myself. That I could go through something like that and survive. I mean, I know it could have been worse—a lot worse—but for me, it was all I could have handled at the time. And I learned from it."

When she finished, I found myself remembering something she'd said. "Was Tim the one who brought you back from the hotel that night?"

She looked up, startled.

"Who else would you call?" I said by way of explanation.

She nodded. "Yeah, I guess you're right. And he was great. To this day, he hasn't asked about the specifics, and I haven't told him. But since then he's been a little protective, and I can't say that I mind."

In the silence, I thought about the courage she had shown, not only that night, but afterward. Had she not told me, I would never have suspected anything bad had ever happened to her. I marveled that despite what happened, she had managed to hold on to her optimistic view of the world.

"I promise to be a perfect gentleman," I said.

She turned to me. "What are you talking about?"

"Tonight. Tomorrow night. Whenever. I'm not like that guy."

She traced a finger along my jaw, and I felt my skin tingle beneath her touch. "I know," she said, sounding amused. "Why do you think I'm here with you now?"

Her voice was so tender, and again, I suppressed the urge to kiss her. It wasn't what she needed, not now, even though it was difficult to think of anything else.

"Do you know what Susan said after that first night? Once you left and I went back to the group?"

I waited.

"She said you looked scary. Like you were the last person on earth she would have ever wanted to be alone with."

I grinned. "I've been told worse," I assured her.

"No, you're missing my point. My point is that I remember thinking that she didn't know what she was talking about, because when you first handed me my bag on the beach, I saw honesty and confidence and even something tender, but nothing frightening at all. I know it sounds crazy, but it felt like I already knew you."

I turned away without responding. Below the streetlamp, mist was rising from the ground, a remnant of the heat of the day. Crickets had begun to sound, singing to one another. I swallowed, trying to soothe the sudden dryness in my throat. I looked at Savannah, then up to the ceiling, then to my feet, and finally back to Savannah again. She squeezed my hand, and I drew a shaky breath, marveling at the fact that while on an ordinary leave in an ordinary place, I'd somehow fallen in love with an extraordinary girl named Savannah Lynn Curtis.

She saw my expression but misinterpreted it. "I'm sorry if I made you uncomfortable," she whispered. "I do that sometimes. Act too forward, I mean. I just blurt out what I'm thinking without taking into account how it might come across to others."

"You didn't make me uncomfortable," I said, turning her face to me. "I've just never had anyone say anything like that to me before."

I almost stopped there, aware that if I kept the words inside, the moment would pass and I would escape without putting my feelings on the line.

"You have no idea how much the last few days have meant to me," I began. "Meeting you has been the best thing that's ever happened to me." I hesitated, knowing that if I stopped now, I'd never be able to say it to anyone. "I love you," I whispered.

I had always imagined the words would be hard to say, but they weren't. In all my life, I'd never been as sure of anything, and as much as I hoped to one day hear Savannah say these words to me, what mattered most was knowing that love was mine to give, without strings or expectations.

Outside, the air was beginning to cool, and I could see pools of water shimmering in the moonlight. The clouds had begun to break up, and between them, an occasional star blinked, as if to remind me of what I'd just admitted.

"Did you ever imagine something like this?" she wondered aloud. "You and me, I mean?"

"No," I said.

"It scares me a little."

My stomach flipped, and all at once, I was sure she didn't feel the same way.

"You don't have to say it back to me," I began. "That's not why I said it—"

"I know," she interrupted. "You don't understand. I wasn't scared because you told me. I got scared because I wanted to say it, too: I love you, John."

Even now, I'm still not sure how it happened. One instant we were talking, and in the next she leaned toward me. For a second, I wondered whether kissing her would break the spell we both were under, but it was too late to stop. And when her lips met mine, I knew that I could live to be a hundred and visit every country in the world, but nothing would ever compare to that single moment when I first kissed the girl of my dreams and knew that my love would last forever.

# Questions and Explanations for Chapters 6 through 8

The ten questions on chapters 6 through 8 focus on grammar and usage, vocabulary, comprehension, literary terms, style, and characterization. Some of the questions combine two or more of these areas, requiring you to synthesize your knowledge, make inferences, and interpret the text. The questions are designed to determine both your current level of understanding of the novel and your ability to answer higher-level questions.

The following sentence tests your ability to recognize grammar and usage errors. The sentence contains either a single error or no error at all. If the sentence contains an error, select the one underlined part that must be changed to make the sentence correct. If there is no error, select choice D.

1. The reason that Savannah <u>shares</u> intimate details about
   <sub>A</sub>
   her horrible experience freshman year is <u>because</u> of
   <sub>B</sub>
   <u>John's</u> honesty and confidence and her sense that she
   <sub>C</sub>
   could trust him. <u>No error</u>
   <sub>D</sub>

Choice A checks your knowledge of the subject-verb agreement between the noun *Savannah* and the verb *shares*. Which is correct, "Savannah share" or "Savannah shares"? Choice B is checking to see if you realize that the words *reason* and *because* should not be used together. To illustrate the rule, think about the sentences, "The *reason* you don't use both words is that it would create a redundancy" or "You don't use both words together *because* that would create a redundancy." The rule of thumb is "the *reason* is never *because*." Choice C questions the use of an apostrophe to show possession. A singular noun demonstrates possession with an apostrophe and an *s*—for example, "the boy's book, the girl's letter, and the surfer's board."

**Question 2 tests your vocabulary. Choose the set of words that, when inserted in the sentence, best fits the meaning of the sentence as a whole.**

2. Although Einstein _____ about the relativity of time, John actually _____ a different type of time drag when waiting for Savannah.

   A. hypothesized...predicted

   B. prophesied...foresaw

   C. postulated...experienced

   D. portended...theorized

This question tests your comprehension and your vocabulary, and the context clues in the statement indicate that the two words have opposite meanings. First, you should recognize that the first word in each of the choices is similar in meaning to the others, so the place to start is with the second word in each pair. Because three of the second-word choices are also similar in nature to each other and to all of the first words, the one word that is different is the correct choice.

**Question 3 asks you to determine the meaning of words and phrases as they are used in the text.**

3. When John's father says that he would like to meet Savannah, what does John mean when he tells the reader his father spoke "in a voice so soft, I barely heard it"?

    A. John actually only imagined his father saying those words.

    B. John wasn't really listening to his father.

    C. John's father didn't really mean what he was saying.

    D. John's father found it difficult to say.

As John is leaving for his date with Savannah, you have to determine if his father actually said he'd like to meet Savannah. If you think he didn't in fact say these words, select choice A. If John barely heard his father because he wasn't paying any attention to him, select choice B. If you think Mr. Tyree spoke softly because he wasn't sincere in his sentiments, select choice C. If you think speaking up is not an easy thing for Mr. Tyree to do, select choice D.

**Question 4 checks your comprehension.**

4. After Savannah states that she is in the mood for a cheeseburger, John found himself "wondering if Savannah was too good to be true." What is significant about her suggestion for dinner?

   A. John was worried that Savannah didn't eat red meat.

   B. John wanted a cheeseburger, although he didn't tell her and instead deferred to Savannah's choice.

   C. For the first time, Savannah makes a decision.

   D. Savannah's domineering nature is starting to take over.

Making connections within and between chapters enables you to understand the development of characters and themes. If you recall that John was worried that Savannah didn't eat red meat, select choice A. If John mentioned wanting to have a cheeseburger but doesn't mention this to Savannah, select choice B. If Savannah has not previously made any decisions, select choice C. If Savannah states her decision in a forceful and overbearing way and continues to act that way, select choice D.

**Question 5 tests your knowledge of literary terms.**

5. As they watch the thunderstorm together, John comments that "her hair smelled sweet, like ripe strawberries." Identify the literary term used in this description.

   A. allusion

   B. metaphor

C. personification

D. simile

An *allusion*, choice A, is an indirect reference. Some of the most common types of allusions are historical (when someone meets his Waterloo, it's a reference to Napoleon); biblical (such as John Coffey in *The Green Mile* being a Christ figure); mythological (a reference to a Greek or Roman myth, such as a character being said to have the Midas touch); and literary (a reference to a character in a work of literature, such as a couple being compared to Romeo and Juliet). A *metaphor*, choice B, is a comparison between two unlike things without using a connective word—for example, "Michael Phelps was a flying fish in the pool." *Personification*, choice C, is giving a nonhuman thing a human characteristic, such as in "Opportunity knocked on the door." And a *simile*, choice D, is a comparison of two unlike things using a connective word, such as *like*, *as*, or *than*—for example, "She looked as fresh as the morning snow."

**Question 6 asks you to make an inference based on textual evidence.**

6. What is the primary purpose of chapter 8?

    A. to develop the conflict

    B. to provide a contrast between the two main characters

    C. to build sympathy for Savannah and her situation

    D. to establish the states of mind of each central character

Think about the dialogue and action (what is said and done) in chapter 8, which will help you answer this question. If there is a growing and expanding gulf between Savannah and John, select choice A. If Savannah and John appear to be polar opposites and all the details and examples seem to indicate that they have nothing in common, select choice B. If the main point of the chapter was to create a human and sympathetic character by revealing what Savannah has endured, select choice C. And if the chapter primarily develops the characters of Savannah and John by revealing their innermost thoughts, through their words and their actions, select choice D.

**Question 7 checks your understanding of literary terms.**

7. When describing a previous relationship, John says, "We were together, but we weren't a couple." This sentence is an example of what?

   A. foreshadowing

   B. hyperbole

   C. paradox

   D. simile

*Foreshadowing*, choice A, is providing hints or clues to future events. For example, when Benvolio suggests to Romeo that finding a new female beauty may help Romeo get over Rosaline, it foreshadows Romeo's falling in love with Juliet when he sees her later in the play.

*Hyperbole*, choice B, is using overexaggeration to illustrate a point. For example, if someone says, "I told you a million times what this is," you know that this person didn't really tell you a million times, just many times.

A *paradox*, choice C, is an apparent contradiction that upon further analysis seemingly makes sense. The famous first line of *A Tale of Two Cities*, "It was the best of times, it was the worst of times," initially doesn't make sense. But when you think about a situation in which both conditions can exist simultaneously, you begin to understand the paradox.

And a *simile*, choice D, is a comparison between two unlike things using a connective word, such as *like*, *as*, or *than*—for example, "She looked as fresh as the morning snow."

**Question 8 tests your knowledge of literary terms.**

8. When sitting in the house that Savannah and her friends were building, John comments that "thunder exploded overhead." What figure of speech is used to describe the sound?

   A. hyperbole
   B. metaphor
   C. onomatopoeia
   D. personification

Again, knowledge of literary terms is essential to answering this question. *Hyperbole*, choice A, is using overexaggeration to make a point—for example, "Everyone who reads this learning guide will know what *hyperbole* is because hyperbole will be explained a bazillion times."

A *metaphor*, choice B, is a comparison made between two unlike things without using a connective word—for example, "Michael Phelps was a flying fish in the pool."

*Onomatopoeia*, choice C, is a word that suggests the very sound it describes, like *buzz, pop,* and *boom.* The word can be used as either a noun or a verb—for example, "The *sizzle* of the bacon indicated that it was almost breakfast time" and "The bacon *sizzled* in the pan."

*Personification*, choice D, is giving a nonhuman thing a human characteristic, such as in "Opportunity knocked on the door."

**Question 9 asks you to make an inference about character and thematic development based on strong and thorough textual evidence.**

9. All of the following definitely support the assertion that John is truly falling in love with Savannah EXCEPT:

   A. his suppression of his desire to kiss her

   B. his jealous feelings when he sees Savannah sitting next to Randy

   C. his sharing of personal information openly and honestly

   D. his taking her to visit his father

Three of the four choices are clearly examples of what a person does or is like when he or she is truly in love and can be eliminated. If respecting the wishes of another while deferring one's own desires is a sign of love, eliminate choice A. If feelings of jealousy are always related to love, then eliminate choice B.

If revealing private information about your life, thoughts, and feelings in a truthful manner indicates true love, eliminate choice C. If doing something you would rather not do because the other person really wants to do it is a sign of love, eliminate choice D.

**Question 10 asks you to analyze how an author's choices contribute to overall structure and meaning.**

10. When Savannah relates to John her horrible experience during her freshman year, she speaks in third person. This achieves all of the following effects EXCEPT:

    A. maintaining the interest of both John and the reader

    B. distancing the speaker from the events

    C. providing an easier means to share the uncomfortable details

    D. making the experience more universal

The question indicates that three of the four choices are effects of telling the story in third person, so eliminate the choices that are effects in order to ascertain the correct answer. If using third person is needed to retain the interest of both John and the reader, eliminate choice A. If speaking in the third person rather than the first enables Savannah to separate herself from the events of that night, eliminate choice B. If talking about the events as if they occurred to another person enables Savannah to tell the story more easily, eliminate choice C. And if telling the story in third person makes it more about some character—any freshman girl—than herself, and thus makes it more general than personal, eliminate choice D.

# Chapter 9

We ended up staying out late. After we left the house, I took Savannah back to the beach, and we walked the long stretch of sand until she began to yawn. I walked her to the door, and we kissed again as moths darted in the porch light.

Although it seemed I'd been thinking about Savannah a lot the day before, it didn't compare with how obsessed I was the following day, though the feeling was different. I found myself smiling for no good reason, something even my father noticed when he got home from work. He didn't comment on it—I hadn't expected him to, of course—but he didn't seem surprised when I patted his back upon learning that he planned on making lasagna. I talked endlessly about Savannah, and after a couple of hours, he wandered back to his den. Even though he'd said little, I think he was happy for me and even more pleased that I'd been willing to share. I was sure of it when I got home later that night and found a platter of fresh-baked peanut-butter cookies on the counter, along with a note that informed me that plenty of milk could be found in the refrigerator.

I took Savannah out for ice cream, then drove her to the touristy part of downtown Wilmington. We strolled through the shops, where I discovered she had an interest in antiques. Later I took her to see the battleship, but we didn't stay long. She'd been right; it was boring. Afterward, I took her home, where we sat around the bonfire with her housemates.

The next two nights, Savannah came over to my house. My dad cooked both evenings. On the first evening, Savannah asked my dad nothing about coins, and conversation was a struggle. My dad mainly listened, and though Savannah kept up a pleasant front and tried to include him, force of habit led the two of us to talk to each other while my dad focused on his plate. When she left, Savannah's brow was creased, and though I didn't want to believe that her initial impression of him had changed, I knew that it had.

Surprisingly, she asked to return the following evening, where once again she and my father found themselves in the den, discussing coins. As I watched them, I wondered what Savannah was making of a situation that I'd long since grown used to. At the same time, I prayed that she would be more understanding than I had once been. By the time we left, I realized that I'd had nothing to worry about. Instead, as we drove back to the beach, she spoke about my dad in glowing terms, particularly praising the job he'd done raising me. While I wasn't sure what to make of it, I breathed a sigh of relief that she seemed to have accepted my dad for who he was.

By the weekend, my appearance at the beach house was becoming a regular occurrence. Most of the people in the house had learned my name, though they still showed little interest in me, exhausted as they were by the day's hard work. Most of them were clustered around the television by seven or eight, instead of drinking and flirting on the beach. Everyone looked sunburned, and all wore Band-Aids on their fingers to cover their blisters.

On Saturday night, people in the house had found additional reservoirs of energy, and I showed up just as a group of guys were unloading case after case of beer from the back of a van. I helped carry them up and realized that since the first night I'd seen Savannah, I hadn't had so much as a sip of alcohol. Like the weekend before, the grill was going and we ate near the bonfire; afterward we went for a walk on the beach. I'd brought a blanket and a picnic basket filled with late night snacks, and while lying on our backs, we watched a show of falling stars, staring in amazement as the flashes of white raced across the sky. It was one of those perfect evenings with just enough breeze to keep us from being either hot or cold, and we talked and kissed for hours before falling asleep in each other's arms.

When the sun began its rise from the sea on Sunday morning, I sat up beside Savannah. Her face was lit with the glow of dawn, and her hair fanned out over the blanket. She had one arm across her chest and another above her head, and all I could think was that I would like to spend every morning for the rest of my life waking up beside her.

We went to church again, and Tim was his regular chipper self, despite the fact that we'd barely spoken a word to him all week. He asked me again whether I'd like to help on the house. I told him that I'd be leaving the following Friday, and therefore I didn't know how much help I could be.

"I think you're wearing him down," Savannah said, smiling at Tim.

He raised his hands. "At least you can't say I didn't try."

It was perhaps the most idyllic week I'd ever spent. My feelings for Savannah had only grown stronger, but as the days wore on, I began to feel a gnawing anxiety at how soon all of this would be ending. Whenever those feelings arose, I tried to force them away, but by Sunday night, I could barely sleep. Instead, I tossed and turned, and thought of Savannah, and tried to imagine how I could be happy knowing she was across the ocean and surrounded by men, one of whom might come to feel exactly the way I did about her.

When I arrived at the house on Monday evening, I couldn't find Savannah. I had someone check her room, and I poked my head into every bathroom. She wasn't on the deck out back or on the beach with the others.

I went down to the beach and asked around, receiving mainly shrugs of indifference. A couple of people hadn't even realized she was gone, but finally one of the girls—Sandy or Cindy, I wasn't sure—pointed down the beach and said they'd seen her head that way about an hour earlier.

It took a long time to find her. I walked the beach in both directions, finally focusing on the pier near the house. On a hunch, I climbed the stairs, hearing the waves crashing below me. When I caught sight of Savannah, I thought she'd come out to the pier to look for porpoises or watch the surfers. She was sitting with her knees pulled up, leaning against a post, and it was only when I got close that I realized she was crying.

I'd never known quite what to do when I saw a girl cry. In all honesty, I never knew what to do when anyone cried. My father never cried, or if he did, it was never in my presence. And the last time I'd cried had been in the third grade, when I'd fallen from the tree house and sprained my wrist. In my unit, I'd seen a couple of the guys cry, and I'd usually pat them on the back and then wander away, leaving the whys and what can I dos to someone with more experience.

Before I could decide what to do, Savannah saw me. She hurriedly swiped at her red and swollen eyes, and I heard her draw a couple of steadying breaths. Her bag, the one I'd rescued from the ocean, was sandwiched between her legs.

"Are you okay?" I asked.

"No," she answered, and my heart clenched.

"Do you want to be alone?"

She considered it. "I don't know," she said at last.

Not knowing what else to do, I stood where I was.

Savannah sighed. "I'll be okay."

I slipped my hands in my pockets as I nodded. "Would you rather be alone?" I asked again.

"Do I really have to tell you?"

I hesitated. "Yeah."

She gave a melancholy laugh. "You can stay," she said. "In fact, it might be nice if you came and sat by me."

I took a seat and then, after a brief period of indecision, slipped my arm around her. For a while, we sat together without saying anything. Savannah inhaled slowly, and her breathing became steadier. She wiped at the tears that continued to slide down her cheeks.

"I bought you something," she said after a while. "I hope you're okay with it."

"I'm sure it's fine," I mumbled.

She sniffled. "Do you know what I was thinking about when I came out here?" She didn't wait for an answer. "I was thinking about us," she said. "The way we met and how we talked that first night, how you flashed your tattoos and gave Randy the evil eye. And your goofy expression when we went surfing the first time, after I rode the wave to shore..."

When she trailed off, I squeezed her waist. "I'm sure there's a compliment in there somewhere."

She tried to rally with a shaky grin but didn't quite succeed. "I remember everything about those first few days," she said. "And the same goes for the whole week. Spending time with your dad, going out for ice cream, even staring at that dumb boat."

"We won't go back," I promised, but she raised her hands to stop me.

"You're not letting me finish," she said. "And you're missing my point. My point is that I loved each and every moment of it, and I didn't expect that. I didn't come here for that, just like I didn't come here to fall in love with you. Or, in a different way, with your father."

Chastened, I said nothing.

She tucked a strand of hair behind her ear. "I think your dad is fantastic. I think he's done a wonderful job raising you, and I know you don't, and..."

When she seemed to run out of words, I shook my head, per-plexed. "And that's why you were crying? Because of the way I feel about my dad?"

"No," she said. "Weren't you listening?"

She paused, as if trying to organize her chaotic thoughts. "I didn't want to fall in love with anyone," she said. "I wasn't ready for that. I've been through that once, and afterwards I was a mess. I know it's different, but you'll be leaving in just a few days and all this will be over...and I'll be a mess again."

"It doesn't have to be over," I protested.

"But it will be," she said. "I know we can write and talk on the phone now and then, and we could see each other when you come home on leave. But it won't be the same. I won't be able to see your silly expressions. We won't be able to lie on the beach together and stare at the stars. We won't be able to sit across from each other and talk and share secrets. And I won't feel your arm around me, like I do now."

I turned away, feeling a rising sense of frustration and panic. Everything she was saying was true.

"It just hit me today," she went on, "while I was browsing in the bookstore. I went there to get you a book, and when I found it, I started imagining how you'd react when I gave it to you. The thing was, I knew that I'd see you in just a couple of hours, and then I *would* know, and that made it okay. Because even if you were upset, I knew that we'd get through it because we could work it out face-to-face. That's what I came to realize while sitting out here. That when we're together, anything is possible." She hesitated, then continued. "Pretty soon, that's not going to be possible anymore. I've known since we met that you'd only be here for a couple of weeks, but I didn't think that it was going to be this hard to say good-bye."

"I don't want to say good-bye," I said, gently turning her face to mine.

Beneath us, I could hear the waves crashing against the pilings. A flock of seagulls passed overhead, and I leaned in to kiss her, my lips barely brushing hers. Her breath smelled of cinnamon and mint, and I thought again of coming home.

Hoping to take her mind off such gloomy thoughts, I gave her a brisk squeeze and pointed at the bag. "So what book did you buy me?"

She seemed puzzled at first, then remembered she'd mentioned it earlier. "Oh yeah, I guess it's time for that, huh?"

By the way she said it, I suddenly knew she hadn't bought me the latest Hiaasen. I waited, but when I tried to meet her eyes, she turned away.

"If I give it to you," she said, her voice serious, "you have to promise me that you'll read it."

I wasn't quite sure what to make of it. "Sure," I said, drawing out the word. "I promise."

Still, she hesitated. Then she reached into her bag and pulled it out. When she handed it to me, I read the title. At first, I didn't know what to think. It was a book—more like a textbook, actually—about autism and Asperger's. I had heard of both conditions and assumed I knew what most people did, which wasn't much.

"It's by one of my professors," she explained. "She's the best teacher I've had in college. Her classes are always filled, and students who aren't registered sometimes drop in to talk to her. She's one of the foremost experts in all forms of developmental disorders, and she's one of the few who focused her research on adults."

"Fascinating," I said, not bothering to hide my lack of enthusiasm.

"I think you might learn something," she pressed.

"I'm sure," I said. "It looks like there's a lot of information there."

"There's more to it than just that," she said. Her voice was quiet. "I want you to read it because of your father. And the way you two get along."

For the first time, I felt myself stiffen. "What's that got to do with anything?"

"I'm not an expert," she said, "but this book was assigned both semesters that I had her, and I must have studied it every night. Like I said, she's interviewed more than three hundred adults with disorders."

I withdrew my arm. "And?"

I knew she heard the tension in my voice, and she studied me with a trace of apprehension.

"I know I'm only a student, but I spend a lot of my lab hours working with children who have Asperger's...I've seen it up close, and I've also had the chance to meet a number of the adults my professor had interviewed." She knelt in front of me, reaching out to touch my arm. "Your father is very similar to a couple of them."

I think I already knew what she was getting at, but for whatever reason, I wanted her to say it directly. "What's that supposed to mean?" I demanded, forcing myself not to pull away.

Her answer was slow in coming. "I think your father might have Asperger's."

"My dad isn't retarded..."

"I didn't say that," she said. "Asperger's is a developmental disorder."

"I don't care what it is," I said, my voice rising. "My dad doesn't have it. He raised me, he works, he pays his bills. He was married once."

"You can have Asperger's and still function..."

As she spoke, I flashed on something she had said earlier. "Wait," I said, trying to remember how she'd phrased it and feeling my mouth go dry. "Earlier, you said you think my dad did a wonderful job in raising me."

"Yeah," she said, "and I mean that..."

My jaw tightened as I figured out what she was really saying, and I stared at her as if seeing her for the first time. "But it's because you think he's like Rain Man. That considering his problem, he did a good job."

"No...you don't understand. There's a spectrum of Asperger's, from mild to severe—"

I barely heard her. "And you respect him for the same reason. But it's not as if you really liked him."

"No, wait—"

I pulled away and got to my feet. Suddenly needing space, I walked to the railing opposite her. I thought of her continual requests to visit with him...not because she wanted to spend time with him. Because she wanted to *study* him.

My stomach knotted, and I faced her. "That's why you came over, isn't it."

"What—"

"Not because you liked him, but because you wanted to know if you were right."

"No—"

"Stop lying!" I shouted.

"I'm not lying!"

"You were sitting there with him, pretending to be interested in his coins, but in reality you were evaluating him like some monkey in a cage."

"It wasn't like that!" she said, rising to her feet. "I respect your dad—"

"Because you think he's got problems and overcame them," I snarled, finishing for her. "Yeah, I get it."

"No, you're wrong. I like your dad..."

"Which is why you ran your little experiment, right?" My expression was hard. "See, I must have forgotten that when you like someone, you do things like that. Is that what you're trying to say?"

She shook her head. "No!" For the first time, she seemed to question what she'd done, and her lip began to quiver. When she spoke again, her voice trembled. "You're right. I shouldn't have done that. But I just wanted you to understand him."

"Why?" I said, taking a step toward her. I could feel my muscles tensing. "I understand him fine. I grew up with him, remember? I lived with him."

"I was trying to help," she said, eyes downcast. "I just wanted you to be able to relate to him."

"I didn't ask for your help. I don't want your help. And why is it any of your damn business, anyway?"

She turned away and swiped at a tear. "It's not," she said. Her voice was almost inaudible. "I thought you'd want to know."

"Know what?" I demanded. "That you think something's wrong with him? That I shouldn't expect to have a normal relationship with him? That I have to talk about coins if I want to talk to him at all?"

I didn't hide the anger in my voice, and from the corner of my eyes, I saw a couple of fishermen turn our way. My gaze kept them from coming closer, which was probably a good thing. As we stared at each other, I didn't expect Savannah to answer, and frankly, I didn't want her to. I was still trying to get my mind around the fact that the hours she had spent with my dad were nothing but a charade.

"Maybe," she whispered.

I blinked, unsure that she'd said what I thought she had. "What?"

"You heard me." She gave a small shrug. "Maybe that's the only thing you'll ever talk about with your father. It might be all he can do."

I felt my hands clench into fists. "So you're saying it's all up to me?"

I didn't expect her to answer, but she did.

"I don't know," she said, meeting my eyes. I could still see her tears, but her voice was surprisingly steady. "That's why I bought the book. So you can read it. Like you said, you know him better than I do. And I never said he's unable to function, because obviously he does. But think about it. His unchanging routines, the fact that he doesn't look at people when he talks to them, his nonexistent social life..."

I whirled away, wanting to hit something. Anything.

"Why are you doing this?" I asked, my voice low.

"Because if it was me, I'd want to know. And I'm not saying it because I wanted to hurt you or insult your father. I told you because I wanted you to understand him."

Her candor made it painfully clear that she believed what she was saying. Even so, I didn't care. I turned and started up the pier. I just wanted to get away. From here, from her.

"Where are you going?" I heard her call out. "John! Wait!"

I ignored her. Instead I picked up the pace, and a minute later I reached the stairs of the pier. I pounded down them, hit the sand, and headed for the house. I had no idea whether Savannah was behind me, and as I neared the group, faces turned toward me. I looked angry, and I knew it. Randy was holding a beer, and he must have seen Savannah approaching because he moved to block my path. A couple of his frat brothers did the same.

"What's going on?" he called out. "What's wrong with Savannah?"

I ignored him and felt him grab my wrist. "Hey, I'm talking to you."

169

Not a wise move. I could smell beer on his breath and knew that the alcohol had given him courage.

"Let go," I said.

"Is she okay?" he demanded.

"Let go," I said again, "or I'll break your wrist."

"Hey, what's going on?" I heard Tim call out from somewhere behind me.

"What did you do to her?" Randy demanded. "Why's she crying? Did you hurt her?"

I could feel the adrenaline surge into my bloodstream. "Last chance," I warned.

"There's no reason for this!" Tim shouted, closer this time. "Just relax, you guys! Knock it off!"

I felt someone try to grab me from behind. What happened next was instinctive, over in a matter of seconds. I drove my elbow hard into his solar plexus and heard a sudden groaning exhale; then I grabbed Randy's hand and quickly twisted it to its snapping point. He screamed and dropped to his knees, and in that instant I felt someone else rushing toward me. I swung an elbow blindly and felt it connect; I felt cartilage crunch as I turned, ready for whoever came next.

"What did you do?" I heard Savannah scream. She must have come running once she saw what was going on.

On the sand, Randy was wincing as he clutched his wrist; the guy who'd grabbed me from behind was gasping and on all fours.

"You hurt him!" she whimpered as she rushed past me. "He was just trying to stop the fight!"

I turned. Tim was sprawled on the ground, holding his face, blood gushing through his fingers. The sight seemed to paralyze everyone except Savannah, who dropped to her knees at his side.

Tim moaned, and despite the hammering in my chest, I felt a pit form in my stomach. Why did it have to be him? I wanted to ask if he was okay; I wanted to tell him I hadn't meant for him to get hurt and that it wasn't my fault. I hadn't started it. But it wouldn't matter. Not now. I couldn't pretend as if they should forgive and forget, no matter how much I wished it hadn't happened.

I could barely hear Savannah fretting as I began to back away. I eyed the others warily, making sure they'd let me leave, not wanting to hurt anyone else.

"Oh, geez...oh, no. You're really bleeding...we've got to get you to a doctor..."

I continued to back away, then turned and climbed the stairs. I moved quickly through the house, then back down to my car. Before I knew it, I was on the street, cursing myself and the entire evening.

# Chapter 10

I didn't know where to go, so I drove around aimlessly for a while, the events of the evening replaying in my mind. I was still angry at myself and what I'd done to Tim—not so much the others, I admit—and angry at Savannah for what had happened on the pier.

I could barely remember how it had started. One minute I was thinking that I loved her more than I'd ever imagined possible, and the next minute we were fighting. I was outraged by her subterfuge yet couldn't understand why I was this angry. It wasn't as if my dad and I were close; it wasn't as if I even thought I really knew him. So why had I been so angry? And why was I still?

*Because,* the little voice inside me asked, *there's a chance she might be right?*

It didn't matter, though. Whether he was or wasn't, so what? How was that going to change anything? And why was it any of her business?

As I drove, I kept veering from anger to acceptance and back to anger again. I found myself reliving the sensation of my elbow crushing Tim's nose, which only made it worse. Why had he come at me? Why not them? I wasn't the one who'd started it.

And Savannah...yeah, I might be able to head over there tomorrow to apologize. I knew she honestly believed what she was saying and that in her own way, she was trying to help. And maybe, if she was right, I did want to know. It would explain things...

But after what I did to Tim? How was she going to react to that? He was her best friend, and even if I swore it had been an accident, would it matter to her? How about what I'd done to the others? She knew I was a soldier, but now that she'd seen a small part of what that meant, would she still feel the same way about me?

By the time I found my way home, it was past midnight. I entered the darkened house, peeked into my dad's den, then proceeded to the bedroom. He wasn't up, of course; he went to bed at the same time every night. A man of routine, as I knew and Savannah had pointed out.

I crawled into bed, knowing I wouldn't sleep and wishing I could start the evening over again. From the moment she'd given me the book, anyway. I didn't want to think about any of it anymore. I didn't want to think about my dad or Savannah or what I'd done to Tim's nose. But all night long I stared at the ceiling, unable to escape my thoughts.

I got up when I heard my dad in the kitchen. I was wearing the same clothes from the evening before, but I doubted he was aware of it.

"Mornin', Dad," I mumbled.

"Hey, John," he said. "Would you like some breakfast?"

"Sure," I said. "Coffee ready?"

"In the pot."

I poured myself a cup. As my dad cooked, I noted the headlines in the newspaper, knowing he would read the front section first, then metro. He would ignore the sports and life section. A man of routine.

"How was your night?" I asked.

"The same," he said. I wasn't surprised when he didn't ask me anything in return. Instead, he ran the spatula through the scrambled eggs. The bacon was already sizzling. In time, he turned to me, and I already knew what he would ask.

"Would you mind putting some bread in the toaster?"

My dad left for work at exactly 7:35.

Once he was gone, I scanned the paper, uninterested in the news, at a loss as to what to do next. I had no desire to go surfing, or even to leave the house, and I was wondering whether I should crawl back into bed to try to get some rest when I heard a car pull up the drive. I figured it might be someone dropping off a flyer offering to clean the gutters or power-wash the mold from the roof; I was surprised when I heard a knock.

Opening the door, I froze, caught completely off guard. Tim shifted his weight from one foot to the other. "Hi, John," he said. "I know it's early, but do you mind if I come in?"

A wide strip of medical tape bridged his nose, and the skin surrounding both eyes was bruised and swollen.

"Yeah...sure," I said, stepping aside, still trying to process the fact that he was here.

Tim walked past me and into the living room. "I almost didn't find your house," he said. "When I dropped you off before, it was late and I can't say I was paying that much attention. I drove by a couple of times before it finally registered."

He smiled again, and I realized he was carrying a small paper sack.

"Would you like some coffee?" I asked, snapping out of my shock. "I think there still might be a cup left in the pot."

"No, I'm fine. I was up most of the night, and I'd rather not have the caffeine. I'm hoping to lie down when I get back to the house."

I nodded. "Hey, listen...about what happened last night," I began. "I'm sorry. I didn't mean..."

He held up his hands to stop me. "It's okay. I know you didn't. And I should have known better. I should have tried to grab one of the other guys."

I inspected him. "Does it hurt?"

"It's okay," he said. "It just happened to be one of those nights in the emergency room. It took a while to see a doctor, and he wanted to call someone else in to set my nose. But they swore it would be good as new. I might have a small bump, but I'm hoping it gives me a more rugged appearance."

I smiled, then felt bad for doing so. "Like I said, I'm sorry."

"I accept your apology," he said. "And I appreciate it. But that's not the reason I came here." He motioned to the couch. "Do you mind if we sit? I still feel a little woozy."

I sat on the edge of the recliner, leaning forward with my elbows on my knees. Tim sat on the sofa, wincing as he got comfortable. He set the paper bag off to the side.

"I want to talk to you about Savannah," he said. "And about what happened last night."

The sound of her name brought it all back, and I glanced away.

"You know we're good friends, right?" He didn't wait for an answer. "Last night in the hospital, we talked for hours, and I just wanted to come here to ask you not to be angry with her for what she did. She knows she made a mistake and that it wasn't her place to diagnose your father. You were right about that."

"Why isn't she here, then?"

"Right now, she's at the site. Someone's got to be in charge while I recuperate. And she doesn't know I'm here, either."

I shook my head. "I don't know why I got so mad in the first place."

"Because you didn't want to hear it," he said, his voice quiet. "I used to feel the same way whenever I heard someone talk about my brother, Alan. He's autistic."

I looked up. "Alan's your brother?"

"Yeah, why?" he asked. "Did Savannah tell you about him?"

"A little," I said, remembering that even more than Alan, she talked about the brother who'd been so patient with him, who'd inspired her to major in special education.

On the couch, Tim winced as he touched the bruising under his eye. "And just so you know," he went on, "I agree with you. It wasn't her place, and I told her so. Do you remember when I said that she was naive sometimes? That's what I meant. She wants to help people, but sometimes it doesn't come across that way."

"It wasn't just her," I said. "It was me, too. Like I said, I over-reacted."

His gaze was steady. "Do you think she might be right?"

I brought my hands together. "I don't know. I don't think so, but..."

"But you don't know. And if so, whether it even matters, right?"

He didn't wait for an answer. "Been there, done that," he

said. "I remember what my parents and I went through with Alan. For a long time we didn't know what, if anything, was wrong with him. And you know what I've decided after all this time? It doesn't matter. I still love him and watch out for him, and I always will. But...learning about his condition did help make things easier between us. Once I knew...I guess I just stopped expecting him to behave in a certain way. And without expectations, I found it easier to accept him."

I digested this. "What if he doesn't have Asperger's?" I asked.

"He might not."

"And if I think he does?"

He sighed. "It's not that simple, especially in milder cases," he said. "It's not as if you can pull a vial of blood and test for it. You might get to the point where you think it's possible, and that's as far as you'll ever get. But you'll never know for sure. And from what Savannah said about him, I honestly don't think much will change. And why should it? He works, he raised you...what more could you expect from a father?"

I considered this while images of my dad flashed through my head.

"Savannah bought you a book," he said.

"I don't know where it is," I admitted.

"I've got it," he said. "I brought it from the house." He handed me the paper bag. Somehow the book felt heavier than it had the night before.

"Thanks."

He rose, and I knew our conversation was nearing the end. He moved to the door but turned with his hand on the knob.

"You know you don't have to read it," he said.

"I know."

He opened the door, then stopped. I knew he wanted to

add something else, but, surprising me, he didn't turn around. "Would you mind if I asked a favor?"

"Go ahead."

"Don't break Savannah's heart, okay? I know she loves you, and I just want her to be happy."

I knew then that I'd been right about his feelings for her. As he walked to the car, I watched him from the window, certain that he was in love with her, too.

I put the book aside and went for a walk; when I got back to the house, I avoided it again. I can't tell you why I did so, other than that it frightened me somehow.

After a couple of hours, however, I forced the feeling away and spent the rest of the afternoon absorbing its contents and reliving memories of my father.

Tim had been right. There wasn't any clear-cut diagnosis, no hard-and-fast rules, and there was no way I'd ever know for certain. Some people with Asperger's had low IQs, while other, even more severely autistic people—like the Dustin Hoffman character in *Rain Man*—were regarded as geniuses in particular subjects. Some could function so well in society that no one even knew; others had to be institutionalized. I read profiles of people with Asperger's who were prodigies in music or mathematics, but I learned that they were as rare as prodigies among the general population. But most important, I learned that when my dad was young, there were few doctors who even understood the characteristics or symptoms and that if something had been wrong, his parents might never have known. Instead, children with Asperger's or autism were often lumped with the retarded or the shy, and if they weren't institutionalized, parents were left to comfort themselves with the hope that one day their child might grow out of it. The difference between Asperger's and autism could sometimes be summed up by the following: A person with autism lives in his own world, while a person with Asperger's lives in our world, in a way of his own choosing.

By that standard, most people could be said to have Asperger's.

But there were some indications that Savannah had been right about my father. His unchanging routines, his social awkwardness, his lack of interest in topics other than coins, his desire to be alone—all seemed like quirks that anyone might have, but with my father it was different. While others might freely make those same choices, my father—like some people with Asperger's—seemed to have been forced to live a life with these choices already predetermined. At the very least, I learned that it *might* explain my father's behavior, and if so, it wasn't that he *wouldn't* change, but that he *couldn't* change. Even with all the implied uncertainty, I found the realization comforting. And, I realized, it might explain two questions that had always plagued me regarding my mother: What had she seen in him? And why had she left?

I knew I'd never know, and I had no intention of delving further. But with a leaping imagination in a quiet house, I could envision a quiet man who struck up a conversation about his rare coin collection with a poor young waitress at a diner, a woman who spent her evenings lying in bed and dreaming of a better life. Maybe she flirted, or maybe she didn't, but he was attracted to her and continued to show up at the diner. Over time, she might have sensed the kindness and patience in him that he would later use in raising me. It was possible that she interpreted his quiet nature accurately as well and knew he would be slow to anger and never violent. Even without love, it might have been enough, so she agreed to marry him, thinking they would sell the coins and live, if not happily ever after, at least comfortably ever after. She got pregnant, and later, when she learned that he couldn't even fathom the idea of selling the coins, she realized that she'd be stuck with a husband who showed little interest in anything she did. Maybe her loneliness got the better of her, or maybe she was just selfish, but either way she wanted out, and after the baby was born, she took the first opportunity to leave.

Or, I thought, maybe not.

I doubted whether I would ever learn the truth, but I really didn't care. I did, however, care about my father, and if he was afflicted with a bit of faulty wiring in his brain, I suddenly understood that he'd somehow formed a set of rules for life, rules that helped him fit into the world. Maybe they weren't quite normal, but he'd nonetheless found a way to help me become the man I was. And to me, that was more than enough.

He was my father, and he'd done his best. I knew that now. And when at last I closed the book and set it aside, I found myself staring out the window, thinking how proud I was of him while trying to swallow the lump in my throat.

When he returned from work, my dad changed his clothes and went to the kitchen to start the spaghetti. I studied him as he went through the motions, knowing I was doing exactly the same thing that I'd grown angry at Savannah for doing. It's strange how knowledge changes perception.

I noted the precision of his moves—the way he neatly opened the box of spaghetti before setting it aside and the way he worked the spatula in careful right angles as he browned the meat. I knew he would add salt and pepper, and a moment later he did. I knew he would open the can of tomato sauce right after that, and again, I wasn't proved wrong. As usual, he didn't ask about my day, preferring to work in silence. Yesterday I'd attributed it to the fact that we were strangers; today I understood that there was a possibility we always would be. But for the first time in my life, it didn't bother me.

Over dinner I didn't ask about his day, knowing he wouldn't answer. Instead, I told him about Savannah and what our time together had been like. Afterward, I helped him with the dishes, continuing our one-sided conversation. Once they were done, he reached for the rag again. He wiped the counter a second time, then rotated the salt and pepper shakers until they were in exactly the same position they'd been in when he arrived home. I had the feeling that he wanted to add to the conversation and didn't know how, but I suppose I was trying to make myself feel better. It didn't matter. I knew he was ready to retreat to the den.

"Hey, Dad," I said. "How about you show me some of the coins you've bought lately? I want to hear all about them."

He stared at me as if uncertain he'd heard me right, then glanced at the floor. He touched his thinning hair, and I saw the growing bald spot on the top of his head. When he looked up at me again, he looked almost scared.

"Okay," he finally said.

We walked to the den together, and when I felt him place a gentle hand on my back, all I could think was that I hadn't felt this close to him in years.

# Chapter 11

The following evening, as I stood on the pier admiring the silver play of moonlight on the ocean, I wondered whether Savannah would show. The night before, after spending hours examining coins with my father and enjoying the excitement in his voice as he described them, I drove to the beach. On the seat beside me was the note I'd written to Savannah, asking her to meet me here. I'd left the note in an envelope I'd placed on Tim's car. I knew that he would pass along the envelope unopened, no matter how much he might not want to. In the short time I'd known him, I'd come to believe that Tim, like my father, was a far better person than I would ever be.

It was the only thing I could think to do. Because of the altercation, I knew I was no longer welcome at the beach house; I also didn't want to see Randy or Susan or any of the others, which made it impossible to contact Savannah. She didn't have a cell phone, nor did I know the phone number at the beach house, which left the note as my only option.

I was wrong. I'd overreacted, and I knew it. Not just with her, but with the others on the beach. I should have simply walked away. Randy and his buddies, even if they lifted weights and considered themselves athletes, didn't stand a chance against someone trained to disable people quickly and efficiently. Had it happened in Germany, I might have found myself locked up for what I'd done. The government wasn't too fond of those who used government-acquired skills in ways the government didn't approve.

So I'd left the note, then watched the clock all the next day, wondering if she would show. As the time I had suggested came and went, I found myself glancing compulsively over my shoulder, breathing a sigh of relief when a figure appeared in the distance. From the way it moved, I knew it had to be Savannah. I leaned against the railing as I waited for her.

She slowed her steps when she spotted me, then came to a stop. No hug, no kiss—the sudden formality made me ache.

"I got your note," she said.

"I'm glad you came."

"I had to sneak away so no one knew you were here," she said. "I've overheard a few people talking about what they would do if you showed up again."

"I'm sorry," I plunged in without preamble. "I know you were just trying to help, and I took it the wrong way."

"And?"

"And I'm sorry for what I did to Tim. He's a great guy, and I should have been more careful."

Her gaze was unblinking. "And?"

I shuffled my feet, knowing I wasn't really sincere in what I

was about to say, but knowing she wanted to hear it anyway. I
sighed. "And Randy and the other guy, too."

Still, she continued to stare. "And?"

I was stumped. I searched my mind before meeting her eyes.
"And..." I trailed off.

"And what?"

"And..." I tried but couldn't come up with anything. "I don't
know," I confessed. "But whatever it is, I'm sorry for that, too."

She wore a curious expression. "That's it?"

I thought about it. "I don't know what else to say," I admitted.

It was half a second before I noticed the tiniest hint of a
smile. She moved toward me. "That's it?" she repeated, her
voice softer. I said nothing. She came closer and, surprising
me, slipped her arms around my neck.

"You don't have to apologize," she whispered. "There's no
reason to be sorry. I probably would have reacted the same way."

"Then why the inquisition?"

"Because," she said, "it let me know that I was right about
you in the first place. I knew you had a good heart."

"What are you talking about?"

"Just what I said," she answered. "Later—after that night, I
mean—Tim convinced me that I had no right to say what I did.
You were right. I don't have the ability to do any sort of professional evaluation, but I was arrogant enough to think I did. As
for what happened on the beach, I saw the whole thing. It wasn't
your fault. Even what happened to Tim wasn't your fault, but
it was nice to hear you apologize anyway. If only to know you
could do it in the future."

She leaned into me, and when I closed my eyes, I knew I
wanted nothing more than to hold her this way forever.

*       *       *

Later, after we'd spent a good part of the night talking and kiss-ing on the beach, I ran my finger along her jaw and whispered, "Thank you."

"For what?"

"For the book. I think I understand my dad a little better now. We had a good time last night."

"I'm glad."

"And thanks for being who you are."

When she wrinkled her brow, I kissed her forehead. "If it wasn't for you," I added, "I wouldn't have been able to say that about my dad. You don't know how much that means to me."

Though she was supposed to work at the site the following day, Tim had been understanding when she explained that it would be the last chance for us to see each other before I returned to Germany. When I picked her up, he walked down the steps of the house and squatted next to the car, at eye level with the window. The bruises had darkened to deep black. He stuck his hand through the window.

"It was a pleasure meeting you, John."

"You too," I said, meaning it.

"Keep safe, okay?"

"I'll try," I answered as we shook hands, struck by the feeling that there was a connection between us.

Savannah and I spent the morning at the Fort Fisher Aquar-ium, bewitched by the strange creatures displayed there. We saw gar with their long noses, and miniature sea horses; in the largest tank were nurse sharks and red drum. We laughed as we handled the hermit crabs, and Savannah bought me a souvenir key chain from the gift shop. For some strange reason there was a penguin on it, which amused her to no end.

Afterward, I took her to a sunny restaurant near the water, and we held hands across the table as we watched the sailboats rocking gently in their slips. Lost in each other, we barely noticed the waiter, who had to come to the table three times before we'd even opened our menus.

I marveled at the easy way Savannah showed her emotions and the tenderness of her expression as I told her about my dad. When she kissed me afterward, I tasted the sweetness of her breath. I reached for her hand.

"I'm going to marry you one day, you know."

"Is that a promise?"

"If you want it to be."

"Well, then you have to promise that you'll come back for me when you get out of the army. I can't marry you if you're not around."

"It's a deal."

Later, we strolled the grounds of the Oswald Plantation, a beautifully restored antebellum home that boasted some of the finest gardens in the state. We walked along the gravel paths, skirting clusters of wildflowers that bloomed a thousand different colors in the lazy southern heat.

"What time do you fly out tomorrow?" she asked. The sun was beginning its gradual descent in the cloudless sky.

"Early," I said. "I'll probably be at the airport before you wake up."

She nodded. "And you'll spend tonight with your dad, right?"

"I was planning on it. I probably haven't spent as much time with him as I should have, but I'm sure he'd understand—"

She shook her head to stop me. "No, don't change your plans. I want you to spend time with your dad. I was hoping you would. That's why I'm with you today."

We walked the length of an elaborate hedge-lined path. "So what do you want to do?" I asked. "About us, I mean."

"It's not going to be easy," she said.

"I know it won't," I said. "But I don't want all this to end." I stopped, knowing words wouldn't be enough. Instead, from behind, I slipped my arms around her and drew her body into mine. I kissed her neck and ear, savoring her velvety skin. "I'll call you as much as I can, and I'll write you when I can't, and I'll get another leave next year. Wherever you are, that's where I'll go."

She leaned back, trying to catch a glimpse of my face. "You will?"

I squeezed her. "Of course. I mean, I'm not happy about leaving you, and I wish more than anything that I was stationed nearby, but that's all I can promise right now. I can request a transfer as soon as I get back, and I will, but you never know how those things go."

"I know," she murmured. For whatever reason, her solemn expression made me nervous.

"Will you write me?" I asked.

"Duh," she teased, and my nervousness disappeared. "Of course I will," she said, smiling. "How can you even bother to ask? I'll write you all the time. And just so you know, I write the best letters."

"I don't doubt it."

"I'm serious," she said. "In my family, that's what we do on just about every holiday. We write letters to those people who we care a lot about. We tell them what they mean to us and how much we look forward to the time when we'll get to see them again."

I kissed her neck again. "So what do I mean to you? And how much are you looking forward to seeing me again?"

She leaned back. "You'll have to read my letters."

I laughed, but I felt my heart breaking. "I'm going to miss you," I said.

"I'll miss you, too."

"You don't sound too broken up about it."

"That's because I already cried about it, remember? Besides, it's not like I'll never see you again. That's what I finally realized. Yeah, it'll be hard, but life moves fast—we'll see each other again. I know that. I can feel that. Just like I can feel how much you care for me and how much I love you. I know in my heart that this isn't over, and that we'll make it through this. Lots of couples do. Granted, lots of couples don't, but they don't have what we have."

I wanted to believe her. I wanted it more than anything, but I wondered if it was really that simple.

When the sun had disappeared below the horizon, we walked back to the car, and I drove her to the beach house. I stopped a little way down the street so no one in the house could see us, and when we got out of the car, I put my arms around her. We kissed and I held her close, knowing for certain that the next year would be the longest in my life. I wished fervently that I'd never joined up, that I were a free man. But I wasn't.

"I should probably be going."

She nodded, beginning to cry. I felt a knot form in my chest.

"I'll write you," I promised.

"Okay," she said. She swiped at her tears and reached into her handbag. She pulled out a pen and a small slip of paper. She began scribbling. "This is my home address and phone number, okay? And my e-mail address, too."

I nodded.

"Remember that I'll be changing dorms next year, but I'll let you know my new address as soon as I get it. But you can always reach me through my parents. They'll forward anything you send."

"I know," I said. "You still have my information, right? Even if I go on a mission somewhere, letters will reach me. E-mail, too. The army's pretty good at setting up computers, even in the middle of nowhere."

She hugged her arms like a forlorn child. "It scares me," she said. "You being a soldier, I mean."

"I'll be okay," I reassured her.

I opened the car door, then reached for my wallet. I slipped the note she scribbled inside, then opened my arms again. She came to me and I held her for a long time, imprinting the feel of her body against mine.

This time, it was she who pulled away. She reached into her handbag again and pulled out an envelope.

"I wrote this for you last night. To give you something to read on the plane. Don't read it until then, okay?"

I nodded and kissed her one last time, then slipped behind the wheel of the car. I started the car, and as I began to pull away, she called out, "Say hello to your father. Tell him that I might stop by sometime in the next couple of weeks, okay?"

She took a step backward as the car began to roll. I could still see her through the rearview mirror. I thought about stopping. My dad would understand. He knew how much Savannah meant to me, and he would want us to have one last evening together.

But I kept moving, watching her image in the mirror grow smaller and smaller, feeling my dream slip away.

*   *   *

Dinner with my dad was quieter than usual. I didn't have the energy to attempt a conversation, and even my dad realized it. I sat at the table as he cooked, but instead of focusing on the preparation, he glanced my way every now and then with muted concern in his eyes. I was startled when he turned off the burner and approached me.

When close, he put a hand on my back. He said nothing, but he didn't have to. I knew he understood that I was hurting, and he stood without moving, as if trying to absorb my pain in the hope of taking it from me and making it his own.

In the morning, Dad drove me to the airport and stood beside me at the gate while I waited for my flight to be called. When it was time, I rose. My dad held out his hand; I hugged him instead. His body was rigid, but I didn't care. "Love you, Dad."

"I love you, too, John."

"Find some good coins, okay?" I added, pulling back. "I want to hear all about them."

He glanced at the floor. "I like Savannah," he said. "She's a nice girl."

It came out of the blue, but somehow it was exactly what I wanted to hear.

On the plane, I sat with the letter Savannah had written me, holding it in my lap. Though I wanted to open it immediately, I waited until we'd lifted off from the runway. From the window, I could see the coastline, and I searched first for the pier, then the house. I wondered whether she was still sleeping, but I wanted to think that she was out on the beach and watching for the plane.

When I was ready, I opened the envelope. In it, she'd placed a photograph of herself, and I suddenly wished I had left her one of me. I stared at her face for a long time, then set it aside. I took a deep breath and began to read.

*Dear John,*

*There's so much I want to say to you, but I'm not sure where I should begin. Should I start by telling you that I love you? Or that the days I've spent with you have been the happiest in my life? Or that in the short time I've known you, I've come to believe that we were meant to be together? I could say all those things and all would be true, but as I reread them, all I can think is that I wish I were with you now, holding your hand and watching for your elusive smile.*

*In the future, I know I'll relive our time together a thousand times. I'll hear your laughter and see your face and feel your arms around me. I'm going to miss all of that, more than you can imagine. You're a rare gentleman, John, and I treasure that about you. In all the time we were together, you never pressed me to sleep with you, and I can't tell you how much that meant to me. It made what we had seem even more special, and that's how I always want to remember my time with you. Like a pure white light, breathtaking to behold.*

*I'll think about you every day. Part of me is scared that there will come a time when you don't feel the same way, that you'll somehow forget about what we shared, so this is what I want to do. Wherever you are and no matter what's going on in your life, when it's the first night of the full moon—like it was the first time we met—I want you to find it in the nighttime sky. I want you to think about me and the week we shared, because wherever I am and no matter what's going on in my life, that's exactly what I'll be doing. If we can't be together, at least we can share that, and maybe between the two of us, we can make this last forever.*

*I love you, John Tyree, and I'm going to hold you to the promise you once made to me. If you come back, I'll marry you. If you break your promise, you'll break my heart.*

*Love,*
*Savannah*

Beyond the window and through the tears in my eyes, I could see a layer of clouds spread beneath me. I had no idea where we were. All I knew was that I wanted to turn around and go back home, to be in the place I was meant to be.

# Questions and Explanations for Chapters 9 through 11

The ten questions on chapters 9 through 11 focus on grammar and usage, vocabulary, literary terms, comprehension, style, and characterization. Some of the questions combine two or more of these areas, requiring you to synthesize your knowledge, make inferences, and interpret the text. The questions are designed to determine both your current level of understanding of the novel and your ability to answer higher-level questions.

**The following sentence tests correctness and effective expression. Part of the following sentence is underlined; beneath the sentence are four ways of phrasing the underlined material. Select the option that produces the best sentence. If you think the original phrasing produces a better sentence than any of the alternatives, select choice A.**

1. When Randy saw John storming back from the pier, he demanded to know <u>if John hurt Savannah</u>.

   A. if John hurt Savannah

   B. if Savannah was hurt by John.

   C. if John had hurt Savannah.

   D. if John did something that hurt Savannah.

This question is testing your ability to express a number of actions accurately. Choice B uses passive voice rather than active voice to express an action—for example, "The door was opened by John" is passive whereas "John opened the door" is active voice (the subject is the doer of the action). Generally, the active voice is preferable to the passive voice. Choice C uses the past perfect tense, indicating that an action occurred at a time in the past prior to another action, which is also in the past—for example, "I had taken the SAT before I enrolled at this high school." Choice D is grammatically correct but is too wordy, creating an unnecessary subordinate clause.

**Question 2 tests your vocabulary. Choose the word that, when inserted in the sentence, best fits the meaning of the sentence as a whole.**

2. Tim's devotion to others, especially Savannah, is truly selfless, demonstrating that he really is a _____ of virtue for others.

   A. paradox

   B. paragon

   C. paramour

   D. paraplegic

The context clues for answering this question reveal that Tim's actions are selfless and serve as a model for others. A *paradox*, choice A, is a seemingly contradictory statement that upon reflection actually makes sense. A *paragon*, choice B, is a model of outstanding mettle, such as a person who provides an example of excellence. A *paramour*, choice C, is an illicit lover. And a *paraplegic*, choice D, is one who has lost the use of his or her legs.

**Question 3 checks your understanding of literary terms.**

3. When responding to Savannah's suggestion that his father might have Asperger's, John tells her, "You think he's like Rain Man." What literary term is used in this simile?

   A. allusion

   B. hyperbole

   C. metaphor

   D. personification

An *allusion*, choice A, is an indirect reference. Some of the most common types of allusions are historical (when someone meets his Waterloo, it's a reference to Napoleon); biblical (such as John Coffey in *The Green Mile* being a Christ figure); mythological (a reference to a Greek or Roman myth, such as a character being said to have the Midas touch); and literary (a reference to a character in a work of literature, such as a couple being compared to Romeo and Juliet). *Hyperbole*, choice B, is using overexaggeration to make a point. An example would be,

"Everyone who reads this learning guide will know what *hyperbole* is because hyperbole will be explained a bazillion times." A *metaphor*, choice C, is a comparison between two unlike things without using a connective word—for example, "Michael Phelps was a flying fish in the pool." *Personification*, choice D, is giving a nonhuman thing a human characteristic, such as in "Opportunity knocked on the door."

**Question 4 checks your understanding of literary terms.**

4. John accuses Savannah of only pretending to be interested in his father while she was actually "evaluating him like some monkey in a cage." What is he using to make his point?

   A. foreshadowing

   B. hyperbole

   C. paradox

   D. simile

*Foreshadowing*, choice A, is providing hints or clues to future events. For example, when Benvolio suggests to Romeo that finding a new female beauty may help Romeo get over Rosaline, it foreshadows Romeo's falling in love with Juliet when he sees her later in the play.

*Hyperbole*, choice B, is using overexaggeration to illustrate a point. For example, if someone says, "I told you a million times what this is," you know that this person really didn't tell you a million times, just many times.

A *paradox*, choice C, is an apparent contradiction that upon further analysis seemingly makes sense. The famous first line of *A Tale of Two Cities*, "It was the best of times, it was the worst of times," initially doesn't make sense. But when you think about a situation in which both conditions can exist simultaneously, you begin to understand the paradox.

And a *simile*, choice D, is a comparison between two unlike things using a connective word, such as *like*, *as*, or *than*—for example, "She looked as fresh as the morning snow."

**Question 5 checks your understanding of literary terms.**

5. When John begins to think about the possibility of his father having Asperger's, he realizes that he doesn't care about the condition, but he does care about his father and whether "he was afflicted with a bit of faulty wiring in his brain." What literary term does John use to help him understand his father's plight?

   A. allusion

   B. metaphor

   C. personification

   D. simile

Knowing about figures of speech will help you answer this question. An *allusion*, choice A, is an indirect reference. Some of the most common types of allusions are historical (when someone meets his Waterloo, it's a reference to Napoleon); biblical (such as John Coffey in *The Green Mile* being a Christ figure); mythological (a reference to a Greek or Roman myth, such as a character being said to have the Midas touch); and literary (a reference to a character in a work of literature, such as a couple being compared to Romeo and Juliet). A *metaphor*, choice

B, is a comparison between two unlike things without using a connective word—for example, "Michael Phelps was a flying fish in the pool." *Personification*, choice C, is giving a nonhuman thing a human characteristic, such as in "Opportunity knocked on the door." And a *simile*, choice D, is a comparison between two unlike things using a connective word, such as *like*, *as*, or *than*—for example, "She looked as fresh as the morning snow."

**Question 6 checks your comprehension.**

6. In Savannah's letter to John, she expresses her love to him and instructs him to think about something that will symbolize their love for one another and serve as a reminder of the week they spent together. What is that something?

   A. the beach

   B. the bonfire

   C. the full moon

   D. the Shrimp Shack

In Savannah's letter to John, not only does she mention something to him, she asks him to do something. This is important for the remainder of the novel. A close reading of the chapter will enable you to know the correct answer. If you are not certain, reread her letter on page 191.

**Question 7 checks your understanding of literary terms.**

7. John's observations and speculations regarding Tim's concern for Savannah and the fact that Tim has consis-

tently served as a physical, emotional, and spiritual friend for Savannah offer us clues as to what may eventually occur in Savannah's personal life. All of these details are examples of what?

A. foreshadowing

B. hyperbole

C. paradox

D. simile

*Foreshadowing*, choice A, is providing hints or clues to future events. For example, when Benvolio suggests to Romeo that finding a new female beauty may help Romeo get over Rosaline, it foreshadows Romeo's falling in love with Juliet when he sees her later in the play.

*Hyperbole*, choice B, is using overexaggeration to illustrate a point. For example, if someone says, "I told you a million times what this is," you know that this person really didn't tell you a million times, just many times.

A *paradox*, choice C, is an apparent contradiction that upon further analysis seemingly makes sense. The famous first line of *A Tale of Two Cities*, "It was the best of times, it was the worst of times," initially doesn't make sense. But when you think about a situation in which both conditions can exist simultaneously, you begin to understand the paradox.

And a *simile*, choice D, is a comparison between two unlike things using a connective word, such as *like*, *as*, or *than*—for example, "She looked as fresh as the morning snow."

**Question 8 asks you to make an inference based on textual evidence.**

199

8. What word best describes John as he awaits Savannah's arrival at the pier, uncertain if she is even going to come?

   A. acrimonious

   B. affable

   C. aloof

   D. apprehensive

Remember that John is waiting for Savannah after their fight and when he is no longer welcome at the beach house. *Acrimonious*, choice A, means severely critical and bitter. *Affable*, choice B, means approachable and friendly. *Aloof*, choice C, means mentally distant and separate, often due to feelings of superiority. And *apprehensive*, choice D, means uneasy, having a feeling of concern or dread.

**Question 9 tests your understanding of irony.**

9. After Savannah suggests to John that his father may have Asperger's, the evening at the pier does not turn out the way John had expected. This is an example of what type of irony?

   A. cosmic irony

   B. dramatic irony

   C. situational irony

   D. verbal irony

Understanding *irony*, the situation of appearance versus reality, is essential to understanding most literary texts. *Cosmic irony*, also known as irony of fate, is the situation where no matter what a character attempts to do, he or she cannot escape his or her fate. The most famous example of this is the Greek myth of Oedipus, who was fated to grow up and kill his father and marry his mother, no matter what he or anyone else tried to do to prevent it. *Dramatic irony* is when the reader knows something that the character in the text does not know. For example, the audience knows that Juliet is not really dead when Romeo discovers her body in the crypt, but he does not, and so he stabs himself. *Situational irony* is the incongruity between the expected outcome and what actually occurs. For example, Macbeth's misinterpretation of the witches' prophecies is an example of situational irony because he expects their words to mean one thing but in reality they mean something else. *Verbal irony* is meaning the opposite of what is said; sarcasm is a form of verbal irony. For example, when Mark Antony is talking about the conspirators as he stands over the body of dead Caesar, he says, "For Brutus is an honorable man." Clearly, Antony does not think Brutus is really honorable.

**Question 10 asks you to analyze how the author's choices contribute to the novel's overall structure and meaning.**

10. What is a valid interpretation as to why the author includes a letter from Savannah in which she expresses her love and a desire to marry John?

    A. The point of view shift enables readers to get inside Savannah's head to know her thoughts and feelings.

    B. John will have a hard copy of her words to carry with him to reread.

201

C. The words are easier to say in writing than in person.

D. all of the above

So far, the novel has been told from John's point of view, for he is the narrator. If the letter enables John and the reader to gain insight and understanding into Savannah's character because it is written from her perspective, select choice A. If the letter provides written words that can be read and reread, select choice B. If the written words provide a means of expression that makes difficult things easier to say, select choice C. And if choices A through C are correct, select choice D.

# Part II

# Chapter 12

Hours later, on that first lonely night back in Germany, I read the letter again, reliving our time together. It was easy; those memories had already begun to haunt me and sometimes seemed more real than my life as a soldier. I could feel Savannah's hand in mine and watched as she shook the ocean water from her hair. I laughed aloud as I recalled my surprise when she rode her first wave to shore. My time with Savannah changed me, and the men in my squad remarked on the difference. Over the next couple of weeks, my friend Tony teased me endlessly, smug in the belief that he'd finally been proven right about the importance of female companionship. It was my own fault for telling him about Savannah. Tony, however, wanted to know more than I was willing to share. While I was reading, he sat in the seat across from me, grinning like an idiot.

"Tell me again about your wild vacation romance," he said.

I forced myself to keep my eyes on the page, doing my best to ignore him.

"Savannah, right? Sa-va-nnah. Damn, I love that name. Sounds so...dainty, but I'll bet she was a tiger in the sack, right?"

"Shut up, Tony."

"Don't give me that. Haven't I been the one watching out for you all this time? Telling you that you gotta get out? You finally listened, and now it's payback time. I want the details."

"It's none of your business."

"But you drank tequila, right? I told you it works every time."

I said nothing. Tony threw up his hands. "Come on—you can tell me that much, can't you?"

"I don't want to talk about it."

"Because you're in love? Yeah, that's what you said, but I'm beginning to think you're making the whole thing up."

"That's right. I made it up. Are we done?"

He shook his head and rose from his seat. "You are one love-sick puppy."

I said nothing, but as he walked away, I knew he was right. I was head over heels crazy about Savannah. I would have done anything to be with her, and I requested a transfer to the States. My hard-bitten commanding officer appeared to give it serious consideration. When he asked why, I told him about my dad instead of Savannah. He listened for a while, then leaned back in his seat and said, "The odds aren't good unless your dad's health is an issue." Walking out of his office, I knew I wasn't going anywhere for at least the next sixteen months. I didn't bother to hide my disappointment, and the next time the moon was full, I left the barracks and wandered out to one of the grassy areas we used for soccer games. I lay on my back and stared at the moon, remembering it all and hating the fact that I was so far away.

From the very beginning, the calls and letters between us were regular. We e-mailed as well, but I soon learned that Savannah preferred to write, and she wanted me to do the same. "I know it's not as immediate as e-mail, but that's what I like about it," she wrote me. "I like the surprise of finding a letter in the mailbox and the anxious anticipation I feel when I'm getting ready to open it. I like the fact that I can take it with me to read at my leisure, and that I can lean against a tree and feel the breeze on my face when I see your words on paper. I like to imagine the way you looked when you wrote it: what you were wearing, your surroundings, the way you held your pen. I know it's a cliché and it's probably off the mark, but I keep thinking of you sitting in a tent at a makeshift table, with an oil lamp burning beside you while the wind blows outside. It's so much more romantic than reading something on the same machine that you use to download music or research a paper."

I'd smiled at that. She was, after all, wrong about the tent and the makeshift table and the oil lamp, but I had to admit that it did paint a more interesting picture than the reality of the fluorescent-lit, government-issued desk inside my wooden barracks.

As the days and weeks wore on, my love for Savannah seemed to grow even stronger. Sometimes I'd sneak away from the guys to be alone. I would take out Savannah's photograph and hold it close, studying every feature. It was strange, but as much as I loved her and remembered our time together, I found that as summer turned to autumn, then changed again to winter, I was more and more thankful for the photograph. Yes, I convinced myself that I could remember her exactly, but when

I was honest with myself, I knew I was losing the specifics. Or maybe, I realized, I'd never noticed them at all. In the photo, for instance, I realized that Savannah had a small mole beneath her left eye, something I'd somehow overlooked. Or that, on close inspection, her smile was slightly crooked. These were imperfections that somehow made her perfect in my eyes, but I hated the fact that I had to use the picture to learn about them.

Somehow, I went on with my life. As much as I thought about Savannah, as much as I missed her, I had a job to do. Beginning in September—owing to a set of circumstances that even the army had trouble explaining—my squad and I were sent to Kosovo for the second time to join the First Armored Division on yet another peacekeeping mission while pretty much everyone else in the infantry was being sent back to Germany. It was relatively calm and I didn't fire my gun, but that didn't mean I spent my days picking flowers and pining for Savannah. I cleaned my gun, kept watch for any crazies, and when you're forced to be alert for hours, you're tired by nightfall. I can honestly say I could go two or three days without wondering what Savannah was doing or even thinking about her. Did this make my love less real? I asked myself that question dozens of times during that trip, but I always decided it didn't, for the simple reason that her image would ambush me when I least expected it, overwhelming me with the same ache I had the day I'd left. Anything might set it off: a friend talking about his wife, the sight of a couple holding hands, or even the way some of the villagers would smile as we passed.

Savannah's letters arrived every ten days or so, and they'd piled up by the time I got back to Germany. None was like the letter I'd read on the plane; mostly they were casual and chatty, and she saved the truth of her feelings until the very end. In the meantime, I learned the details of her daily life: that they'd finished the first house a little behind schedule, which made things tougher when it came to building the second house. For that one, they had to work longer hours, even though everyone involved had grown more efficient at their tasks. I learned that after they completed the first house, they had thrown a big party for the entire neighborhood and that they'd been toasted over and over as the afternoon wore on. I learned that the work crew had celebrated by going to the Shrimp Shack and that Tim had pronounced it to have the greatest atmosphere of any restaurant he'd been to. I learned that she got most of her fall classes with the teachers she'd requested and that she was excited to be taking adolescent psychology with a Dr. Barnes, who'd just had a major article published in some esoteric psychology journal. I didn't need to believe that Savannah thought of me every time she pounded a nail or was helping to slide a window into place, or think that in the midst of a conversation with Tim, she would always wish it were me she was talking to. I liked to think that what we had was deeper than that, and over time, that belief made my love for her grow even stronger.

Of course, I did want to know that she still cared about me, and in this, Savannah never let me down. I suppose that was the reason I saved every letter she ever sent. Toward the end of each letter, there would always be a few sentences, maybe even a paragraph, where she would write something that made me pause, words that made me remember, and I would find myself rereading passages and trying to imagine her voice as I read them. Like this, from the second letter I received:

*When I think of you and me and what we shared,*
*I know it would be easy for others to dismiss our time*

together as simply a by-product of the days and nights spent by the sea, a "fling" that, in the long run, would mean absolutely nothing. That's why I don't tell people about us. They wouldn't understand, and I don't feel the need to explain, simply because I know in my heart how real it was. When I think of you, I can't help smiling, knowing that you've completed me somehow. I love you, not just for now, but for always, and I dream of the day that you'll take me in your arms again.

Or this, from the letter after I'd sent her a photograph of me:

And finally, I want to thank you for the picture. I've already put it in my wallet. You look healthy and happy, but I have to tell you that I cried when I saw it. Not because it made me sad—though it did, since I know I won't be able to see you—but because it made me happy. It reminded me that you're the best thing that's ever happened to me.

And this, from a letter she'd written while I'd been in Kosovo:

I have to say that your last letter worried me. I want to hear about it, I need to hear about it, but I find myself holding my breath and getting scared for you whenever you tell me what your life is really like. Here I am, getting ready to go home for Thanksgiving and worrying about tests, and you're someplace dangerous, surrounded by people who want to hurt you. I just wish those people could know you like I know you, because then you'd be safe. Just like I feel safe when I'm in your arms.

Christmas that year was a dismal affair, but it's always dismal when you're far from home. It wasn't my first Christmas alone during my years in the service. Every holiday had been spent in Germany, and a couple of guys in our barracks had rigged up a tree of sorts—a green tarp braced with a stick and decorated with blinking lights. More than half of my buddies had gone home—I was one of the unlucky ones who had to stay in case our friends the Russians got it in their heads that we were still mortal enemies—and most of the others trooped into town to celebrate Christmas Eve by getting bombed on quality German beer. I'd already opened the package Savannah had sent me—a sweater that reminded me of something Tim would wear and a batch of homemade cookies—and knew she'd already received the perfume I'd sent her. But I was alone, and as a gift to myself, I splurged on a phone call to Savannah. She hadn't expected the call, and I replayed the excitement in her voice for weeks afterward. We ended up talking for more than an hour. I had missed the sound of her voice. I'd forgotten her lilting accent and the twang that grew more pronounced whenever she started speaking quickly. I leaned back in my chair, imagining that she was with me and listening as she described the falling snow. At the same time, I realized it was snowing outside my window as well, which, if only for an instant, made it feel as if we were together.

By January 2001, I had begun to count down the days to when I'd see her again. My summer leave was coming in June, and I'd be out of the army in less than a year. I'd wake up in the morning and literally tell myself that there were 360 days left, then 359 and 358 till I was out, but I'd see Savannah in 178, then 177 and 176 and so on. It was tangible and real, close enough to allow me to dream of moving back to North Carolina; on the other hand, it unfortunately made time slow down. Isn't that the way it always is when you really want something? It reminded me of being a kid and the lengthening days as I waited for summer vacation. Had it not been for Savannah's letters, I have no doubt that the wait would have seemed much longer.

My dad wrote as well. Not with the frequency of Savannah, but on his own regular monthly schedule. To my surprise, his letters were two or three times longer than the page or so I'd been used to. The additional pages were exclusively about coins. In my spare time, I'd visit the computer center and do a bit of research on my own. I'd search for certain coins, collect the history, and send the information back in a letter of my own. I swear, the first time I did that, I thought I saw tears on the next letter he sent me. No, not really—I know it was just my imagination since he never even mentioned what I'd done—but I wanted to believe that he pored over the data with the same intensity he used when studying the *Greysheet*.

In February, I was shipped off on maneuvers with other NATO troops: one of those "pretend we're in a battle in 1944 exercises," in which we were supposedly facing an onslaught of tanks through the German countryside. Kind of pointless, if you ask me. Those kinds of wars are long since over, gone the way of Spanish galleons blasting their close-range cannons and the U.S. Cavalry riding horseback to the rescue. These days, they never say who the enemies are supposed to be, but everyone knows it's the Russians, which makes even less sense, since they're supposed to be our allies now. But even if they weren't, the simple fact is that they don't have that many working tanks anymore, and even if they were secretly building thousands at some plant in Siberia with the intent of overrunning Europe, any advancing wave of tanks would most likely be confronted with air strikes and our own mechanized divisions instead of the infantry. But what did I know, right? The weather was miserable, too, with some freakishly angry cold front moving down from the arctic just as the maneuvers started. It was epic, with snow and sleet and hail and winds topping fifty miles an hour, making me think of Napoleon's troops on the retreat from Moscow. It was so cold that frost formed on my eyebrows, it hurt to breathe, and my fingers would stick to the gun barrel if I touched it accidentally. It stung like hell getting them unstuck, and I lost a good bit of skin on the tips in the process. But I kept my face covered and my hand on the stock after that and marched through icy mud brought on by the endless snow showers, trying my best not to become an ice statue while we pretended to fight the enemy.

We spent ten days doing that. Half my men got frostbite, the other half suffered from hypothermia, and by the time we finished, my squad was reduced to just three or four men, all of whom ended up in the infirmary once we got back to base. Including me. The whole experience was just about the most ridiculous and idiotic thing the army ever made me do. And that's saying something, because I've done a lot of idiotic things for good old Uncle Sam and the Big Red One. At the end, our commander walked through the ward, congratulating my squad on a job well done. I wanted to tell him that maybe our time would have been better spent learning modern war tactics or, at the very least, tuned in to the Weather Channel. But instead I offered a salute and an acknowledgment, being the good army grunt I am.

After that, I spent the next few uneventful months on base. Sure, we did the occasional class on weapons or navigation, and every now and then I'd wander into town for a beer with the guys, but for the most part I lifted tons of weights, ran hundreds of miles, and kicked Tony's ass whenever we stepped into the boxing ring.

Spring in Germany wasn't as bad as I thought it would be after the disaster we went through on maneuvers. Snow melted, flowers came out, and the air began to warm. Well, not really warm, but it rose above freezing, and that was enough for most of my buddies and me to throw on shorts and play Frisbee or softball outside. As June finally rolled around, I found myself getting antsy to return to North Carolina. Savannah had graduated and was already in summer school doing classes for her master's degree, so I planned to travel to Chapel Hill. We would have two glorious weeks together—even when I went to see my dad in Wilmington, she planned to come with me—and I found myself feeling alternately nervous and excited and scared at the thought.

Yes, we'd corresponded through the mail and talked on the phone. Yes, I'd gone out to stare at the moon on the first night it was full, and in her letters she told me she had, too. But I hadn't seen her in nearly a year, and I didn't have any idea how she'd react when we were face-to-face again. Would she rush into my arms when I got off the plane, or would her reaction be more restrained, perhaps a gentle kiss on the cheek? Would we fall into easy conversation immediately, or would we find ourselves talking about the weather and feeling awkward around each other? I didn't know, and I'd lie awake at night imagining a thousand different scenarios.

Tony knew what I was going through, though he knew better than to call obvious attention to it. Instead, as the date approached, he slapped me on the back.

"Gonna see her soon," he said. "You ready for that?"

"Yeah."

He smirked. "Don't forget to pick up some tequila on the way home."

I made a face, and Tony laughed.

"It's going to be just fine," he said. "She loves you, man. She's got to, considering how much you love her."

# Chapter 13

In June 2001, I was given my leave and left for home immediately, flying from Frankfurt to New York, then on to Raleigh. It was a Friday evening, and Savannah had promised to pick me up at the airport before bringing me to Lenoir to meet her parents. She'd dropped that little surprise on me the day before the flight. Now, I had nothing against meeting her parents, mind you. I was sure they were wonderful people and all that, but if I had my way, I would rather have had Savannah all to myself at least for the first few days. It's kind of hard to make up for lost time with the parents around. Even if we didn't get physical—and knowing Savannah, I was pretty sure we wouldn't, though I kept my fingers crossed—how would her parents treat me if I kept their daughter out until the wee hours, even if all we did was lie under the stars? Granted, she was an adult, but parents were funny when it came to their own kids, and I was under no illusions that they'd be understanding about the whole thing. She would always be their little girl, if you know what I mean.

But Savannah had had a point when she explained it to me. I had two weekends free, and if I planned to see my dad on the second weekend, I had to see hers the first weekend. Besides, she sounded so excited about the whole thing that all I could say was that I was looking forward to meeting them. Still, I wondered if I'd even be able to hold her hand, and I speculated about whether I could talk her into taking a little detour on the way to Lenoir.

As soon as the plane landed, my anticipation grew and I could feel my ticker booming. But I didn't know how to act. Should I jog toward her as soon as I spotted her or stroll casually, cool and in control? I still wasn't sure, but before I could dwell on it, I was in the cattle chute, moving up the aisle. I slung my duffel bag over my shoulder as I emerged from the ramp that accessed the terminal. I didn't see her at first—too many folks milling around. When I scanned the area a second time, I saw her off to the left and realized instantly that all my worries had been pointless, for she spotted me and came running at full tilt. I barely had time to drop my duffel bag before she jumped into my arms, and the kiss that followed was like its own magic kingdom, complete with its special language and geography, fabulous myths and wonders for the ages. And when she pulled back and whispered, "I missed you so much," I felt as if I'd been put back together after spending a year cut in half.

I don't know how long we stood together, but when we finally began moving toward the baggage claim, I slipped my hand into hers knowing that I loved her not only more than the last time I'd seen her, but more than I would ever love anyone.

On the drive we talked easily, but we did make a small

detour. After pulling into a rest stop, we made out like teen-agers. It was great—let's leave it at that—and a couple of hours later, we arrived at her house. Her parents were waiting on the porch of a neat, two-story Victorian. Surprising me, her mother hugged me as soon as I got close, then offered me a beer. I declined, mostly because I knew I'd be the only one drinking, but I appreciated the effort. Savannah's mom, Jill, was a lot like Savannah: friendly, open, and a lot sharper than she first came across. Her dad was exactly the same, and I actually had a good time visiting with them. It didn't hurt that Savannah held my hand the whole time and seemed completely at ease doing so. Toward the end of the evening, she and I went for a long moonlit walk. By the time we got back to the house, it felt almost as if we'd never been apart at all.

It went without saying that I slept in the guest room. I hadn't expected otherwise, and the room was a lot better than most places I'd stayed, with classic furniture and a comfortable mat-tress. The air was stuffy, though, and I opened the window, hop-ing the mountain air would bring welcome cool. It had been a long day—I was still on German time—and I fell asleep imme-diately, only to wake up an hour later when I heard my door squeak open. Savannah, wearing comfy cotton pajamas and socks, closed the door behind her and started toward the bed, tiptoeing across the floor.

She held a finger to her lips to keep me quiet. "My parents would kill me if they knew I was doing this," she whispered. She crawled into bed beside me and adjusted the covers, pulling them up to her neck as if she were camping in the arctic. I put my arms around her, loving the feel of her body against mine.

We kissed and giggled for most of the night, then she sneaked back to her room. I fell asleep again, probably before she reached her room, and awakened to the sight of sunlight streaming in the window. The smell of breakfast came wafting into the room, and I tossed on a T-shirt and jeans and went down to the kitchen. Savannah was at the table, talking with her mom while her dad read the paper, and I felt the weight of their presence when I entered. I took a place at the table, and Savannah's mom poured me a cup of coffee before setting a plate of bacon and eggs in front of me. Savannah, who was sitting across from me already showered and dressed, was chipper and impossibly fresh-looking in the soft morning light.

"Did you sleep okay?" she asked, her eyes shining with mischief.

I nodded. "Actually, I had the most wonderful dream," I said.

"Oh?" her mom asked. "What was it about?"

I felt Savannah kick me under the table. She shook her head almost imperceptibly. I have to admit that I enjoyed the sight of Savannah squirming, but enough was enough. I feigned concentration. "I can't remember now," I said.

"I hate when that happens," her mother said. "Is breakfast okay?"

"It smells great," I said. "Thank you." I glanced at Savannah. "What's on the agenda today?"

She leaned across the table. "I was thinking we might go horseback riding. Do you think you'd be up for that?"

When I hesitated, she laughed. "You'll be fine," she added. "I promise."

"Easy for you to say."

She rode Midas; for me, she suggested a quarter horse named Pepper, which her dad usually rode. We spent most of the day walking up trails, galloping through open fields, and exploring this part of her world. She'd prepared a picnic lunch, and we ate at a spot that overlooked Lenoir. She pointed out the schools she'd attended and homes of the people she knew. It dawned on me then that not only did she love it here, she never wanted to live anywhere else.

We spent six or seven hours in the saddle, and I did my best to keep up with Savannah, though that was close to impossible. I didn't end up with my face planted in the dirt, but there were a few dicey moments here and there when Pepper acted up and it took everything I could do to hold on. It wasn't until Savannah and I were getting ready for dinner that I realized what I'd gotten myself into, however. Little by little, I began to realize that my walking resembled waddling. The inside muscles of my legs felt as if Tony had pounded them for hours.

On Saturday night, Savannah and I went to dinner at a cozy little Italian place. Afterward, she suggested we go dancing, but by then I could barely move. As I limped toward the car, she adopted a concerned expression and reached out to stop me.

Leaning over, she grasped my leg. "Does it hurt when I squeeze right here?"

I jumped and screamed. For some reason, she found this amusing.

"Why'd you do that? That hurt!"

She smiled. "Just checking."

"Checking what? I already told you—I'm sore."

"I just wanted to see if little old me could make a big, tough army guy like you scream."

I rubbed my leg. "Yeah, well, let's not test that anymore, okay?"

"Okay," she said. "And I'm sorry."

"You don't sound sorry."

"Well, I am," she said. "But it is kind of funny, don't you think? I mean, I rode just as long as you, and I'm fine."

"You ride all the time."

"I haven't ridden in over a month."

"Yeah, well."

"Come on. Admit it. It was kind of funny, wasn't it?"

"Not at all."

On Sunday, we attended church with her family. I was too sore to do much else the rest of the day, so I plopped myself on the couch and watched a baseball game with her dad. Savannah's mom brought in sandwiches, and I spent the afternoon wincing every time I tried to get comfortable while the game went into extra innings. Her dad was easy to talk to, and the conversation drifted from army life to teaching to some of the kids he coached and his hopes for their future. I liked him. From my seat, I could hear Savannah and her mom chatting in the kitchen, and every now and then, Savannah would come into the living room with a basket of laundry to fold while her mother started another load in the washing machine. Though technically a college graduate and an adult, she still brought her dirty clothes home to Mom.

That night, we drove back to Chapel Hill, and Savannah showed me her apartment. It was sparse in the furniture department, but it was relatively new, and it had both a gas fireplace and small balcony that offered a view of the campus. Despite the warm weather, she got the fire going, and we snacked on cheese and crackers, which, aside from cereal, was about all she had to offer. It felt indescribably romantic to me, though I'd come to realize that being alone with Savannah always struck me as romantic. We talked until nearly midnight, but Savannah was quieter than usual. In time, she wandered to the bedroom. When she didn't return, I went to find her. She was sitting on the bed, and I stopped in the doorway.

She squeezed her hands together and drew a long breath. "So...," she began.

"So...," I responded when she remained silent.

She drew another long breath. "It's getting late. And I've got an early class tomorrow."

I nodded. "You should probably get some sleep."

"Yeah," she said. She nodded as if she hadn't considered it and turned toward the window. Through the blinds, I could see shafts of light streaming in from the parking lot. She was cute when she was nervous.

"So...," she said again, as if speaking to the wall.

I held up my hands. "Why don't I sleep on the couch, okay?"

"You wouldn't mind?"

"Not at all," I said. Actually, it wasn't what I preferred, but I understood.

Still staring toward the window, she made no move to get up. "I'm just not ready," she said, her voice soft. "I mean, I thought I was, and part of me really wants to. I've been thinking about it for the last few weeks, and I made up my mind and it just seemed right, you know? I love you and you love me, and this is what people do when they're in love. It was easy to tell myself when you weren't here, but now..." She trailed off.

"It's okay," I said.

At last she turned toward me. "Were you scared? Your first time?"

I wondered how best to answer that. "I think it's different for men and women," I said.

"Yeah. I suppose so." She pretended to adjust the blankets. "Are you mad?"

"Not at all."

"But you're disappointed."

"Well . . . ," I admitted, and she laughed.

"I'm sorry," she said.

"There's no reason to apologize."

She thought about it. "Then why does it feel like I have to apologize?"

"Well, I am a lonely soldier," I pointed out, and she laughed again. I could still hear the nervousness in it.

"The couch isn't very comfortable," she fretted. "And it's small. You won't be able to stretch out. And I don't have any extra blankets. I should have grabbed a couple from home, but I forgot."

"That is a problem."

"Yeah," she said. I waited.

"I suppose you could sleep with me," she ventured.

I waited while she continued her own internal debate. Finally she shrugged. "You want to give it a try? Just sleeping, I mean?"

"Whatever you say."

For the first time, her shoulders relaxed. "Okay, then. We've got that settled. Just give me a minute to change."

She rose from the bed, crossed the room, and opened a drawer. The pajamas she chose were similar to the ones she'd worn at her parents', and I left her to go back to the living room, where I slipped on some of my workout shorts and a T-shirt. By the time I returned, she was already under the covers. I went to the other side and crawled in beside her. She shuffled the covers before turning out the light, then lay on her back, staring toward the ceiling. I lay on my side, facing her.

"Good night," she whispered.

"Good night."

I knew I wouldn't sleep. Not for a while, anyway. I was too... worked up for that. But I didn't want to toss and turn, in case she could.

"Hey," she finally whispered again.

"Yes?"

She rolled over to face me. "I just want you to know this is my first time that I've ever slept with a man. All night, I mean. That's a step closer, right?"

"Yeah," I said. "It's a step closer."

She brushed my arm. "And now if anyone asks, you'll be able to tell them that we've slept together."

"True," I said.

"But you won't tell anyone, will you? I mean, I don't want to get a reputation, you know."

I stifled a laugh. "I'll keep it our little secret."

The next few days fell into an easy, relaxing pattern. Savannah had classes in the morning and usually finished up a little after lunch. Theoretically, I suppose it gave me the opportunity to sleep in—something that all army recruits dream about when they talk about going on leave—but years of rising before dawn was a habit impossible to break. Instead, I woke before she did and would start a pot of coffee before trotting down to the corner to pick up the newspaper. Occasionally, I grabbed a couple of bagels or croissants; other times, we simply had cereal at the house, and it was easy to view our little routine as a preview of the first years of our future life together, effortless bliss that was almost too good to be true.

Or, at least, I tried to convince myself of that. When we

stayed with her parents, Savannah was exactly the girl I remembered. Same thing on our first night alone. But after that...I began to notice differences. I guess I hadn't fully realized that she was living a life that seemed complete and fulfilling, even without me. The calendar she kept on the refrigerator door listed something to do almost every day: concerts, lectures, half a dozen parties for various friends. Tim, I noted, was penciled in for the occasional lunch as well. She was taking four classes and teaching another as a graduate assistant, and on Thursday afternoons, she worked with a professor on a case study, one she was sure would be published. Her life was exactly the way she'd described it in her letters, and when she returned to the apartment, she'd tell me about her day while she made herself something to eat in the kitchen. She loved the work she was doing, and the pride in her tone was evident. She would talk animatedly while I listened, and I asked just enough questions to keep the flow of conversation going.

Nothing unusual in that, I admitted. I knew enough to realize that it would have been a bigger problem if she'd said nothing about her day at all. But with every new story, I'd get this sinking feeling, one that made me think that as much as we'd kept in touch, as much as we cared about each other, she'd somehow zigged while I had zagged. Since I'd last seen her, she'd completed her degree, tossed her cap into the air at commencement, found work as a graduate assistant, and moved into, and furnished, her own apartment. Her life had entered a new phase, and while I suppose it was possible to say the same thing about me, the simple fact was that nothing much had changed on my end, unless you counted the fact that I now knew how to assemble and disassemble eight types of weapons instead of six and I'd increased my bench press by another thirty pounds.

And, of course, I'd done my part in giving the Russians something to think about if they were debating whether or not to invade Germany with dozens of mechanized divisions.

Don't get me wrong. I was still head over heels for Savannah, and there were times when I still sensed the strength of her feelings for me. Lots of times, in fact. For the most part, it was a wonderful week. While she was gone, I'd walk the campus or jog around the sky blue track near the field house, taking advantage of some much needed downtime. Within a day I'd found a gym that would allow me to work out for the time I was there, and because I was in the service, they didn't even charge me. I'd usually be finished working out and showering by the time Savannah got back to the apartment, and we'd spend the rest of the afternoon together. On Tuesday night, we joined a group of her classmates for dinner in downtown Chapel Hill. It was more fun than I'd thought it would be, especially considering I was hanging out with a bunch of summer school eggheads and most of the conversation centered on the psychology of adolescents. On Wednesday afternoon, Savannah gave me a tour of her classes and introduced me to her professors. Later that afternoon, we met up with a couple of people I'd been introduced to the night before. That evening, we picked up some Chinese food and sat at the table in her apartment. She was wearing one of those strappy tank tops that accentuated her tan, and all I could think was that she was the sexiest woman I'd ever seen.

By Thursday, I wanted to spend some one-on-one time with her and decided to surprise her with a special night out. While she was in class and working on the case study, I went to the mall and dropped a small fortune on a new suit and tie and another small fortune on shoes. I wanted to see her dressed up, and I made dinner reservations at this restaurant the shoe salesman had told me was the best in town. Five stars, exotic menu, nattily dressed waiters, the whole shebang. Granted, I didn't tell Savannah about it beforehand—it was supposed to be a surprise, after all—but as soon as she walked in the door, I found out she'd already made plans to spend another evening with the same friends we'd seen during the last couple of days. She sounded so excited about it that I never bothered to tell her what I'd planned.

Still, I wasn't just disappointed, I was angry. To my way of thinking, I was more than happy to spend an evening with her friends, even an additional afternoon. But almost every day? After a year apart, when we had so little time left together? It bothered me that she didn't seem to share the same desire. For the past few months, I'd been imagining that we'd spend as much time together as we could, making up for our year apart. But I was coming to the conclusion that I might have been mistaken. Which meant...what? That I wasn't as important to her as she was to me? I didn't know, but given my mood, I probably should have stayed at the apartment and let her go by herself. Instead I sat off to the side, refused to take part in the conversation, and pretty much stared down everyone who looked my way. I've become good at intimidation over the years, and I was in rare form that night. Savannah could tell I was angry, but every time she asked if something was bothering me, I was at my passive-aggressive best in denying that anything was wrong at all.

"Just tired," I said instead.

She tried to make things better, I'll give her that. She reached for my hand now and then, flashed a quick smile my way when she thought I'd see it, and plied me with soda and chips. After a while, though, she got tired of my attitude and pretty much gave up. Not that I blame her. I'd made my point, and somehow the fact that she started getting angry with me left me feeling flush with tit-for-tat satisfaction. We barely talked on the way home, and when we got into bed, we slept on opposite sides of the mattress. In the morning I was over it, ready to move on. Unfortunately, she wasn't. While I was out getting the paper, she left the apartment without touching breakfast, and I ended up drinking my coffee alone.

I knew I'd gone too far, and I planned to make it up to her as soon as she got home. I wanted to come clean about my concerns, tell her about the dinner I'd planned, and apologize for my behavior. I assumed she'd understand. We'd put it all behind us over a romantic dinner out. It was just what I thought we needed, since we would be leaving for Wilmington the next day to spend the weekend with my dad.

Believe it or not, I wanted to see him, and I figured he was looking forward to my visit, too, in his own way. Unlike Savannah, Dad got a pass when it came to expectations. It might not have been fair, but Savannah had a different role to play in my life then.

I shook my head. Savannah. Always Savannah. Everything on this trip, everything about my life, I realized, always led back to her.

By one o'clock, I'd finished working out, cleaned up, packed most of my things, and called the restaurant to renew my reservation. I knew Savannah's schedule by then and assumed that she would be rolling in any minute. With nothing else to do, I sat on the couch and turned on the television. Game shows, soap operas, infomercials, and talk shows were interspersed with commercials from ambulance-chasing lawyers. Time dragged as I waited. I kept wandering out on the patio to scan the parking lot for her car, and I checked my gear three or four times. Savannah, I thought, was surely on the way home, and I occupied myself with clearing out the dishwasher. A few minutes later, I brushed my teeth for the second time, then peeked out the window again. Still no Savannah. I turned on the radio, listened to a few songs, and changed the station six or seven times before turning it off. I walked to the patio again. Nothing. By then, it was coming up on two o'clock. I wondered where she was, felt the remnants of anger starting to rise again, but forced them away. I told myself that she probably had a legitimate explanation and repeated it again when it didn't take hold. I opened my bag and pulled out the latest from Stephen King. I filled a glass with ice water, made myself comfortable on the couch, but when I realized I was reading the same sentence over and over, I put the book aside.

Another fifteen minutes passed. Then thirty. By the time I heard Savannah's car pulling into the lot, my jaw was tight and I was grinding my teeth. At a quarter past three, she pushed open the door. She was all smiles, as if nothing were wrong.

"Hey, John," she called out. She went to the table and started unloading her backpack. "Sorry I was late, but after my class, a student came up to tell me that she loved my class, and because of me, she wanted to major in special education. Can you believe that? She wanted advice on what to do, what classes to take, what teachers were the best . . . and the way she listened to my answers . . ." Savannah shook her head. "It was . . . so rewarding. The way this girl was hanging on everything I was saying . . . well, it just makes me feel like I was really making a difference to someone. You hear professors talk about experiences like that, but I never imagined that it would happen to me."

I forced a smile, and she took it as a cue to go on.

"Anyway, she asked if I had some time to really discuss it, and even though I told her I only had a few minutes, one thing led to another and we ended up going to lunch. She's really something—only seventeen, but she graduated a year early from high school. She passed a bunch of AP exams, so she's already a sophomore, and she's going to summer school so she can get even further ahead. You have to admire her."

She wanted an echo of her enthusiasm, but I couldn't muster it.

"She sounds great," I said instead.

At my answer, Savannah seemed to really look at me for the first time, and I made no effort to hide my feelings.

"What's wrong?" she asked.

"Nothing," I lied.

She set her backpack aside with a disgusted sigh. "You don't want to talk about it? Fine. But you should know that it's getting a little tiring."

"What's that supposed to mean?"

She whirled toward me. "This! The way you're acting," she said. "You're not that hard to read, John. You're angry, but you don't want to tell me why."

I hesitated, feeling defensive. When I finally spoke, I forced myself to keep my voice steady. "Okay," I said, "I thought you'd be home hours ago..."

She threw up her hands. "That's what this is about? I explained that. Believe it or not, I have responsibilities now. And if I'm not mistaken, I apologized for being late as soon as I walked in the door."

"I know, but..."

"But what? My apology wasn't good enough?"

"I didn't say that."

"Then what is it?"

When I couldn't find the words, she put her hands on her hips. "You want to know what I think? You're still mad about last night. But let me guess—you don't want to talk about that either, right?"

I closed my eyes. "Last night, you—"

"Me?" she broke in, and began shaking her head. "Oh no—don't blame me for this! I didn't do anything wrong. I wasn't the one who started this! Last night could have been fun—would have been fun—but you had to sit around acting as if you wanted to shoot someone."

She was exaggerating. Or then again, maybe she wasn't. Either way, I kept quiet.

She went on. "Do you know that I had to make excuses for you today? And how that made me feel? Here I was, singing your praises all year long, telling my friends what a nice guy you were, how mature you were, how proud I am of the job you're doing. And they ended up seeing a side of you that even I've never seen before. You were just...rude."

"Did you ever think that I might have been acting that way because I didn't want to be there?"

That stopped her, but only for an instant. She crossed her arms. "Maybe the way you acted last night was the reason I was late today."

Her statement caught me off guard. I hadn't considered that, but that wasn't the point.

"I'm sorry about last night—"

"You should be!" she cried, cutting me off again. "Those are my friends!"

"I know they're your friends!" I snapped, pushing myself up from the couch. "We've been with them all week!"

"What's that supposed to mean?"

"Just what I said. Maybe I wanted to be alone with you. Did you ever think of that?"

"You want to be alone with me?" she demanded. "Well, let me tell you, you're sure not acting like it. We were alone this morning. We were alone when I walked in the door just now. We were alone when I tried to be nice and put this all behind us, but all you wanted to do is fight."

"I don't want to fight!" I said, doing my best not to shout but knowing I'd failed. I turned away, trying to keep my anger in check, but when I spoke again, I could hear the ominous undercurrent in my voice. "I just want things to be like they were. Like last summer."

"What about last summer?"

I hated this. I didn't want to tell her that I no longer felt important. What I wanted was akin to asking someone to love you, and that never worked. Instead, I tried to dance around the subject.

"Last summer, it just felt like we had more time together."

"No, we didn't," she countered. "I worked on houses all day long. Remember?"

She was right, of course. At least partially. I tried again. "I'm not saying it makes much sense, but it seems like we had more time to talk last year."

"And that's what's bothering you? That I'm busy? That I have a life? What do you want me to do? Ditch my classes all week? Call in sick when I have to teach? Skip my homework?"

"No..."

"Then what do you want?"

"I don't know."

"But you're willing to humiliate me in front of my friends?"

"I didn't humiliate you," I protested.

"No? Then why did Tricia pull me aside today? Why did she feel the need to tell me that we had nothing in common and that I could do a lot better?"

That stung, but I'm not sure she realized how it came across. Anger sometimes makes that impossible, as I was well aware.

"I just wanted to be alone with you last night. That's all I'm trying to say."

My words had no effect on her.

"Then why didn't you tell me that?" she demanded instead. "Say something like 'Would it be okay if we do something else? I'm not really in the mood to hang out with people.' That's all you would have had to say. I'm not a mind reader, John."

I opened my mouth to answer but said nothing. Instead, I turned away and walked to the other side of the room. I stared out the patio door, not angered so much by what she'd said, just…*sad*. It struck me that I had somehow lost her, and I didn't know whether it was because I'd been making too much of nothing or because I understood all too well what was really happening between us.

I didn't want to talk about it anymore. I was never good at talking, and I realized that what I really wanted was for her to cross the room and put her arms around me, to say that she understood what was really bothering me and that I had nothing to worry about.

But none of those things happened. Instead I spoke to the window, feeling strangely alone. "You're right," I said. "I should have told you. And I'm sorry about that. And I'm sorry about the way I acted last night, and I'm sorry about being upset that you were late. It's just that I really wanted to see you as much as I could this trip."

"You say that like you don't think I want the same thing."

I turned around. "To be honest," I said, "I'm not sure you do." With that, I headed for the door.

I was gone until nightfall.

I didn't know where to go or even why I left, other than that I needed to be alone. I started for campus beneath a sweltering sun and found myself moving from one shade tree to the next. I didn't check to see if she was following; I knew that she wouldn't be.

In time, I stopped and bought an ice water at the student center, but even though it was relatively empty and the cool air refreshing, I didn't stay. I felt the need to sweat, as if to purify myself from the anger and sadness and disappointment I couldn't shake.

One thing was certain: Savannah had walked in the door ready for an argument. Her answers had come too quickly, and I realized that they seemed less spontaneous than rehearsed, as if her own anger had been simmering most of the day. She'd known exactly how I would be acting, and though I might have deserved her anger based on the way I'd acted last night, the fact that she hadn't appeared to care about her own culpability or my feelings gnawed at me for most of the afternoon.

Shadows lengthened as the sun began to go down, but I still wasn't ready to go back. Instead, I bought a couple of slices of pizza and a beer from one of those tiny storefront places that depended on students to survive. I finished eating, walked some more, and finally began the trek back to her apartment. By then it was nearly nine, and the emotional roller coaster

I'd been on left me feeling drained. Approaching the street, I noticed Savannah's car was still in the same spot. I could see a lamp blazing from inside the bedroom. The rest of the apartment was black.

I wondered whether the door would be locked, but the knob turned freely when I tried. The bedroom door was halfway closed, light spilled down the hallway, and I debated whether to approach or stay in the living room. I didn't want to face her anger, but I took a deep breath and made my way down the short hallway. I poked my head in. She was sitting on the bed in an oversize shirt, one that reached to midthigh. She looked up from a magazine, and I offered a tentative smile.

"Hey," I said.

"Hey."

I crossed the room and sat on the edge of the bed.

"I'm sorry," I said. "For everything. You were right. I was a jerk last night, and I shouldn't have embarrassed you in front of your friends. And I shouldn't have been so angry that you were late. It won't happen again."

She surprised me by patting the mattress. "Come here," she whispered.

I moved up the bed, leaned against the bed frame, and slipped my arm around her. She leaned against me, and I could feel the steady rise and fall of her chest.

"I don't want to argue anymore," she said.

"I don't either."

When I stroked her arm, she sighed. "Where'd you go?"

"Nowhere, really," I said. "Just walked the campus. Had some pizza. Did a lot of thinking."

"About me?"

"About you. About me. About us."

She nodded. "Me too," she said. "Are you still mad?"

"No," I said. "I was, but I'm too tired to be mad anymore."

"Me too," she repeated. She lifted her head to face me. "I want to tell you something about what I was thinking while you were gone," she said. "Can I do that?"

"Of course," I said.

"I realized that I'm the one who should have been apologizing. About spending so much time with my friends, I mean. I think that's why I got so mad earlier. I knew what you were trying to say, but I didn't want to hear it because I knew you were right. Partly, anyway. But your reasoning was wrong."

I looked at her uncertainly. She went on.

"You think that I made you spend so much time with my friends because you weren't as important to me as you used to be, right?" She didn't wait for an answer. "But that's not the reason. It's really the opposite. I was doing that because you're so important to me. Not so much because I wanted you to get to know my friends, or so they could get to know you, but because of me."

She halted uncertainly.

"I don't know what you're trying to say."

"Do you remember when I told you that I draw strength from being with you?"

When I nodded, she skated her fingers along my chest. "I wasn't kidding about that. Last summer meant so much to me. More than you can ever imagine, and when you left, I was a wreck. Ask Tim. I barely worked on the houses. I know I sent you letters that made you think all was well and good, but it wasn't. I cried every night, and every day I'd sit at the house and keep imagining and hoping and wishing that you'd come strolling up the beach. Every time I saw someone with a crew cut, I'd feel my heart start beating faster, even though I knew it wasn't you. But that was the thing. I wanted it to be you. Every time. I know that what you do is important, and I understand that you're posted overseas, but I don't think I understood how hard it was going to be once you weren't around. It seemed like it was almost killing me, and it took a long time to even begin to feel normal again. And on this trip, as much as I wanted to see you, as much as I love you, there's this part of me that's terrified that I'm going to go to pieces again when our time is up. I'm being pulled in two directions, and my response was to do anything I could so I wouldn't have to go through what I did last year again. So I tried to keep us busy, you know? To keep my heart from being broken again."

I felt my throat tighten but said nothing. In time, she went on.

"Today, I realized that I was hurting you in the process. That wasn't fair to you, but at the same time, I'm trying to be fair to me, too. In a week, you'll be gone again, and I'm the one who's going to have to figure out how to function afterwards. Some people can do that. You can do that. But for me..."

She stared at her hands, and for a long time it was quiet.

"I don't know what to say," I finally admitted.

Despite herself, she laughed. "I don't want an answer," she said, "because I don't think there is one. But I do know that I don't want to hurt you. That's all I know. I just hope I can find a way to be stronger this summer."

"We could always work out together," I joked halfheartedly, and was gratified to hear the sound of her laugh.

"Yeah, that'll work. Ten chin-ups and I'll be good as new, right? I wish it were that easy. But I'll make it. It might not be easy, but at least it's not going to be a full year this time. That's what I kept reminding myself today. That you'll be home for Christmas. A few more months and all this will be over."

237

I held her then, feeling the warmth of her body against my own. I could feel her fingers through the thin fabric of my shirt and felt her tug gently, exposing the skin of my stomach. The sensation was electric. I savored her touch and leaned in to kiss her.

There was a different kind of passion to her kiss, something vibrant and alive. I felt her tongue against my own, conscious of the way her body was responding, and breathed deeply as her fingers began to drift toward the snap on my jeans. When I slid my hands lower, I realized that she was naked beneath the shirt. She undid the snap, and though I wanted nothing more than to continue, I forced myself to pull back, to stop before this went too far, to prevent something I still wasn't sure she was ready for.

I sensed my own hesitation, but before I could dwell on it, she suddenly sat up and slipped off her shirt. My breaths quickened as I stared at her, and all at once, she leaned forward and lifted my shirt. She kissed my navel and my ribs, then my chest, and I could feel her hands begin to tug at my jeans.

I stood up from the bed and pulled off my shirt, then let my jeans fall to the floor. I kissed her neck and shoulders and felt the warmth of her breath in my ear. The sensation of her skin against mine was like fire, and we began to make love.

It was everything I had dreamed it would be, and when we were finished, I wrapped my arms around Savannah, trying to record the memory of every sensation. In the dark, I whispered to her how much I loved her.

We made love a second time, and when Savannah finally fell asleep, I found myself staring at her. Everything about her was exquisitely peaceful, but for some reason, I couldn't escape a nagging sense of dread. As tender and exciting as it had been, I couldn't help wondering whether there had been a trace of desperation in our actions, as if we were both clinging to the hope that this would sustain our relationship through whatever the future would bring.

# Questions and Explanations for Chapters 12 and 13

The ten questions on chapters 12 and 13 focus on grammar and usage, vocabulary, literary terms, comprehension, style, and characterization. Some of the questions combine two or more of these areas, requiring you to synthesize your knowledge, make inferences, and interpret the text. The questions are designed to determine both your current level of understanding of the novel and your ability to answer higher-level questions.

The following sentence tests your ability to recognize grammar and usage errors. The sentence contains either a single error or no error at all. If the sentence contains an error, select the one underlined part that must be changed to make the sentence correct. If there is no error, select choice D.

1. John was under no <u>allusion</u> that <u>Savannah's</u> parents
   A           B
   would be understanding about <u>his</u> keeping their daugh-
   C
   ter out until the wee hours of the morning. <u>No error</u>
   D

Choice A checks your knowledge of the homophones *allusion* and *illusion*. An *allusion* is a reference to something—for example, "Many works of literature are filled with historical *allusions*." An *illusion* is a mistaken idea—for example, "In spite of the evidence to the contrary, the ardent fan clung to her *illusion* regarding the team's athletic prowess."

Choice B checks the use of an apostrophe to show possession. A singular noun demonstrates possession with an apostrophe and an s—for example, "the boy's book, the girl's letter, the surfer's board."

Choice C checks the use of a pronoun before a word ending in -*ing*. When a word that is typically used as a verb ends in -*ing* and is acting as a noun in a sentence, that word is a gerund. When a pronoun precedes a gerund, it takes the possessive case—for example, "Savannah admired John's surfing."

**Question 2 tests your vocabulary. Choose the set of words that, when inserted in the sentence, best fits the meaning of the sentence as a whole.**

2. Although John was _____ about his leave and being able to spend time with Savannah, he was also _____ about seeing her after being apart for nearly a year.

   A. bitter...morose

   B. concerned...lugubrious

C. excited…uneasy

D. euphoric…ecstatic

This question tests your comprehension and your vocabulary. The context clues in the statement indicate that the two words have opposite meanings, and both words need to fit the context of the sentence. John is clearly not *bitter* about his leave, so eliminate choice A. Even though he is *concerned* about his upcoming leave, he is not mournful (nor is *lugubrious* an antonym for the word *concerned*), so eliminate choice B.

Although you can differentiate between *excited* and *euphoric*, it is easier to determine the correct second word in each pair. *Uneasy*, choice C, means apprehensive, and *ecstatic*, choice D, means to be in a state of delight.

**Question 3 tests your knowledge of literary terms.**

3. While John reads his letter from Savannah, Tony sits across from him, grinning like an idiot. What literary term is used to describe Tony?

   A. allusion

   B. hyperbole

   C. metaphor

   D. simile

An *allusion*, choice A, is an indirect reference. Some of the most common types of allusions are historical (when someone meets his Waterloo, it's a reference to Napoleon); biblical (such as John Coffey in *The Green Mile* being a Christ figure); mythological (a reference to a Greek or Roman myth, such as a character being said to have the Midas touch); and literary (a reference to a character in a work of literature, such as a couple being compared to Romeo and Juliet). *Hyperbole*, choice B, is using overexaggeration to make a point. An example would be, "Everyone who reads this learning guide will know what *hyperbole* is because hyperbole will be explained a bazillion times." A *metaphor*, choice C, is a comparison between two unlike things without using a connective word—for example, "Michael Phelps was a flying fish in the pool." A *simile*, choice D, is a comparison between two unlike things using a connective word, such as *like*, *as*, or *than*—for example, "She looked as fresh as the morning snow."

**Question 4 tests your knowledge of literary terms.**

4. John notices that Savannah's smile "was slightly crooked," yet claims, "These were imperfections that somehow made her perfect." His assertion is an example of what?

   A. foreshadowing

   B. hyperbole

   C. paradox

   D. simile

*Foreshadowing*, choice A, is providing hints or clues to future events. For example, when Benvolio suggests to Romeo that finding a new female beauty may help Romeo get over Rosaline, it foreshadows Romeo's falling in love with Juliet when he sees her later in the play.

*Hyperbole*, choice B, is using overexaggeration to illustrate a point. For example, if someone says, "I told you a million times what this is," you know that this person really didn't tell you a million times, just many times.

A *paradox*, choice C, is an apparent contradiction that upon further analysis seemingly makes sense. The famous first line of *A Tale of Two Cities*, "It was the best of times, it was the worst of times," initially doesn't make sense. But when you think about a situation in which both conditions can exist simultaneously, you begin to understand the paradox.

And a *simile*, choice D, is a comparison between two unlike things using a connective word, such as *like*, *as*, or *than*—for example, "My love is like a red, red rose."

**Question 5 tests your knowledge of literary terms.**

5. When describing his duty during Christmas, John says that "most of the others trooped into town to celebrate Christmas Eve by getting bombed on quality German beer." The word *bombed* is slang for getting drunk; thus, in this context, it's an example of a what?

   A. hyperbole

   B. onomatopoeia

   C. personification

   D. pun

Again, knowledge of literary terms is essential to answering this question. *Hyperbole*, choice A, is using overexaggeration to make a point—for example, "Everyone who reads this learning guide will know what *hyperbole* is because hyperbole will be explained a bazillion times."

*Onomatopoeia*, choice B, is a word that suggests the very sound it describes, like *buzz*, *sizzle*, and *boom*.

*Personification*, choice C, is giving a nonhuman thing a human characteristic, such as in "Opportunity knocked on the door."

A *pun*, choice D, is a play on words that is humorous because a word or phrase has more than one definition—for example, "The orthopedist slipped outside for a break."

**Question 6 asks you to make an inference based on textual evidence.**

6. What is the mood—or atmosphere—in the apartment when Savannah arrives home over two hours late?

   A. eerie

   B. peaceful

   C. playful

   D. tense

John expected Savannah to arrive home a lot earlier, and Savannah spent the day being annoyed at John. The attitude of the characters works with the setting to create the atmosphere, or mood, of the text. An *eerie* mood, choice A, creates a sense of superstitious fear. A *peaceful* mood, choice B, is free from conflict. A *playful* mood, choice C, creates a feeling of fun. A *tense* mood, choice D, results in (or is the result of) mental and emotional strain.

**Question 7 asks you to make an inference based on words used in context.**

7. Although Savannah wants John to affirm her enthusiasm regarding the student who came to see her after class, John is unable to do so. Instead, he says, "She sounds great." What is the probable tone of John's words?

   A. bitter and ironic

   B. loving and kind

   C. serene and soothing

   D. tepid and forced

A *bitter* and *ironic* tone, choice A, is harsh, disagreeable, and not to be taken seriously. A *loving* and *kind* tone, choice B, is warmly affectionate. A *serene* and *soothing* tone, choice C, is calm and tranquil. And a *tepid* and *forced* tone, choice D, demonstrates a lukewarm response that lacks enthusiasm.

**Question 8 checks your understanding of literary terms.**

8. John was more sad than angry when Savannah told him she wasn't a mind reader. He thinks to himself, "I understood all too well what really was happening between us." This statement is an example of what?

   A. foreshadowing

   B. hyperbole

   C. paradox

   D. simile

*Foreshadowing*, choice A, is providing hints or clues to future events. For example, when Benvolio suggests to Romeo that finding a new female beauty may help Romeo get over

Rosaline, it foreshadows Romeo's falling in love with Juliet when he sees her later in the play.

*Hyperbole*, choice B, is an overexaggeration used to illustrate a point. For example, if someone says, "I told you a million times what this is," you know that this person really didn't tell you a million times, just many times.

A *paradox*, choice C, is an apparent contradiction that upon further analysis seemingly makes sense. The famous first line of *A Tale of Two Cities*, "It was the best of times, it was the worst of times," initially doesn't make sense. But when you think about a situation in which both conditions can exist simultaneously, you begin to understand the paradox.

And a *simile*, choice D, is a comparison between two unlike things using a connective word, such as *like*, *as*, or *than*—for example, "The maid was as busy as a bee."

**Question 9 asks you to make an inference about character and thematic development based on strong and thorough textual evidence.**

9. The fight between John and Savannah illustrates all of the following EXCEPT that:

   A. Savannah has changed.

   B. Savannah no longer loves John.

   C. John and Savannah each have different expectations.

   D. Lack of communication can hurt a relationship.

Characters in a novel—like real people—fight for a variety of reasons. If you think that Savannah has changed during her time apart from John and that is part of the reason they are fighting, eliminate choice A. If you think that by fighting with John, Savannah is demonstrating that she no longer loves him, eliminate choice B. If you think John and Savannah each envision their time together being different than it is and that unmet expectations leads to the quarrel, eliminate choice C. And if you think the fight is due in part to lack of communication, eliminate choice D.

**Question 10 asks you to analyze how an author's choices contribute to overall structure and meaning.**

10. What is the best description of the scene created in the final paragraph of chapter 13 with John and Savannah lying in bed together after making love for the first time?

   A. It is the juxtaposition of their physical closeness with their emotional distance.

   B. It is an image of a couple who have never been closer.

   C. It is an image that represents the culmination of their romance.

   D. It is proof that even people who truly love one another fight once in a while.

Although you might be able to make a case for more than one answer, the *best* answer will incorporate aspects of other responses that may also seem correct. If you think the final image of the chapter contrasts the closeness and distance that currently exists in John and Savannah's relationship, select choice A. If you think the concluding image demonstrates that

John and Savannah have now achieved a physical closeness that matches their emotional and spiritual connection, select choice B. If the concluding image represents the highest point of their romance, select choice C. If you think the closing scene symbolizes all love relationships and provides sufficient evidence of the love between John and Savannah despite the fact that they had a fight, select choice D.

# Chapter 14

Our remaining time together on my leave was much as I had originally hoped. Aside from the weekend with my father—during which he cooked for us and spoke endlessly about coins—we were alone as much as possible. Back in Chapel Hill, once Savannah was finished with her classes for the day, our afternoons and evenings were spent together. We walked through the stores along Franklin Street, went to the North Carolina Museum of History in Raleigh, and even spent a couple of hours at the North Carolina Zoo. On my second to last evening in town, we went to dinner at the fancy restaurant the shoe salesman had told me about. She wouldn't let me peek while she was getting ready, but when she finally emerged from the bathroom, she was positively glamorous. I stared at her in between bites, thinking how lucky I was to be with her.

We didn't make love again. After our night together, I woke

the next morning to find Savannah studying me, tears running down her cheeks. Before I could ask what was wrong, she put a finger to my lips and shook her head, willing me not to speak.

"Last night was wonderful," she said, "but I don't want to talk about it." Instead, she wrapped herself around me and I held her for a long time, listening to the sound of her breath. I knew then that something had changed between us, but at the time, I didn't have the courage to find out what.

On the morning I left, Savannah drove me to the airport. We sat at the gate together, waiting for my flight to be called, her thumb tracing small circles on the back of my hand. When it was time for me to board the plane, she fell into my arms and started to cry. When she saw my expression, she forced a laugh, but I could hear the sorrow in it.

"I know I promised," she said, "but I can't help it."

"It's going to be okay," I said. "It's only six months. With all that's going on in your life, you'll be amazed how fast that goes."

"Easy to say," she said, sniffling. "But you're right. I'm going to be stronger this time. I'll be okay."

I scrutinized her face for signs of denial but saw none.

"Really," she said. "I'll be fine."

I nodded, and for a long moment we simply stared at each other.

"Will you remember to watch for the full moon?" she asked.

"Every single time," I promised.

We shared one last kiss. I held her tight and whispered that I loved her, then I forced myself to release her. I slung my gear over my shoulder and headed up the ramp. Peeking over my shoulder, I realized that Savannah was already gone, hidden somewhere in the crowd.

On the plane, I leaned back in the seat, praying that Savannah had been telling the truth. Though I knew she loved and cared for me, I suddenly understood that even love and caring weren't always enough. They were the concrete bricks of our relationship, but unstable without the mortar of time spent together, time without the threat of imminent separation hanging over us. Although I didn't want to admit it, there was much about her I didn't know. I hadn't realized how my leaving last year had affected her, and despite anxious hours thinking about it, I wasn't sure how it would affect her now. Our relationship, I felt with a heaviness in my chest, was beginning to feel like the spinning movement of a child's top. When we were together, we had the power to keep it spinning, and the result was beauty and magic and an almost childlike sense of wonder; when we separated, the spinning began inevitably to slow. We became wobbly and unstable, and I knew I had to find a way to keep us from toppling over.

I'd learned my lesson from the year before. Not only did I write more letters from Germany during July and August, but I called Savannah more frequently as well. I listened carefully during the calls, trying to pick up any signs of depression and longing to hear any words of affection or desire. In the beginning, I was nervous before making those calls; by the end of the summer, I was waiting for them. Her classes went well. She spent a couple of weeks with her parents, then began the fall semester. In the first week of September, we began the countdown of days I had left until my discharge. There were one hundred to go. It was easier to talk of days rather than weeks or months; somehow it made the distance between us shrink to something far more intimate, something that both of us knew we could handle. The hard part was behind us, we reminded each other, and I found that as I flipped the days on the calendar, the worries I'd had about our relationship began to diminish. I was certain there was nothing in the world that could stop us from being together.

Then came September 11.

# Chapter 15

This I am sure of: The images of September 11 will be with me forever. I watched the smoke billowing from the Twin Towers and the Pentagon and saw the grim faces of the men around me as they watched people jump to their deaths. I witnessed the buildings' collapse and the massive cloud of dust and debris that rose in their place. I felt fury as the White House was evacuated.

Within hours, I knew that the United States would respond to the attack and that the armed services would lead the way. The base was put on high alert, and I doubted there was ever a time that I was prouder of my men. In the days that followed, it was as if all personal differences and political affiliations of any kind melted away. For a short period of time, we were all simply Americans.

Recruiting offices began to fill around the country with men wanting to enlist. Among those of us already enlisted, the desire to serve was stronger than ever. Tony was the first of the men in my squad to reup for an additional two years, and one by one, every other man followed his lead. Even I, who was expecting my honorable discharge in December and had been counting the days until I could go home to Savannah, caught the fever and found myself reenlisting.

It would be easy to say that I was influenced by what was going on around me and that was the reason I made the decision I did. But that's just an excuse. Granted, I was caught up in the same patriotic wave, but more than that, I was bound by the twin ties of friendship and responsibility. I knew my men, I cared about my men, and the thought of abandoning them at a time like this struck me as impossibly cowardly. We'd been through too much together for me to even contemplate leaving the service in those waning days of 2001.

I called Savannah with the news. Initially, she was supportive. Like everyone else, she'd been horrified by what had happened, and she understood the sense of duty that weighed on me, even before I tried to explain it. She said she was proud of me.

But reality soon set in. In choosing to serve my country, I'd made a sacrifice. Though the investigation into the perpetrators was completed quickly, 2001 drifted to an uneventful close for us. Our infantry division played no role in the overthrow of the Taliban government in Afghanistan, a disappointment to everyone in my squad. Instead, we spent most of winter and spring drilling and preparing for what everyone knew was the future invasion of Iraq.

It was, I suppose, around this time that the letters from Savannah began to change. Where once they came weekly, they started arriving every ten days, and then, as the days began to lengthen, they came only every other week. I tried to console myself with the fact that the tone of the letters hadn't changed, but in time even that did. Gone were long passages in which she described the way she envisioned our life together, passages that in the past had always filled me with anticipation. We both knew that dream was now two years distant. Writing about a future so far off reminded her of how long we had to go, something painful for both of us to contemplate.

As May swept in, I consoled myself that at least we would be able to see each other on my next leave. Fate, however, conspired against us again just a few days before I was to return home. My commanding officer requested a meeting, and when I presented myself in the office, he instructed me to take a seat. My dad, he told me, had just suffered a major heart attack, and he'd already gone ahead and granted the additional emergency leave. Instead of heading to Chapel Hill and two glorious weeks with Savannah, I traveled to Wilmington and spent my days by my dad's bedside, breathing in the antiseptic odor that always made me think less of healing than of death itself. When I arrived, my dad was in the intensive care unit; he stayed there most of my leave. His skin had a grayish pallor, and his breathing was rapid and weak. For the first week, he drifted in and out of consciousness, but when he was awake, I saw emotions in my father that I'd seen only rarely and never in combination: desperate fear, momentary confusion, and a heartbreaking gratitude that I was beside him. More than once, I reached for his hand, another first in my life. Because of a tube inserted into his throat, he couldn't speak, so I did all the talking for us. Though I told him a little of what was going on back on base, I spoke to him mainly about coins. I read him the *Greysheet*; when that was done, I went to his house and retrieved the old copies he kept filed in his drawer and read those to him as well. I researched coins on the Internet—at sites like David Hall Rare Coins and Legend Numismatics—and recited what was being offered as well as the latest prices. The prices amazed me and I suspected that my father's collection, despite the fall in coin prices since gold was in its heyday, was probably ten times as valuable as the house he'd owned outright for years. My father, unable to master the art of even simple conversation, had become richer than anyone I knew.

My dad was uninterested in their value. His eyes would dart away whenever I mentioned it, and I soon remembered what I'd somehow forgotten: that to my dad, the pursuit of the coins was far more interesting than the coins themselves, and to him each coin was representative of a story with a happy ending. With that in mind, I racked my brain, doing my best to remember those coins that we had found together. Because my dad kept exceptional records, I would scan those before going to sleep, and little by little, those memories came back. The following day, I would recall for him stories of our trips to Raleigh or Charlotte or Savannah. Despite the fact that even the doctors weren't sure whether he was going to make it, my dad smiled more in those weeks than I ever remember him doing. He made it back home the day before I was set to leave, and the hospital made arrangements for someone to look in on him while he continued to recover.

But if my stay in the hospital strengthened my relationship with my dad, it did nothing for my relationship with Savannah. Don't get me wrong—she joined me as often as she could, and she was both supportive and sympathetic. But because I spent so much time in the hospital, it did little to heal the fissures that had begun to form in our relationship. To be honest, I wasn't sure what I even wanted from her: When she was there, I felt as if I wanted to be alone with my dad, but when she wasn't, I wanted her by my side. Somehow, Savannah navigated this minefield without reacting to any stress I redirected her way. She seemed to know what I was thinking and anticipate what I wanted, even better than I did.

Still, what we needed was time together. Time alone. If our relationship was a battery, my time overseas was continually draining it, and we both needed time to recharge. Once, while sitting with my dad and listening to the steady beep of the heart monitor, I realized that Savannah and I had spent only 4 of the last 104 weeks together. Less than 5 percent. Even with letters and phone calls, I would sometimes find myself staring into space, wondering how we'd survived as long as we had.

We did make it out for occasional walks, and we dined together twice. But because Savannah was teaching and taking classes again, it was impossible for her to stay. I tried not to blame her for that, except when I did, and we ended up arguing. I hated that, as did she, but neither of us seemed to be able to stop it. And though she said nothing, and even denied it when confronted, I knew the underlying issue was the fact that I was supposed to be home for good and wasn't. It was the first and only time that Savannah ever lied to me.

We put the argument behind us as best we could, and good-bye was another tearful affair, though less so than the last time. It would be comforting to think that it was because we were getting used to it, or that we were both growing up, but as I sat on the plane, I knew that something irrevocable had changed between us. Fewer tears had been shed because the intensity of the feeling between us had waned.

It was a painful realization, and on the night of the next full moon, I found myself wandering out onto the deserted soccer field. And just as I'd promised, I remembered my time with Savannah on my first leave. I thought of my second leave as well, but strangely, I didn't want to think about the third leave, for even then I think I knew what it portended.

As the summer wore on, my dad continued to improve, albeit slowly. In his letters, he wrote that he'd taken to walking around the block three times a day, every day, each journey lasting exactly twenty minutes, but even that was hard on him. If there was a positive side to all this, it was that it gave him something to build his days around now that he was retired—something aside from coins, that is. In addition to sending letters even more frequently, I began to phone him on Tuesdays and Fridays at exactly one o'clock his time, just to make sure he was okay. I listened for any signs of fatigue in his voice and reminded him constantly about eating well, sleeping enough, and taking his medication. I always did most of the talking. Dad found phone conversations even more painful than face-to-face communication and always sounded as if he wanted nothing more than to hang up the phone as quickly as he could. In time, I took to teasing him about this, but I was never sure if he knew I was kidding. This amused me, and I sometimes laughed; though he didn't laugh in response, his tone would immediately lighten, if only temporarily, before he lapsed back into silence. That was okay. I knew he looked forward to the calls. He always answered on the first ring, and I had no trouble imagining him staring at the clock and waiting for the call.

August turned to September, then October. Savannah finished her classes at Chapel Hill and moved back home while she began hunting for a job. In the newspapers, I read about the United Nations and how European countries wanted to find a way to keep us from going to war with Iraq. Things were tense in the capitals of our NATO allies; on the news, there were demonstrations from the citizens and forceful proclamations from their leaders that the United States was about to make a terrible mistake. Meanwhile, our leaders tried to change their minds. I and everyone in my squad just kept going about our business, training for the inevitable with grim determination. Then, in November, my squad and I went back to Kosovo *again*. We weren't there long, but it was more than enough. I was tired of the Balkans by then, and I was tired of peacekeeping, too. More important, I and everyone else in the service knew that war in the Middle East was coming, whether Europe wanted it or not.

During that time, the letters from Savannah still came somewhat regularly, as did my phone calls to her. Usually I'd call her before dawn, as I always had—it was around midnight her time—and though I'd always been able to reach her in the past, more than once she wasn't home. Though I tried to convince myself she was out with friends or her parents, it was difficult to keep my thoughts from running wild. After hanging up the phone, I sometimes found myself imagining that she'd met another man she cared about. Sometimes I would call two or three more times in the next hour, growing angrier with every ring that went unanswered.

When she would finally answer, I could have asked her where she'd been, but I never did. Nor did she always volunteer the information. I know I made a mistake in keeping quiet, simply because I found it impossible to banish the question from my mind, even as I tried to focus on the conversation at hand. More often than not, I was tense on the phone, and her responses were tense as well. Too often our conversations were less a joyous exchange of affection than a rudimentary exchange of information. After hanging up, I always hated myself for the jealousy I'd been feeling, and I'd beat myself up for the next couple of days, promising that I wouldn't let it happen again.

Other times, however, Savannah came across as exactly the same person I remembered, and I could tell how much she still cared for me. Throughout it all, I loved her as much as I always had, and I found myself aching for those simpler times in the past. I knew what was happening, of course. As we were drifting apart, I was becoming more desperate to save what we once had shared; like a vicious circle, however, my desperation made us drift apart even further.

We began to have arguments. As with the argument we had in her apartment on my second leave, I had trouble telling her what I was feeling, and no matter what she said, I couldn't escape the thought that I was being baited by her or that she wasn't even attempting to alleviate my concerns. I hated these calls even worse than I hated my jealousy, even though I knew the two were intertwined.

Despite our troubles, I never doubted that we would make it. I wanted a life with Savannah more than I ever wanted anything. In December, I began calling more regularly and did my best to keep my jealousy in check. I forced myself to be upbeat on the phone, in the hope that she would want to hear from me. I thought things were getting better, and on the surface they were, but four days before Christmas, I reminded her that I'd be home in a little less than a year. Instead of the excited response I expected, she grew quiet. All I could hear was the sound of her breathing.

"Did you hear me?" I asked.

"Yeah," she said, her tone soft. "It's just that I've heard that before."

It was the truth, and we both knew it, but I didn't sleep well for nearly a week.

The full moon fell on New Year's Day, and though I went out to stare at it and remembered the week when we fell in love, those images were fuzzy, as if blurred by the overwhelming sadness I felt inside. On the walk back, dozens of men were clustered in circles or leaning against buildings while smoking cigarettes, as though they had no cares at all. I wondered what they thought when they saw me walking by. Did they sense that I was losing all that mattered to me? Or that I wished again that I could change the past?

I don't know, and they didn't ask. The world was changing fast. The orders we'd been waiting for were given the following morning, and a few days later, my squad found itself in Turkey as we began preparing to invade Iraq from the north. We sat in meetings where we learned our assignments, studied the topography, and went over battle plans. There was little free time, but when we did venture outside of camp, it was hard to ignore the hostile glares of the populace. We heard rumors that Turkey was planning to deny access to our troops for use in the invasion and that talks were under way to make sure they wouldn't. We'd long ago learned to listen to rumors with a grain of salt, but this time the rumors were accurate, and my squad and others were sent to Kuwait to start all over.

We landed in midafternoon under a cloudless sky and found ourselves surrounded by sand on every side. Almost immediately we were loaded on a bus, drove for hours, and ended up in what was essentially the largest tent city I'd ever seen. The army did its best to make it comfortable. The food was good and the PX had everything you might need, but it was boring. Mail delivery was poor—I received no letters at all—and the lines for the phone were always a mile long. In between drills, my men and I either sat around trying to guess when the invasion would start or practiced getting into our chemical suits as quickly as we could. The plan was for my squad to augment other units from different divisions on a hard push to Baghdad. By February, after what already felt like a zillion years in the desert, my squad and I were as ready as we'd ever be.

At that point, a lot of soldiers had been in Kuwait since mid-November, and the rumor mill was in full swing. No one knew what was coming. I heard about biological and chemical weapons; I heard that Saddam had learned his lesson in Desert Storm and was retrenching the Republican Guard around Baghdad, in the hope of making a bloody last stand. On March 17, I knew there would be war. On my last night in Kuwait, I wrote letters to those I loved, in case I didn't make it: one to my father and one to Savannah. That evening, I found myself part of a convoy that stretched a hundred miles into Iraq.

Fighting was sporadic, at least initially. Because our air force dominated the skies, we had little to fear overhead as we rolled up mainly deserted highways. The Iraqi army, for the most part, was nowhere to be seen, which only increased the tension I felt as I tried to anticipate what my squad would face later in the campaign. Here and there, we'd get word of enemy mortar fire, and we'd scramble into our suits, only to learn it was a false alarm. Soldiers were tense. I didn't sleep for three days.

Deeper in Iraq, skirmishes began to break out, and it was then I learned the first law associated with Operation Iraqi Freedom: Civilians and enemies often looked exactly alike. Shots would ring out, we'd attack, and there were times we weren't even sure who we were shooting at. As we reached the Sunni Triangle, the war began to intensify. We heard about battles in

Fallujah, Ramadi, and Tikrit, all being fought by other units in other divisions. My squad joined the Eighty-second Airborne in an assault on Samawah, and it was there that my squad and I had our first taste of real combat.

The air force had paved the way. Bombs, missiles, and mortars had been exploding since the day before, and as we crossed the bridge into the city, my first thought was amazement at the stillness. My squad was assigned to an outlying neighborhood, where we were to move from house to house to help clear the area of the enemy. As we moved, images came quickly: the charred remains of a truck, the driver's lifeless body beside it; a partially demolished building; ruins of cars smoking here and there. Sporadic rifle fire kept us on edge. As we patrolled, civilians occasionally rushed out with their arms up, and we tried our best to save the wounded.

By early afternoon, we were getting ready to head back, but we were assaulted by heavy fire coming from a building up the street. Pinned against a wall, we were in a precarious position. Two men covered while I led the rest of my squad through the shooting gallery to a safer spot on the other side of the street; it struck me as almost miraculous that no one was killed. From there, we sank a thousand rounds into the enemy's position, laying absolute waste to it. When I thought it was safe, we began our approach to the building, moving cautiously. I used a grenade to blast open the front door. I led my men to the door and poked my head in. Smoke was heavy, and sulfur hung in the air. The interior was destroyed, but at least one Iraqi soldier had survived, and as soon as we were close, he began shooting from the crawl space beneath the floor. Tony got clipped in the hand, and the rest of us responded with hundreds of rounds. The sound was so loud that I couldn't hear myself screaming, but I kept my finger squeezed, aiming everywhere from the floor to the walls to the ceiling. Chips of plaster and brick and wood were flying as the interior was decimated. When we finally stopped firing, I was sure that no one could have survived, but I threw another grenade into an opening that led to the crawl space just to make sure, and we braced ourselves outside for the explosion.

After twenty minutes of the most intense experience of my life, the street was quiet, except for the ringing in my ears and the sounds of my men as they puked or cussed or rehashed the experience. I wrapped Tony's hand, and when I thought everyone was ready, we began backing out the way we'd come. In time, we made our way to the railroad station, which our troops had secured, and we collapsed. That night, we received our first batch of mail in almost six weeks.

In the mail, there were six letters from my father. But from Savannah there was only one, and in the dim light, I began to read.

*Dear John,*

*I'm writing this letter at the kitchen table, and I'm struggling because I don't know how to say what I'm about to tell you. Part of me wishes that you were here with me so I could do this in person, but we both know that's impossible. So here I am, groping for words with tears on my cheeks and hoping that you'll somehow forgive me for what I'm about to write.*

*I know this is a terrible time for you. I try not to think about the war, but I can't escape the images, and I'm scared all the time. I watch the news and scour newspapers, knowing you're in the midst of all of it, trying to find out where you are and what you're going through. I pray every night that you'll make it home safely, and I always will. You and I shared something wonderful, and I never want you to forget that. Nor do I want you to believe that you didn't mean as much to me as I did to you. You're rare and beautiful, John. I fell in love with you, but more than that, meeting you made me realize what true love really means. For the past two and a half years, I've been staring at every full moon and remembering everything we've been through together. I remember how talking to you that first night felt like coming home, and I remember the night we made love. I'll always be glad that you and I shared ourselves like that. To me, it means that our souls will be linked together forever.*

*There's so much more, too. When I close my eyes, I see your face; when I walk, it's almost as if I can feel your hand in mine. Those things are still real to me, but where they once brought comfort, now they leave me with an ache. I understood your reason for staying in the army, and I respected your decision. I still do, but we both know our relationship changed after that. We changed, and in your heart, I think you realized it, too. Maybe the time apart was too much, maybe it was just our different worlds. I don't know. Every time we fought I hated myself for it. Somehow, even though we still loved each other, we lost that magical bond that kept us together.*

*I know that sounds like an excuse, but please believe me when I say that I didn't mean to fall in love with someone else. If I don't really understand how it happened, how can you? I don't expect you to, but because of all we've been through, I just can't continue lying to you. Lying would diminish everything we've shared, and I don't want to do that, even though I know you will feel betrayed.*

*I'll understand if you never want to talk to me again, just as I'll understand if you tell me that you hate me. Part of me hates me, too. Writing this letter forces me to acknowledge that, and when I look in the mirror, I know I'm looking at someone who isn't sure she deserves to be loved at all. I mean that.*

*Even though you may not want to hear it, I want you to know that you'll always be a part of me. In our time together, you claimed a special place in my heart, one I'll carry with me forever and that no one can ever replace. You're a hero and a gentleman, you're kind and honest, but more than that, you're the first man I ever truly loved. And no matter what the future brings, you always will be, and I know that my life is better for it.*

*I'm so sorry—*
*Savannah*

# Questions and Explanations for Chapters 14 and 15

The ten questions on chapters 14 and 15 focus on grammar and usage, vocabulary, literary terms, comprehension, style, and characterization. Some of the questions combine two or more of these areas, requiring you to synthesize your knowledge, make inferences, and interpret the text. The questions are designed to determine both your current level of understanding of the novel and your ability to answer higher-level questions.

**The following sentence tests correctness and effective expression. Part of the following sentence is underlined; beneath the sentence are four ways of phrasing the underlined material. Select the option that produces the best sentence. If you think the original phrasing produces a better sentence than any of the alternatives, select choice A.**

1. John, along with many of the men in his company, <u>were caught up</u> in the fever of patriotism following September 11, which made reenlisting an easy thing for them to do.

   A. were caught up

   B. who were

   C. were

   D. was caught up

Choice A uses the plural form of the verb, *were*, instead of the singular form, *was*, yet the subject of the sentence, as written, is John. Choice B incorrectly adds the pronoun *who* while maintaining the plural form of the verb. Choice C eliminates the phrase *caught up* in an attempt to tighten the writing, yet still maintains the plural form of the verb. Choice D changes the form of the verb from plural to singular in order to have subject and verb agreement.

**Question 2 tests your vocabulary. Choose the word that, when inserted in the sentence, best fits the meaning of the sentence as a whole.**

2. After John had to spend his leave with his sick father and noticed that fewer tears were shed when he and Savannah said good-bye, he realized that the intensity of feeling between the two of them had _____.

   A. alleviated

   B. forestalled

   C. waned

   D. waxed

This question checks your comprehension as well as your vocabulary. The context clues indicate that the missing word is related to "fewer" tears. *Alleviated*, choice A, means relieved. *Forestalled*, choice B, means prevented by having taken action in advance. *Waned*, choice C, means to have decreased, and *waxed*, choice D, means to have increased.

**Question 3 checks your understanding of literary terms.**

3. John learns that "love and caring weren't always enough" and refers to those elements as "the concrete bricks of our relationship, but unstable without the mortar of time spent together." What is the figure of speech being used to help readers—and himself—understand their relationship?

   A. allusion

   B. hyperbole

   C. metaphor

   D. simile

An *allusion*, choice A, is an indirect reference. Some of the most common types of allusions are historical (when someone meets his Waterloo, it's a reference to Napoleon); biblical (such as John Coffey in *The Green Mile* being a Christ figure); mythological (a reference to a Greek or Roman myth, such as a character being said to have the Midas touch); and literary (a reference to a character in a work of literature, such as a couple being compared to Romeo and Juliet). *Hyperbole*, choice B, is using overexaggeration to make a point. An example would be,

"Everyone who reads this learning guide will know what *hyperbole* is because hyperbole will be explained a bazillion times." A *metaphor*, choice C, is a comparison between two unlike things without using a connective word—for example, "Michael Phelps was a flying fish in the pool." And a *simile*, choice D, is a comparison between two unlike things using a connective word, such as *like*, *as*, or *than*—for example, "She looked as fresh as the morning snow."

**Question 4 asks you to analyze an author's stylistic choices and their impact on the text as a whole.**

4. John compares his relationship to the "spinning movement of a child's top." This simile is effective for all of the following reasons EXCEPT:

   A. He and Savannah had the power to keep it spinning.
   B. Their love was beautiful and magical with a childlike sense of wonder.
   C. Their separation resulted in the slowing down of the spinning.
   D. Their relationship was immature and childish.

Because the question indicates that three of the four choices are reasons why the simile is effective, it might be easier to eliminate choices. If Savannah and John have the ability to keep their relationship moving, eliminate choice A. If John considers the love that exists between Savannah and himself to be something wondrous and magical that is awe-inspiring, eliminate choice B. If being apart hurt their relationship, and thus the top stopped spinning, eliminate choice C. And if the comparison reveals that their summer romance and attempt at a long-distance relationship was juvenile, eliminate choice D.

**Question 5 asks you to analyze an author's stylistic choices and their impact on the text as a whole.**

5. The last sentence of chapter 14, "Then came September 11," achieves each of the following effects EXCEPT:

   A. developing Savannah's character

   B. building suspense

   C. establishing the significance of setting

   D. foreshadowing conflict

A character is developed directly and indirectly through words and actions. Building *suspense* means adding excitement and interest to the narrative, providing the readers with a desire and interest to keep reading to find out what is going to happen. *Setting* refers to time and place. *Foreshadowing* is providing hints or clues to future events. For example, when Benvolio suggests to Romeo that finding a new female beauty may help Romeo get over Rosaline, it foreshadows Romeo's falling in love with Juliet when he sees her later in the play. And *conflict* refers to the problem. Conflict is either internal, external, or a combination of the two.

The final single-sentence paragraph of chapter 14 is creating three of these four choices as effects. You can determine the correct answer by either eliminating the choices you know are accurate descriptions or realizing which one is a false description.

**Question 6 checks your understanding of literary terms.**

6. John states that his relationship to Savannah "was a battery" and "my time overseas was continually draining it." What figure of speech is being used here to describe their relationship?

   A. allusion

   B. hyperbole

   C. metaphor

   D. simile

An *allusion*, choice A, is an indirect reference. Some of the most common types of allusions are historical (when someone meets his Waterloo, it's a reference to Napoleon); biblical (such as John Coffey in *The Green Mile* being a Christ figure); mythological (a reference to a Greek or Roman myth, such as a character being said to have the Midas touch); and literary (a reference to a character in a work of literature, such as a couple being compared to Romeo and Juliet). *Hyperbole*, choice B, is using overexaggeration to make a point. An example would be, "Everyone who reads this learning guide will know what *hyperbole* is because hyperbole will be explained a bazillion times." A *metaphor*, choice C, is a comparison between two unlike things without using a connective word—for example, "Michael Phelps was a flying fish in the pool." And a *simile*, choice D, is a comparison between two unlike things using a connective word, such as *like*, *as*, or *than*—for example, "Without her glasses, she was as blind as a bat."

**Question 7 checks your understanding of literary terms.**

7. When describing his time in Baghdad, John says, "After what already felt like a zillion years in the desert, my squad and I were as ready as we'd ever be." What figure of speech is he using within the simile to intensify his comparison?

    A. foreshadowing

    B. hyperbole

    C. paradox

    D. onomatopoeia

*Foreshadowing*, choice A, is providing hints or clues to future events. For example, when Benvolio suggests to Romeo that finding a new female beauty may help Romeo get over Rosaline, it foreshadows Romeo's falling in love with Juliet when he sees her later in the play.

*Hyperbole*, choice B, is using overexaggeration to illustrate a point. For example, if someone says, "I have a ton of home-work," that does not refer to an accurate weight but rather a large amount.

A *paradox*, choice C, is an apparent contradiction that upon further analysis seemingly makes sense. The famous first line of *A Tale of Two Cities*, "It was the best of times, it was the worst of times," initially doesn't make sense. But when you think about a situation in which both conditions can exist simultaneously, you begin to understand the paradox.

*Onomatopoeia*, choice D, is a word that suggests the very sound it describes, like *buzz*, *sizzle*, and *boom*.

**Question 8 checks your understanding of literary terms.**

8. While in Iraq, John receives a letter from Savannah that begins, "Dear John," in which she breaks up with him. In this context, the phrase "Dear John" is an example of what?

    A. hyperbole

    B. onomatopoeia

    C. personification

    D. pun

Again, knowledge of literary terms is essential to answering this question. *Hyperbole*, choice A, is using overexaggeration to make a point—for example, "Everyone who reads this learning guide will know what *hyperbole* is because hyperbole will be explained a bazillion times."

*Onomatopoeia*, choice B, is a word that suggests the very sound it describes, like *buzz, sizzle,* and *boom.*

*Personification*, choice C, is giving a nonhuman thing a human characteristic, such as in "Opportunity knocked on the door."

A *pun*, choice D, is a play on words that is humorous because a word or phrase has more than one definition—for example, "She got fired from the hot dog stand for putting her hair in a bun."

**Question 9 checks your understanding of literary terms.**

9. The Dear John letter in chapter 14 serves as what part of the plot?

A. exposition

B. inciting incident

C. climax

D. denouement

The *exposition*, choice A, is the background information, which answers all the questions that a reporter asks—*who, what, where, when, why*, and *how?* The *inciting incident*, choice B, introduces the central conflict, or problem. The *climax*, choice C, refers to when the conflict reaches a high point of suspense or interest. The *denouement*, choice D, ties up the loose ends after the resolution of the conflict.

**Question 10 asks you to analyze how the author's choices contribute to the novel's overall structure and meaning.**

10. Stylistically, concluding part 2 with a Dear John letter achieves each of the following effects EXCEPT:

    A. having a chapter and larger section of the novel end as the love relationship ends

    B. providing symmetry with the end of part 1, which also ended with a letter to John from Savannah

    C. building suspense, for John already told the reader in the prologue that he ended their relationship

    D. revealing John to be an unreliable narrator

Three out of the four choices can be eliminated. If the chapter and part 2 both are ended just as the relationship has ended, eliminate choice A. If part 1 also ended with a letter, eliminate choice B. If John did indeed tell the reader in the prologue that he ended their relationship, eliminate choice C. An *unreliable* narrator is one of two things: someone who cannot or does not fully understand the world around him or her, which means his or her judgments cannot be trusted by the reader, *or* someone who may have a reason to be purposely misleading the reader. For example, Huckleberry Finn is too young to fully understand the significance of events that he is narrating in *The Adventures of Huckleberry Finn*. The term *unreliable narrator* does not mean that the character is immoral or a liar; rather, he or she may just be naive. And if the letter demonstrates that John has not been a trustworthy narrator, eliminate choice D.

# *Part III*

# Chapter 16

*S*he *was in love with someone else.*

I knew that even before I finished reading the letter, and all at once the world seemed to slow down. My first instinct was to ram my fist into a wall, but instead I crumpled up the letter and threw it aside. I was incredibly angry then; more than feeling betrayed, I felt as if she'd crushed everything that had any meaning in the world. I hated her, and I hated the nameless, faceless man who'd stolen her from me. I fantasized what I would do to him if he ever crossed my path, and the picture wasn't pretty.

At the same time, I longed to talk to her. I wanted to fly home immediately, or at least call her. Part of me didn't want to believe it, couldn't believe it. Not now, not after everything we'd been through. We had only nine more months left—after almost three years, was that so impossible?

But I didn't go home, and I didn't call. I didn't write her back, nor did I hear from her again. My only action was to retrieve the letter I'd crumpled. I straightened it as best I could, stuffed it back in the envelope, and decided to carry it with me like a wound I'd received in battle. Over the next few weeks, I became the consummate soldier, escaping into the only world that still seemed real to me. I volunteered for any mission regarded as dangerous, I barely spoke to anyone in my unit, and for a while it took everything I had not to be too quick with the trigger while out on patrol. I trusted no one in the cities, and although there were no unfortunate "incidents"—as the army likes to call civilian deaths—I'd be lying if I claimed to have been patient and understanding while dealing with Iraqis of any kind. Though I barely slept, my senses were heightened as we continued our spearhead to Baghdad. Ironically, only while risking my life did I find relief from Savannah's image and the reality that our relationship had ended.

My life followed the shifting fortunes of the war. Less than a month after I received the letter, Baghdad fell, and despite a brief period of initial promise, things got worse and more complicated as the weeks and months wore on. In the end, I figured, this war was no different from any other. Wars always come back to the quest for power among the competing interests, but this understanding didn't make life on the ground any easier. In the aftermath of Baghdad's fall, every soldier in my squad was thrust into the roles of policeman and judge. As soldiers, we weren't trained for that.

From the outside and with hindsight, it was easy to second-guess our activities, but in the real world, in real time, decisions weren't always easy. More than once, I was approached by Iraqi civilians and told that a certain individual had stolen this or that item, or committed this or that crime, and was asked to do something about it. That wasn't our job. We were there to keep some semblance of order—which basically meant killing insurgents who were trying to kill us or other civilians—until the locals could take over and handle it themselves. That particular process was neither quick nor easy, even in places where calm was more frequent than chaos. In the meantime, other cities were disintegrating into chaos, and we were sent in to restore order. We'd clear a city of insurgents, but because there weren't enough troops to hold the city and keep it safe, the insurgents would occupy it again soon after we cleared out. There were days when all of my men wondered at the futility of that particular exercise, even if they didn't question it openly.

My point is, I don't know how to describe the stress and boredom and confusion of those next nine months, except to say that there was a lot of sand. Yeah, I know it's a desert, and yeah, I spent a lot of time at the beach so I should have been used to it, but the sand was different over there. It got in your clothes, in your gun, in locked boxes, in your food, in your ears and up your nose and between your teeth, and when I spat, I always felt the grit in my mouth. People can at least relate to that, and I've learned that they don't want to hear the real truth, which is that most of the time Iraq wasn't so bad but sometimes it was worse than hell. Did people really want to hear that I watched a guy in my unit accidentally shoot a little kid who just happened to be in the wrong place at the wrong time? Or that I'd seen soldiers get torn into pieces when they hit an IED—improvised explosive device—on the roads near Baghdad? Or that I'd seen blood pooling in the streets like rain, flowing past body parts? No, people would rather hear about sand, because it kept the war at a safe distance.

I did my duty as best I knew how, reupped again, and stayed

in Iraq until February 2004, when I was finally sent back to Germany. As soon as I got back, I bought a Harley and tried to pretend that I'd left the war unscarred; but the nightmares were endless, and I woke most mornings drenched in sweat. During the day I was often on edge, and I got angry at the slightest things. When I walked the streets in Germany, I found it impossible not to carefully survey groups of people loitering near buildings, and I found myself scanning windows in the business district, watching for snipers. The psychologist—everyone had to see one—told me that what I was going through was normal and that in time these things would pass, but I sometimes wondered whether they ever would.

After I left Iraq, my time in Germany felt almost meaningless. Sure, I worked out in the morning and I took classes on weapons and navigation, but things had changed. Because of the hand wound, Tony was given a discharge along with his Purple Heart, and he was sent back to Brooklyn right after Baghdad fell. Four more of my guys were honorably discharged in late 2003 when their time was up; in their minds—and mine—they'd done their duty, and it was time for them to get on with the rest of their lives. I, on the other hand, had reupped again. I wasn't sure it was the right decision, but I didn't know what else to do.

But now, looking at my squad, I realized that I suddenly felt out of place. My squad was full of newbies, and though they were great kids, it wasn't the same. They weren't the friends I'd lived with through boot camp and the Balkans, I hadn't gone to war with them, and deep down, I knew I'd never be as close to them as I'd been to my former squad. For the most part, I was a stranger, and I kept it that way. I worked out alone and avoided personal contact as much as possible, and I knew what my squad thought of me when I walked past them: I was the crusty old sergeant, the one who claimed to want nothing more than to ensure that they got back to their moms in one piece. I told my squad that all the time while we drilled, and I meant it. I would do what it took to keep them safe. But like I said, it wasn't the same.

With my friends gone, I devoted myself to my dad as best I could. After my tour of combat, I spent an extended leave with him in spring 2004, then another leave with him later that summer. We spent more time together in those four weeks than we had in the previous ten years. Because he was retired, we were free to spend the day however we wished. I fell easily into his routines. We had breakfast, went for our three walks, and had dinner together. In between, we talked about coins and even bought a couple while I was in town. The Internet made that far easier than it had once been, and though the search wasn't quite as exciting, I don't know that it made any difference to my dad. I found myself talking to dealers I hadn't spoken with in over fifteen years, but they were as friendly and informative as they'd ever been and remembered me with pleasure. The coin world, I realized, was a small one, and when our order arrived— they were always shipped via overnight delivery—my dad and I would take turns examining the coins, pointing out any existing flaws, and usually agreeing with the grade that they had been assigned by the Professional Coin Grading Service, a company that evaluates the quality of any coin submitted. Though my mind would eventually wander to other things, my dad could stare at a single coin for hours, as if it held the secret of life.

We didn't talk about much else, but then, we didn't really need to. He had no desire to talk about Iraq, and I had no desire to talk about it, either. Neither of us had a social life to speak of—Iraq hadn't been conducive to that—and my dad...well, he was my dad, and I didn't even bother asking.

Nonetheless, I was worried about him. On his walks, his breathing was labored. When I suggested that twenty minutes was perhaps too long, even at his slow pace, he said that the doctor had told him that twenty minutes was just what he needed, and I knew there was nothing I could do to convince him otherwise. Afterward, he was far more tired than he should have been, and it usually took an hour for the deep color in his cheeks to fade. I spoke to the doctor, and the news wasn't what I had hoped. My dad's heart, I was told, had sustained major damage, and—in the doctor's opinion—it was pretty much a miracle that he was moving as well as he was. Lack of exercise would be even worse for him.

It might have been that conversation with the doctor, or maybe it was just that I wanted an improved relationship with my dad, but we got along better on those two visits than we ever had. Instead of pressing him for constant conversation, I'd simply sit with him in his den, reading a book or doing crossword puzzles while he looked at coins. There was something peaceful and honest about my lack of expectation, and I think my dad was slowly coming to grips with the newfound change between us. Occasionally, I caught him peeking at me in a way that seemed almost foreign. We would spend hours together, most of the time saying nothing at all, and it was in this quiet, unassuming way that we finally became friends. I often found myself wishing that my dad hadn't thrown away the photograph of us, and when it was time for me to return to Germany, I knew that I would miss him in a way I never had before.

Autumn of 2004 passed slowly, as did the winter and spring of 2005. Life dragged on uneventfully. Occasionally, rumors of my eventual return to Iraq would interrupt the monotony of my days, but since I'd been there before, the thought of my return affected me little. If I stayed in Germany, that was fine. If I went back to Iraq, that was fine as well. I kept up with what was going on in the Middle East like everyone else, but as soon as I put down the newspaper or turned off the television, my mind wandered to other things.

I was twenty-eight by then, and I couldn't escape the feeling that even though I'd experienced more than most people my age, my life was still on hold. I'd joined the army to grow up, and although a case could be made that I had, I sometimes wondered whether it was true. I owned neither a house nor a car, and aside from my dad, I was completely alone in the world. While my peers stuffed their wallets with photographs of their children and their wives, my wallet held a single fading snapshot of a woman I'd loved and lost. I heard soldiers talking of their hopes for the future, while I was making no plans at all. Sometimes I wondered what my men thought of my life, for there were times I caught them staring at me curiously. I never told them about my past or shared personal information. They knew nothing of Savannah or my dad or my friendship with Tony. Those memories were mine and mine alone, for I'd learned that some things are best kept secret.

In March 2005, my dad had a second heart attack, which led to pneumonia and another stint in the ICU. Once he was released, the medication he was on prohibited driving, but the hospital social worker helped me find someone to pick up the groceries he needed. In April, he went back to the hospital, where he learned he'd have to give up his daily walks as well. By May, he was taking a dozen different pills a day, and I knew he was spending most of his time in bed. The letters he wrote became almost illegible, not only because he was weak, but because his hands had begun to tremble. After a bit of prodding and begging on the phone, I persuaded a neighbor of my dad's—a nurse who worked at the local hospital—to look in on him regularly, and I breathed a sigh of relief while counting down the days until my leave in June.

But my dad's condition continued to worsen over the next few weeks, and on the phone I could hear a weariness that seemed to deepen every time I spoke with him. For the second time in my life, I asked for a transfer back home. My commanding officer was more sympathetic than he had been before. We researched it—even got as far as filing the papers to get me posted at Fort Bragg for airborne training—but when I spoke to the doctor again, I was told that my proximity wouldn't do much to help my dad and that I should consider placing him in an extended care facility. My dad needed more care than could be provided at home, he assured me. He'd been trying to convince my father of that for some time—he was eating only soup by then—but my father refused to consider it until I returned for my leave. For whatever reason, the doctor explained, my dad was determined to have me visit him at home one last time.

The realization was crushing, and in the cab from the airport, I tried to convince myself that the doctor was exaggerating. But he wasn't. My father was unable to rise from the couch when I pushed open the door, and I was struck by the thought that in the single year since I'd seen him last, he seemed to have aged thirty years. His skin was almost gray, and I was shocked by how much weight he'd lost. With a hard knot in my throat, I put down my bag just inside the door.

"Hey, Dad," I said.

At first, I wondered whether he even recognized me, but eventually I heard a ragged whisper. "Hey, John."

I went to the couch and sat beside him. "You okay?"

"Okay," was all he said, and for a long time we sat together without saying anything.

Eventually I rose to inspect the kitchen but found myself blinking when I got there. Empty soup cans were stacked everywhere. There were stains on the stove, the garbage was overflowing, and moldy dishes were piled in the sink. Stacks of unopened mail flooded the small kitchen table. It was obvious that the house hadn't been cleaned in days. My first impulse was to storm over to confront the neighbor who'd agreed to look in on him. But that would have to wait.

Instead, I located a can of chicken noodle soup and heated it up on the filthy stove. After filling a bowl, I brought it to my father on a tray. He smiled weakly, and I could see his gratitude. He finished the bowl, scraped at the sides for every morsel, and I filled another bowl, growing even angrier and wondering how long it had been since he'd eaten. When he polished off that bowl, I helped him lie back on the couch, where he fell asleep within minutes.

The neighbor wasn't home, so I spent most of the afternoon and evening cleaning the house, starting with the kitchen and the bathroom. When I went to change the sheets on his bed and found them soiled, I closed my eyes and stifled the urge to wring the neighbor's neck.

After the house was reasonably clean, I sat in the living room, watching my dad sleep. He looked so small beneath the blanket, and when I reached out to stroke his hair, a few strands came out. I began to cry then, knowing with certainty that my dad was dying. It was the first time I'd cried in years, and the only time in my life I'd ever cried for my dad, but for a long time the tears wouldn't stop.

I knew that my dad was a good man, a kind man, and though he'd led a wounded life, he'd done the best he could in raising me. Never once had he raised his hand in anger, and I began to torment myself with the memories of all those years I'd wasted blaming him. I remembered my last two visits home, and I ached at the thought that we would never share those simple times again.

Later, I carried my dad to bed. He was light in my arms, too light. I pulled the covers up around him and made my bed on the floor beside him, listening to him wheeze and rasp. He woke up coughing in the middle of the night and seemed unable to stop; I was getting ready to bring him to the hospital when the coughing finally subsided.

He was terrified when he realized where I wanted to take him. "Stay ... here," he pleaded, his voice weak. "Don't want to go."

I was torn, but in the end I didn't bring him. To a man of routine, I realized, the hospital was not only foreign, but a dangerous place, one that took more energy to adjust to than he knew he could summon. It was then that I realized he'd soiled himself and the sheets again.

When the neighbor came by the following day, the first words out of her mouth were an apology. She explained that she hadn't cleaned the kitchen for several days because one of her daughters had been taken ill, but she'd been changing the sheets daily and making sure he had plenty of canned food. As she stood before me on the porch, I could see the exhaustion in her face, and all the words of reproach I'd been rehearsing drained away. I told her that I appreciated what she'd already done more than she would ever know.

"I was glad to help," she said. "He's been so nice over the years. He never complained about the noise my kids made when they were teenagers, and he always bought whatever they were selling when they needed to raise money for school trips or things like that. He keeps the yard just right, and whenever I asked him to watch my house, he was always there for me. He's been the perfect neighbor."

I smiled. Encouraged, she went on.

"But you should know that he doesn't always let me inside anymore. He told me that he didn't like where I put things. Or how I clean. Or the way I moved a stack of papers on his desk. Usually I ignore it, but sometimes, when he's feeling okay, he's quite adamant about keeping me out and he threatened to call the police when I tried to get past him. I just don't . . ."

She trailed off, and I finished for her.

"You just don't know what to do."

Guilt was written plainly on her face.

"It's okay," I said. "Without you, I don't know what he would have done."

She nodded with relief before glancing away. "I'm glad you're home," she began hesitantly, "because I wanted to talk to you about his situation." She brushed at invisible lint on her clothing. "I know this great place that he could go where he could be taken care of. The staff is excellent. It's almost always at capacity, but I know the director, and he knows your dad's doctor. I know how hard this is to hear, but I think it's what's best for him, and I wish . . ."

When she stopped, letting the rest of her statement hang, I felt her genuine concern for my dad, and I opened my mouth to respond. But I said nothing. This wasn't as easy a decision as it sounded. His home was the only place my father knew, the only place he felt comfortable. It was the only place his routines made sense. If staying in the hospital terrified him, being forced to live someplace new would likely kill him. The question came down to not only where he should die, but how he should die. Alone at home, where he slept in soiled sheets and possibly starved to death? Or with people who would feed and clean him, in a place that terrified him?

With a quiver in my voice I couldn't quite control, I asked, "Where is it?"

I spent the next two weeks taking care of my dad. I fed him the best I could, read him the *Greysheet* when he was awake, and slept on the floor beside his bed. He soiled himself every evening, forcing me to purchase adult diapers for him, much to his embarrassment. He slept most of the afternoon.

While he rested on the couch, I visited a number of extended care facilities: not just the one that the neighbor had recommended, but those within a two-hour radius. In the end, the neighbor was right. The place she mentioned was clean, and the staff came across as professional, but most important, the director seemed to have taken a personal interest in my dad's care. Whether that was because of the neighbor or my dad's doctor, I never found out.

Price wasn't an issue. The facility was notoriously expensive, but because my dad had a government pension, Social Security, Medicare, and private insurance to boot (I could imagine him signing on the insurance salesman's dotted line years before without really understanding what he was paying for), I was assured that the only cost would be emotional. The director—fortyish and brown haired, whose kindly manner somehow reminded me of Tim—understood and didn't press for an immediate decision. Instead, he handed me a stack of information and assorted forms and wished my dad the best.

That evening, I raised the subject of moving to my dad. I was leaving in a few days and didn't have a choice, no matter how much I wanted to avoid it.

He said nothing while I spoke. I explained my reasons, my worries, my hope that he would understand. He asked no questions, but his eyes remained wide with shock, as if he'd just heard his own death sentence.

When I finished, I desperately needed a moment alone. I patted him on the leg and went to the kitchen to get a glass of water. When I returned to the living room, my dad was hunched over on the couch, downcast and trembling. It was the first time I ever saw him cry.

In the morning, I began to pack my dad's things. I went through his drawers and his files, the cupboards and closets. In his sock drawer, I found socks; in his shirt drawer, only shirts. In his file cabinet, everything was tabbed and ordered. It shouldn't have been surprising, but in its own way it was. My dad, unlike most of humanity, had no secrets at all. He had no hidden vices, no diaries, no embarrassing interests, no box of private things he kept all to himself. I found nothing that further enlightened me about his inner life, nothing that might help me understand him after he was gone. My dad, I knew then, was just as he'd always seemed to be, and I suddenly realized how much I admired him for that.

When I finished gathering his things, my dad lay awake on the couch. After a few days of eating regularly, he'd regained a bit of strength. There was the faintest gleam in his eyes, and I noticed a shovel leaning against the end table. He held out a scrap of paper. On it was what appeared to be a hastily scrawled map, labeled "BACKYARD" in a shaky hand.

"What's this for?"

"It's yours," he said. He pointed to the shovel.

I picked up the shovel, followed the directions on the map to the oak tree in the backyard, marched off paces, and began to dig. Within minutes the shovel sounded on metal, and I retrieved a box. And another one, beneath it. And another to the side. Sixteen heavy boxes in all. I sat on the porch and wiped the sweat from my face before opening the first.

I already knew what I'd find, and I squinted at the reflection of gold coins shimmering in the harsh sunlight of a southern summer. At the bottom of that box, I found the 1926-D buffalo nickel, the one we'd searched for and found together, knowing it was the only coin that really meant anything to me.

The next day, my last day on leave, I made arrangements for the house: turning off the utilities, forwarding the mail, finding someone to keep the lawn mowed. I stored the unearthed coins in a safe-deposit box at the bank. Handling those details took most of the day. Later, we shared a final bowl of chicken noodle soup and soft-cooked vegetables for dinner before I brought him to the extended care facility. I unpacked his things, decorated the room with items I thought he'd want, and placed a dozen years' worth of the *Greysheet* on the floor beneath his desk. But it wasn't enough, and after explaining the situation to the director, I went back to the house again to collect even more knickknacks, all the while wishing I knew my dad well enough to tell what really mattered to him.

No matter how much I reassured him, he remained paralyzed with fear, his eyes tearing me apart. More than once, I was stricken with the notion that I was killing him. I sat beside him on his bed, conscious of the few hours remaining before I had to leave for the airport.

"It's going to be okay," I said. "They're going to take care of you."

His hands continued to tremble. "Okay," he said in a barely audible voice.

I felt the tears beginning to form. "I want to say something to you, okay?" I drew breath, focusing my thoughts. "I just want you to know that I think you're the greatest dad ever. You had to be great to put up with someone like me."

My dad didn't respond. In the silence, I felt all those things I'd ever wanted to say to him forcing their way to the surface, words that had been a lifetime in the making.

"I mean it, Dad. I'm sorry about all the crappy things I put you through, and I'm sorry that I was never here for you enough. You're the best person I've ever known. You're the only one who never got angry with me, you never judged me, and somehow you taught me more about life than any son could possibly ask. I'm sorry that I can't be here for you now, and I hate myself for doing this to you. But I'm scared, Dad. I don't know what else to do."

My voice sounded hoarse and uneven to my own ears, and I wanted nothing more than for him to put his arm around me.

"Okay," he finally said.

I smiled at his response. I couldn't help it.

"I love you, Dad."

To this he knew exactly what to say, for it had always been part of his routine.

"I love you, too, John."

I hugged him, then rose and brought him the latest issue of the *Greysheet*. When I reached the door, I stopped once more and faced him.

For the first time since he'd been there, the fear was almost gone. He held the paper close to his face, and I could see the page shaking slightly. His lips were moving as he concentrated on the words, and I forced myself to study him, hoping to memorize his face forever.

It was the last time I ever saw him alive.

# Chapter 17

My dad died seven weeks later, and I was granted an emergency leave to attend the funeral.

The flight back to the States was a blur. All I could do was stare out the window at the formless gray of the ocean thousands of feet below me, wishing I could have been with him in his final moments. I hadn't shaved or showered or even changed my clothes since I'd heard the news, as if going about my daily life meant that I fully accepted the idea that he was gone.

In the terminal and on the ride back to my house, I found myself growing angry at the everyday scenes of life around me. I saw people driving or walking or heading in and out of stores, acting normal, but for me nothing seemed normal at all.

It was only when I got back to the house that I remembered I'd turned off the utilities almost two months earlier. Without lights, the house seemed strangely isolated on the street, as if it didn't quite belong. Like my dad, I thought. Or me, I realized. Somehow that thought made it possible to approach the door.

Wedged in the door frame of our house, I found the business card of a lawyer named William Benjamin; on the back, he claimed to represent my dad. With phone service disconnected, I called from the neighbor's house and was surprised when he showed up at the house early the following morning, briefcase in hand.

I led him inside the dim house, and he took a seat on the couch. His suit must have cost more than I earned in two months. After introducing himself and apologizing for my loss, he leaned forward.

"I'm here because I liked your dad," he said. "He was one of my first clients, so there's no charge for this, by the way. He came to me right after you were born to make up a will, and every year, on the same day, I'd get a certified letter in the mail from him that listed all the coins he'd purchased. I explained to him about estate taxes, so he's been gifting them to you ever since you were a kid."

I was too shocked to speak.

"Anyway, six weeks ago he wrote me a letter informing me that you finally had the coins in your possession, and he wanted to make sure everything else was in order, so I updated his will one last time. When he told me where he was living, I figured he wasn't doing well, so I called him. He didn't say much, but he did give me permission to talk to the director. The director promised that he'd let me know when or if your dad passed away so I could meet you. So here I am."

He started rifling through his briefcase. "I know you're dealing with the funeral arrangements, and it's a bad time. But your dad told me you might not be here for very long and that I should handle his affairs. Those were his words, by the way, not mine. Okay, here it is." He handed over an envelope, heavy with papers. "His will, a list of every coin in the collection, including quality and the date of purchase, and all the arrangements for the funeral—which is prepaid, by the way. I promised him that I'd see the estate all the way through probate, too, but that won't be a problem, since the estate is small and you're his only child. And if you want, I can find someone to haul away anything you don't want to keep and make arrangements to sell the house, too. Your dad said you might not have time for that, either." He closed his briefcase. "As I said, I liked your dad. Usually you have to convince people of the importance of this stuff, but not your dad. He was one methodical man."

"Yeah." I nodded. "He was."

As the lawyer said, everything had been taken care of. My dad had chosen the type of graveside service he wanted, he'd had his clothing dropped off, and he'd even picked his own coffin. Knowing him, I guess I should have expected it, but it only reinforced my belief that I never really understood him.

His funeral, on a warm, rainy August day, was only sparsely attended. Two former co-workers, the director of the extended care facility, the lawyer, and the neighbor who'd helped take care of him were the only ones beside me at the graveside service. It broke my heart—absolutely broke it into a million pieces—that in all the world, only these people had seen the worthiness of my dad. After the pastor finished the prayers, he whispered to me to see if I wanted to add anything. By then my throat was tight as a drum, and it took everything I had to simply shake my head and decline.

*  *  *

Back at home, I sat tentatively on the edge of my dad's bed. By then the rain had stopped, and gray sunlight slanted through the window. The house had a musty, almost moldy odor, but I could still smell the scent of my dad on his pillow. Beside me was the envelope the lawyer had brought me. I poured out the contents. The will was on top, as were some other documents. Beneath it, however, was the framed photograph that my dad had removed from his desk so long ago, the only existing photograph of the two of us.

I brought it to my face and stared at it until tears filled my eyes.

Later that afternoon, Lucy, my long-ago ex, arrived. When she first stood at my doorstep, I didn't know what to say. Gone was the suntanned girl from my wild years; in her place was a woman dressed in a dark, expensive pantsuit and a silk blouse.

"I'm sorry, John," she whispered, coming toward me. We hugged, holding each other close, and the sensation of her body against mine was like a glass of cool water on a hot summer day. She wore the lightest trace of perfume, one I couldn't place, but it made me think of Paris, even though I'd never been there.

"I just read the obituary," she said after pulling back. "I'm sorry I couldn't make it to the funeral."

"It's okay," I said. I motioned to the couch. "You want to come in?"

She sat beside me, and when I noticed she wasn't wearing her wedding ring, she subconsciously moved her hand.

"It didn't work out," she said. "I got divorced last year."

"I'm sorry."

300

"I am, too," she said, reaching for my hand. "You doing okay?"

"Yeah," I lied. "I'm okay."

We talked for a while about old times; she was skeptical of my claim that her final phone call had led me to join the army. I told her that it was exactly what I needed at the time. She spoke about her career—she helped design and set up retail spaces in department stores—and asked what Iraq was like. I told her about the sand. She laughed and then asked no more about it. In time, our conversation slowed to a trickle as we realized how much we both had changed. Maybe it was because we'd been close once, or maybe it was because she was a woman, but I could feel her scrutinizing me and already knew what she would ask next.

"You're in love, aren't you," she whispered.

I folded my hands in my lap and faced the window. Outside, the sky was again dark and cloudy, portending even more rain. "Yes," I admitted.

"What's her name?"

"Savannah," I said.

"Is she here?"

I hesitated. "No."

"Do you want to talk about it?"

No, I wanted to say. I don't want to talk about it. I'd learned in the army that stories like ours were both boring and predictable, and though everyone asked, no one really wanted to hear them.

But I told her the story from beginning to end, in more detail than I should have, and more than once, she reached for my hand. I hadn't realized how hard it had been to keep it inside, and by the time I trailed off, I think she knew I needed to be alone. She kissed me on the cheek as she left, and when she was gone, I paced the house for hours. I drifted from room to room, thinking of my dad and thinking of Savannah, feeling like a foreigner, and gradually coming to the realization that there was somewhere else I had to go.

# Chapter 18

That night, I slept in my dad's bed, the only time I'd done that in my life. The storm had passed, and the temperature had risen to miserable levels. Even opening the windows wasn't enough to keep me cool, and I tossed and turned for hours. When I crawled out of bed the next morning, I found my dad's car keys on the peg-board in the kitchen. I threw my gear into the back of his car and picked out a few things from the house that I wanted to keep. Aside from the photograph, there wasn't much. After that, I called the lawyer and took him up on his offer to find someone to haul away the rest and sell the house. I dropped the house key in the mail.

In the garage, it took a few seconds for the engine to catch. I backed the car out of the drive, closed the garage door, and locked up. From the yard, I stared at the house, thinking of my father and knowing that I'd never see this place again.

※　　※　　※

I drove to the extended care facility, picked up my dad's things, then left Wilmington, heading west along the interstate, moving on autopilot. It had been years since I'd seen this stretch of road, and I was only dimly aware of the traffic, but the sense of familiarity came back in waves. I passed the towns of my youth and headed through Raleigh toward Chapel Hill, where memories flashed with painful intensity, and I found myself pushing the accelerator, trying to leave them behind.

I drove on through Burlington, Greensboro, and Winston-Salem. Aside from a single gas stop earlier in the day where I'd also picked up a bottle of water, I pressed forward, sipping water but unable to stomach the thought of eating. The photograph of my father and me lay on the seat beside me, and every now and then I would try to recall the boy in the picture. Eventually I turned north, following a small highway that wound its way through blue-tipped mountains spreading north and south, a gentle swell in the crust of the earth.

It was late afternoon by the time I pulled the car to a stop and checked into a shabby motel just off the highway. My body was stiff, and after taking a few minutes to stretch, I showered and shaved. I put on a clean pair of jeans and a T-shirt and debated whether or not to get something to eat, but I still wasn't hungry. With the sun hanging low, the air had none of the sultry humid heat of the coast, and I caught the scent of conifers drifting down from the mountains. This was the place of Savannah's birth, and somehow I knew she was still here.

Though I could have gone to her parents' house and asked, I discarded the idea, uncertain how they'd react to my presence. Instead I drove the streets of Lenoir, passing through the retail district, complete with the assorted collection of fast-food restaurants, and began to slow the car only when I reached the less generic part of town. Here was the part of Lenoir that hadn't changed, where newcomers and tourists were welcome to visit but would never be considered locals. I pulled into a run-down pool hall, a place that reminded me of some of my own youthful haunts. Neon signs advertising beer hung in the windows, and the parking lot was full out front. It was in a place like this that I would find the answer I needed.

I went inside. Hank Williams blared from the jukebox, and ribbons of cigarette smoke drifted in the air. Four pool tables were clustered together; every player was wearing a baseball hat, and two had obvious wads of chewing tobacco parked in their cheeks. Trophy bass had been mounted on the walls, surrounded by NASCAR memorabilia. There were photos taken at Talladega and Martinsville, North Wilkesboro and Rockingham, and though my opinion of the sport hadn't changed, the sight put me strangely at ease. At the corner of the bar, below the smiling face of the late Dale Earnhardt, was a jar filled with cash, asking for donations to help a local victim of cancer. Feeling an unexpected pull of sympathy, I threw in a couple of dollars.

I took a seat at the bar and struck up a conversation with the bartender. He was about my age, and his mountain accent reminded me of Savannah's. After twenty minutes of easy conversation, I took Savannah's picture from my wallet and explained that I was a friend of the family. I used her parents' names and asked questions that implied I'd been there before.

He was wary, and rightfully so. Small towns protect their own, but it turned out that he'd spent a couple of years in the Marine Corps, which helped. In time, he nodded.

"Yeah, I know her," he said. "She lives out on Old Mill Road, next to her parents' place."

It was just after eight in the evening, and the sky was graying as dusk began to settle in. Ten minutes later, I left a big tip on the bar and made my way out the door.

My mind was curiously blank as I headed into horse country. At least, that's how I remembered thinking of it the last time I was here. The road I drove slanted ever upward, and I began to recognize the landmarks of the area; I knew that in a few minutes I'd pass Savannah's parents' house. When I did, I leaned over the steering wheel, watching for the next break in the fence before turning onto a long gravel road. As I made the turn, I saw a hand-painted sign for something called "Hope and Horses."

The crackle of my tires as they rolled over gravel was oddly comforting, and I pulled to a stop beneath a willow tree, next to a small battered pickup truck. I looked toward the house. Steep roofed and square, with flaking white paint and a chimney pointing toward the sky, it seemed to rise from the earth like a ghostly image a hundred years in the making. A single bulb glowed above the battered front door, and a small potted plant hung near an American flag, both moving gently in the breeze. Off to the side of the house was a weathered barn and a small corral; beyond that, an emerald-covered pasture enclosed by a tidy white fence stretched toward a line of massive oak trees. Another shedlike structure stood near the barn, and in the shadows I could see the outlines of aging field equipment. I found myself wondering again what I was doing here.

It wasn't too late to leave, but I couldn't force myself to turn the car around. The sky flared red and yellow before the sun dipped below the horizon, casting the mountains in moody darkness. I emerged from the car and began to approach the house. The dew on the grass moistened the tips of my shoes, and I caught the scent of conifers once more. I could hear the sounds of crickets chirping and the steady call of a nightingale. The sounds seemed to give me strength as I stepped onto the porch. I tried to figure out what I would say to her if she answered the door. Or what I would say to him. While I was trying to decide what to do, a tail-wagging retriever approached me.

I held out my hand, and his friendly tongue lapped against it before he turned and trotted down the steps again. His tail continued to swish back and forth as he headed around the house, and hearing the same call that had brought me to Lenoir, I left the porch and followed him. He dipped low, skimming his belly as he crawled beneath the lowest rung of the fence, and trotted into the barn.

As soon as the dog had disappeared, I saw Savannah emerge from the barn with rectangles of hay clamped beneath her arms. Horses from the pasture began to canter toward her as she tossed the hay into various troughs. I continued moving forward. She was brushing herself off and getting ready to head back into the barn when she inadvertently glanced my way. She took a step, looked again, and then froze in place.

For a long moment, neither of us moved. With her gaze locked on mine, I realized that it was wrong to have come, to have shown up without warning like this. I knew I should say something, anything, but nothing came to mind. All I could do was stare at her.

The memories came rushing back then, all of them, and I noticed how little she'd changed since I'd last seen her. Like me, she was wearing jeans and a T-shirt, smudged with dirt, and her cowboy boots were scuffed and worn. Somehow the hardscrabble look gave her an earthy appeal. Her hair was longer than I remembered, but she still had the slight gap between her front teeth that I had always loved.

"Savannah," I finally said.

It wasn't until I spoke that I realized she'd been as spellbound as I. All at once, she broke into a wide smile of innocent pleasure.

"John?" she cried.

"It's good to see you again."

She shook her head, as if trying to clear her mind, then squinted at me again. When at last she was convinced I wasn't a mirage, she jogged to the gate and bounded through it. A moment later I could feel her arms around me, her body warm and welcoming. For a second it was as if nothing between us had changed at all. I wanted to hold her forever, but when she pulled back, the illusion was shattered, and we were strangers once more. Her expression held the question I'd been unable to answer on the long trip here.

"What are you doing here?"

I looked away. "I don't know," I said. "I just needed to come."

Though she asked nothing, there was a mixture of curiosity and hesitation in her expression, as if she weren't sure she wanted a further explanation. I took a small step backward, giving her space. I could see the shadowy outlines of the horses in the darkness and felt the events of the last few days coming back to me.

"My dad died," I whispered, the words seeming to come from nowhere. "I just came from his funeral."

She was quiet, her expression softening into the spontaneous compassion I'd once been so drawn to.

"Oh, John . . . I'm so sorry," she murmured.

She drew near again, and there was an urgency to her embrace this time. When she pulled back, her face was half in shadow.

"How did it happen?" she asked, her hand lingering on mine.

I could hear the authentic sorrow in her voice, and I paused, unable to sum up the last couple of years into a single statement. "It's a long story," I said. In the glare of the barn lights, I thought I could see in her gaze traces of memories that she wanted to keep buried, a life from long ago. When she released my hand, I saw her wedding band glinting on her left finger. The sight of it doused me with a cold splash of reality.

She recognized my expression. "Yes," she said, "I'm married."

"I'm sorry," I said, shaking my head. "I shouldn't have come."

Surprising me, she gave a small wave of her hand. "It's okay," she said, tilting her head. "How'd you find me?"

"It's a small town." I shrugged. "I asked someone."

"And they just . . . told you?"

"I was persuasive."

It was awkward, and neither of us seemed to know what to say. Part of me fully expected to continue standing there while we caught up like old friends on everything that had happened in our lives since we'd last seen each other. Another part of me expected her husband to pop out of the house any minute and either shake my hand or challenge me to fight. In the silence a horse neighed, and over her shoulder I could see four horses with their heads lowered into the trough, half in shadow, half in the circle of the barn's light. Three other horses, including Midas, were staring at Savannah, as if wondering whether she'd forgotten them. Savannah finally motioned over her shoulder.

"I should get them going, too," she said. "It's their feeding time, and they're getting antsy."

When I nodded, Savannah took a step backward, then turned. Just as she reached the gate, she beckoned. "Do you want to give me a hand?"

I hesitated, glancing toward the house. She followed my gaze.

"Don't worry," she said. "He's not here, and I could really use the help." Her voice was surprisingly steady.

Though I wasn't sure what to make of her response, I nodded. "I'd be glad to."

She waited for me and shut the gate behind us. She pointed to a pile of manure. "Watch out for their droppings. They'll stain your shoes."

I groaned. "I'll try."

In the barn, she separated a chunk of hay and then two more and handed them both to me.

"Just toss those in the troughs next to the others. I'm going to get the oats."

I did as she directed, and the horses closed in. Savannah came out holding a couple of pails.

"You might want to give them a little room. They might accidentally knock you over."

I stepped away, and Savannah hung a couple of pails on the fence. The first group of horses trotted toward them. Savannah watched them, her pride evident.

"How many times do you have to feed them?"

"Twice a day, every day. But there's more than just feeding. You'd be amazed at how clumsy they can be sometimes. We have the veterinarian on speed dial."

I smiled. "Sounds like a lot of work."

"They are. They say owning a horse is like living with an anchor. Unless you have someone else help out, it's tough to get away, even for a weekend."

"Do your parents pitch in?"

"Sometimes. When I really need them. But my dad's getting older, and there's a big difference between taking care of one horse and taking care of seven."

"I'll take your word for it."

In the warm embrace of the night, I listened to the steady hum of cicadas, breathing in the peace of this refuge, trying to still my racing thoughts.

"This is just the kind of place I imagined you'd live," I finally said.

"Me too," she said. "But it's a lot harder than I thought it would be. There's always something that needs to be repaired. You can't imagine how many leaks there were in the barn, and big stretches of the fence collapsed last winter. That's what we worked on during the spring."

Though I heard her use of "we" and assumed she was talking about her husband, I wasn't ready to talk about him yet. Nor, it seemed, was she.

"But it is beautiful here, even if it's a lot of work. On nights like this, I like to sit on the porch and just listen to the world. You hardly ever hear cars driving by, and it's just so . . . peaceful. It helps to clear the mind, especially after a long day."

As she spoke, I felt for the measure of her words, sensing her desire to keep our conversation on safe footing.

"I'll bet."

"I need to clean some hooves," she announced. "You want to help?"

"I don't know what to do," I admitted.

"It's easy," she said. "I'll show you." She vanished into the barn and walked out carrying what looked to be a couple of small curved nails. She handed one to me. As the horses were eating, she moved toward one.

"All you have to do is grab near the hoof and tug while you tap the back of his leg here," she said, demonstrating. The horse, occupied with his hay, obediently lifted his hoof. She propped the hoof between her legs. "Then, just dig out the dirt around the shoe. That's all there is to it."

I moved toward the horse beside her and tried to replicate her actions, but nothing happened. The horse was both exceedingly large and stubborn. I tugged again at the foot and tapped in the right place, then tugged and tapped some more. The horse continued to eat, ignoring my efforts.

"He won't lift his foot," I complained.

She finished the hoof she was working on, then bent next to my horse. A tap and tug later, the hoof was in place between her legs. "Sure he will. He just knows you don't know what you're doing and that you're uncomfortable around him. You have to be confident about this." She let the hoof drop, and I took her place, trying again. The horse ignored me once more.

"Watch what I do," she said carefully.

"I was watching," I protested.

She repeated the drill; the horse lifted his foot. A moment later I mimicked her exactly, and the horse ignored me. Though I couldn't claim to read the mind of a horse, I had the strange notion that this one was enjoying my travails. Frustrated, I tapped and tugged relentlessly until finally, as if by magic, the horse's foot lifted. Despite the minimal nature of my accomplishment, I felt a surge of pride. For the first time since I'd arrived, Savannah laughed.

"Good job. Now just scrape the mud out and go to the next hoof."

Savannah had finished the other six horses by the time I finished one. When we were done, she opened the gate and the horses trotted into the darkened pasture. I wasn't sure what to expect, but Savannah moved toward the shed. She had two shovels in hand.

"Now it's time to clean up," she said, handing me a shovel.

"Clean up?"

"The manure," she said. "Otherwise it can get pretty rank around here."

I took the shovel. "You do this every day?"

"Life's a peach, isn't it?" she teased. She left again and returned with a wheelbarrow.

As we began scooping the manure, the sliver of a moon began its rise over the treetops. We worked in silence, the clink and scrape of her shovel a steady rhythm that filled the air. In time we both finished, and I leaned on my shovel, inspecting her. In the shadows of the barnyard, she seemed as lovely and elusive as a wraith. She said nothing, but I could feel her evaluating me.

"Are you okay?" I finally asked.

"Why are you here, John?"

"You already asked me that."

"I know I did," she said. "But you didn't really answer."

I studied her. No, I hadn't. I wasn't sure I could explain it myself and shifted my weight from one foot to the other. "I didn't know where else to go."

Surprising me, she nodded. "Uh-huh," she acknowledged.

It was the unqualified acceptance in her voice that made me go on.

"I mean it," I said. "In some ways, you were the best friend I've ever had."

I could see her expression soften. "Okay," she said. Her response reminded me of my father, and after she answered, perhaps she realized it as well. I forced myself to survey the property.

"This is the ranch you dreamed of starting, isn't it?" I asked. "Hope and Horses is for autistic kids, isn't it?"

She ran a hand through her hair, tucking a strand behind her ear. She seemed pleased that I remembered. "Yes," she said. "It is."

"Is it everything you thought it would be?"

She laughed and threw up her hands. "Sometimes," she said. "But don't think for a second it earns enough to pay the bills. We both have jobs, and every day I realize that I didn't learn as much in school as I thought I did."

"No?"

She shook her head. "Some of the kids who show up here, or at the center, are difficult to reach." She hesitated, trying to find the right words. Finally she shook her head. "I guess I thought they'd all be like Alan, you know?" She looked up. "Do you remember when I told you about him?"

When I nodded, she went on. "It turns out that Alan's situation was special. I don't know—maybe it was because he'd grown up on a ranch, but he adapted to this a lot more easily than most kids."

When she didn't continue, I gave her a quizzical look. "That's not the way I remember you telling it to me. From what I remember, Alan was terrified at first."

"Yeah, I know, but still... he did get used to it. And that's the thing. I can't tell you how many kids we have here who never adapt at all, no matter how long we work with them. This isn't just a weekend thing; some kids have come here regularly for more than a year. We work at the developmental evaluation center, so we've spent a lot of time with most of the kids, and when we started the ranch, we insisted on opening it up to kids no matter how severe their condition. We felt it was an important commitment, but with some kids... I just wish I knew how to get through to them. Sometimes it feels like we're just spinning our wheels."

I could see Savannah cataloging her memories. "I don't mean that we feel like we're wasting our time," she went on. "Some kids really benefit from what we're doing. They come out here and spend a couple of weekends, and it's like... a flower bud slowly blossoming into something beautiful. Just like it did with Alan. It's like you can sense their minds opening up to new ideas and possibilities, and when they're riding with a great big smile on their faces, it's like nothing else matters in the world. It's a heady feeling, and you want it to happen over and over with every child who comes here. I used to think it was a matter of persistence, that we could help everyone, but we can't. Some of the kids never even get close to the horse, let alone ride it."

"You know that's not your fault. I wasn't too thrilled with the idea of riding, either, remember?"

She giggled, sounding remarkably girlish. "Yeah, I remember. The first time you got on a horse, you were more scared than a lot of the kids."

"No, I wasn't," I protested. "And besides, Pepper was frisky."

"Ha!" she cried. "Why do you think I let you ride him? He's just about the easiest horse you can imagine. I don't think he's ever so much as shimmied when someone rode him."

"He was frisky," I insisted.

"Spoken like a true rookie," she teased. "But even if you're wrong, I'm touched that you still remember it."

Her playfulness summoned a tidal wave of memories.

"Of course I remember," I said. "Those were some of the best days of my life. I won't ever forget them." Over her shoulder, I could see the dog wandering in the pasture. "Maybe that's why I'm still not married."

At my words, her gaze faltered. "I still remember them, too."

"Do you?"

"Of course," she said. "You might not believe it, but it's true."

The weight of her words hung heavy in the air.

"Are you happy, Savannah?" I finally asked.

She offered a wry smile. "Most of the time. Aren't you?"

"I don't know," I said, which made her laugh again.

"That's your standard answer, you know. When you're asked to look into yourself for the answer? It's like a reflex with you. It always has been. Why don't you ask me what you really wanted to ask."

"What did I really want to ask?"

"Whether or not I love my husband. Isn't that what you mean?" she asked, looking away for a moment.

For an instant I was speechless, but I realized her instincts were correct. It was the real reason I was here.

"Yes," she said at last, reading my mind again. "I love him."

The unmistakable sincerity in her tone stung, but before I could dwell on it, she turned to face me again. Anxiety flickered in her expression, as if she were remembering something painful, but it passed quickly.

"Have you eaten yet?" she asked.

I was still trying to make sense of what I'd just seen. "No," I said. "Actually, I didn't have breakfast or lunch, either."

She shook her head. "I've got some leftover beef stew in the house. Do you have time for dinner?"

Though I wondered again about her husband, I nodded. "I'd like that," I said.

We started toward the house and stopped when we reached a porch lined with muddy and worn cowboy boots. Savannah reached for my arm in a way that struck me as being remarkably easy and natural, using me for balance as she slipped off her boots. It was, perhaps, her touch that emboldened me to really look at her, and though I saw the mysteriousness and maturity that had always made her attractive, I noticed a hint of sadness and reticence as well. To my aching heart, the combination made her even more beautiful.

# Questions and Explanations for Chapters 16 through 18

The ten questions on chapters 16 through 18 focus on grammar and usage, vocabulary, literary terms, comprehension, style, and characterization. Some of the questions combine two or more of these areas, requiring you to synthesize your knowledge, make inferences, and interpret the text. The questions are designed to determine both your current level of understanding of the novel and your ability to answer higher-level questions.

The following sentence tests your ability to recognize grammar and usage errors. The sentence contains either a single error or no error at all. If the sentence contains an error, select the one underlined part that must be changed to make the sentence correct. If there is no error, select choice D.

1. Because <u>John's</u> assignment was in the desert, he <u>should</u>
   <sub>A</sub>                                             <sub>B</sub>

   <u>of</u> been <u>used to</u> all the sand. <u>No error</u>
   <sub>C</sub>                                  <sub>D</sub>

Understanding what is being evaluated will help assist you in making your determination of whether or not there is an error in this sentence. Choice A is checking the use of the apostrophe. A singular noun demonstrates possession with an apostrophe and an *s*—for example, "the boy's book, the girl's letter, the surfer's board."

Choice B is asking about the accuracy of the phrase "should of." Sometimes when a word or phrase is spoken, it sounds like there are two or more different spellings for it. For example, the phrase "could have" is the same as the contraction "could've." This phrase might sound like "could of" or "coulda" when spoken out loud.

Choice C is asking you to differentiate between "use to" and "used to." You use the form "use to" when paired with a helping verb—for example, "John didn't *use to* ride a horse before meeting Savannah." You use the form "used to" when meaning to be accustomed to. For example, "Because John wasn't *used to riding*, he was extremely sore the next day."

**Question 2 tests your vocabulary. Choose the set of words that, when inserted in the sentence, best fits the meaning of the sentence as a whole.**

2. When John was attempting to clean the horse's hoof, he thought the horse not only realized the _____ of his actions but was rather enjoying his _____.

A. ineffectiveness...indolence

B. effectiveness...sloth

C. competence...toils

D. futility...travails

This question tests your comprehension and your vocabulary. The context clues in the sentence indicate that John is "attempting" to clean the hoof, reminding you that he is not being successful and allowing you to eliminate two of the possible answer choices. Because *effectiveness*, choice B, and *competence*, choice C, both indicate contrary conditions, you can eliminate these choices. Either of the first words in choices A and D could fit, so you must determine which of the second words is the correct choice. *Indolence*, choice A, suggests that little effort is being exerted, and *travails*, choice D, indicates burdensome work.

**Question 3 tests your knowledge of literary terms.**

3. John carries his Dear John letter "like a wound I'd received in battle." What literary device does he use to make his point?

   A. foreshadowing

   B. hyperbole

   C. paradox

   D. simile

*Foreshadowing*, choice A, is providing hints or clues to future events. For example, when Benvolio suggests to Romeo that finding a new female beauty may help Romeo get over Rosaline, it foreshadows Romeo's falling in love with Juliet when he sees her later in the play.

*Hyperbole*, choice B, is using overexaggeration to illustrate a point. For example, if someone says, "I told you a million times what this is," you know that this person really didn't tell you a million times, just many times.

A *paradox*, choice C, is an apparent contradiction that upon further analysis seemingly makes sense. The famous first line of *A Tale of Two Cities*, "It was the best of times, it was the worst of times," initially doesn't make sense. But when you think about a situation in which both conditions can exist simultaneously, you begin to understand the paradox.

And a *simile*, choice D, is a comparison of two unlike things using a connective word, such as *like*, *as*, or *than*—for example, "She looked as fresh as the morning snow."

**Question 4 tests your knowledge of literary terms.**

4. John claims that the army uses the word *incidents* to refer to civilian deaths. This is an example of what?

   A. euphemism

   B. foreshadowing

   C. hyperbole

   D. paradox

A *euphemism*, choice A, substitutes a milder expression for one that may seem to be too bold, direct, or offensive—for example, often people don't refer to someone as dying, instead they "pass away."

*Foreshadowing*, choice B, is providing hints or clues to future events. For example, when Benvolio suggests to Romeo that finding a new female beauty may help Romeo get over Rosaline, it foreshadows Romeo's falling in love with Juliet when he sees her later in the play.

*Hyperbole*, choice C, is using overexaggeration to illustrate a point. For example, after the holiday season, someone might claim, "I have an endless pile of bills." Although he or she may have many, the pile isn't literally without end.

A *paradox*, choice D, is an apparent contradiction that upon further analysis seemingly makes sense. The famous first line of *A Tale of Two Cities*, "It was the best of times, it was the worst of times," initially doesn't make sense. But when you think about a situation in which both conditions can exist simultaneously, you begin to understand the paradox.

**Question 5 checks your comprehension.**

5. How and why are John and his father able to become friends?

   A. John begins to appreciate coin collecting.

   B. John's father gives up his pretensions.

   C. John finally lowers his expectations for his father.

   D. John's father's sickness forces them to spend a lot of time together.

Becoming friends with his father is an important part of John's growth as a character and is also important to the development of plot and theme in *Dear John*. If you're not sure of the answer, reread the section of chapter 16 that discusses John's time home on leave in 2004.

**Question 6 checks your comprehension.**

6. Why does John talk about sand when people ask him about the war?

    A. It's too difficult for him to state the truth.

    B. People would rather hear about the natural environment of the Middle East.

    C. John is too scared to process the events that he experienced.

    D. John is not permitted to share any of his battle experiences with civilians.

This is another important question about John's character development and his realization of what people want to know and are able to handle when they ask about his time in Iraq. Not only does John explain his thoughts in the beginning of chapter 16, he illustrates them during his conversation with Lucy in chapter 17.

**Question 7 asks you to analyze how an author's choices contribute to overall structure and meaning.**

7. The single-sentence paragraph that ends chapter 16, "It was the last time I ever saw him alive," produces each of the following effects EXCEPT:

    A. preparing the reader for Mr. Tyree's death

B. having the finality of the chapter parallel the finality of Mr. Tyree's life

C. indicating the growth and change in John's relationship with his father

D. establishing the conflict for the rest of the novel

The question indicates that three of the four choices are effects of the single-sentence paragraph, and thus they can be eliminated. If the statement specifically prepares readers for John's father's death, eliminate choice A. If the sentence occurs at both the end of a chapter and at the end of Mr. Tyree's life, eliminate choice B. If the tone and sentiment of the sentence indicates how John feels about his relationship with his father—especially as compared to his younger days—eliminate choice C. And if his father's death is the problem that John is going to have to deal with for the remainder of the novel, eliminate choice D.

**Question 8 asks you to make an inference about character and thematic development based on strong and thorough textual evidence.**

8. What is the most significant result of John spending time with his father after his father's second heart attack?

A. John receives the 1926-D buffalo nickel.

B. Lucy reappears in John's life.

C. John inherits the photograph of his father and himself.

D. The subplot mirrors the main thematic topic of the novel—John discovers what true love is.

The question asks for the most significant result of John's time with his father. Although all of these choices are events that occur in this section, the best answer is the one that supports the development of character and theme. In this case, the broadest answer, which may incorporate some of the others, is the best choice.

**Question 9 asks you to make an inference based on the stylistic choices of the author.**

9. Chapter 17 is full of plot, character, and thematic development. What inference can you make about the stylistic choices that affect the pacing of the plot throughout this chapter?

    A. The long chapter parallels the long days that John experiences following his father's death.

    B. The pace of the chapter is slow for both John and the reader.

    C. The quick tempo parallels John's experiences in the days following the news of his father's death.

    D. The surprises John learns about his father after the death support the assertion that John's father continued to astonish him, even after his death.

If chapter 17 is particularly long and is mirroring the long days that follow for John after the death of Mr. Tyree, select choice A. If the chapter reads very slowly, demonstrating that time was essentially standing still for John, select choice B. If the chapter reads very quickly, just like time is passing in a blur for John, select choice C. If John is surprised to learn that his father made decisions about his own burial and the settlement of his estate, select choice D.

**Question 10 asks you to make an inference regarding character development.**

10. The words and actions of Savannah at Hope and Horses suggest which of the following?

   A. Savannah doesn't love her husband.

   B. Savannah definitely regrets breaking up with John.

   C. Savannah hasn't changed at all during the past two years.

   D. Savannah is going through a tough time in her personal life.

If you can support the assertion that Savannah is not in love with her husband, select choice A. If you can state unequivocally that she regrets breaking up with John, select choice B. If she is exactly the same person she was before she broke up with John, select choice C. And if there is any indication that she is experiencing some personal difficulties, select choice D.

# Chapter 19

Her small kitchen was what one would expect from an old house that had probably been remodeled half a dozen times over the last century: ancient linoleum floors that were peeling slightly near the walls; functional, unadorned white cabinets—thick with countless paint jobs—and a stainless-steel sink set beneath a wood-framed window that probably should have been replaced years ago. The countertop was cracking, and against one wall stood a woodstove as old as the house itself. In places, it was possible to see the modern world encroaching: a large refrigerator and dishwasher near the sink; a microwave propped kitty-corner near a half-empty bottle of red wine. In some ways, it reminded me of my dad's place.

Savannah opened a cupboard and removed a wineglass. "Would you like a glass of wine?"

I shook my head. "I've never been much of a wine drinker."

I was surprised when she didn't return the glass. Instead, she retrieved the half-empty bottle of wine and poured a glass; she set the glass on the table and took a seat before it.

We sat at the table as Savannah took a sip.

"You've changed," I observed.

She shrugged. "A lot of things have changed since I last saw you."

She said nothing more and set her glass back on the table. When she spoke again, her voice was subdued. "I never thought I'd be the kind of person who looked forward to a glass of wine in the evenings, but I do."

She began rotating the glass on the table, and I found myself wondering what had happened to her.

"You know the funny thing?" she said. "I actually care how it tastes. When I had my first glass, I didn't know what was good or what was bad. Now when it comes to buying, I've become pretty selective."

I didn't fully recognize the woman who sat before me, and I wasn't sure how to respond.

"Don't get me wrong," she went on. "I still remember everything my folks taught me, and I hardly ever have more than a glass a night. But since Jesus himself turned water into wine, I figured that it can't be much of a sin."

I smiled at her logic, recognizing how unfair it was to cling to the time-capsule version I held of her. "I wasn't asking."

"I know," she said. "But you were wondering."

For a moment, the only sound in the kitchen was the low hum of the refrigerator. "I'm sorry about your dad," she said, tracing a crack in the tabletop. "I really am. I can't tell you how many times I've thought about him in the past few years."

"Thank you," I said.

Savannah began rotating her glass again, seemingly lost in the swirl of liquid. "Do you want to talk about it?" she asked.

I wasn't sure I did, but as I leaned back in my chair, the words came surprisingly easily. I told her about my dad's first heart attack, and the second, and the visits we'd shared in the past couple of years. I told her about our growing friendship, and the comfort I felt with him, the walks that he began taking and then eventually gave up. I recounted my final days with him and the agony of committing him to an extended care facility. When I described the funeral and the photograph I found in the envelope, she reached for my hand.

"I'm glad he saved it for you," she said, "but I'm not surprised."

"I was," I said, and she laughed. It was a reassuring sound.

She squeezed my hand. "I wish I'd have known. I would have liked to go to the funeral."

"It wasn't much."

"It didn't have to be. He was your dad, and that's all that matters." She hesitated before releasing my hand and took another sip of wine.

"Are you ready to eat?" she asked.

"I don't know," I said, flushing at the memory of her earlier comment.

She leaned forward with a grin. "How about I heat you up a plate of stew and we'll see what happens."

"Is it any good?" I asked. "I mean . . . when I knew you before, you never mentioned that you knew how to cook."

"It's our special family recipe," she said, pretending to be offended. "But I've got to be honest—my mom made it. She brought it over yesterday."

"The truth comes out," I said.

"That's the funny thing about the truth," she said. "It usually does." She rose and opened the refrigerator, bending over as she scanned the shelves. I found myself wondering about the ring on her finger and where her husband was as she pulled out the Tupperware. She scooped some of the stew into a bowl and placed it in the microwave.

"Do you want anything else with that? How about some bread and butter?"

"That would be great," I agreed.

A few minutes later, the meal was spread before me, and the aroma reminded me for the first time of how hungry I actually was. Surprising me, Savannah took her place again, holding her glass of wine.

"Aren't you going to eat?"

"I'm not hungry," she said. "Actually, I haven't been eating much lately." She took a sip as I took my first bite and I let her comment pass.

"You're right," I said. "It's delicious."

She smiled. "Mom's a good cook. You'd think I would have learned more about cooking, but I didn't. I was always too busy. Too much studying when I was young, and then lately, too much remodeling." She motioned toward the living room. "It's an old house. I know it doesn't look like it, but we've done a lot of work in the past couple of years."

"It looks great."

"You're just being polite, but I appreciate it," she replied. "You should have seen the place when I moved in. It was kind of like the barn, you know? We needed a new roof, but it's funny— no one ever thinks of roofs when they're imagining what to remodel. It's one of those things that everyone expects a house to have but never thinks might one day need replacing. Almost everything we've done falls into that category. Heat pumps, thermal windows, fixing the termite damage... there were a lot of long days." She wore a dreamy expression on her face. "We did most of the work ourselves. Like with the kitchen here. I know we need new cabinets and flooring, but when we moved in, there were puddles in the living room and bedrooms every time it rained. What were we supposed to do? We had to prioritize, and one of the first things we did was to tear all the old shingles from the roof. It must have been a hundred degrees and I'm up there with a shovel, scraping shingles off, getting blisters. But... it just felt right, you know? Two young people starting out in the world, working together and repairing their home? There was such a sense of... togetherness about it. It was the same thing when we did the floor in the living room. It must have taken a couple of weeks to sand it down and get it level again. We stained it and added a layer of varnish, and when we finally walked across it, it felt like we'd laid the foundation for the rest of our lives."

"You make it sound almost romantic."

"It was, in a way," she agreed. She tucked a strand of hair behind her ear. "But lately it's not so romantic. Now, it's just getting old."

I laughed unexpectedly, then coughed and found myself reaching for a glass that wasn't there.

She pushed back from her chair. "Let me get you some water," she said. She filled a glass from the faucet and placed it before me. As I drank, I could feel her watching me.

"What?" I asked.

"I just can't get over how different you look."

"Me?" I found it hard to believe.

"Yeah, you," she insisted. "You're... older somehow."

"I am older."

"I know, but it's not that. It's your eyes. They're...more serious than they used to be. Like they've seen things they shouldn't have. Weary, somehow."

To this, I said nothing, but when she saw my expression, she shook her head, looking embarrassed. "I shouldn't have said that. I can only imagine what you've been through lately."

I ate another bite of stew, thinking about her comment. "Actually I left Iraq in early 2004," I said. "I've been in Germany ever since. Only a small part of the army is ever there at any one time, and we rotate through. I'll probably end up going back, but I don't know when. Hopefully things will have calmed down by then."

"Weren't you supposed to be out by now?"

"I reupped again," I said. "There wasn't any reason not to."

We both knew the reason why, and she nodded. "How long now?"

"I'm in until 2007."

"And then?"

"I'm not sure. I might stay in for a few more years. Or maybe I'll go to college. Who knows—I might even pick up a degree in special education. I've heard great things about the field."

Her smile was strangely sad, and for a while, neither of us said anything. "How long have you been married?" I asked.

She shifted in her seat. "It'll be two years next November."

"Were you married here?"

"As if I had a choice." She rolled her eyes. "My mom was really into the whole perfect wedding thing. I know I'm their only daughter, but in hindsight, I would have been just as happy with something a lot smaller. A hundred guests would have been perfect."

"You consider that small?"

"Compared with what we ended up with? Yeah. There weren't enough seats in the church for everyone, and my dad keeps reminding me that he'll be paying it off for years. He's just teasing, of course. Half the guests were friends of my parents, but I guess that's what you get when you get married in your hometown. Everyone from the mailman to the barber gets an invitation."

"But you're glad to be back home?"

"It's comfortable here. My parents are close by, and I need that, especially now."

She didn't elaborate, content to let her comment stand. I wondered about that—and a hundred other things—as I rose from the table and brought my plate to the sink. After rinsing it, I heard her call out behind me.

"Just leave it there. I haven't unloaded the dishwasher yet. I'll get it later. Do you want anything else, though? My mom left a couple of pies on the counter."

"How about a glass of milk?" I said. As she started to rise, I added, "I can get it. Just point me to the glasses."

"In the cupboard by the sink."

I pulled a glass from the shelf and went to the refrigerator. Milk was on the top shelf; on the shelves below were at least a dozen Tupperware containers filled with food. I poured a glass and returned to the table.

"What's going on, Savannah?"

With my words, she came back to me. "What do you mean?"

"Your husband," I said.

"What about him?"

"When can I meet him?"

Instead of answering, Savannah rose from the table with her

wineglass. She poured the remains into the sink, then retrieved a coffee cup and a box of tea.

"You've already met him," she said, turning around. She squared her shoulders. "It's Tim."

I could hear the spoon tapping against the cup as Savannah sat across from me again.

"How much of this do you want to hear?" she murmured, staring into her teacup.

"All of it," I said. I leaned back in my chair. "Or none of it. I'm not sure yet."

She snorted. "I guess that makes sense."

I brought my hands together. "When did it start?"

"I don't know," she said. "I know that sounds crazy, but it didn't happen like you probably think. It wasn't as if either of us planned it." She set her spoon on the table. "But to give some kind of answer, I guess it started in early 2002."

A few months after I'd reupped, I realized. Six months before my father had his first heart attack and right around the time I noticed that her letters to me had begun to change.

"You know we've been friends. Even though he was a graduate student, we ended up having a couple of classes in the same building during my last year in college, and afterwards, we'd have coffee or end up studying together. It's not like we dated, or even held hands. Tim knew I was in love with you...but he was there, you know? He listened when I talked about how much I missed you and how hard it was to be apart. And it *was* hard. I thought you'd be home by then."

When she looked up, her eyes were filled with...What? Regret? I couldn't tell.

"Anyway, we spent a lot of time together, and he was good at consoling me whenever I got down. He'd always remind me that you'd be back on leave before I knew it, and I can't tell you how much I wanted to see you again. And then your dad got sick. I know you had to be with him—I would never have forgiven you if you hadn't stayed by his side—but it wasn't what we needed. I know how selfish that sounds, and I hate myself for even thinking it. It just felt like fate was conspiring against us."

She put her spoon in the tea and stirred again, collecting her thoughts.

"That fall, right after I finished up with all my classes and moved back home to work at the developmental evaluation center here in town, Tim's parents were in a horrible accident. They were driving back from Asheville when they lost control of their car and swerved into oncoming traffic on the highway. A semi ended up hitting them. The driver of the truck wasn't hurt, but both of Tim's parents died on impact. Tim had to quit school—he was trying to get his PhD—so he could come back here to take care of Alan." She paused. "It was awful for Tim. Not only was he trying to come to terms with the loss—he adored his parents—but Alan was inconsolable. He screamed all the time, and he began pulling out his hair. The only one who could stop him from hurting himself was Tim, but it took all the energy Tim had. I guess that's when I first started coming over here. You know, to help out."

When I frowned, she added, "This was Tim's parents' house. Where Tim and Alan grew up."

As soon as she said it, the memory came back. Of course it was Tim's—she'd once told me that Tim lived on the ranch next to hers.

"We just ended up consoling each other. I tried to help him, and he tried to help me, and we both tried to help Alan. And little by little, I guess, we began to fall in love."

For the first time, she met my eyes.

"I know you want to be angry with Tim or me. Probably both of us. And I guess we deserve it. But you don't know what it was like back then. So much was going on—it was just so emotional all the time. I felt guilty about what was happening, Tim felt guilty. But after a while, it just began to feel like we were a couple already. Tim started working at the same developmental evaluation center where I did and then decided that he wanted to start a weekend ranch program for autistic kids. His parents always wanted him to do that, so I signed on to work on the ranch, too. After that, we were together almost all the time. Setting up the ranch gave us both something to focus on, and it helped Alan, too. He loves horses, and there was so much to do that he gradually got used to the fact that his parents weren't around. It's like we were all leaning on each other....He proposed later that year."

When she stopped, I turned away, trying to digest her words. We sat in silence for a while, each of us wrestling with our thoughts.

"Anyway, that's the story," she concluded. "I don't know how much more you want to hear."

I wasn't sure, either.

"Does Alan still live here?" I asked.

"He's got a room upstairs. Actually, it's the same room he's always had. It's not as hard as it sounds, though. After he's finished feeding and brushing the horses, he usually spends most of his time alone. He loves video games. He can play for hours. Lately I haven't been able to get him to stop. He'd play all night long if I'd let him."

"Is he here now?"

She shook her head. "No," she said. "Right now he's with Tim."

"Where?"

Before she could answer, the dog scratched insistently at the door, and Savannah got up to open it. The dog padded in, tongue out and tail still wagging. He trotted toward me and nuzzled my hand.

"He likes me," I said.

Savannah was still near the door. "She likes everyone. Her name's Molly. Worthless as a guard dog, but sweeter than candy. Just try to avoid the drool. She'll drip all over you if you let her."

I glanced at my jeans. "I can see that."

Savannah motioned over her shoulder. "Listen, I just realized I've still got to put some things away. It's supposed to rain tonight. It shouldn't take long."

I noted that she hadn't answered the question about Tim. Nor, I realized, did she plan to.

"Need a hand?"

"Not really. But you're welcome to come. It's a beautiful night."

I followed her out, and Molly trotted ahead of us, completely forgetting that she'd just begged to come inside. When an owl broke from the trees, Molly galloped into the darkness and vanished. Savannah pulled on her boots again.

We walked toward the barn. I thought about everything she'd told me and wondered again why I'd come. I wasn't sure if I was happy that she'd married Tim—since they'd seemed so perfect for each other—or upset for exactly the same reason. Nor was I glad that I finally knew the truth; somehow, I realized, it was easier not to know. All at once, I simply felt tired.

And yet...there was something I knew she wasn't telling me. I heard it in her voice, in the hint of sadness that wouldn't go away. As the darkness surrounded us, I was acutely aware of how close we were walking together, and I wondered whether she felt the same. If she did, she gave no sign.

The horses were mere shadows in the distance, shapes without recognizable form. Savannah retrieved a couple of bridles and brought them to the barn, hanging them on a couple of pegs. While she did, I collected the shovels we'd been using and set them with the rest of the tools. On our way out, she made sure to shut the gate.

Glancing at my watch, I saw it was nearly ten o'clock. It was late, and we were both conscious of the hour.

"I guess I should probably get going," I said. "It's a small town. I don't want to start any rumors."

"You're probably right." Molly wandered up, appearing from nowhere, and sat between us. When she lapped at Savannah's leg, she stepped to the side. "Where are you staying?" she asked.

"Something or other motor court. Just off the highway."

Her nose crinkled, if only for an instant. "I know the place."

"It is kind of a dive," I admitted.

She smiled. "I can't say I'm surprised. You always did have a way of finding the most unique places."

"Like the Shrimp Shack?"

"Exactly."

I pushed my hands into my pockets, wondering whether this was the last time I'd ever see her. If so, it struck me as absurdly anticlimactic; I didn't want it to end in small talk, but I couldn't think of anything else to say.

On the road out front, the headlights of an approaching car flashed over the property as it sped past the house.

"I guess that's it, then," I said, at a loss. "It was good seeing you again."

"You, too, John. I'm glad you came by."

I nodded again. When she looked away, I took it as my cue to leave.

"Good-bye," I said.

"Bye."

I turned from the porch and started toward my car, dazed at the thought it was really and truly over. I wasn't sure I'd expected anything different, but the finality brought to the surface all those feelings I'd been repressing since I'd read her last letter.

I was opening the door when I heard her call out.

"Hey, John?"

"Yeah?"

She stepped off the porch and started toward me. "Are you going to be around tomorrow?"

As she drew near, her face half in shadow, I knew with certainty that I was still in love with her. Despite the letter, despite her husband. Despite the fact that we could never be together now.

"Why?" I asked.

"I was wondering if you'd like to drop by. Around ten. I'm sure Tim would like to see you..."

I was shaking my head even before she finished. "I'm not sure that's such a good idea—"

"Could you do it for me?"

I knew she wanted me to see that Tim was still the same man I remembered, and in a sense, I knew she was asking because she wanted forgiveness. Still...

She reached out to take my hand. "Please. It would mean a lot to me."

Despite the warmth of her hand, I didn't want to come back.

I didn't want to see Tim, I didn't want to see the two of them together or sit around the table pretending that all seemed right in the world. But there was something plaintive about her request that made it impossible to turn her down.

"Okay," I said. "Ten o'clock."

"Thank you."

A moment later, she turned. I stayed in place, watching her climb onto the porch before I got in the car. I turned the key and backed out. Savannah turned on the porch, waving one last time. I waved, then headed out to the road, her image growing smaller in the rearview mirror. Watching her, I felt a sudden dryness in my throat. Not because she was married to Tim, and not at the thought of seeing them both tomorrow. It came from watching Savannah as I was driving away, standing on her porch, crying into her hands.

# Chapter 20

The following morning, Savannah was standing on the porch, and she waved as I pulled in the drive. She stepped forward as I brought the car to a stop. I half expected Tim to appear in the doorway behind her, but he was nowhere to be seen.

"Hey," she said, touching my arm. "Thanks for coming."

"Yeah," I said, giving a reluctant shrug.

I thought I saw a flash of understanding in her eyes before she asked, "Did you sleep okay?"

"Not really."

At that, she gave a wry smile. "Are you ready?"

"As I'll ever be."

"Okay," she said. "Just let me get the keys. Unless you'd like to drive."

I didn't catch her meaning at first. "We're leaving?" I nodded toward the house. "I thought we were going to see Tim."

"We are," she said. "He's not here."

"Where is he?"

It was as if she hadn't heard me. "Do you want to drive?"

"Yeah, I guess so," I said, not bothering to hide my confusion but somehow knowing she'd clear things up when she was ready. I opened the door for her and went around the driver's side to slide behind the wheel. Savannah was running her hand over the dashboard, as if trying to prove to herself it was real.

"I remember this car." Her expression was nostalgic. "It's your dad's, right? Wow, I can't believe it's still running."

"He didn't drive all that much," I said. "Just to work and the store."

"Still."

She put on her seat belt, and despite myself, I wondered whether she'd spent the night alone.

"Which way?" I asked.

"At the road, take a left," she said. "Head toward town."

Neither of us spoke. Instead, she stared out the passenger window with her arms crossed. I might have been offended, but there was something in her expression that told me her preoccupation had nothing to do with me, and I left her alone with her thoughts.

On the outskirts of town, she shook her head, as if suddenly conscious of how quiet it was in the car. "I'm sorry," she said. "I guess my company leaves a lot to be desired."

"It's okay," I said, trying to mask my growing curiosity.

She pointed toward the windshield. "At the next corner, take a right."

"Where are we going?"

She didn't answer right away. Instead, she turned and gazed out the passenger window.

"The hospital," she finally said.

\*　　\*　　\*

I followed her through seemingly endless corridors, finally stopping at the visitors' check-in. Behind the desk, an elderly volunteer held out a clipboard. Savannah reached for the pen and began signing her name automatically.

"You holdin' up, Savannah?"

"Trying," Savannah murmured.

"It'll all turn out okay. You've got the whole town prayin' for him."

"Thanks," Savannah said. She handed back the clipboard, then looked at me. "He's on the third floor," she explained. "The elevators are just down the hall."

I followed her, my stomach churning. We reached the elevator just as someone was getting off, and stepped inside. When the doors closed, it felt as if I were in a tomb.

When we reached the third floor, Savannah started down the hallway with me trailing behind. She stopped in front of a room with a door propped open and then turned to face me.

"I think I should probably go in first," she said. "Can you wait here?"

"Of course."

She flashed her appreciation, then turned away. She drew a long breath before entering the room. "Hey, honey," I heard her call out, her tone bright. "You doing okay?"

I didn't hear any more than that for the next couple of minutes. Instead I stood in the hallway, absorbing the same sterile, impersonal surroundings I'd noticed while visiting with my father. The air reeked of a nameless disinfectant, and I watched as an orderly wheeled a cart of food into a room down the hall. Halfway up the corridor, I saw a group of nurses clustered in the station. Behind the door across the hallway, I could hear someone retching.

"Okay," Savannah said, poking her head out. Beneath her brave appearance, I could still see her sadness. "You can come in. He's ready for you."

I followed her in, bracing myself for the worst. Tim sat propped up in the bed with an IV connected to his arm. He looked exhausted, and his skin was so pale that it was almost translucent. He'd lost even more weight than my father had, and as I stared at him, all I could think was that he was dying. Only the kindness in his eyes was unaffected. On the other side of the room was a young man—late teens or early twenties, maybe—rolling his head from side to side, and I knew immediately it was Alan. The room was crowded with flowers: dozens of bouquets and greeting cards stacked on every available tabletop and ledge. Savannah sat on the bed beside her husband and reached for his hand.

"Hey, Tim," I said.

He looked too tired to smile, but he managed. "Hey, John. Good to see you again."

"You too," I said. "How are you?"

As soon as I said it, I knew how ridiculous it sounded. Tim must have been used to it, for he didn't flinch.

"I'm okay," he said. "I'm feeling better now."

I nodded. Alan continued to roll his head, and I found myself watching him, feeling like an intruder in events I wished I could have avoided.

"This is my brother, Alan," he said.

"Hi, Alan."

When Alan didn't respond, I heard Tim whisper to him, "Hey, Alan? It's okay. He's not a doctor. He's a friend. Go say hello."

It took a few seconds, but Alan finally rose from his seat. He walked stiffly across the room, and though he wouldn't meet my eyes, he extended his hand. "Hi, I'm Alan," he said in a surprisingly deep monotone.

"Nice to meet you," I said, taking his hand. It was limp; he pumped once, then let go and went back to his seat.

"There's a chair if you'd like to sit," Tim said.

I wandered farther into the room and took a seat. Before I could even ask, I heard Tim already answering the question on my mind.

"Melanoma," he said. "In case you're wondering."

"But you'll be okay, right?"

Alan's head rolled even faster, and he began to slap his thighs. Savannah turned away. I already knew I shouldn't have asked.

"That's what the doctors are for," Tim replied. "I'm in good hands." I knew the answer was more for Alan than me, and Alan began to calm down.

Tim closed his eyes, then opened them again, as if trying to concentrate his strength. "I'm glad to see you made it back in one piece," he said. "I prayed for you the whole time you were in Iraq."

"Thank you," I said.

"What have you been up to? Still in the army, I guess."

He nodded toward my crew cut, and I ran my hand over it. "Yeah. Seems like I'm becoming a lifer."

"Good," he said. "The army needs people like you."

I said nothing. The scene struck me as surreal, like watching yourself in a dream. Tim turned to Savannah. "Sweetheart— would you walk with Alan and get him a soda? He hasn't had anything to drink since earlier this morning. And if you can, maybe you can talk him into eating."

"Sure," she said. She kissed him on the forehead and rose

from the bed. She stopped in the doorway. "Come on, Alan. Let's get something to drink, okay?"

To me, it seemed as if Alan were slowly processing the words. Finally, he got up and followed Savannah; she placed a gentle hand on his back on the way out the door. When they were gone, Tim faced me again.

"This whole thing is really hard on Alan. He's not taking it well."

"How can he?"

"Don't let the rolling of his head fool you, though. It's got nothing to do with autism or his intelligence. It's more like a tic he gets when he's nervous. The same thing when he started slapping his thighs. He knows what's going on, but it affects him in ways that usually make other people uncomfortable."

I clasped my hands. "It didn't make me uncomfortable," I said. "My dad had his things, too. He's your brother, and it's obvious that he's worried. It makes sense."

Tim smiled. "That's kind of you to say. A lot of people get frightened."

"Not me," I said, shaking my head. "I know I could take him."

Remarkably, he laughed, although it seemed to take a lot out of him.

"I'm sure you could," he said. "Alan's gentle. Probably too gentle. He won't even swat flies."

I nodded, recognizing that all this small talk was just his way of making me feel more comfortable. It wasn't working.

"When did you find out?"

"A year ago. A mole on the back of my calf started to itch, and when I scratched at it, it started to bleed. Of course, I didn't think much of it then, until it bled again the next time I scratched at it. Six months ago, I went to the doctor. That was on a Friday. I had surgery on Saturday and started interferon on Monday. Now, I'm here."

"You've been in the hospital all this time?"

"No. I'm here only off and on. Usually, interferon is done on an outpatient basis, but me and the interferon don't get along. I don't tolerate it that well, so now they do it here. In case I get too sick and become dehydrated. Like I did yesterday."

"I'm sorry," I said.

"I am, too."

I looked around the room, my eyes landing on a cheaply framed bedside photo of Tim and Savannah standing with their arms around Alan. "How's Savannah holding up?" I asked.

"Like you'd expect." Tim traced a crease in his hospital sheet with his free hand. "She's been great. Not only with me, but with the ranch, too. She's had to handle everything lately, but she never complains about it. And whenever she's around me, she tries to be strong. She keeps telling me that it's all going to work out." He formed the ghost of a smile. "Half the time, I even believe her."

When I didn't respond, he struggled to sit up higher in the bed. He winced, but the pain passed, and he became himself again. "Savannah told me you had dinner at the ranch last night."

"Yeah," I said.

"I'll bet she was glad to see you. I know she's always felt bad that it ended the way it did, and so did I. I owe you an apology."

"Don't." I raised my hands. "It's okay."

He formed a wry grin. "You're only saying that because I'm sick, and we both know it. If I was healthy, you'd probably want to break my nose again."

"Maybe," I admitted, and though he laughed again, this time I could hear the sound of sickness in it.

"I deserve it," he said, oblivious to my thoughts. "I know you might not believe it, but I feel bad about what happened. I know you two really cared about each other."

I leaned forward, propping myself on my elbows. "Water under the bridge," I said.

I didn't believe it, and he didn't believe me when I said it. But it was enough for both of us to put it to rest. "What brought you here? After all this time?"

"My dad passed away," I said. "Last week."

Despite his condition, his face reflected genuine sympathy. "I'm sorry, John. I know how much he meant to you. Was it sudden?"

"At the end, it always is. But he'd been sick for a while."

"It doesn't make it any easier."

I found myself wondering whether he was referring just to me or to Savannah and Alan as well.

"Savannah told me you lost both your parents."

"A car accident," he said, drawing out the words. "It was... unbelievable. We'd just had dinner with them a couple of nights before, and the next thing you know, I'm making arrangements for their funerals. It still doesn't seem real. Whenever I'm at home, I keep expecting to see my mom in the kitchen or my dad puttering around the garden." He hesitated, and I knew he was replaying those images. At last he shook his head. "Did that happen to you? When you were home?"

"Every single minute."

He leaned his head back. "I guess it's been a rough couple of years for both of us. It's enough to test your faith."

"Even for you?"

He gave a halfhearted grin. "I said test. I didn't say that it ended it."

"No, I don't suppose it would have."

I heard a nurse's voice approaching, and though I thought she was going to enter, she passed by on her way to another room.

"I'm glad you came to see Savannah," he said. "I know it sounds trite considering all that you two have been through, but she needs a friend right now."

My throat was tight. "Yeah," was all I could think to say.

He grew quiet, and I knew he would say no more about it. In time, he drifted off to sleep, and I sat there watching him, my mind curiously blank.

"I'm sorry I didn't tell you yesterday," Savannah said to me an hour later. When she and Alan had returned to the room to find Tim sleeping, she'd motioned for me to follow her downstairs to the cafeteria. "I was surprised to see you, and I knew I should have said something, but every time I tried, I just couldn't."

Two cups of tea were on the table, since neither of us felt like eating. Savannah lifted her cup and set it back down again.

"It had just been one of those days, you know? I'd spent hours in the hospital, and the nurses kept giving me those piti-ful looks and...well, they just feel like they're killing me little by little. I know that sounds ridiculous considering what Tim is going through, but it's so hard to watch him get sick. I hate it. I know I have to be there to support him, and the thing is, I want to be there, but it's always worse than I expect. He was so sick after his treatment yesterday that I thought he was dying. He couldn't stop vomiting, and when nothing else would come up, he just kept dry heaving. Every five or ten minutes, he'd start to moan and move around the bed trying to prevent it, but there was nothing he could do. I'd hold him and comfort him, but I can't even begin to describe how helpless it made me feel." She lifted her bag of tea in and out of the water. "It's like that every time," she said.

I fiddled with the handle of my cup. "I wish I knew what to say."

"There's nothing you can say, and I know that. That's why I'm talking to you. Because I know that you can handle it. I don't really have anyone else. None of my friends can even relate to what I'm going through. My mom and dad have been great... kind of. I know they'd do anything that I ask, and they're always offering to help, and Mom brings over our meals, but every time she drops off the food, she's just a bundle of nerves. She's always on the verge of crying. It's like she's terrified of saying or doing anything wrong, so when she's trying to help, it's like I have to support her, too, instead of the other way around. Added to everything else, it's almost too much sometimes. I hate to say that about her because she's doing her best and she's my mom and I love her, but I just wish she'd be stronger, you know?"

Remembering her mother, I nodded. "How about your dad?"

"The same, but in a different way. He avoids the topic. He doesn't want to talk about it at all. When we're together, he talks about the ranch or my job—anything but Tim. It's like he's trying to make up for Mom's incessant worrying, but he never asks what's been going on or how I'm holding up." She shook her head. "And then there's Alan. Tim's so good with him, and I like to think I'm getting better with him, but still...there are times when he starts hurting himself or breaking things, and I just end up crying because I don't know what to do. Don't get me wrong—I try, but I'm not Tim, and we both know it."

Her eyes held mine for a moment before I looked away. I took a sip of tea, trying to imagine what her life was like now.

"Did Tim tell you what's going on? With his melanoma?"

"A little," I said. "Not enough to know the whole story. He told me he found a mole and that it was bleeding. He put it off for a while, then finally went to see a doctor."

She nodded. "It's one of those crazy things, isn't it? I mean, if Tim spent a lot of time in the sun, maybe I could have understood it. But it was on the back of his leg. You know him—can you imagine him in Bermuda shorts? He's hardly ever worn shorts, even at the beach, and he's always the one who nagged us about wearing sunscreen. He doesn't drink, he doesn't smoke, he's careful about what he eats. But for whatever reason, he got melanoma. They cut out the area around the mole, and because of its size, they took out eighteen of his lymph nodes. Out of the eighteen, one was positive for melanoma. He started interferon—that's the standard treatment, and it lasts a full year—and we tried to stay optimistic. But then things started going wrong. First with the interferon, and then a few weeks after surgery, he got cellulitis near the groin incision."

When I frowned, she caught herself.

"Sorry. I'm just so used to talking to doctors these days. Cellulitis is a skin infection, and Tim's was pretty serious. He spent ten days in the intensive care unit for that. I thought I was going to lose him, but he's a fighter, you know? He got through it and continued with his treatment, but last month we found cancerous lesions near the site of his original melanoma. That, of course, meant another round of surgery, but even worse, it meant that the interferon probably wasn't working as well as it could. So he got a PET scan and an MRI, and sure enough, they found some cancerous cells in his lung."

She stared into her coffee cup. I felt speechless and drained, and for a long time, we were quiet.

"I'm sorry," I finally whispered.

My words brought her back. "I'm not going to give up," she said, her voice beginning to crack. "He's such a good man. He's sweet and he's patient, and I love him so much. It's just not fair. We haven't even been married for two years."

She looked at me and took a few deep breaths, trying to regain her composure.

"He needs to get out of here. Out of this hospital. All they can do here is interferon, and like I said, it's not working as well as it should. He needs to go someplace like MD Anderson or the Mayo Clinic or Johns Hopkins. There's cutting-edge research going on in those places. If interferon isn't doing the job like it should, there might be another drug they can add—they're always trying different combinations, even if they're experimental. They're doing biochemotherapy and clinical trials at other places. MD Anderson is even supposed to start testing a vaccine in November—not for prevention like most vaccines, but for treatment—and the preliminary data has shown good results. I want him to be part of that trial."

"So go," I urged.

She gave a short laugh. "It's not that easy."

"Why? It sounds pretty clear to me. Once he's out of here, you hop in the car and go."

"Our insurance won't pay for it," she said. "Not now, anyway. He's getting the appropriate standard of care—and believe it or not, the insurance company has been pretty responsive so far. They've paid for all the hospitalizations, all the interferon, and all the extras without hassle. They've even assigned me a personal caseworker, and believe me, she's sympathetic to our plight. But there's nothing she can do, since our doctor thinks it's best that we give the interferon a little more time. No insurance company in the world will pay for experimental treatments. And no insurer will agree to pay for treatments outside the standard of care, especially if they're in other states and are attempting new things on the off chance that they *might* work."

"Sue them if you have to."

"John, our insurer hasn't batted an eyelash at all the costs for intensive care and extra hospitalizations, and the reality is that Tim *is* getting the appropriate treatment. The thing is, I can't prove that Tim would get better in another place, receiving alternate treatments. I *think* it might help him, I *hope* it will help him, but no one knows for sure that it would." She shook her head. "Anyway, even if I did sue and the insurance company ended up paying for everything I demanded, that would take time . . . and that's what we don't have." She sighed. "My point is, it's not just a money problem, it's a time problem."

"How much are you talking about?"

"A lot. And if Tim ends up in the hospital with an infection and in the intensive care unit—like he has before—I can't even begin to guess. More than I could ever hope to pay, that's for sure."

"What are you going to do?"

"Get the money," she said. "I don't have a choice. And the community's been supportive. As soon as word about Tim got out, there was a segment on the local news and the newspaper did a story, and people all over town have promised to start collecting money. They set up a special bank account and everything. My parents helped. The place we worked at helped. Parents of some of the kids we worked with helped. I've heard that they've even got jars out in a lot of the businesses."

My mind flashed to the sight of the jar at the end of the bar in the pool hall, the day I arrived in Lenoir. I'd thrown in a couple of dollars, but suddenly it felt completely inadequate.

"Are you close?"

"I don't know." She shook her head, as if unwilling to think about it. "All this just started happening a little while ago, and since Tim had his treatment, I've been here and at the ranch. But we're talking about a lot of money." She pushed aside her cup of tea and offered a sad smile. "I don't even know why I'm telling you this. I mean, I can't guarantee that any of those other places can even help him. All I can tell you is that if we stay, I know he's not going to make it. He might not make it any-place else, either, but at least there's a chance... and right now, that's all I have."

She stopped, unable to continue, staring sightlessly at the stained tabletop.

"You want to know what's crazy?" she asked finally. "You're the only one I've told this to. Somehow, I know that you're the only one who can possibly understand what I'm going through, without having to feel like I have to be careful about what I say." She lifted her cup, then set it down again. "I know it's unfair considering your dad..."

"It's okay," I reassured her.

"Maybe," she said. "But it's selfish, too. You're trying to work through your own emotions about losing your dad, and here I am, saddling you with mine about something that might or might not happen." She turned to look out the cafeteria's window, but I knew she wasn't seeing the sloping lawn beyond.

"Hey," I said, reaching for her hand. "I meant it. I'm glad you told me, if only so you could get it off your chest."

In time, Savannah shrugged. "So that's us, huh? Two wounded warriors looking for support."

"That sounds about right."

Her eyes rose to meet mine. "Lucky us," she whispered.

Despite everything, I felt my heart skip a beat.

"Yeah," I echoed. "Lucky us."

We spent most of the afternoon in Tim's room. He was asleep when we got there, woke for a few minutes, then slept again. Alan kept vigil at the foot of his bed, ignoring my presence while he focused on his brother. Savannah alternately stayed beside Tim on the bed or sat in the chair next to mine. When she was close, we spoke of Tim's condition, of skin cancer in general, the specifics of possible alternative treatments. She'd spent weeks researching on the Internet and knew the details of every clinical trial in progress. Her voice never rose above a whisper; she didn't want Alan to overhear. By the time she was finished, I knew more about melanoma than I imagined possible.

It was a little after the dinner hour when Savannah finally rose. Tim had slept for most of the afternoon, and by the tender way she kissed him good-bye, I knew she believed he'd sleep most of the night as well. She kissed him a second time, then squeezed his hand and motioned toward the door. We crept out quietly.

"Let's head to the car," she said once we were out in the hallway.

"Are you coming back?"

"Tomorrow. If he does wake, I don't want to give him a reason to feel like he has to stay awake. He needs his rest."

"What about Alan?"

"He rode his bike," she said. "He rides here every morning and comes back late at night. He won't come with me, even if I ask. But he'll be okay. He's been doing the same thing for months now."

A few minutes later, we left the hospital parking lot and turned into the flow of evening traffic. The sky was turning a thickening gray, and heavy clouds were on the horizon, portending the same kinds of thunderstorms common to the coast. Savannah was lost in thought and said little. In her face, I saw reflected the same exhaustion that I felt. I couldn't imagine having to come back tomorrow, and the next day, and the day after that, all the while knowing there was a possibility he could get better somewhere else.

When we pulled in the drive, I looked over at Savannah and noticed a tear trickling slowly down her cheek. The sight of it nearly broke my heart, but when she saw me staring at her, she swiped at the tear, looking surprised at its appearance. I pulled the car to a stop beneath the willow tree, next to the battered truck. By then, the first few drops of rain were beginning to hit the windshield.

As the car idled in place, I wondered again whether this was good-bye. Before I could think of something to say, Savannah turned toward me. "Are you hungry?" she asked. "There's a ton of food in the fridge."

Something in her gaze warned me that I should decline, but I found myself nodding. "I would love something to eat," I said.

"I'm glad," she said, her voice soft. "I don't really want to be alone tonight."

We got out of the car as the rain began to fall harder. We made a dash for the front door, but by the time we reached the porch, I could feel the wetness soaking through the fabric of my clothes. Molly heard us, and as Savannah pushed open the door, the dog surged past me through the kitchen to what I assumed was the living room. As I watched the dog, I thought about my arrival the day before and how much had changed in the time we'd been apart. It was too much to process. Much the way I had while on patrol in Iraq, I steeled myself to focus only on the present yet remain alert to what might come next.

"We've got a bit of everything," she called out on her way to the kitchen. "That's how my mom's been handling all of this. Cooking. We have stew, chili, chicken pot pie, barbecued pork, lasagna . . ." She poked her head out of the refrigerator as I entered the kitchen. "Does anything sound appetizing?"

"It doesn't matter," I said. "Whatever you want."

At my answer, I saw a flash of disappointment on her face and knew instantly that she was tired of having to make decisions. I cleared my throat.

"Lasagna sounds good."

"Okay," she said. "I'll get some going right now. Are you super hungry or just hungry?"

I thought about it. "Hungry, I guess."

"Salad? I've got some black olives and tomatoes I could add. It's great with ranch dressing and croutons."

"That sounds terrific."

"Good," she said. "It won't take long."

I watched as Savannah pulled out a head of lettuce and tomato from the bottom drawer of the fridge. She rinsed them under the faucet, diced the tomato and the lettuce, and added both to a wooden bowl. Then she topped off the salad with olives and set it on the table. She scooped out generous portions of lasagna onto two plates and popped the first into the microwave. There was a steady quality to her movements, as if she found the simple task at hand reassuring.

"I don't know about you, but I could use a glass of wine." She pointed to a small rack on the countertop near the sink. "I've got a nice Pinot Noir."

"I'll try a glass," I said. "Do you need me to open it?"

"No, I've got it. My corkscrew is kind of temperamental."

She opened the wine and poured two glasses. Soon she was sitting across from me, our plates before us. The lasagna was steaming, and the aroma reminded me of how hungry I actually was. After taking a bite, I motioned toward it with my fork.

"Wow," I commented. "This is really good."

"It is, isn't it?" she agreed. Instead of taking a bite, however, she took a sip of wine. "It's Tim's favorite, too. After we got married, he was always pleading with my mom to make him a batch. She loves to cook, and it makes her happy to see people enjoying her food."

Across the table, I watched as she ran her finger around the rim of her glass. The red wine trapped the light like the facet of a ruby.

"If you want more, I've got plenty," she added. "Believe me, you'd be doing me a favor. Most of the time, the food just goes to waste. I know I should tell her to bring less, but she wouldn't take that well."

"It's hard for her," I said. "She knows you're hurting."

"I know." She took another drink of wine.

"You are going to eat, aren't you?" I gestured at her untouched plate.

"I'm not hungry," she said. "It's always like this when Tim's in the hospital . . . I heat something up, I look forward to eating, but as soon as it's in front of me, my stomach shuts down." She stared at her plate as if willing herself to try, then shook her head.

"Humor me," I urged. "Take a bite. You've got to eat."

"I'll be okay."

I paused, my fork halfway up. "Do it for me, then. I'm not used to people watching me eat. This feels weird."

"Fine." She picked up her fork, scooped a tiny wedge onto it, and took a bite. "Happy now?"

"Oh yeah," I snorted. "That's exactly what I meant. That makes me feel a whole lot more comfortable. For dessert, maybe we can split a couple of crumbs. Until then, though, just keep holding the fork and pretending."

She laughed. "I'm glad you're here," she said. "These days, you're the only one who would even think of talking to me like that."

"Like what? Honestly?"

"Yes," she said. "Believe it or not, that's exactly what I meant." She set down her fork and pushed her plate aside, ignoring my request. "You were always good like that."

"I remember thinking the same thing about you."

She tossed her napkin on the table. "Those were the days, huh?"

The way she was looking at me made the past come rushing back, and for a moment I relived every emotion, every hope and dream I'd ever had for us. She was once again the young woman I'd met on the beach with her life ahead of her, a life I wanted to make part of my own.

Then she ran a hand through her hair, causing the ring on her finger to catch the light. I lowered my eyes, focusing on my plate.

"Something like that."

I shoveled in a bite, trying and failing to erase those images. As soon as I swallowed, I stabbed at the lasagna again.

"What's wrong?" she asked. "Are you mad?"

"No," I lied.

"You're acting mad."

She was the same woman I remembered—except that she was married. I took a gulp of wine—one gulp, I noticed, was equivalent to all the sips she'd taken. I leaned back in my chair. "Why am I here, Savannah?"

"I don't know what you mean," she said.

"This," I said, motioning around the kitchen. "Asking me in for dinner, even though you won't eat. Bringing up the old days. What's going on?"

"Nothing's going on," she insisted.

"Then what is it? Why did you ask me in?"

Instead of answering the question, she rose and refilled her glass with wine. "Maybe I just needed someone to talk to," she whispered. "Like I said, I can't talk to my mom or dad; I can't even talk to Tim like this." She sounded almost defeated. "Everybody needs somebody to talk to."

She was right, and I knew it. It was the reason I'd come to Lenoir.

"I understand that," I said, closing my eyes. When I opened them again, I could feel Savannah evaluating me. "It's just that I'm not sure what to do with all this. The past. Us. You being married. Even what's happening to Tim. None of this makes much sense."

Her smile was full of chagrin. "And you think it makes sense to me?"

When I said nothing, she set aside her glass. "You want to know the truth?" she asked, not waiting for an answer. "I'm just trying to make it through the day with enough energy to face tomorrow." She closed her eyes as if the admission were painful, then opened them again. "I know how you still feel about me, and I'd love to tell you that I have some secret desire to know everything you've been through since I sent you that awful letter, but to be honest?" She hesitated. "I don't know if I really want to know. All I know is that when you showed up yesterday, I felt...okay. Not great, not good, but not bad, either. And that's the thing. For the last six months, all I've done is feel bad. I wake up every day nervous and tense and angry and frustrated and terrified that I'm going to lose the man I married. That's all I feel until the sun goes down," she went on. "Every single day, all day long, for the past six months. That's my life right now, but the hard part is that from here on in, I know it's only going to get worse. Now there's the added responsibility of trying to find some way to help my husband. Of trying to find a treatment that might help. Of trying to save his life."

She paused and looked closely at me, trying to gauge my reaction.

I knew there were words to comfort Savannah, but as usual, I didn't know what to say. All I knew was that she was still the woman I'd once fallen in love with, the woman I still loved but could never have.

"I'm sorry," she said eventually, sounding spent. "I don't mean to put you on the spot." She gave a fragile smile. "I just wanted you to know that I'm glad you're here."

I focused on the wood grain of the table, trying to keep my feelings on a tight leash. "Good," I said.

She wandered toward the table. She added some wine to my glass, though I'd yet to drink more than that one gulp. "I pour out my heart and all you do is say, 'Good'?"

"What do you want me to say?"

Savannah turned away and headed toward the door of the kitchen. "You could have said that you're glad you came, too," she said in a barely audible voice.

With that, she was gone. I didn't hear the front door open, so I surmised that she had retreated to the living room.

Her comment bothered me, but I wasn't about to follow her.

Things had changed between us, and there was no way they could be what they once were. I forked lasagna into my mouth with stubborn defiance, wondering what she wanted from me. She was the one who'd sent the letter, she was the one who'd ended it. She was the one who got married. Were we supposed to pretend that none of those things had happened?

I finished eating and brought both plates to the sink and rinsed them. Through the rain-splattered window, I saw my car and knew I should simply leave without looking back. It would be easier that way for both of us. But when I reached into my pockets for the keys, I froze. Over the patter of the rain on the roof, I heard a sound from the living room, a sound that defused my anger and confusion. Savannah, I realized, was crying.

I tried to ignore the sound, but I couldn't. Taking my wine, I crossed into the living room.

Savannah sat on the couch, cupping the glass of wine in her hands. She looked up as I entered.

Outside, the wind had begun to pick up, and the rain started coming down even harder. Beyond the living room glass, lightning flashed, followed by the steady rumble of thunder, long and low.

Taking a seat beside her, I put my glass on the end table and looked around the room. Atop the fireplace mantel stood photographs of Savannah and Tim on their wedding day: one where they were cutting the cake and another taken in the church. She was beaming, and I found myself wishing that I were the one beside her in the picture.

"Sorry," she said. "I know I shouldn't be crying, but I can't help it."

"It's understandable," I murmured. "You've got a lot going on."

In the silence, I listened to the sheets of rain batter the windowpanes.

"It's quite a storm," I observed, grasping for words that would fill the taut silence.

"Yeah," she said, barely listening.

"Do you think Alan's going to be okay?"

She tapped her fingers against the glass. "He won't leave until it stops raining. He doesn't like lightning. But it shouldn't last long. The wind will push the storm toward the coast. At least, that's the way it's been lately." She hesitated. "Do you remember that storm we sat out? When I took you to the house we were building?"

"Of course."

"I still think about that night. That was the first time I told you that I loved you. I was remembering that night just the other day. I was sitting here just like I am now. Tim was in the hospital, Alan was with him, and while I watched the rain, it all came back. The memory was so vivid, it felt like it had just happened. And then the rain stopped and I knew it was time to feed the horses. I was back in my regular life again, and all at once, it felt like I had just imagined the whole thing. Like it happened to someone else, someone I don't even know anymore."

She leaned toward me. "What do you remember the most?" she asked.

"All of it," I said.

She looked at me beneath her lashes. "Nothing stands out?"

The storm outside made the room feel dark and intimate, and I felt a shiver of guilty anticipation about where all this might be leading. I wanted her as much as I'd ever wanted anyone, but in the back of my mind, I knew Savannah wasn't mine anymore. I could feel Tim's presence all around me, and I knew she wasn't really herself.

I took a sip of wine, then set the glass back on the table.

"No." I kept my voice steady. "Nothing stands out. But that's why you always wanted me to look at the moon, right? So that I could remember all of it?"

What I didn't say was that I still went out to stare at the moon, and despite the guilt I was feeling about being here, I wondered whether she did, too.

"You want to know what I remember most?" she asked.

"When I broke Tim's nose?"

"No." She laughed, then turned serious. "I remember the times we went to church. Do you realize that they're still the only times I ever saw you in a tie? You should get dressed up more often. You looked good." She seemed to reflect on that before turning her eyes to me again.

"Are you seeing anyone?" she asked.

"No."

She nodded. "I didn't think so. I figured you would have mentioned it."

She turned toward the window. In the distance, I could see one of the horses galloping in the rain.

"I'm going to have to feed them in a little while. I'm sure they're wondering where I am already."

"They'll be okay," I assured her.

"Easy for you to say. Trust me—they can get as cranky as people when they're hungry."

"It must be hard handling all this on your own."

"It is. But what choice do I have? At least our employer's been understanding. Tim's on a leave of absence, and whenever he's

in the hospital, they let me take however much time I need."
Then, in a teasing tone, she added, "Just like the army, right?"

"Oh yeah. It's exactly the same."

She giggled, then became sober again. "How was it in Iraq?"

I was about to make my usual crack about the sand, but instead I said, "It's hard to describe."

Savannah waited, and I reached for my glass of wine, stalling. Even with her, I wasn't sure I wanted to go into it. But something was happening between us, something I wanted and yet didn't want. I forced myself to look at Savannah's ring and imagine the betrayal she would no doubt feel later. I closed my eyes and started with the night of the invasion.

I don't know how long I talked, but it was long enough for the rain to have ended. With the sun still drifting in its slow descent, the horizon glowed the colors of a rainbow. Savannah refilled her glass. By the time I finished, I was entirely spent and knew I'd never speak of it again.

Savannah had remained quiet as I spoke, asking only the occasional question to let me know she was listening to everything I said.

"It's different from what I imagined," she remarked.

"Yeah?" I asked.

"When you scan the headlines or read the stories, most of the time, names of soldiers and cities in Iraq are just words. But to you, it's personal . . . it's real. Maybe too real."

I had nothing left to add, and I felt her hand reach for mine. Her touch made something leap inside me. "I wish you'd never had to go through all that."

I squeezed her hand and felt her respond in kind. When she finally let go, the sensation of her touch lingered, and like an old habit rediscovered, I watched her tuck a strand of hair behind her ear. The sight made me ache.

"It's strange how fate works," she said, her voice almost a whisper. "Did you ever imagine that your life would turn out like it did?"

"No," I said.

"I didn't either," she said. "When you first went back to Germany, I just knew that you and I would be married one day. I was more sure of that than anything in my life."

I stared into my glass as she went on.

"And then, on your second leave, I was even more sure. Especially after we made love."

"Don't . . ." I shook my head. "Let's not go there."

"Why?" she asked. "Do you regret it?"

"No." I couldn't bear to look at her. "Of course not. But you're married now."

"But it happened," she said. "Do you want me to just forget it?"

"I don't know," I said. "Maybe."

"I can't," she said, sounding surprised and hurt. "That was my first time. I'll never forget it, and in its own way, it will always be special to me. What happened between us was beautiful."

I didn't trust myself to respond, and after a moment, she seemed to collect herself. Leaning forward, she asked, "When you found out that I had married Tim, what did you think?"

I waited to answer, wanting to choose my words with care. "My first thought was that in a way, it made sense. He's been in love with you for years. I knew that from the moment I met him." I ran a hand over my face. "After that, I felt . . . conflicted. I was glad that you picked someone like him, because he's a nice guy and you two have a lot in common, but then I was just . . .

sad. We didn't have that long to go. I would have been out of the army for almost two years now."

She pressed her lips together. "I'm sorry," she murmured.

"I am, too." I tried to smile. "If you want my honest opinion, I think you should have waited for me."

She laughed uncertainly, and I was surprised by the look of longing on her face. She reached for her glass of wine.

"I've been thinking about that, too. Where we would have been, where we'd be living, what we'd be doing in our lives. Especially lately. Last night after you left, that's all I could think about. I know how terrible that makes me sound, but these past couple of years, I've been trying to convince myself that even if our love was real, it never would have lasted." Her expression was forlorn. "You really would have married me, wouldn't you?"

"In a heartbeat. And I still would if I could."

The past suddenly seemed to loom over us, overwhelming in its intensity.

"It was real, wasn't it?" Her voice had a tremor. "You and me?"

The gray light of dusk was reflected in her eyes as she waited for my answer. In the moments that elapsed, I felt the weight of Tim's prognosis hanging over both of us. My racing thoughts were morbid and wrong, but they were there nonetheless. I hated myself for even thinking about life after Tim, willing the thought away.

Yet I couldn't. I wanted to take Savannah in my arms, to hold her, to recapture everything we had lost in our years apart. Instinctively, I began to lean toward her.

Savannah knew what was coming but didn't pull away. Not at first. As my lips neared hers, however, she turned quickly and the wine she was holding splashed onto both of us.

She jumped to her feet, setting her glass on the table and pulling her blouse away from her skin.

"I'm sorry," I said.

"It's okay," she said. "I'm going to change, though. I've got to get this soaking. It's one of my favorites."

"Okay," I said.

I watched as she left the living room and went down the hall. She turned into the bedroom on the right, and when she was gone, I cursed. I shook my head at my own stupidity, then noticed the wine on my shirt. I stood and started down the hall, looking for the bathroom.

Turning a random doorknob, I came face-to-face with myself in the bathroom mirror. In the reflected background, I could see Savannah through the cracked door of the bedroom across the hall. She was topless with her back to me, and though I tried, I couldn't turn away.

She must have sensed me staring at her, for she looked over her shoulder toward me. I thought she would suddenly close the door or cover herself, but she didn't. Instead, she caught my eyes and held them, willing me to continue watching her. And then, slowly, she turned around.

We stood there facing each other through the reflection in the mirror, with only the narrow hallway separating us. Her lips were parted slightly, and she lifted her chin a bit; I knew that if I lived to be a thousand, I would never forget how exquisite she looked at that moment. I wanted to cross the hallway and go to her, knowing that she wanted me as much as I wanted her. But I stayed where I was, frozen by the thought that she would one day hate me for what we both so obviously wanted.

And Savannah, who knew me better than anyone else, dropped her eyes as if suddenly coming to the same understanding. She turned back around just as the front door crashed open and I heard a loud wail pierce the darkness.

Alan...

I turned and rushed to the living room; Alan had already vanished into the kitchen, and I could hear the cupboard doors being opened and slammed while he continued to wail, almost as if he were dying. I stopped, not knowing what to do. A moment later, Savannah rushed past me, tugging her shirt back into place.

"Alan! I'm coming!" she shouted, her voice frantic. "It's going to be okay!"

Alan continued to wail, and the cupboards continued to slam shut.

"Do you need help?" I called to her.

"No." She gave a hard shake of her head. "Let me handle this. It happens sometimes when he gets home from the hospital."

As she rushed into the kitchen, I could barely hear her beginning to talk to him. Her voice was almost lost in the clamor, but I heard the steadiness in it, and moving off to the side, I could see her standing next to him, trying to calm him. It didn't seem to have any effect, and I felt the urge to help, but Savannah remained calm. She continued to talk steadily to him, then placed a hand on top of his, following along with the slamming.

Finally, after what seemed like forever, the slamming began to slow and become more rhythmic; from there it slowly faded away. Alan's cries followed the same pattern. Savannah's voice was softer now, and I could no longer hear distinct words.

I sat on the couch. A few minutes later, I rose and went to the window. It was dark; the clouds had passed, and above the mountains was a swirl of stars. Wondering what was going on, I moved to a spot in the living room that afforded a glimpse into the kitchen.

Savannah and Alan were sitting on the kitchen floor. Her back was leaning against the cupboards, and Alan rested his head on her chest as she ran a tender hand through his hair. He was blinking rapidly, as if wired to always be in motion. Savannah's eyes gleamed with tears, but I could see her look of concentration, and I knew she was determined not to let him know how much she was hurting.

"I love him," I heard Alan say. Gone was the deep voice from the hospital; this was the aching plea of a frightened little boy.

"I know, sweetie. I love him, too. I love him so much. I know you're scared, and I'm scared, too."

I could hear from her tone how much she meant it.

"I love him," Alan repeated.

"He'll be out of the hospital in a couple of days. The doctors are doing everything they can."

"I love him."

She kissed the top of his head. "He loves you, too, Alan. And so do I. And I know he's looking forward to riding the horses with you again. He told me that. And he's so proud of you. He tells me all the time what a good job you do around here."

"I'm scared."

"I am, too, sweetie. But the doctors are doing everything they can."

"I love him."

"I know. I love him, too. More than you can ever imagine."

I continued to watch them, knowing suddenly that I didn't belong here. In all the time I stood there, Savannah never looked up, and I felt haunted by all that we had lost.

I patted my pocket, pulled out my keys, and turned to leave, feeling tears burning at the back of my eyes. I opened the door, and despite the loud squeak, I knew that Savannah wouldn't hear anything.

I stumbled down the steps, wondering if I'd ever been so tired in my life. And later, as I drove to my motel and listened to the car idle as I waited for the stoplights to change, I knew that passersby would see a man crying, a man whose tears felt as if they would never stop.

I spent the rest of the evening alone in my motel room. Outside, I could hear strangers passing by my door, wheeled luggage rolling behind them. When cars pulled into the lot, my room would be illuminated momentarily by headlights casting ghostly images against the walls. People on the go, people moving forward in life. As I lay on the bed, I was filled with envy and wondered whether I would ever be able to say the same.

I didn't bother trying to sleep. I thought about Tim, but oddly, instead of the emaciated figure I'd seen in the hospital room, I saw only the young man I'd met at the beach, the clean-cut student with an easy smile for everyone. I thought about my dad and wondered what his final weeks were like. I tried to imagine the staff listening to him as he talked about coins and prayed that the director had been right when he told me that my dad had passed away peacefully in his sleep. I thought about Alan and the foreign world his mind inhabited. But mostly I thought about Savannah. I replayed the day we'd spent, and I dwelled endlessly on the past, trying to escape an emptiness that wouldn't go away.

In the morning, I watched the sun come up, a golden marble emerging from the earth. I showered and loaded the few belongings I'd brought into the room back in the car. At the diner across the street, I ordered breakfast, but when the plate arrived steaming before me, I pushed it aside and nursed a cup of coffee, wondering if Savannah was already up, feeding the horses.

It was nine in the morning when I showed up at the hospital. I signed in and rode the elevator to the third floor; I walked the same corridor I'd walked the day before. Tim's door was half-way open, and I could hear the television.

He saw me and smiled in surprise. "Hey, John," he said, turning off the television. "Come in. I was just killing time."

As I took a seat in the same chair I'd sat in the day before, I noticed that his color was better. He struggled to sit up higher in the bed before focusing on me again.

"What brings you here so early?"

"I'm getting ready to head out," I said. "I've got to catch a flight tomorrow back to Germany. You know how it is."

"Yeah, I know." He nodded. "Hopefully I'll be getting out later today. I had a pretty good night last night."

"Good," I said. "I'm glad to hear it."

I studied him, looking for any sign of suspicion in his gaze, any inkling of what had nearly happened the night before, but I saw nothing.

"Why are you really here, John?" he asked.

"I'm not sure," I confessed. "I just felt like I needed to see you. And that maybe you wanted to see me, too."

He nodded and turned toward the window; from his room, there was nothing to see except a large air-conditioning unit. "You want to know what the worst thing about all this is?" He didn't wait for an answer. "I worry about Alan," he said. "I know what's happening to me. I know the odds aren't good and that there's a good chance I won't make it. I can accept that. Like I told you yesterday, I've still got my faith, and I know—or at least I hope—there's something better waiting for me. And Savannah...I know that if something does happen to me, she'll be crushed. But you know what I learned when I lost my parents?"

"That life isn't fair?"

"Yeah, that, of course. But I also learned that it's possible to go on, no matter how impossible it seems, and that in time, the grief...lessens. It may not ever go away completely, but after a while it's not overwhelming. That's what's going to happen to Savannah. She's young and she's strong, and she'll be able to move on. But Alan...I don't know what's going to happen to him. Who's going to take care of him? Where's he going to live?"

"Savannah will take care of him."

"I know she would. But is that fair to her? To expect her to shoulder that responsibility?"

"It won't matter whether it's fair. She won't let anything happen to him."

"How? She's going to have to work—who watches Alan then? Remember, he's still young. He's only nineteen. Do I expect her to take care of him for the next fifty years? For me, it was simple. He's my brother. But Savannah..." He shook his head. "She's young and beautiful. Is it fair to expect that she'll never get married again?"

"What are you talking about?"

"Would her new husband be willing to take care of Alan?"

When I said nothing to that, he raised his eyebrows. "Would you?" he added.

I opened my mouth to answer, but no words came out. His expression softened.

"That's what I think about when I'm lying here. When I'm

not sick, I mean. Actually, I think about a lot of things. Including you."

"Me?"

"You still love her, don't you?"

I kept my expression steady, but he read me anyway. "It's okay," he said. "I already know. I've always known." He looked almost wistful. "I can still remember Savannah's face the first time she talked about you. I'd never seen her like that. I was happy for her because there was something about you that I trusted right away. That whole first year you were gone, she missed you so much. It was like her heart was breaking a little bit every single day. You were all she could think about. And then she found out you weren't coming home and we ended up in Lenoir and my parents died and..." He didn't finish. "You always knew I was in love with her, too, didn't you?"

I nodded.

"I thought so." He cleared his throat. "I've loved her since I was twelve years old. And gradually, she fell in love with me, too."

"Why are you telling me this?"

"Because," he said, "it wasn't the same. I know she loves me, but she's never loved me the way she loved you. She never had that burning passion for me, but we were making a good life together. She was so happy when we started the ranch...and it just made me feel so good that I could do something like that for her. Then I got sick, but she's always here, caring for me the same way I'd care for her if it was happening to her." He stopped then, struggling to find the right words, and I could see the anguish in his expression.

"Yesterday, when you came in, I saw the way she was looking at you, and I knew that she still loved you. More than that,

I know she always will. It breaks my heart, but you know what? I'm still in love with her, and to me that means that I want nothing more than for her to be happy in life. I want that more than anything. It's all I've ever wanted for her."

My throat was so dry that I could barely speak. "What are you saying?"

"I'm saying don't forget Savannah if anything happens to me. And promise that you'll always treasure her the same way I do."

"Tim..."

"Don't say anything, John." He raised a hand, either to stop me or in farewell. "Just remember what I said, okay?"

When he turned away, I knew our conversation was over.

I stood then and walked quietly out of the room, shutting the door behind me.

Outside the hospital, I squinted in the harsh morning sunlight. I could hear birds chirping in the trees, but even though I searched for them, they remained hidden from me.

The parking lot was half full. Here and there, I could see people walking to the entrance or back to their cars. All looked as weary as I felt, as if the optimism they showed to loved ones in the hospital vanished the moment they were alone. I knew that miracles were always possible no matter how sick a person might be, and that women in the maternity ward were feeling joy as they held their newborns in their arms, but I sensed that, like me, most of the hospital visitors were barely holding it together.

I sat on the bench out front, wondering why I'd come and wishing that I hadn't. I replayed my conversation with Tim over and over, and the image of his anguish made me close my eyes. For the first time in years, my love for Savannah felt some-how... *wrong*. Love should bring joy, it should grant a person peace, but here and now, it was bringing only pain. To Tim, to Savannah, even to me. I hadn't come to tempt Savannah or ruin her marriage... or had I? I wasn't sure I was quite as noble as I thought I was, and the realization left me feeling as empty as a rusted paint can.

I removed the photograph of Savannah from my wallet. It was creased and worn. As I stared at her face, I found myself wondering what the coming year would bring. I didn't know whether Tim would live or die, and I didn't want to think about it. I knew that no matter what happened, the relationship between Savannah and me would never be what it once was. We'd met at a carefree time, a moment full of promise; in its place now were the harsh lessons of the real world.

I rubbed my temples, struck by the thought that Tim knew what had almost happened between Savannah and me last night, that maybe he'd even expected it. His words made that clear, as did his request that I promise to love her with the devo-tion he felt. I knew exactly what he was suggesting that I do if he died, but somehow his permission made me feel even worse.

I finally stood and began the slow walk to my car. I wasn't sure where I wanted to go, other than that I needed to get as far away from the hospital as I could. I needed to leave Lenoir, if only to give myself a chance to think. I dug my hands into my pockets and fished out my keys.

It was only when I got close to my car that I realized Savan-nah's truck was parked next to mine. Savannah was sitting in the front seat, and when she saw me coming, she opened the door and got out. She waited for me, smoothing her blouse as I drew near.

I stopped a few feet away.

"John," she said, "you left without saying good-bye last night."

"I know."

She nodded slightly. We both understood the reason.

"How did you know I was here?"

"I didn't," she said. "I went by the motel and they told me you'd checked out. When I came here, I saw your car and decided to wait for you. Did you see Tim?"

"Yeah. He's doing better. He thinks he'll be getting out of the hospital later today."

"That's good news," she said. She motioned to my car. "Are you leaving town?"

"Gotta get back. My leave's up."

She crossed her arms. "Were you going to come say good-bye?"

"I don't know," I admitted. "I hadn't thought that far ahead."

I saw a flash of hurt and disappointment on her face. "What did you and Tim talk about?"

I looked over my shoulder at the hospital, then back at her. "You should probably ask him that question."

Her mouth formed a tight line, and her body seemed to stiffen. "So this is good-bye?"

I heard a car honk on the road out front and saw a number of cars suddenly slow. The driver of a red Toyota veered into the other lane, doing his best to get around the traffic. As I watched, I knew I was stalling and that she deserved an answer.

"Yes," I said, slowly turning back to her. "I think it is."

Her knuckles stood out white against her arms. "Can I write to you?"

I forced myself not to look away, wishing again that the cards had fallen differently for us. "I'm not so sure that's a good idea."

"I don't understand."

"Yes, you do," I said. "You're married to Tim, not me." I let that sink in while gathering my strength for what I wanted to say next. "He's a good man, Savannah. A better man than me, that's for sure, and I'm glad you married him. As much as I love you, I'm not willing to break up a marriage for it. And deep down, I don't think you are, either. Even if you love me, you love him, too. It took me a little while to realize that, but I'm sure of it."

Left unspoken was Tim's uncertain future, and I could see her eyes beginning to fill with tears.

"Will we ever see each other again?"

"I don't know." The words burned in my throat. "But I'm hoping we don't."

"How can you say that?" she asked, her voice beginning to crack.

"Because it means that Tim's going to be okay. And I have a feeling that it's all going to turn out the way it should."

"You can't say that! You can't promise that!"

"No," I said, "I can't."

"Then why does it have to end now? Like this?"

A tear spilled down her face, and despite the fact that I knew I should simply walk away, I took a step toward her. When I was close, I gently wiped it away. In her eyes I could see fear and sadness, anger and betrayal. But most of all, I saw them pleading with me to change my mind.

I swallowed hard.

"You're married to Tim, and your husband needs you. All of you. There's no room for me, and we both know there shouldn't be."

As more tears started flowing down her face, I felt my own

eyes fill up. I leaned in and kissed Savannah gently on the lips, then took her in my arms and held her tight.

"I love you, Savannah, and I always will," I breathed. "You're the best thing that's ever happened to me. You were my best friend and my lover, and I don't regret a single moment of it. You made me feel alive again, and most of all, you gave me my father. I'll never forget you for that. You're always going to be the very best part of me. I'm sorry it has to be this way, but I have to leave, and you have to see your husband."

As I spoke, I could feel her shaking with sobs, and I continued to hold her for a long time afterward. When we finally separated, I knew that it would be the last time I ever held her.

I backed away, my eyes holding Savannah's.

"I love you, too, John," she said.

"Good-bye." I raised a hand.

And with that, she wiped her face and began walking toward the hospital.

Saying good-bye was the hardest thing I ever had to do. Part of me wanted to turn the car around and race back to the hospital, to tell her that I would always be there for her, to confide in her the things Tim had said to me. But I didn't.

On the way out of town, I stopped at a small convenience store. I needed gas and filled the tank; inside, I bought a bottle of water. As I approached the counter, I saw a jar that the owner had set out to collect money for Tim, and I stared at it. It was filled with change and dollar bills; on the label, it listed the name of an account at a local bank. I asked for a few dollars in quarters, and the man behind the counter obliged.

I was numb as I made my way back to the car. I opened the door and began fishing through the documents that the lawyer had given me, looking also for a pencil. I found what I needed, then went to the pay phone. It was located near the road, with cars roaring past. I dialed information and had to press the receiver hard against my ear to hear the computerized voice give me the number I'd requested. I scrawled it on the documents, then hung up. I dropped some coins into the slot, dialed the long-distance number, and heard another computer-generated voice request even more money. I dropped in a few more coins. Soon I could hear the phone ringing.

When it was answered, I told the man who I was and asked if he remembered me.

"Of course I do, John. How are you?"

"Fine, thanks. My dad passed away."

There was a short pause. "I'm sorry to hear that," he said. "You doing okay?"

"I don't know," I said.

"Is there anything I can do?"

I closed my eyes, thinking of Savannah and Tim and hoping somehow that my dad would forgive me for what I was about to do. "Yes," I said to the coin dealer, "actually there is. I want to sell my dad's coin collection, and I need the money as quickly as you can get it to me."

# Epilogue

What does true love really mean?

I think about the question again as I sit on the hillside and watch Savannah moving among the horses. For a moment, I flash to the night I showed up at the ranch to find her . . . but that visit, a year ago now, feels more and more like a dream to me.

I sold the coins for less than they were worth, and piece by piece, I knew that the remains of my dad's collection would be distributed to people who would never care as much about them as he did. In the end, I saved only the buffalo head nickel, for I simply couldn't bear to give it up. Aside from the photo, it's all I have left of my dad, and I always carry it with me. It's a talisman of sorts, one that carries with it all my memories of my dad; every now and then, I remove it from my pocket and stare at it. I'll run my fingers over the plastic case that holds the coin, and all at once, I can see my dad reading the *Greysheet* in his office or smell the bacon as it sizzles in the kitchen. I find that it makes me smile, and for a moment, I feel that I'm no longer alone.

But I am, and part of me knows that I always will be. I hold this thought as I search out the figures of Savannah and Tim in the distance, holding hands as they walk to the house; I see them touch in a way that speaks of their genuine affection for each other. They look good as a couple, I have to admit. When Tim calls to Alan, he joins them, and the three of them head inside. I wonder for a moment what they're talking about as they enter, for I'm curious about the little details of their lives, but I'm fully aware that it's none of my business. I have heard, however, that Tim is no longer receiving treatment and that most people in town expect him to recover.

I learned this through the local lawyer I hired on my last visit to Lenoir. I'd entered his office with a cashier's check and asked him to deposit it in the account that had been set up for Tim's treatment. I knew all about attorney-client privilege, and I knew he would say nothing to anyone in town. It was important not to let Savannah know what I'd done. In any marriage, there's room for only two people.

I did, however, ask the lawyer to keep me informed, and during the past year, I spoke with him several times from Germany. He told me that when he contacted Savannah to tell her that a client wanted to make an anonymous donation—but wanted to be kept informed of Tim's progress—she broke down and cried when he told her the amount. He told me that within a week, she'd brought Tim to MD Anderson and learned that Tim was an ideal candidate for the vaccine trial MD Anderson planned to start in November. He told me that prior to joining the clinical trial, Tim was treated with biochemotherapy and adjuvant therapy and that the doctors were hopeful the treatments would kill the cancerous cells massing in his lungs. A couple of months ago, the lawyer called to tell me that the treatment had been more successful than even the doctors hoped and that now Tim was technically in remission.

It didn't guarantee that he would live to an old age, but it did guarantee him a fighting chance, and that's all I wanted for both of them. I wanted them to be happy. I wanted her to be happy. And from what I had witnessed today, they were. I'd come because I needed to know that I'd made the right choice in selling the coins for Tim's treatment, that I'd done the right thing in never contacting her again, and from where I sat, I knew that I had.

I sold the collection because I finally understood what true love really meant. Tim had told me—and shown me—that love meant that you care for another person's happiness more than your own, no matter how painful the choices you face might be. I'd left Tim's hospital room knowing that he'd been right. But doing the right thing wasn't easy. These days, I lead my life feeling that something is missing that I somehow need to make my life complete. I know that my feeling about Savannah will never change, and I know I will always wonder about the choice I made.

And sometimes, despite myself, I wonder if Savannah feels the same way. Which of course explains the other reason I came to Lenoir.

I stare at the ranch as evening settles in. It's the first night of the full moon, and for me, the memories will come. They always do.

I hold my breath as the moon begins its slow rise over the mountain, its milky glow edging just over the horizon. The trees turn liquid silver, and though I want to return to those bittersweet memories, I turn away and look at the ranch again.

For a long time, I wait in vain. The moon continues its slow arc across the sky, and one by one, the lights in the house wink out. I find myself focusing anxiously on the front door, hoping for the impossible. I know that she won't appear, but I still can't force myself to leave. I breathe in slowly, as if hoping to draw her out.

And when I see her finally emerge from the house, I feel a strange tingling in my spine, one I've never experienced before. She pauses on the steps, and I watch as she turns and seems to stare in my direction. I freeze for no reason—I know she can't possibly see me. From my perch, I watch as Savannah closes the door quietly behind her. She slowly descends the steps and wanders to the center of the yard.

She pauses then and crosses her arms, glancing over her shoulder to make sure no one has followed her. Finally, she seems to relax. And then I feel as if I'm witnessing a miracle, as ever so slowly she raises her face toward the moon. I watch her drink in the sight, sensing the flood of memories she's unleashed and wanting nothing more than to let her know I'm here. But instead I stay where I am and stare up at the moon as well. And for the briefest instant, it almost feels like we're together again.

# Questions and Explanations for Chapter 19 through the Epilogue

$T$he ten questions on chapter 19 through the epilogue focus on grammar and usage, vocabulary, literary terms, comprehension, style, and characterization. Some of the questions combine two or more of these areas, requiring you to synthesize your knowledge, make inferences, and interpret the text. The questions are designed to determine both your current level of understanding of the novel and your ability to answer higher-level questions.

**The following sentence tests correctness and effective expression. Part of the following sentence is underlined; beneath the sentence are four ways of phrasing the underlined material. Select the option that produces the best sentence. If you think the original phrasing produces a better sentence than any of the alternatives, select choice A.**

1. John observes Savannah looking up <u>at the full moon,
   that is evidence suggesting</u> that she is still in love with
   him.

   A. at the full moon, that is evidence suggesting
   B. at the full moon; evidence suggesting
   C. at the full moon; which is evidence suggesting
   D. at the full moon; that evidence suggests

The original wording, choice A, is an example of a comma
splice. A comma splice is when a comma is used to connect
two main clauses without using a coordinating conjunction. A
comma splice is also one kind of a run-on sentence—for example, "John likes *The Lord of the Rings*, Jane prefers *Twilight*."
Each clause in this example is a complete thought, so connecting them with only a comma is incorrect. The error can be
corrected in two different ways: by using a comma and a coordinating conjunction such as *but* to create a *compound sentence*,
one with two or more main clauses ("John likes *The Lord of the
Rings*, but Jane prefers *Twilight*"), or by using a comma and a
subordinating conjunction to create a *complex sentence*, a sentence with one main clause and at least one dependent clause
("John likes *The Lord of the Rings*, although Jane prefers *Twilight*"). Stylistically, a complex sentence is usually preferable to
a compound sentence.

Choices B, C, and D attempt to eliminate the comma splice
by using a semicolon to create a compound sentence. In order
for either of these choices to be correct, everything to the right
of the semicolon must be a complete sentence. Select the sentence that correctly joins two independent clauses (complete
sentences) with a semicolon.

**Question 2 tests your vocabulary. Choose the word that, when inserted in the sentence, best fits the meaning of the sentence as a whole.**

2. After John admits that he didn't sleep well, Savannah flashes him a _____ smile and tells him that they are leaving.

    A. belligerent

    B. dubious

    C. wry

    D. zealous

This question tests both your comprehension and your vocabulary. *Belligerent*, choice A, means quarrelsome. *Dubious*, choice B, means filled with doubt. *Wry*, choice C, means mischievous. And *zealous*, choice D, means enthusiastic.

**Question 3 checks your understanding of literary terms.**

3. As John prepares to leave Savannah's ranch, he tells the reader, "I knew with certainty that I was still in love with her. Despite the letter, despite her husband. Despite the fact that we could never be together now." What literary device is used to emphasize John's realization?

    A. alliteration

    B. anaphora

    C. personification

    D. polysyndeton

*Alliteration,* choice A, is the repetition of a word's initial sound—for example, "Becky bought Bill a bad bugle." *Anaphora,* choice B, is the repetition of a word or group of words at the beginning of successive clauses or lines. An example of this might be, "I want you to know the word *anaphora.* I want you to recognize the effect of anaphora in a passage. I want you to attempt to use anaphora in your own writing." *Personification,* choice C, is giving a nonhuman thing a human characteristic, such as in "Opportunity knocked on the door." *Polysyndeton,* choice D, is the use of a number of conjunctions (*and, but, or, for, nor, so, yet*) in close succession, when one or more of them could be eliminated—for example, "lions *and* tigers *and* bears" and "neither snow *nor* rain *nor* heat *nor* gloom of night."

**Question 4 asks you to make an inference regarding characterization.**

4. Why doesn't Savannah immediately tell John where Tim is?

   A. She is embarrassed.

   B. She is teasing John.

   C. She doesn't want to upset John.

   D. She finds it too difficult to talk about.

Even though Savannah asks John to visit the next morning, she does not immediately answer his question as to Tim's location. If it is because the answer makes her uncomfortable or self-conscious, select choice A. If not telling John is a type of playful teasing, select choice B. If Savannah is concerned that the information will disturb John, select choice C. If talking about her husband's illness with her former boyfriend is something that is not easy for Savannah to do, select choice D.

**Question 5 asks you to analyze the impact of specific details on meaning.**

5. Before she visits Tim in the hospital, John notices that Savannah "drew a long breath before entering the room." Why does she do that?

   A. to present a positive front for Tim

   B. to hide her feelings from John

   C. to disguise the fact that she is hungover

   D. to pretend that she still loves her husband

If Savannah realizes that she needs to be outwardly strong for her husband's sake, select choice A. If Savannah is trying to hide the truth from John, select choice B. If she drank too much wine last night with John but doesn't want Tim to know that, select choice C. And if her deep breath enables her to gather the strength to make believe that she is still in love with Tim, select choice D.

**Question 6 checks your understanding of literary terms.**

6. In the morning, John watches "the sun come up, a golden marble emerging from the earth." What literary device is used in this description?

A. allusion

B. hyperbole

C. metaphor

D. simile

An *allusion*, choice A, is an indirect reference. Some of the most common types of allusions are historical (when someone meets his Waterloo, it's a reference to Napoleon); biblical (such as John Coffey in *The Green Mile* being a Christ figure); mythological (a reference to a Greek or Roman myth, such as a character being said to have the Midas touch); and literary (a reference to a character in a work of literature, such as a couple being compared to Romeo and Juliet). *Hyperbole*, choice B, is using overexaggeration to make a point. An example would be, "Everyone who reads this learning guide will know what *hyperbole* is because hyperbole will be explained a bazillion times." A *metaphor*, choice C, is a comparison between two unlike things without using a connective word—for example, "Michael Phelps was a flying fish in the pool." And a *simile*, choice D, is a comparison between two unlike things using a connective word, such as *like*, *as*, or *than*—for example, "She looked as fresh as the morning snow."

**Question 7 asks you to analyze the development of a central idea.**

7. Tim makes an important thematic statement that "it's possible to go on, no matter how impossible it seems, and that in time, the grief...lessens." Identify all the characters to whom this statement applies.

A. John

B. Savannah

C. Tim

D. all of the above

The question indicates that more than one answer may be correct. A central idea, or theme, is one of the most important aspects of literary analysis. Select any character who has to move on after experiencing grief.

**Question 8 checks your understanding of literary terms.**

8. After talking to Tim in the hospital, John sits alone, "feeling as empty as a rusted paint can." What literary term illustrates what John is experiencing?

A. allusion

B. metaphor

C. personification

D. simile

Knowing about figures of speech will help you answer this question. An *allusion*, choice A, is an indirect reference. Some of the most common types of allusions are historical (when someone meets his Waterloo, it's a reference to Napoleon); biblical (such as John Coffey in *The Green Mile* being a Christ figure); mythological (a reference to a Greek or Roman myth, such as a character being said to have the Midas touch); and literary (a reference to a character in a work of literature, such as a couple being compared to Romeo and Juliet). A *metaphor*, choice B, is a comparison between two unlike things without using a connective word—for example, "Michael Phelps was a flying fish in the pool." *Personification*, choice C, is giving a nonhuman thing a human characteristic, such as in "Opportunity knocked on the door." And a simile, choice D, is a comparison between two unlike things using a connective word, such as *like*, *as*, or *than*—for example, "She looked as fresh as the morning snow."

**Question 9 asks you to recognize the development of central ideas.**

9. Which of the following is an essential thematic topic in *Dear John*?

    A. Loves means that you care for another person's happiness more than your own.

    B. Doing the right thing isn't easy.

    C. Life isn't fair.

    D. all of the above

Remember that a *central idea*, or theme, is expressed in a complete sentence. By definition, a theme states an opinion, but it is an opinion about a topic, not about a specific person or event. For example, the sentences "Spring break passed by too quickly" and "You are my best friend" are both statements of opinion, but they are not themes. Literary works have multiple, interrelated themes.

Even though all the choices are examples of central ideas,

you have to determine if they apply to the novel *Dear John* as a whole. If a central idea applies to more than one character and can be supported by multiple pieces of support—details and evidence from the text—select that choice.

**Question 10 asks you to recognize the development of a motif.**

10. The concluding image of the novel is that of John and Savannah both staring at the full moon. What is the significance of this motif throughout the novel as a whole? Mark all that apply.

    A. The full moon represents their time together.

    B. The full moon symbolizes that even though they are apart, John and Savannah are together.

    C. In an ever-changing world, some things remain constant.

    D. all of the above

A *motif* is a recurring object, idea, symbol, image, etc., in a literary work. For example, throughout the Twilight series, there are a number of recurring elements, such as choices, love, good versus evil, and fear. Also, images of light and darkness permeate the Twilight saga; these are also motifs. Motifs serve as unifying components of a text.

The question asks you to "mark all that apply," indicating that there may be more than one correct answer. If the full moon is significant to the time John and Savannah spent together during the summer when they first met, select choice

A. If the full moon represents an action that the two can share even if they are apart, select choice B. And if the cycle of the moon is constant from month to month, just as John or Savannah can choose to stare at it from month to month, select choice C. If all choices are correct, select choice D.

# Post-Reading Questions and Writing Assignments

## Critical Reading Questions

Answer the questions below based on the information in the following passage.

Like all cities, Wilmington is rich in places and poor in others, and since my dad had one of the steadiest, solid-citizen jobs on the planet—he drove a mail delivery route for the post office—we did okay. Not great, but okay. We weren't rich, but we lived close enough to the rich area for me to attend one of the best high schools in the city. Unlike my friends' homes, though, our house was old and small; part of the porch had begun to sag, but the yard was its saving grace. There was a big oak tree in the backyard, and when I was eight years old, I built a tree house with scraps of wood I collected from a construction site. My dad didn't help me with the project (if he hit a nail with a hammer, it could honestly be called an accident); it was the same summer I taught myself to surf. I suppose I should have realized then how different I was from my dad, but that just shows how little you know about life when you're a kid.

My dad and I were as different as two people could possibly be. Where he was passive and introspective, I was always in motion and hated to be alone; while he placed a high value on education, school for me was like a social club with sports added in. He had poor posture and tended to shuffle when he walked; I bounced from here to there, forever asking him to time how long it took me to run to the end of the block and back. I was taller than him by the time I was in eighth grade and could beat him in arm-wrestling a year later. Our physical features were completely different, too. While he had sandy hair, hazel eyes, and freckles, I had brown hair and eyes, and my olive skin would darken to a deep tan by May. Our differences struck some of our neighbors as odd, which made sense, I suppose, considering that he'd raised me by himself. As I grew older, I sometimes heard them whispering about the fact that my mom had run off when I was less than a year old. Though I later suspected my mom had met someone else, my dad never confirmed this. All he'd say was that she'd realized she made a mistake in getting married so young, and that she wasn't ready to be a mother. He neither heaped scorn on her nor praised her, but he made sure that I included her in my prayers, no matter where she was or what she'd done. "You remind me of her," he'd say sometimes. To this day, I've never spoken a single word to her, nor do I have any desire to do so.

1. The main ideas in this passage are primarily developed through which rhetorical pattern?

    A. argumentation

    B. cause and effect

    C. comparison and contrast

    D. description

    E. narration

2. The line, "if he hit a nail with a hammer, it could honestly be called an accident" (line 3) suggests that

    A. the narrator's father isn't skillful with his hands

    B. the narrator is a stand-up comedian

    C. the narrator resents his father

    D. the narrator's father is prone to accidents

    E. the speaker is an unreliable narrator

3. The author makes use of all of the following devices in the first paragraph EXCEPT

    A. compound-complex sentence

    B. dashes

    C. parentheses

    D. sentence fragment

    E. simple sentence

4. According to the passage, the narrator and his father differ in all of the following areas EXCEPT

   A. athletic ability

   B. manual dexterity

   C. physical features

   D. religious views

   E. value of education

5. Based on the details in this passage, the narrator would most likely characterize his father as

   A. active

   B. careful

   C. lively

   D. rude

   E. worried

6. The tone of the final sentence, "To this day, I've never spoken a single word to her, nor do I have any desire to do so," is best described as

   A. cynical

   B. emotional

   C. guarded

   D. petty

   E. wistful

Answer the questions below based on the information in the accompanying passage.

The crackle of my tires as they rolled over gravel was oddly comforting, and I pulled to a stop beneath a willow tree, next to a small battered pickup truck. I looked toward the house. Steep roofed and square, with flaking white paint and a chimney pointing toward the sky, it seemed to rise from the earth like a ghostly image a hundred years in the making. A single bulb glowed above the battered front door, and a small potted plant hung near an American flag, both moving gently in the breeze. Off to the side of the house was a weathered barn and a small corral; beyond that, an emerald-covered pasture enclosed by a tidy white fence stretched toward a line of massive oak trees. Another shedlike structure stood near the barn, and in the shadows I could see the outlines of aging field equipment. I found myself wondering again what I was doing here.

It wasn't too late to leave, but I couldn't force myself to turn the car around. The sky flared red and yellow before the sun dipped below the horizon, casting the mountains in moody darkness. I emerged from the car and began to approach the house. The dew on the grass moistened the tips of my shoes, and I caught the scent of conifers once more. I could hear the sounds of crickets chirping and the steady call of a nightingale. The sounds seemed to give me strength as I stepped onto the porch. I tried to figure out what I would say to her if she answered the door. Or what I would say to him. While I was trying to decide what to do, a tail-wagging retriever approached me.

I held out my hand, and his friendly tongue lapped against it before he turned and trotted down the steps again. His tail continued to swish back and forth as he headed around the house, and hearing the same call that had brought me to Lenoir, I left the porch and followed him. He dipped low, skimming his belly as he crawled beneath the lowest rung of the fence, and trotted into the barn.

1. The first two paragraphs are primarily developed through which rhetorical pattern?

   A. argumentation

   B. cause and effect

   C. comparison and contrast

   D. description

   E. narration

2. "The crackle of my tires as they rolled over gravel was oddly comforting" contains an example of which literary device?

   A. hyperbole

   B. metaphor

   C. onomatopoeia

   D. personification

   E. simile

3. One can infer from this passage that:

   A. the narrator has been here many times before

   B. the narrator is eager to visit

C. no one is home

D. the house is brand-new

E. the narrator is apprehensive

4. The second paragraph makes use of many sensory details, using all senses EXCEPT:

    A. smell

    B. sight

    C. hearing

    D. taste

    E. touch

5. What is the primary function of the retriever?

    A. to serve as a contrast to the speaker

    B. to guide the narrator to the barn

    C. to remind the narrator of his past

    D. to prove that someone is home

    E. to symbolize the speaker's fear

6. One can infer that the primary function of the setting in this passage is:

    A. to provide background for the period

    B. to help create an atmosphere

    C. to develop the conflict within the plot

    D. to develop a theme

    E. to mirror the emotional nature of the narrator

## Short Answer Questions (paragraph response)

1. In a manner similar to Romeo and Juliet, John and Savannah seemingly fall in love at first sight and then seem to suffer at the hands of fate, unable to live happily ever after together. Does love at first sight truly exist, or is it merely a dream of hopeless romantics?

2. Two opposite clichés or adages address the notion of those who are separated from the ones they love: "absence makes the heart grow fonder" and "out of sight, out of mind." Which saying is more realistic? Which one is more thematically supported by *Dear John*?

3. Which is more important to demonstrate—love for country or love for another person?

4. What primary function does Mr. Tyree serve in the novel?

5. *Dear John* concludes with a somewhat ambiguous ending. Even if the outcome of the plot isn't what you would like it to be, is the conclusion satisfying?

## Writing Assignments (essay response)

1. One important thematic topic in *Dear John* is the relationship between fate and free will. Consider the actions and events in the novel that appear to be

fate versus those that are the result of choices a character made using his or her own free will. Then, using specific details and examples from the text, write an essay in which you analyze the novel's view of the relationship between fate and free will. Avoid mere plot summary.

2. Select a moment or scene from *Dear John* that you find especially memorable. Write an essay in which you identify the passage, explain its relationship to the text as a whole, and analyze the reasons for its effectiveness.

3. The opening line of *Dear John* asks, "What does it mean to truly love another?" The question is revisited in the epilogue. How is it answered in the novel? What does John learn regarding what it means to truly love another? How do the lessons John learns transcend the pages of the novel and apply to the real world?

4. Select a character from *Dear John* who functions as an agent for the suffering of others. Write an essay in which you detail how the suffering that character brings to another relates to the thematic significance of the novel as a whole. Do not merely summarize the plot.

5. What important roles do minor characters play in *Dear John*? Be sure to consider how they contribute to the development of the main characters (John and Savannah), plot, and theme.

## Rubric for Essays

| CATEGORY | OUTSTANDING | STRONG | MEETS EXPECTATIONS | EMERGING | UNACCEPTABLE |
|---|---|---|---|---|---|
| Thesis | A clearly stated, focused, and persuasive opinion | A clearly stated and focused claim | Although the opinion may be legitimate, it is too broad for the scope of the assignment | More of a topic than thesis OR thesis does not address assignment | No thesis evident OR thesis is a retelling of plot |
| Organization | Introduction grabs attention; variety of transitions used within and between paragraphs; topic sentences have ample support; meaningful conclusion ties essay together well | Introduction sparks some interest; some variety of transitions used within and between paragraphs; topic sentences have support; satisfying conclusion completes the argument | Evidence of an introduction, body paragraphs, and a conclusion; transitions used within and between paragraphs | Introduction and/or conclusion does not flow with rest of argument; body paragraphs lack topic sentences or support; few transitions used | Introduction and/or conclusion missing; topic sentences not evident OR topic sentences are summaries; transitions not used |

| | | | | | |
|---|---|---|---|---|---|
| Support from the Text | Every body paragraph has multiple supports from text; evidence from text persuasively supports your argument; all citations are incorporated smoothly | Every body paragraph has some support from text; evidence supports your argument; most citations are incorporated smoothly | Every body paragraph has support from text, though the evidence may be superficial; some citations stand alone | Evidence does not support topic sentences; most citations stand alone and are not incorporated smoothly into argument | Little or no textual support |
| Analysis | All support material is introduced and commented upon; cumulative weight of the evidence is convincing | Most support material is introduced and commented upon; analysis is clearly connected to thesis | Ideas support thesis but are obvious and basic | Analysis misrepresents evidence OR is an illogical argument OR ideas are not fully developed | Analysis not attempted OR restates evidence OR does not address the assignment |
| MUGS (Mechanics, Usage, Grammar, Spelling) | Varied sentences; sophisticated vocabulary; no editing errors | Some variety in sentence structure; advanced vocabulary; few editing errors | Little sentence variety; adequate vocabulary; some editing errors | Lack of sentence variety and clarity; limited vocabulary; many editing errors | Fragments and/or run-ons; errors with word choice; editing errors handicap readers |

## Understanding the Rubric

It is important to understand the various sections of the rubric and to use it while you are drafting your essay. The following sections are designed to help you understand the rubric for your literary essay.

*Thesis*

A strong essay relies on the quality of its thesis. Thus, a strong thesis—a precise opinion about a limited topic, a debatable claim, a main idea, or a central idea—is essential for a strong, interpretative, analytical essay.

A strong thesis has the following characteristics:

- a clearly defined opinion
- one idea
- something worth saying
- specific terms

A thesis may be weak if it is a retelling of the plot: An example of a weak thesis is "*Dear John* is a novel that recounts the relationship between a soldier and the woman he falls in love with during leave." It is also weak if it merely mentions a topic. An example of this type of weak thesis is "*Dear John* is a novel about the difficulties of sustaining a long-distance romance."

Your thesis must not be too broad: "In *Dear John*, Sparks shows the true nature of love." Instead, focus your topic: "*Dear John* demonstrates that true love sometimes means sacrificing your wants for the needs of another."

A strong thesis is clearly stated and focused: "In his

novel *Dear John,* Sparks explores the difficulties of a long-distance love relationship in order to demonstrate that true love sometimes means sacrificing your wants for the needs of another."

An outstanding thesis is not only clearly stated and focused but also persuasive: "*Dear John* illustrates that almost every negative situation can be used to create good."

*Organization*

An essay has three distinct sections: the introduction, the body, and the conclusion. The introduction should be about 15 percent of your paper; the body should be about 75 percent; and the conclusion should comprise about 10 percent of the entire essay.

*INTRODUCTION*

The introduction should contain the following elements:

- motivator
- title and author
- basic plot summary/overview
- thesis

The *motivator* is the first part of your introduction. It is something that captures your reader's attention and entices him or her to keep reading. A good introduction announces the topic and sets the tone—for example, an amusing anecdote is not appropriate for a paper about political torture or a Shakespearean tragedy. You want to entice your reader (motivate him or her) to keep reading. And you want to state—either explicitly or implicitly—your opinion. Here are some suggestions for possible motivators:

- general background
- history
- definitions
- quotation
- anecdote
- personal experience
- arresting statement
- interesting details (facts, figures, statistics)
- directly stated thesis
- a question

Here are some examples of poor beginnings:

- In this paper I intend to...
- Wars have always affected mankind.
- As you may know, having too little time is a problem for many of us.
- In the modern world today...

Here are some examples of stronger beginnings:

- Although Mr. Tyree is an important minor character in *Dear John*, readers are not privy to his interior world; rather, we—like John—are dependent on his words and actions in order to get to know the real person.
- Nicholas Sparks's control over pacing and his ability to intertwine the past with the present in *Dear John* are

essential to his success developing the idea that doing the right thing isn't easy.

• Nicholas Sparks introduces an important idea from the onset of his novel *Dear John* by opening with the question, "What does it mean to truly love another?"

• Is it better to have loved and lost than to have never loved at all? Nicholas Sparks explores this question in his novel *Dear John* as his soldier protagonist finds and then loses the girl of his dreams—only to meet up with her again.

*BODY*

Each body paragraph should have a topic sentence—that is, a sentence that states the main idea of the paragraph. All of the topic sentences in your essay should develop and illustrate your thesis. If they do, your essay will have unity. Within the paragraph, all of your details and examples should develop and illustrate your topic sentence. If they do, then your paragraph will have unity.

In order to allow your reader to follow your train of thought, you need to use transitions—standard devices and hooks to connect ideas—that give your essay coherence. Use transitions within and between paragraphs.

*CONCLUSION*

Your conclusion is your last chance to make your case. Think of it as an attorney's closing argument in a trial. Rather than restating your thesis and main support for it, you should demonstrate how the cumulative weight of the evidence in your essay works together to prove your point.

## Support from the Text

Support from the text can come in one of three forms: summaries, paraphrases, or direct quotations. The most effective support is a direct quotation because you are using the exact words of the original text in support of your assertions.

None of your citations should be used as a stand-alone sentence in your essay; rather, you should incorporate citations into your own sentences.

## Analysis

Although having citations in your essay is important, citations alone are not enough. You must be certain that you are using the citations to develop your ideas.

You do this by following a four-part process:

1. Introduce
2. Use
3. Cite
4. Comment upon

When you make the cited material a part of your own sentence, you integrate it smoothly into your essay by introducing the quoted material before you use it. This prepares the reader of your essay for the information that is going to follow.

After introducing the source material, you use it. Make sure you use quotation marks for all passages that you cite verbatim—that is, exactly—from the novel.

Follow the documentation style required by your teacher, which is typically MLA (Modern Language Association). Sometimes you may be asked to use the *Chicago Manual of Style* or APA (American Psychological Association) documentation guidelines, including footnotes or endnotes. Although the specific formats vary, all documentation styles exist to indicate the location of the cited material in the original text and to credit the original text properly. If in doubt, ask your teacher for documentation guidelines.

The most important aspect of using citations is your explanation of the significance of the text evidence you are citing. When you discuss the passage, quoting lines from the novel helps develop your interpretation. Providing individual instances of textual support is a good thing, and when all of the quotations in your essay work together, they create a cohesive whole.

Another part of your analysis is addressing details and examples that may initially indicate a counterinterpretation. The best interpretations are those that address and incorporate the significant words and actions on both sides of the argument.

## *MUGS*

MUGS refers to the editing portion of your essay. MUGS stands for "mechanics, usage, grammar, and spelling." This is the last step of the writing process, when you clean up any surface-level errors.

Mechanics are the rules regarding how you put a sentence together—using capital letters and punctuation marks. In addition, they require you to use a variety of sentence types. Sometimes a simple sentence, such as "John loves Savannah," is effective. Other times, a complex sentence is more effective, such as "Although John loves Savannah, he realizes that he can't be with her because she is married to Tim."

Usage refers to various forms of agreement—subject and verb agreement (*he is, they are*) and pronoun and antecedent agreement (*not* "Savannah and me are going to go surfing" or "Everybody has their board")—as well as dangling and misplaced modifiers. A dangling modifier is using a word or group of words to modify something that isn't in the sentence—for example, "Walking along the beach, a dolphin came into view." In this sentence, the dolphin wasn't walking along the beach, so the phrase "walking along the beach" is considered dangling. To correct the error, rewrite the sentence: "Walking along the beach, John and Savannah spotted a dolphin" or "While John and Savannah were walking along the beach, a dolphin came into view." A vague pronoun reference occurs when a pronoun could possibly reference more than one word, which can create confusion—for example, "John tossed a stick at the window and broke it." Did he break the stick or the window?

Grammar is the overarching term that covers all the rules of language and composition, and spelling is self-evident.

## Three Sample Essays and Application of the Rubric

Below is a copy of essay question 3 and three sample essays, each written at different and improving levels, based on the rubric. Sample Essay 1 is an example of a below-average essay. Sample Essay 2 takes some of the shortcomings (as identified on the rubric) from Sample Essay 1, makes some revisions based on the rubric, and thus improves the essay. Sample Essay 3 is an outstanding essay fully utilizing the essential elements of the rubric and thus improving Sample Essay 2.

Essay Question 3. The opening line of *Dear John* asks, "What does it mean to truly love another?" The question is revisited in the epilogue. How is it answered in the novel? What does John learn regarding what it means to truly love another? How do the lessons John learns transcend the pages of the novel and apply to the real world?

*Sample Essay 1 (example of a poor essay)*

In "Dear John," Nicholas Sparks uses the character of John to answer the question, "What does it mean to love another?" (1) In fact, that is the first sentence of the hole novel. John learns what it means to truly love through two important but very different love relationships. The first relationship that I will talk about is with the woman he wants to marry, Savannah, and the second one ends up being quite a surprise. It's his father! John's words and actions have an effect on the reader as well as to the real world.

In the prologue we find out that John was in love with Savannah but was also the one "who ended it" (4), meaning his relationship with Savannah. John first says, "It meant that I'd care for Savannah more deeply than I cared for myself and that we'd spend the rest of our lives together" (3). But things don't work out the way the John plans on them doing.

After the attacks on the World Trade Center on September 11, John, a good soldier and patriot, extends his time in the service. This understandably puts a strain on his long-distance relationship with Savannah. Not only can't she handle their time apart, she can't wait two more years for him, so she ends up writing to him less and less and eventually sends John a Dear John letter telling him that she fell in love with someone else. In the letter she writes, "even though we still loved each other, we lost that magical bond that kept us together" (266). John learns that sometimes love isn't enough and sometimes you can't be with the one you love.

John did continue to love Savannah, though, even after she broke up with him. But he has the war in Iraq to fight, and then his father had another heart attack. John ends up having to take care of his father. And ends up having to put his father in an extended care facility. He doesn't want to put his father in the home, but learns that sometimes love makes you do things you don't want to do. His father was unable to care for himself any longer, and John wasn't always on leave, so he had to do it. John tells his father, "You're the greatest dad ever. You had to be great to put up with someone like me" (295).

What John learns about true love transcends the pages of the novel because we as readers can learn the same things. Sometimes we can love someone but if they don't love us back or fall in love with someone else, then all our love isn't enough. We also learn that our parents put up with a lot of stuff from their kids, especially high school kids, and they do it because they love us, so we learn what true love is from them when we follow their example.

*Dear John* is a good book that talks about the nature of true love, and when John sees Savannah that last night, when she "raises her face toward the moon" (384), he knows that she still is in love with him, and that is almost good enough for him to know.

Below is a list of reasons why this essay is subpar:

- first direct quotation is not copied verbatim from the novel

- too much retelling of the plot
- most citations stand alone and are not incorporated smoothly into argument
- analysis restates evidence and does not fully address the prompt
- little sentence variety
- some editing errors

*Sample Essay 2 (example of a competent essay)*

"What does it mean to truly love another?" (3) asks John Tyree in the opening sentence of the Prologue of Nicholas Sparks's novel *Dear John*. He answers his own question in the next paragraph, claiming, "There was a time in my life when I thought I knew the answer" (3), yet his notions of love were based on things that would lead to his happiness and were not necessarily indicative of true love. Most of the novel proper takes place via flashback, recounting the developing and disintegrating relationship between John and Savannah. But *Dear John* is more than just the story of their doomed relationship; rather, it's the chronicle of John's maturation. He learns what true love is not only through his relationship with Savannah, the girl of his dreams, but through his relationship with his father, the man whom he ignored and disregarded for early years of his adult life. By the end of *Dear John*, both John and readers realize that to truly love another, the focus of the relationship is on the other person and not one's self.

Before John even knows Savannah's name, only identifying her as "the brunette" (29), he jumps off a pier to save her purse. This small action is actually a great representation of the way a true love relationship works—John is doing something for another without thinking about himself. Granted, he appreciates Savannah's smile and her laugh, but diving in the water for a complete stranger without the expectation of anything in return is a selfless action. When Randy asks if John wants a reward, he replies, "No. Just glad to help" (42); he does the right thing for the right reason, and the result of his unselfish act, he begins to develop a relationship with Savannah.

As they spend time together during his week on leave from the army, John and Savannah fall in love because they get to know each other without the pressure and stress of a physical relationship. When describing how she views their developing relationship, Savannah tells John that "spending time with you just feels...right, somehow. Easy, like the way it's supposed to be" (134). She then compares their budding relationship to the one her parents have. Savannah captures the essence of their week together in the letter she writes to John, the one he reads on the plane on the way back to Germany. She instructs John to find the first night of the full moon, to look up in the nighttime sky, and to remember their week together, with the stated desire that if she does the same, "we can make this last forever" (192). Both John and Savannah believe that their relationship isn't just a summer fling, but rather, it's the basis for a lifelong commitment to one another.

Unfortunately, their relationship suffers from typical and not-so-typical growing pains: spending most of their time apart, having to share their time together with friends and family members, trying to recapture the magic of that first week together. But true love isn't living in the past. True love isn't about stagnation; it's about growth and change. Unfortunately for their relationship, John is caught up in the patriotism following the attacks of September 11, and when he reenlists, although logically it makes sense, Savannah emotionally has a hard time accepting the situation—not his decision but rather, the resulting effects of his decision. When attending to his sick father during his leave, John realizes that "Savannah and I had spent only 4 of the last 104 weeks together" (258). Being apart from one another is no way to strengthen and maintain a relationship. Ultimately, the distance took its toll, and John receives his Dear John letter from Savannah, ending their relationship.

The time apart doesn't kill John's love for Savannah, however. After his father's death, John shares the details of his lost love with Lucy and realizes that he must see Savannah. Savannah, who is going through tough times of her own, would have succumbed to the temptation of their feelings had John not "stayed where I was, frozen by the thought that she would one day hate me for what we both so obviously wanted" (368). John loves Savannah too much to take advantage of her vulnerable position. John then sells the coins he inherited from his father to benefit the rival of his heart's affection, which is, in and of itself, indicative of his love for Savannah. But, not revealing to Savannah that he is the anonymous benefactor demonstrates the truly selfless nature of the action and his true love for her.

And one of the reasons John is able to demonstrate this unselfish behavior is that he had a model for it—his father. Mr. Tyree removed the one picture that he had of his only son because he didn't want to upset John, and even though he didn't understand John's contempt for coin collecting, stops talking about coins with John because that is what his son demands. Mr. Tyree ends up providing everything for John without judging him, even accepting the tough decision that John has to make, consenting to the move to the extended care facility without complaining. John, having only his father to spend time with on leave after Savannah breaks off their relationship, learns that "there was something peaceful and honest" (286) about his lack of expectation from his father. He ends up giving his father what Mr. Tyree needs from the relationship rather than what John wants from the relationship. Then, they finally become friends. True to form, Mr. Tyree takes care of the details and arrangements for his own funeral, not wanting to burden his son with anything, even after his own death. Although he doesn't realize it growing up, John learns from his father's example what true love really is.

Readers, like John, also learn the nature of true love. For those readers who have already experienced it—as either parents, spouses, or those who had to sacrifice their own wants for the needs of another—*Dear John* is an affirmation of that love. For those who have not yet experienced true love, *Dear John* provides a blueprint of how to treat the one you love.

- a clearly stated and focused claim
- introduction sparks some interest
- some variety of transitions used within and between paragraphs
- topic sentences have support
- a conclusion exists
- most support material is introduced and commented upon
- analysis is clearly connected to thesis
- some variety in sentence structure
- few editing errors

*Sample Essay 3 (example of an outstanding essay)*

"What does it mean to truly love another?" (3) asks John Tyree in the opening sentence of the Prologue of Nicholas Sparks's novel *Dear John.* He answers his own question in the next paragraph, claiming, "There was a time in my life when I thought I knew the answer" (3), yet his notions of love were based on things that would lead to his happiness but were not necessarily indicative of true love. This opening question is also answered both explicitly and implicitly through the course of the novel, as the major and minor characters and the primary and secondary story lines all converge to create a narrative that explores the development of true love across all types of relationships. Most of the novel proper takes place via flashback, recounting the developing and disintegrating relationship between John and Savannah. But *Dear John* is more than just the story of their doomed relationship; rather, it's the chronicle of John's maturation. He learns what true love is not only through his relationship with Savannah, the girl of his dreams, but also through his relationship with his father, the man whom he ignored and disregarded for the early years of his adult life. By the end of *Dear John*, both John and the reader realize that true love is not synonymous with romantic love—but rather, to truly love another, one's focus must be on the other person in the relationship and not one's self.

Tim is the first character in *Dear John* who embodies the ideals of true love. When John first meets Tim, he thinks that Tim's feelings for Savannah "ran a little

*Motivator includes direct quotation as well as title and author*

*Insight about structure*

*Introduction has a thesis that addresses the prompt*

*Topic sentence incorporates transition and supports thesis*

deeper than he was letting on" (52), and he is right. But during their time at the beach house, Tim never reveals these feelings nor treats John differently. Tim drives John home and acts as a courier for John, even after John accidentally breaks Tim's nose. Tim is a good friend to Savannah, and as such, he realizes when she's exploring different romantic relationships, his role is that of a supportive friend. When Savannah tells John about calling someone to give her a ride back from a bad hotel experience, John correctly guesses that Tim was the friend. Savannah reveals that "to this day, he hasn't asked about the specifics" (145), indicating that Tim does what a friend needs, when she needs it, without needing to know all the details.

*Explanation of support* }

In addition to demonstrating true love as a friend, Tim also demonstrates true love in the other relationships he has. As a brother, he helps Alan both before and after the death of their parents. As a son, he assumes the role of parent and guardian for his autistic brother after their parents' tragic car accident. And when he is seemingly on his deathbed, his concern for his wife and brother consumes his thoughts. He articulates his understanding of true love when he tells John he knows that Savannah is still in love with John and is okay with her feelings as he asserts, "I want nothing more than for her to be happy in life. I want that more than anything. It's all I've ever wanted for her" (375). The last thing Tim says to John is a request for him not to forget Savannah if something were to happen to him. Tim puts the happiness, well-being, and welfare of others before his own, the mark of true love.

*Standard device transition* }

*Introduces direct quotation and integrates it into analysis* }

When John first meets Savannah, he has no idea what true love is. But before he even knows her name, only identifying her as "the brunette" (29), he jumps off a pier to save her purse. This small action is actually a great representation of the way people in a mature love relationship act—John is doing something for another without thinking about himself. Granted, he appreciates Savannah's smile and her laugh, but diving in the water for a complete stranger without the expectation of anything in return is a selfless action. When Randy asks if John wants a reward, he replies, "No. Just glad to help" (42); he does the right thing for the right reason, and the result of his unselfish act is that he begins to develop a relationship with Savannah.

*Direct quotations develop both character and theme*

As they spend time together during his week on leave from the army, John and Savannah fall in love without the pressure and stress of a physical relationship. When describing how she views their developing relationship, Savannah tells John that "spending time with you just feels...right, somehow. Easy, like the way it's supposed to be" (134). She then compares their budding relationship to the one her parents have, which represents the ideal, committed relationship. An important part of Savannah's identity, one that comes from her parents, is the role God and religion play in her life. She takes John to church and explicitly states the importance of God in her life when she tells him that she doesn't believe in casual sex and asks him, "Shouldn't you save things like that for someone you love?" (101). Savannah attempts to live a life of faith, basing her decisions on the Bible. One of the most famous passages from the Bible that discusses the nature of true love is in 1 Corinthians, which provides this description of love: "Love is patient, love is kind…it is not self-seeking, it is not easily angered" (1 Cor 13:4–5, NIV). This description of love captures the essence of the newly forming relationship between Savannah and John and serves as a model for what a perfect relationship based on love would look like.

Savannah expresses her understanding of their week together in the letter she writes to John, the one he reads on the plane on the way back to Germany. She instructs John to find the first night of the full moon each month, to look up in the nighttime sky, and to remember their week together, with the stated desire that if she does the same, "we can make this last forever" (192). Because what they shared is real, Savannah wants John not only to remember it, but also to keep it alive. The letter represents a shift in point of view. Up until this time, the entire novel has been narrated from John's perspective, and readers have only been privy to his thoughts and feelings, but the letter enables Savannah to share her thoughts and feelings with both John and the reader. Both John and Savannah believe that their relationship isn't just a summer fling, but rather the basis for a lifelong commitment to one another.

*Provides a balance between textual evidence and explanation of evidence*

Unfortunately, their relationship suffers from typical and not-so-typical growing pains; their difficulties include spending most of their time apart, having to share their time together with friends and family members, and trying to recapture the magic of the week they first met. But true love isn't living in the past.

And it isn't about stagnation; it's about growth and change. When John is caught up in the patriotism following the attacks of September 11 and reenlists, his actions make sense to Savannah logically, although emotionally she has a hard time accepting the results of his decision. When attending to his sick father during his next leave, John realizes that "Savannah and I had spent only 4 of the last 104 weeks together" (258). Being apart from one another is no way to strengthen and maintain a relationship. Ultimately, the distance takes its toll, and John receives his Dear John letter from Savannah, ending their relationship, a relationship that was essentially over before the letter is even written.

The Dear John letter doesn't kill John's love for Savannah, however. After his father's death, John shares the details of his lost love with Lucy and realizes that he must see Savannah. Although when he finally tracks her down, he has difficulty explaining why he needed to come. He mumbles, "In some ways, you were the best friend I've ever had" (314). This admission clarifies for John and Savannah that love doesn't necessarily die just because one person decides to end a relationship. The next day over dinner, Savannah tells John, "Everybody needs somebody to talk to" (360), and John concurs. He realizes that Savannah is still in love with him, but his love for her enables him to not succumb to temptation because John is "frozen by the thought that she would one day hate me for what we both so obviously wanted" (368). John loves Savannah too much to take advantage of her vulnerable position.

He puts her needs as a wife ahead of his physical desire. Just as he didn't pressure her to sleep with him during their first week together, John doesn't initiate any sexual contact at Savannah's house. John then sells the coins he inherited from his father to benefit the rival of his heart's affection, which is in and of itself indicative of his love for Savannah. But not revealing to Savannah that he is the benefactor demonstrates the truly selfless nature of the action. John is in a position to help Tim and Savannah, and his love for her makes this happen, even though it essentially ends any possibility of him ever resuming his relationship with Savannah.

One of the reasons John is able to demonstrate this unselfish behavior is that he had a model for it— his father. Mr. Tyree also has a religious background, for he made sure John as a child included his absent mother in his daily prayers and doesn't ever bad-mouth his ex-wife. When John screams, "I'm sick and tired of hearing about coins" (17), Mr. Tyree not only stops talking about them, he removes the one picture that he had of him and his only son because he didn't want to upset John. Although Mr. Tyree doesn't understand John's contempt for coin collecting, he stops talking about his passion with John because that is what John demands. Mr. Tyree ends up providing everything for John without judging him. Years later, when John is home on leave, instead of having dinner with his father, John makes plans to go out two nights in a row. When John apologizes, his father simply says, "It's okay...I understand" (89) and holds out the car keys. Although Mr. Tyree would like to spend time with his only son, he recognizes that his son has other needs and desires and does not stand in his way. A few years later, Mr. Tyree even accepts the tough decision that John has to make, consenting to the move to the extended care facility without complaining. John, having only his father to spend time with on leave after Savannah breaks off their relationship, learns that "there was something peaceful and honest" (286) about his lack of expectation from his father. He ends up giving his father what Mr. Tyree needs from the relationship rather than what John wants from the relationship, and they finally become friends. True to form, Mr. Tyree takes care of the details and arrangements for his own funeral, not wanting to burden his son with anything, even after his own death. <u>Although he doesn't realize it growing up, John learns from his father's example what true love really is.</u>

*Uses minor character as support for thesis and to demonstrate protagonist's growth*

Readers, like John, also observe the nature of true love. For those readers who have already experienced it—as either parents, spouses, or those who had to sacrifice their own wants for the needs of another—*Dear John* is an affirmation of that love. For those who have not yet experienced true love, *Dear John* provides a blueprint of how to treat the one you love. The novel opens and closes with the query, "<u>What does true love really mean?</u>" (381) and spends the chapters in between answering the question.

*Returns to motivator to give essay sense of completeness*

425

# About the Author

With over 80 million copies of his books in print worldwide, Nicholas Sparks is one of the world's most beloved storytellers. His novels include eleven #1 *New York Times* best sellers, and all his books, including *Three Weeks with My Brother*, the memoir he wrote with his brother, Micah, have been *New York Times* and international best sellers and were translated into more than forty languages. Eight of Nicholas Sparks's novels—*Safe Haven, The Lucky One, The Last Song, Dear John, Nights in Rodanthe, Message in a Bottle, A Walk to Remember,* and *The Notebook*—were also adapted into major motion pictures. The author lives in North Carolina with his wife and family. You can visit him at www.nicholassparks.com.

# Available Books in the Novel Learning Series

*Novel Learning Series:*
*A Bend in the Road*
by Nicholas Sparks
ISBN: 978-1-4555-2942-1

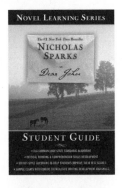

*Novel Learning Series:*
*Dear John*
by Nicholas Sparks
ISBN: 978-1-4555-2944-5

*Novel Learning Series:*
*Frankenstein*
by Mary Shelley
ISBN: 978-1-4555-2943-8

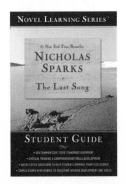

*Novel Learning Series:*
*The Last Song*
by Nicholas Sparks
ISBN: 978-1-4555-1560-8

*Novel Learning Series:*
*The Notebook*
by Nicholas Sparks
ISBN: 978-1-4555-1559-2

*Novel Learning Series:*
*Three Weeks with My Brother:*
*A Memoir*
by Nicholas and Micah Sparks
ISBN: 978-1-4555-1561-5

*Novel Learning Series:*
*A Walk to Remember*
by Nicholas Sparks
ISBN: 978-1-4555-0856-3

**For more information and teachers' resources, visit**
www.novellearningseries.com.